SMOKEOUT

ALSO BY S. V. DATE

Speed Week

Final Orbit

S. V. Date

SMOKEOUT

G. P. Putnam's Sons

New York

G. P. Putnam's Sons
Publishers Since 1838
a member of
Penguin Putnam Inc.
375 Hudson Street
New York, NY 10014

Library of Congress Cataloging-in-Publication Data

Date, S. V. (Shirish V.)
Smokeout / S. V. Date.
p.   cm.
ISBN 0-399-14649-0
1. Florida—Fiction.   I. Title.
PS3554.A8237 S62   2000   00-028056
813'.54—dc21

Printed in the United States of America

1   3   5   7   9   10   8   6   4   2

Book design by Victoria Kuskowski

For Orion and Rigel

Thanks again to Neil Nyren for seeing the forest for the trees, to Monika Gonzalez for help with my dismal español, to Orion for playing relatively quietly with his choo-choos on at least the occasional morning, to Senator Jim King for teaching me how Tallahassee really works, and to Mary Beth for everything.

SMOKEOUT

THURSDAY

Trademark smile affixed on carefully made-up face, Dorothy Marie Nichols gazed serenely upon a polished mahogany armoire where, inside, on closed-circuit television, a small bald man in a canary sport coat presided over highway robbery.

With each strand of auburn hair carefully lacquered in place, she watched toady after toady in the bald man's clique propose transferring a million or two or three from the Transportation Department budget to a particular swine festival or catfish farm or alfalfa project in a particular hometown. With every crease of carefully pressed wool suit still razor-sharp, she kept mental tally as the bald man muttered "without objection" and pointed to the next of his pals waiting with microphone held high.

And so it was, perfect smile, perfect coif and perfect attire, that she finally turned away from the TV and toward the neatly tailored, outwardly polite and yet somehow vulgar man who for the past half hour had held her hostage in the Senate president's suite with his allegorical carrots and sticks.

"Senator Nichols? Madame Rules Chair? Not boring you, are we?"

Dolly Nichols maintained an inscrutable smile, and appraised Bartholomew Simons' single raised eyebrow. A trick he'd no doubt picked up at a management seminar somewhere. Coolly she studied his egg-shaped head, the narrow gray eyes peering through designer steel frames, an ordinary yet confident chin. He was shiny on top but made no attempt to comb over.

Had, in fact, trimmed the remaining ring of blond hair to a buzz cut. She noticed again the gold and scarlet handprints on his mauve tie.

"Not at all." Her smile dissolved into a grateful laugh. "You've been so kind as to remind us exactly how much Roper-Joyner Holdings has given our campaigns these six years you've been in charge, and how much RJH corporately has contributed to the Party. I know I speak for my colleagues when I say: Thank you."

Behind Simons she saw House Speaker Jon Powers' malignant, tiny-eyed glare aimed her way, heard Senate President Walter Soffit's nervous snicker. Calmly, she blinked through the silence and addressed Simons: "Pretty tie. Leukemia Fund? Or Cancer Society?"

Simons grinned neutrally. "Children designed it."

Powers cleared his throat pompously, removed square horn-rims to wipe them on a silk handkerchief as he fashioned a look conveying the appropriate degree of steadfast loyalty. "Well, Mr. Simons, I'm proud to say that you ain't got a worry in the world over in my House. We got a solid ninety-five votes lined up outta a hundred twenty. That's fifteen more than we need. And I don't use that word lightly: solid." He nodded once, solidly. "I ain't too modest to tell you I run a tight ship over there."

Dolly let her gaze fall back to the television as Soffit quickly jumped in to brag about *his* equally impressive command over the Senate. Soffit had a month earlier declared his candidacy for state insurance commissioner, a factor Dolly and everyone else in Tallahassee knew would only weaken an already malleable nature when it came to big-money contributors.

Inside Soffit's armoire, the bald man approved an amendment moving the Transportation Department's District 1 headquarters from Pensacola, the Panhandle's largest city, to Chipley, the bald man's hometown. And now Dolly discerned a pattern. For every pork barrel project Senator T. C. Tuttle approved for one of his cronies, he approved one for himself. One hand washed the other. You steal a cookie, I steal a cookie, no one tells Mom.

"I'm sure Madame Rules Chairman would agree," Soffit finished with a flourish. "Right?"

Dolly had a while ago lost track of what exactly Soffit was promising. "You realize, don't you, Walter, that you've left the Floor without adult supervision?"

Cast adrift, Soffit managed a shrug and a she's-such-a-kidder laugh. Nervously, he ran a hand through his mousey brown hair and over his round, accommodating face as he reached onto his desk for a single sheet of paper.

"Mr. Simons, I look at the votes again here and can tell you there's no need for concern." Soffit offered the piece of paper to Simons, then returned it to the desk when it became clear Simons had no intention of touching it. "True, we don't enjoy the overwhelming majority in the Senate that Jon has over in the House, but I assure you that we, too, know how to make the trains run on time."

Before Dolly could stop it, the remark had tumbled out of her mouth: "You mean run a tight ship, Walter. Trains running on time, that was Mussolini."

Suddenly Simons uncrossed his legs and stood, an act which sent his unintroduced, neurotic-looking flunky into a furious round of note-taking. Simons walked past Powers, patting him on the shoulder. He nodded once at Soffit, but avoided even glancing Dolly's way. "Roper-Joyner," he began importantly, "last year saw net profits of $814 million, on sales of $4.3 billion. We are in lawn chemicals, transdermal pharmaceuticals, outpatient clinics, processed food products, beer and, of course, tobacco—"

"I was meaning to ask about that," Dolly cut in, still smiling. "Nicotine patches, cancer clinics and cigarettes: Isn't that a vertical monopoly? Does the Justice Department know?"

"—both cigarettes and snuff under a variety of brand names. The point here is I'm a busy man. There is a subpoena demanding my presence in West Palm Beach on April second in the matter of the State of Florida versus RJH Inc. I frankly have better things to do than waste a single day, let alone a week, God forbid a month, in some courtroom answering some hick lawyer's questions, all because some two-bit governor snuck a law past his legislature letting him rob my shareholders blind."

Dolly casually turned back to the TV. Her peripheral vision caught Simons' eyes flash at the gesture, saw Soffit quickly move between them, hands in the air.

"And that's exactly what we're assuring you, sir," Soffit simpered. "By the end of next week, this legislature will have repealed the Medicaid Third-Party Liability Act and returned tobacco to a level pla—"

"Medicaid Third-Party Liability Act," Simons mocked. "You mean the Let's-Make-Tobacco-Take-It-up-the-Ass Act. Let's cut the bullshit here, ladies and gentlemen. As Speaker Powers says, the House will not be a problem. And you, Walter, I can see you're on board."

In the armoire's polished wood, Dolly saw Simons addressing her back.

"But from what I understand, your system down here gives your incoming president-*designate* as much clout as the outgoing president? His, or her, vote can drag a considerable number with it, am I correct? And I have yet to hear from Madame President-*designate* a clear explanation of her views."

A silence fell over Soffit's suite, broken only by the background chatter as Tuttle moved beyond the Transportation Department in ever bolder forays. Dolly kept her eyes on the television as she took a deep breath. "You realize, Walter, that T.C.'s run amok? That last amendment moved the Florida State Fair to Chipley. This amendment now moves the Orange Bowl there. . . ."

Finally she turned toward the others, casually reached into a handbag to remove a checkbook. "Mr. Simons? I'm trying to recall how much you said you and your fellow executives and your secretaries and your janitors and your janitors' wives have given my campaign over the years. Was it $322,000?" All eyes locked onto the checkbook in horror as Dolly put pen to paper.

"Uh, $322,400, ma'am," the flunky offered helpfully, before catching a glare from Simons.

"Thank you." Dolly continued writing. "So we avoid any misunderstanding? This covers the principal. I'll have my accountant look up the exact dates of your contributions so he can calculate the interest. Prime plus four percent sound fair?"

She tore off the check and held it toward Simons, who eyed the piece of paper icily. "And that's supposed to mean . . . what, exactly?"

"It means, mister, that I don't know where you're from, but bribery is illegal in Florida. Says so right in our Constitution." She maintained the ever-pleasant smile, despite the words. "So if you're expecting certain treatment because of all the money you've donated, then—"

And Soffit cut in quickly with a louder, more-nervous-than-usual laugh, pushed the hand proffering the check back at Dolly. "Senator Nichols! Dolly! There's *really* no need!" A steady titter continued through his clenched teeth. "Of *course* there's no quid pro quo here, expressed or implied! That would be against the law! Mr. Simons, like anyone else, is simply expressing his constitutionally protected freedom to contribute financially to the political candidates of his choice." Soffit released Dolly's hand, clapped Simons timidly on the shoulder. "Who, in this particular instance, happen to agree with him one hundred ten percent!"

Dolly rolled her eyes, tuned out Soffit's stroking and returned her attention to the television, where T. C. Tuttle had just approved an amendment moving the Kennedy Space Center to Chipley Stables. Chipley Stables, wholly owned by a trust controlled by T. C. Tuttle.

For just a moment, Simons sucked air through clenched teeth before softly clearing his throat. "Madame Chairman, if I have offended in any way, please accept my heartfelt apologies. I intended this as a courtesy call, to answer questions, provide information. . . ."

With Tuttle once more pointing at and yielding the Floor to a crony, Dolly slowly gathered her handbag, shoved the crumpled-up check inside and stood; she could almost feel the invisible daggers on the patch of bare skin between pearl necklace and silk blouse. With a final breath, she turned to face Soffit's sweat-beaded brow, Powers' poisonous smile and Simons' relaxed grin.

"Mr. Simons, I don't have any questions. Nor should you." She said it pleasantly, a schoolteacher addressing her children. "I, you might remember, was a Republican back when most of my party mates in Florida were still Yellow Dog Democrats. They have any of those up north? Folks who'd rather vote for a yellow dog than a Republican?"

She broadened her smile a hair for the benefit of Soffit and Powers, was rewarded with the beginnings of a tic from one, a steady, hateful glare from the other. "Look, y'all at Roper-Joyner don't know me, so let me save you some time. In eighteen years here, I've never promised anyone a vote. I'm not about to start. But before you get too excited, you might want to look up my record, connect the dots a little bit. You might also remember that when T.C. sponsored the law last year as a technical amendment of quote no consequence unquote, I was the only one warning that words like 'statistical analyses' and 'market share' seemed odd in a bill supposedly deleting obsolete language. I said: Don't let this in. We don't know what it does."

Dolly started past Soffit and Powers toward the door. "But everyone's tired. It's eleven at night, the last day of session, everyone wanting to go home. So we approve the amendment and we go home. And a week later the governor sues RJH." She shrugged, put a hand on the doorknob.

She nodded at Simons. "What I'm trying to say is that changing the rules to sue a legal industry isn't right. No one puts a gun to people's heads and makes them smoke. No one keeps them from quitting. Either we believe in individual freedom or we don't."

Simons nodded graciously. "So in other words—"

Dolly pushed open the door to Soffit's office as she flashed a final smile. "Me? I happen to believe. Always have. With or without a dime of campaign money. Now if you'll excuse me, someone needs to retake the Floor before T.C. moves Disney World to Chipley."

———

Her mouth still chattering about her spring internship in House bill drafting, her two years as an analyst in Senate Finance and Taxation, her four semesters at law school, Jeena Golden began to sense yet another interview slipping away.

On the other side of the cluttered oak desk, the toughest, hardest-ass woman in the lobbying corps clearly had lost interest. Eyes as sharp as flint now only occasionally glanced up at Jeena, remaining for ever longer stretches on a dog-eared draft of a bill that lay atop the heap of paper.

Suddenly, Ruth Ann Bronson stood, walked to a stained coffee machine on a side table, and Jeena knew it was pointless, wondered what she'd been thinking when she applied for the job or, for that matter, when she'd decided to leave law school and come back to Tallahassee. Just a couple of feet away, Bronson's dark-brown legs rose from three-inch black heels, with sinuous muscle stretching from sculpted calves through slim buttocks, back and shoulders, each curve on display through a skin-tight navy miniskirt and rib-hugging knit top. Jeena tugged self-consciously at the high collar of her blouse, uncrossed her legs to hide a long, dowdy skirt and scuffed flats behind the wing chair beside her.

To find a woman more unlike herself would have been impossible, Jeena realized. This woman had the world before her, anything she wanted for the taking. The face was strikingly angular and world-weary, a perfect foil to the shameless display of sexual energy of her body. In contrast, Jeena was college-girl soft: honey-blond hair framing a pleasantly fresh face, shapeless clothes cloaking an anonymous figure.

Ruth Ann Bronson sat back down and began studying Jeena anew with furrowed brow. Jeena felt pangs of anxiety shoot up and down her spine. She realized she'd stopped talking, wondered whether it had been mid-sentence, decided it didn't matter. The more quickly this ended, the better, and she could slink out and away before any more harm was done. Ruth Ann picked up Jeena's resume, studied it, turned back to Jeena's face, studied *it,* and said finally: "Women of the ACC, 1992, right?"

And Jeena was standing, holding her breath, suppressing tears, mumbling incomprehensibly, searching for her briefcase. Coming back hadn't just been a mistake, it had been a huge, gigantic, enormous mistake. Not only had no one forgotten, but they were taking mean pleasure in reminding her! Unable to find her briefcase—where could it have gone in such a small office?—she headed for the door, apologizing constantly, when she felt the hand on her wrist.

She was crying, the last shred of control gone, just like earlier in her car, after the last appointment, only now there was a piece of tissue before her eyes. Jeena turned to see Ruth Ann offering the entire box, muttering her own apologies. Then, unprompted, Jeena began explaining about the keg party the afternoon of the last final, and how drunk everyone got, and how the photographer had shown up at the house looking for roommate Melanie. Melanie the exhibitionist, the one who sunbathed nude on the sloping roof in full view of the engineering building. How in the spirit of the moment, her other roommate, Judy, had volunteered, too, had goaded Jeena into posing as well. Jeena, too liberated by the end of finals, too unused to the strong German beer to say no. How they'd signed their releases and stripped: Melanie getting the whole $250 for the full frontal, Judy earning $150 for her boobs, while Jeena, the demure one, took a mere $100 for revealing only her derriere to a million loyal subscribers. How six months later, her small-town parents had for a time disowned her when, lo and behold, her photo actually made the magazine—a one-in-a-thousand chance, the ever-so-professional photographer had told them—and the neighbors and co-workers had started with the smirks and the averted eyes.

And finally how just a few hours earlier, during her last job interview, Tallahassee's premiere lobbyist had, as she was explaining about needing a break from law school, reached down and pulled the November 1992 issue out of a drawer, opened it to her page and told her, leering, that she had the job, provided she was willing to use *all* her assets—get it? wink, wink—on behalf of his clients. And then, even as she was stumbling for the door after a moment of stunned silence, he'd called out to her, begging: "Please, at *least* autograph the picture!"

Ruth Ann let Jeena rest her head on her shoulder, the last of the sobs diminishing, Ruth Ann muttering, "That asshole, that asshole," over and over again, until Jeena eventually pulled away, dabbed at her cheeks, began apologizing anew.

"I'm *so* sorry. I don't even know you, and here I am—"

Ruth Ann threw a hand up, stood to walk back around her desk. "Forget it. And forget about the picture, too, all right? We all make mistakes." She rifled through a bottom drawer, then finally straightened, holding an ancient copy of the magazine, and threw it on the pile of papers. "Co-eds of Florida, 1974. That's what we were back then: co-eds."

Jeena could only stare at the magazine in disbelief. After a few moments, she reached for it, paged through it, thumbed through to a pictorial of early-seventies college girls. Long straight hair, funky clothes unbuttoned to the waist or draped carelessly over a shoulder. And there suddenly was the hard-as-nails woman who would be her boss, lounging naked in a field, a wild-flower in one hand held to her nose.

"Back in another life, I used to be a nurse." Ruth Ann lit a long, thin cigarette, paused for a first puff. "One day, one of the doctors I worked with found out about that picture. He dug up a copy and pinned it up in the scrub room, the son of a bitch."

In the photo, Ruth Ann had shiny brown hair that reflected streaks of red in the sunshine, perfect, milky white skin, pert little breasts that pointed triumphantly skyward. Jeena suddenly was aware of the awkwardness of the moment, blushed violently and laid the closed magazine back on the desk. "It's, uh, it's a nice picture."

Ruth Ann snorted, scooped up the magazine and stuffed it back into a drawer. "It's the most ridiculous thing I've ever done, and it'll haunt me until the day I die." She took another drag from the cigarette, a Princess, Jeena could see, from the soft-sided packet on the desk. "I'm sorry I embarrassed you, but I remembered your face. I remember all the Florida State girls who get snookered into taking off their clothes with the dream of landing a big modeling contract."

She leaned to the ashtray on a side table to tap the end of her cigarette. "So let's talk about this job. There's a reason my dear friend Martin Remy always keeps a stable full of hot young chicks, and here it is: Hundred and sixty legislators in this town, hundred and twenty-three of 'em are men. Up here two months a year, away from the wife . . . You do the math."

Ruth Ann threw tanned, shapely legs up on the corner of the desk. "That's how come I look like this. Every morning, five o'clock, in the gym for an hour and a half. I pay with sweat and blood to stay competitive. So here's the deal. You've got the body to get in the door, and the brains to get the job done once you're there. And unlike Mr. Remy, I don't expect you to sleep with the client. Only to dress like you might. That's key." She blew a gray stream toward the ceiling. "Also to know every word, every punctuation mark of every bill you're working." She paused a moment, thinking. "Oh, and no panty lines or bra straps. That's also key."

Jeena blinked at this, found herself studying Ruth Ann's chest and realized, sure enough, that she could see the outline of each areola through the clingy fabric. She glanced up with a gulp to Ruth Ann's gaze.

"I don't ask of my employees anything I wouldn't do myself." She laid the cigarette on the lip of the ashtray and leaned back in her chair, hands locked behind her head. "As you probably know, I'm one of the lobbyists RJH hired to get the override through the Senate, and I've got a half dozen shaky votes. You understand that's what we're doing here, right? Working for tobacco? I see on your resume you interned once for the Cancer Society in college. This isn't going to be a conflict for you? I need a pro. . . ."

It began to dawn on Jeena that this woman was actually offering her a job. Nine interviews in three days with male bosses, and the most they'd wanted was a spring intern, another pretty face to get them through legislative session. Quickly, she shook her head. "No problem. Business is business, and I want to learn."

"Good. I can offer seventy-six thousand a year, five weeks' vacation, full medical, a 401(k) plan, the works. We got a deal?"

Senator Agustin Cruz watched through narrowed eyes as the white-haired receptionist slowly took a phone message and stuck it in a revolving tree on her desk before answering yet another call in a sleepy North Florida drawl: "Good afternoon, office of Governor Bolling Waites, how may I help you?"

He watched as she punched a blinking light on her phone, told Waites' secretary that the governor had an important call, then rang the first line through. Gus bit back resentment. An Anglo, no doubt. Cracker governor always had time for Anglos.

Gus watched as the old lady went back to a stack of mail and resumed sorting it into various bins on the long leaf of her desk. She'd been the governor's gatekeeper, he remembered somebody telling him, through the eighteen years he was a United States senator, plus the twelve years before that as a state legislator. Sweet as honey on the outside, tough as a bulldog when she needed to be, was how she was described. Dumb old cracker was more like it, he thought. Just like the old man.

He forced his eyes back to the magazine he held, tried to read some endlessly boring article about election fraud in Miami, the writer trying to make it sound like some great big hairy deal, when a tall redheaded man in cowboy boots and a string tie strode into the reception area, to the door leading to the inner offices and, with a nod to the receptionist, pulled the doorknob when it buzzed and slipped inside. Another Anglo. Figured. More than an hour on this stupid couch, and not one Cuban in or out of the governor's office the whole time. He should call a press conference, was what he should do. Get *The Miami Herald* to write a story about the Hispanic-hating governor. See how the old fool liked *that*.

"Ma'am, are you sure he knows I'm here?" He made a show of checking his watch. "That I'm a state *senator*?"

Another white person, this time a middle-aged woman in a gray suit and a briefcase, stood in front of the door until the receptionist buzzed her in. "Yes, sir, Senator Cruz. He's been in meetings all afternoon. It'll be just a few more minutes."

Gus returned to his magazine, stewed about the locked door. He'd wait for a group of people to get buzzed in, then slip in before the door swung shut. That's what he'd do: strike up a conversation with one of them and walk on back like he belonged. Even better, he would just lean over that desk, press the button and buzz himself back. Now *that* would teach her—

And suddenly the door was open, a tall, liver-spotted man with thinning silver hair and plaid madras shirt striding through, followed by a gaggle of aides. They were out the double doors opening onto the Capitol lobby before Gus could jump up and start after him, falling in behind the pack of young men and women, each of them muttering something or thrusting a clipboard at him to sign before peeling away.

"Governor, sir," he began, before yet another aide cut him off with some papers, and he was crowded into the elevator down to the parking garage, and then out across the concrete, only two aides left now as they neared the white Ford Expedition with the "FLORIDA 1" license plate, and even they left, leaving Waites to climb into the truck with his Florida Department of Law Enforcement guard.

"Governor, sir, please," Gus shouted.

Waites stopped, stood on the running board and stared over the truck at Gus, who was speechless now that he had the old man's attention. "The tobacco vote, sir," he blurted.

Waites nodded once, then slipped inside. Gus tugged at the handle and climbed into the backseat beside Waites, as the FDLE driver pulled out of the parking spot and turned up the ramp toward Jefferson Street. Waites nodded at him again as he checked the contents of a small overnight bag in his lap. Immediately, Gus launched into the pitch he'd rehearsed in his head for days.

"Governor, sir, you and I can be of great benefit to each other." He flashed a conspiratorial grin at Waites, who had his head bent over the overnight bag and therefore missed it. "You, sir, face a great battle over the tobacco law, and I face a great battle of my own." Gus allowed his voice to quaver with emotion: "One which is shared by a great many of my countrymen. The struggle for a free Cuba."

Still the governor said nothing, and Gus continued. "What I propose is this: I will support your veto to preserve Florida's historic lawsuit against tobacco. I think I could be your fourteenth vote. The difference between victory and defeat."

Waites grunted, reached over the seat into the cargo area, sat back down with a black nylon case on his lap. Gus watched with curiosity, then alarm, as Waites unzipped the case and removed a spear gun.

"In, ah, consideration, I merely ask that you support my foreign trade office for Cuba's government-in-exile. A first-year appropriation of twenty-five thousand dollars to the Cuban-American Freedom Association to provide office space and support staff for our government-in-exile for the day, which we can all hope is not so far now, that Castro is gone and Cuba returns to democracy and capitalism." Gus swallowed as Waites cocked the complicated weapon. "Going fishing, sir?"

Waites glanced up brusquely, then quickly returned his attention to the spear gun's firing mechanism. "Grouper. Nothin' like the taste of fresh grouper, swimmin' around in the coral one minute, on your plate a half hour later. Goin' to Key West for the Southeastern Governors Association conference, might as well do something productive." He poked his little finger into a slot above the trigger, wiggled it around. "You were saying about your twenty-five thousand dollars?"

Gus told him how the money would be used for outreach, to develop a constitution for the freed Cuba, when Waites pulled the trigger and the spear gun fired with a loud *snap*. Gus swallowed and tried to control his pounding heart. The gun's business end had been pointed at his spleen when it had gone off, and for a moment he imagined the metal stick emerging from his torso.

Gus looked around and realized they'd arrived at the state air pool, an asphalt apron spread before a rusting corrugated steel hangar. A six-seat

Beechcraft Kingair had its boarding ladder down, its starboard propeller already whirring noisily as Gus followed Waites to the foot of the ladder, shouting over the din about the unbelievable value to Florida businesses a free Cuba represented, and how CAFA was uniquely poised to make such a thing happen.

Waites stood on the bottom step as his driver removed luggage from the rear of the truck and loaded it into a cargo compartment under the plane. He considered Gus for a long minute, his tongue exploring around inside his mouth. "Gus, you're chairman of this Cuba association, right?"

Gus nodded enthusiastically. "Cuban-American *Freedom* Association, sir."

"And the sole employee?"

Suddenly Gus had a bad feeling about where things were headed. He swallowed, nodded again, more weakly this time.

"But you're actually from New Jersey, right? Not Cuba?"

Gus could only shrug. "I think we could work together, Governor."

Waites nodded at the thumbs-up from his driver, then climbed the remaining stairs, and addressed Gus without turning. "I'll have someone get back to you on that."

Then he pulled up the staircase behind him as the plane lurched forward and taxied to the top of the runway. Gus cursed under his breath, berated himself for his clumsy approach. He'd have to think of a way to salvage it, and soon. *Damn!* What had gone wrong? Too much money, that must have been it. Well, he'd show the old man he was nothing if not reasonable. Twenty-five grand too much? Okay, how about twenty? Fifteen, even ten, was better than nothing!

Glumly, he watched the plane climb into the sinking sun before banking left. He finally turned around and only then realized that the governor's driver had gone. He was all alone at the now deserted general-aviation side of the airport, three miles from the passenger terminal. He let out a pained groan, cursed aloud now with no one to hear him, then pulled off the polyester suitcoat that chafed at his underarms and slung it over a shoulder.

With a final curse for the disappearing plane, he started walking.

Murphy Moran didn't even have to pay close attention, the walls were so thin. Over and over, a Midwest accent disparaged somebody in low tones, then at the whole backwoods political culture down here. He'd gone to an actual fish-fry the past weekend, for Christ's sake, would you believe it? They *fry* their fish!

A politician, Murphy thought from the context, and a woman, based on the gender-specific epithets, although he supposed he couldn't be certain.

Murphy continued reading the magazine in his lap, idly picking at the rawhide lace on his boat shoes. They were fraying at the tips. Eventually, soon, he would have to make an actual effort to replace them. Perhaps this week-end, if he could find some time. If whatever he was doing didn't consume the whole three days. If, that is, his client on the other side of the wall ever got around to explaining what exactly he *was* supposed to be doing. He'd been sitting in the outer room of the hotel penthouse for some forty-five minutes, he and a receptionist who occupied the rented desk guarding the suite's inner room. She'd buzzed in on the intercom when he'd arrived, then told him to have a seat.

The midwesterner's tone was more animated now, and Murphy peeked over his magazine at the receptionist, ready to trade a raised eyebrow and an embarrassed smile, but the woman kept working intently on some paperwork, like she hadn't heard a thing. A perfect company secretary, hearing nothing that wasn't meant to be heard. Or maybe, Murphy thought after a moment, she actually was hard of hearing.

He toyed with staging an experiment to find out but instead shifted his legs to pick at the lace on the other shoe and began wondering again whether he'd made a colossal mistake. Here it was, the spring after a general election, a rare chance to get away, grab some precious time for himself before the governors' races and the midterm elections began again. Yet here he was, once again in a small town state capital. The call had come out of the blue: How would he like to run publicity for a major legislative battle? A battle with national implications? A battle that would last two weeks, tops, and pay a guaranteed million, with another million if they prevailed?

He'd caught the next flight down from Washington. Two million was two million, equal to the earnings from two full campaign cycles consisting of eight months of eighty-hour weeks. Two weeks of highly concentrated sleaze in Florida paying the same as two years of run-of-the-mill, campaign-trail sleaze, allowing him to chuck it all and retire how many years sooner?

His mind ran through the familiar calculations: $5 million returning a before-tax yield of seven percent in the bond market, maybe ten percent in a good mix of large-cap stocks. In the alternative, maybe three or four percent in tax-free munis. Either way he was looking at a few hundred thousand a year, after taxes. He recalled a time when one million, a single lousy million, had been the magic number. A million in the bank and he could retire on fifty or sixty grand a year. And then he'd started pulling in three and four hundred thousand a year, and began wondering how he could possibly survive on just fifty. He'd raised his target to three million, then five.

He supposed at some point it had dawned on him that he had no idea what he would do with himself if he *did* retire. Three years back, he'd splurged, bought himself a gorgeous, perfectly maintained fifty-four-foot Hinckley Sou'wester. Because he'd taken delivery in the middle of a presidential race and couldn't make the time to learn to sail her, he'd bought himself a captain, too, and now *Dark Horse* happily plied the Atlantic circuit each year: Bermuda and the Azores each spring, Gibraltar, the Italian Riviera, the Greek Isles and the Balearics each summer, the Canaries in the fall and the eastern Caribbean each winter. Murphy had so far found time for a week, at most ten days, afloat each year, thus turning over a million-dollar yacht to his twenty-eight-year-old skipper and whatever nineteen-year-old "cook" he happened to be shacking up with at the moment.

Chasing sunsets, he'd eventually decided, played better as a long-term dream. Even better, as his old man's dream. For now, amazingly, even though he typically loathed the people he did it for, he'd actually come to enjoy what he did, not to mention that he was damn good at it. Hell, just last summer, hadn't *U.S. News* ranked him among the top five political consultants in the country? And hadn't RJH called and offered to double his net worth in a matter of two weeks?

Murphy leaned back and stroked a perfectly trimmed mustache-goatee combo, when he picked up on the discussion in the other room, heard a scared voice say that the chairman had called and had wanted to know if there were any new details about the memo. And the midwesterner was in a tirade again. For the last time, there was no fucking memo, never had been. Abruptly he changed subjects, and Murphy realized the new target of his wrath was him: *Where is that goddamned political expert, whatsisname, Muller, Morgan . . .*

Moran, the other voice corrected.

Whatever. Should have been here an hour ago.

Actually, sir, I believe it has been an hour. You don't recall? Mrs. Kennedy buzzed?

She did? Why the fuck . . .

Murphy stood, stretched, put his magazine back on the table and started walking as the intercom on the receptionist's desk buzzed. She nodded him toward the door, and Murphy entered a large corner room with windows looking south and west toward a still-orange horizon. A balding, barrel-chested man in rolled-up shirtsleeves arose from an enormous desk arrayed with three different computers, hooked his thumbs under his suspenders and nodded confidently.

"Mr. Moran. Well, well. Have a seat."

Murphy glanced around the room, wondered for a moment whether the guy had been talking to himself, and finally noticed a mousy-looking man with a notepad standing against the wall.

"Sorry to have kept you," Simons said, sitting back down. "At the rate I'm paying you, you don't know *how* sorry. Good flight?"

"Not bad. Can't get to heaven or hell without changing in Atlanta." Murphy smiled, remembering the hitchhiker. "Funny thing coming into town. There's this smarmy-looking guy walking down the road in a Sears suit, thumb out, sweating like a dog. Says he's a state senator." Murphy pulled a business card from his pocket. "Turns out he is. Senator Agustin Cruz. But I can call him Gus. If I'm ever in Little Havana and need anything, he's my man."

Simons cleared his throat, the niceties concluded. "So here it is. Last year, the good Governor Waites snuck a law through letting him sue me. Three weeks ago, the legislature—"

"Repealed the law," Murphy cut in. "Waites vetoed the repeal. On Monday, the vetoed bill comes back to the legislature. If they override, the law is off the books, the suit gets thrown out, and Roper-Joyner saves hundreds of millions of hard-earned, shareholder dollars."

"Right." Simons nodded approvingly, then looked down to some paperwork. "Done your homework. Good."

Murphy slid forward to the edge of his seat. "In fact, I've already started working up scripts for some broadcast ads. You know, to give this thing a higher profile. Maybe set up phone banks to generate some constituent calls." Murphy waited for a response, but Simons was engrossed in some report on his desk. "Also, I went through the list of lobbyists you usually use and added a couple of names a friend of mine said would be good. I, ah, also deleted a couple of people with a black mark or two on their record. I thought we'd want to run as clean a fight as possible, give the opposition—"

"In the interest of time, allow me to be crass: I don't give a fuck what kind of fight you run, as long as I win." Simons looked up with a hard grin. "Hire who you want, don't hire who you don't want. Spend however much you need. Just make damn sure that when they take that vote in the Senate, we have the two-thirds majority necessary for an override. Understood?"

Murphy shrugged. "Sure. It's just—well, I'm sure you know of my reputation. My ads tend to go for the jugular. You know, real grab-you-by-the-collar type stuff, even if that means we take a little poetic license with the facts. I just need to know if you're going to be okay with that."

Simons set down his pen with a thoughtful look. "Mr. Moran, have you ever read Nietzsche? The will to power? *Thus Spake Zarathustra?*"

Murphy couldn't help a blink. "Sure. In college. It's been a while."

"Do you consider yourself a common man? Or a superman?"

Murphy stared a moment, then realized the question wasn't rhetorical. Simons actually expected an answer. "Well, given the choices . . . superman, I guess."

Simons returned to his reading. "Good. So do I. I'm fifty-two years old, but I'm the same weight I was when I wrestled at Dartmouth. I bench-press two-eighty. I do five hundred sit-ups in ten minutes. I don't drink, smoke or consume red meat. What I do is win. What any superman does is win, regardless of the obstacles in his way. I expect you to win. That said, I expect I can allow you to go about your business, and I will return to mine."   .

Behind him Murphy heard the little man against the wall scribbling on his notepad. That and the ticking of a clock. It dawned on him slowly that, as abruptly as it had started, his briefing with the chief executive officer of one of the world's largest tobacco conglomerates was now finished. More than a little puzzled, he arose and turned for the door. "I'll, uh, get those ads done over the weekend for you to sign off on."

"That will be marvelous."

Simons never looked up, and Murphy nodded at the acolyte with the notebook and left the room.

The red and green lights receded slowly, eventually becoming a single point of green as the plane banked right high above the Capitol, then eased earthward, dropping out of sight amid the trees. Last flight in for the night, Simons guessed. Getting up on nine, if the plane was on time.

In the darkened office, he eyed three idle computers arrayed on the curved walnut desktop. It would be any time now.

He refilled his ice-tea glass from a pitcher of chilled mineral water and turned to the picture windows. Before him was spread Florida's capital city, insofar as a small, basically South Georgia town could be considered a city.

Four square blocks of "downtown" surrounded by old neighborhoods shaded by sprawling live oaks and towering long-leaf pines. The seventies-era rectangular Capitol high-rise stood out like a sore thumb, particularly right beside the antebellum Old Capitol with its columns and dome. He'd visited only once previously, a few years earlier for a series of fund-raisers for the Republican gubernatorial candidate, and had thoroughly enjoyed it, even allowing himself the rare indulgence of one of the many young, beautiful ladies who disproportionately populated the staffs of the various power-brokers.

This visit, of course, there would be no time for that. This time would be all work, no play, thanks to the conniving Bolling Waites, whose leadership had made genteel Tallahassee the first state capital to bite the hand that fed it. Until Waites' law, a state hoping to sue tobacco had had the impossible burden of proving that a particular brand of cigarette had caused a particular cancer in a particular smoker. But now, in Florida, the shysters would only have to show a statistical increase in disease among smokers and then apportion blame by market share.

It was a rigged game, the company lawyers had warned the Board, and the rules had to be changed back or Roper-Joyner brands' historical dominance in Florida would come to bite them in the ass. How bad a bite? the chairman had asked. Hundreds of millions, the lawyers had shrugged. Unless of course they got punitive damages by showing a conspiracy . . . for example, hiding in-house medical studies about the effects of smoking or, for instance, targeting minors with advertising. Then the sky was the limit. Ten billion. More. Years and years of net profit.

The chairman had stared at the lawyer for what seemed like ages, and then had gone off, the other directors nodding like children, a stenographer taking it all down, about how it was now and always had been against the Roper-Joyner canon of ethics even to contemplate such things. About how such things were not tolerated at the company, not at any level. Simons had left the meeting gritting his teeth and on the flight from Durham back to New York had rearranged his schedule so as to personally spend the whole of the month in Tallahassee directing the legislative fight and, unofficially, continuing the hunt for MRK93-1321, goddamned MRK93-1321.

He took a deep breath. No point in getting worked up about it. Not yet, anyway. In a few moments, the message he'd been waiting for might very well flash across his computer, giving him an "all clear" on MRK93-1321 and letting him concentrate on the relatively easier task of pinning down the stubborn Ms. Nichols and defeating the uppity Governor Waites.

Still, Simons couldn't help just a little bit of resentfulness. Putting something like that down on paper had been—who else's?—the chairman's idea. The same man who'd dreamed up the idiotic "Smokers Care!" campaign, with its RJH-emblazoned Sharper Image smokeless ashtrays, given away to employers from coast to coast. A feeble attempt to counter the workplace smoking bans that had spread like a cancer across the nation.

As Simons had predicted, the idea had been a total flop. More than 800,000 of the silly things had been shipped, unit cost $72.16 plus freight. Yet as far as Simons knew, auto parts stores and some mini-marts in the South were the only workplaces left in America you could still light up. But would the moron admit he'd been wrong? Of course not, the hypocrite. If company stock went up, it was because *he* was a genius. If it went down, well, that was management's fault. Like that "canon of ethics" bullshit he'd pulled at that meeting: Where in hell did the man think new smokers came from? Did adult smokers just magically appear at age eighteen, ready to puff an average 1.6 packs per day each for an average 38.7 years?

And like snagging kids, or fudging medical research, or flat-out destroying it, for that matter, was somehow the worst thing the company had ever done in the name of shareholder value. Like a dozen congressmen weren't enjoying mistresses, all expenses paid, thanks to a company slush fund and another couple dozen weren't fully "leverageable," thanks to the work of company investigators and photographers. Like their competitors hadn't suffered the occasional unlucky catastrophe at their research centers. Like a whistleblower or two hadn't boarded a doomed commuter flight.

Simons peered into the night and saw another set of airplane lights approach from the west, slowly turn and head south over the red blinking lights on top of the Capitol. A private plane, from the sound of it, zipping low over the building before banking to line up on the runway.

That's what would've done the trick a year earlier: a company plane and a pilot ready to make the ultimate sacrifice. It would have been the perfect teachable moment for all the other governors and attorneys general thinking about suing the industry. Let's see how eager they would have been to mess with Roper-Joyner as they watched their CNN *Headline News,* saw the blackened bodies of turncoat legislators pulled from the rubble of Florida's statehouse.

But no, instead, their intelligence had failed them. His director of legislative affairs had been blindsided, and Simons himself had been overseas on a trade mission, had come home to an emergency Board meeting to learn of the evil little law Florida's governor had snuck through in the wee hours. Which meant that now a plane or bomb or similar means of mass destruction would be pointless, even counterproductive, if it left Waites' law on the books. A judge had the case, a jury was already hearing it. If the thing didn't go away, and soon, the jury would hear too damn much, and then it would be all over. The high-seven-figure salary, the lower-eight-figure stock options, the mid-eight-figure retirement package: gone.

He sipped his ice water and pushed the doom and gloom from his mind. He had things in hand now and could guide his own destiny. Hell, the worst-case scenario was still doable, and he most likely wouldn't even be facing that. In another week, it would all be over, like it had never happened, and he could get on with the business of catapulting Roper-Joyner into the number-two position like he'd promised—

The Toshiba laptop chimed softly, and Simons turned to it with the beginnings of a grimace. He'd been hoping it would come on either the Compaq or the Dell, both configured to receive company e-mail, rather than the laptop, which was his personal machine. A note on a company computer would have suggested things could be talked about in the open. This, to his personal e-mail account . . .

With an index finger, he moved the pencil-eraser nub in the center of the keyboard, clicked with his thumb. His grimace hardened as he read the note from his former fraternity housemate who was now Roper-Joyner's general counsel. Subject: MRK93-1321. Company shorthand for a memorandum originating in the Marketing Department in 1993, the one-thousand three-hundred twenty-first such document created that year, the whereabouts or destruction of which he still could not definitively say but which in increasing likelihood had inadvertently been included in a shipment of documents sent to Tallahassee a week earlier. In regards to Simons' other query: The federal sentencing guideline range for perjury was eighteen to thirty-six months in prison. However, that could be adjusted upward at the judge's discretion. . . .

Simons read the message through twice, realized he was sucking air through his teeth. He willed himself to stop, then heard a new noise, the gentlest tapping at the door. He read the message a third time, then hit the delete key.

"Come in, Andrews."

His assistant entered meekly, shut the door behind him. "Sorry to disturb you, sir, but I finished that project you wanted. I thought you'd want to know."

Simons spun to face him, switching on his desktop lamp en route. The fucking thing was in Tallahassee. Of all the places it could have gone . . . He watched Andrews for half a minute, then began rapping his fingers on the desktop. "Well?"

Andrews cleared his throat and began reading from his clipboard. "About Senator Nichols, sir. I looked up her voting record, like you wanted. She was one of three votes against the Medicaid Third-Party Liability Act last spring. According to the *Senate Journal,* she was the only one to speak against it during floor debate. And also, let's see . . . that guy from that business group, United Industries, he gives her an A-1 rating. Says that over eighteen years, on eight hundred sixteen separate votes, her record is a hundred percent in favor of private enterprise over government regulation. He says he considers her a safe vote."

Simons squinted. "Really. A safe vote. Why, then, does she fuck with us?"

Andrews shifted nervously, like it was his advice that was under question. "Well, sir, he said that's just how she is. She's real serious about her office and her constituents and that kind of stuff."

Simons snorted and leaned back in his chair to remove his glasses and squeeze the bridge of his nose. "Serious about the office. Of course. Why didn't I see it myself?" He squeezed until the pain built behind his eyes, became a vivid, red thing. First this Nichols woman, now the damned memo. It should have been easy, this. The company had collectively given the Florida legislature $16 million in the last six years. That ought to buy something. And of course if that memo got out . . . Christ. Eighteen months. More if the judge happened to be pissed off that day.

Well, it simply wasn't going to happen. That was all there was to it. He would get the memo back, then strategically erase its existence from living memory. And as to Madame Chairman Nichols, Miss Hundred-Percent Voting Record . . . He recalled with a wince the last goody-two-shoes, vote-my-conscience politician he'd dealt with. A New York State assemblyman, also with a perfect voting record, also with the always suspect my-vote's-not-for-sale attitude, who'd ultimately rolled to the other side to become the swing vote on a cigarette tax increase. Well, that's what history was there for. To learn from.

He released his fingers and the pain disappeared. He put his glasses back on and opened his eyes. "I want Lambert. He should still be down in South America. Find him."

Andrews went pale, shifted his feet again. "Sir, I uh . . . Well, I thought the chairman didn't want Lambert back in the States, not so soon after Limpkin—"

Simons blinked twice and affected a smile. "Oh, I'm sorry. For a moment I was under the delusion that I was the CEO and you were the flunky, but here I seem to have got that backwards." He let Andrews stare at the floor for a few long seconds. "Oh, wait, I wasn't wrong. I *am* the CEO, aren't I?"

Andrews, eyes still downcast, reached behind him for the doorknob. "I'll get right on it."

Staying low, one arm around his back to keep the contents of his field pack from rattling and giving away his position, Colonel Marvin Lambert moved from tree to tree, always in shadow opposite the moonlight. Getting in unnoticed was crucial. He could easily find himself outnumbered, and the element of surprise would be the only thing in his favor.

He cleared another clump of pines and there, finally, was the top of the ridge he'd been climbing since dusk. Thirty-one hundred vertical feet and more than eight miles, a glance at his GPS position finder told him. Clear up the side of the valley from the road where an astonished bus driver had let off the *norteamericano loco,* and shouted warnings of *guerrillas* and *narcotraficantes* had gone unheeded.

He was close, he knew, and let himself breathe through his mouth for the final sprint. Ahead he could finally see the next moonlit ridge, and he dropped to his belly to crawl the rest of the way. A few minutes of slithering through leaves and underbrush, and there: Target Area Romeo. He breathed deeply with his mouth closed, settling into position, letting his eyes grow accustomed to the pattern of shadows in the next valley, comparing them in his mind's eye to the aerials he'd studied in his hotel room in Cartagena, the one that showed the subtle, greener-than-the-surroundings square that hinted of a human presence.

Based on the plane's altitude when the photo was shot, the square was one-quarter mile by one-quarter mile, about forty acres. It would take four to five hours to get everything set up, so he didn't have much time to waste.

A flicker appeared for an instant several hundred yards away. Lambert slid the heavy pack off his back, removed the night-vision binocs and focused. Through the infrared glasses, there appeared a glowing wooden shanty. In front of it, a man, holding a small bright light to his lips. A cigarette. Lambert smiled, congratulating himself on his navigation. He'd arrived, as intended, at the northwest corner of the square, where even from the grainy photo he'd deduced that a tiny smudge was in fact the guard shack now before him.

Slowly, Lambert moved the glasses over the target, then back to the solitary sentry. Quietly, he shed all his gear save for the knife on his calf and the Glock on his hip, sank to the soft carpet of leaves and pine needles, and started crawling downslope toward the edge of the square two hundred meters south of the lone smoker.

Soon he could see that his interpretation of the aerial was correct: Ahead stood a line of bamboo poles, each supporting an edge of a giant camouflage net covering rows and rows of plants. He smiled to himself again. He'd done it. Two months ago, they'd said that without a break from their source at enemy headquarters, finding this site would be next to impossible. Well, here he was, once again *doing* the impossible!

Yes, it was definitely time to strike out on his own. Leaving on a high note was best, and what could possibly be higher than this: a one-man infiltration, deep in enemy territory? With the footage from this op, his demo tape would be downright irresistible: proof positive that Lambert Security Ltd. and its president, Colonel Marvin Lambert, were new forces to be reckoned with in the crowded world of security consulting.

He cleared his mind to concentrate on the job at hand, reminding himself he was well behind lines now and therefore in constant peril. Stealthily, he crawled, sacrificing speed for silence, until he was under the net, approaching the first row of mature, potted plants. He peered down toward the guard shack, rose to his knees to tear off a single leaf. He held it to his nose and breathed in deeply.

The grin widened as the aroma filled him. Yessir, the killer weed. He was in business.

Hours later, Lambert stared down into the darkness for a moment and allowed a warm sense of satisfaction to bathe him. He was almost finished, and he wanted to savor the feeling of watching a carefully executed project come to fruition. Soon would be the powerful finale, followed by the hasty exit, and although the adrenaline rush those provided was great, he wanted to enjoy the subtlety behind it, too.

Finally, he turned away from the valley and down to his pack. He removed a microwave transmitter, opened a panel in back to insert a battery and tested the circuitry. Then he walked back to the low-light videocamera he'd mounted on a tripod. He peered through the viewfinder one last time, hit the record button, and walked back to his field pack and picked up the radio. It was showtime.

God, he loved this part. With a deep breath of cool, pine mountain air, he gazed into the darkness below and flicked his thumb over the red toggle switch.

Flashes of light instantly lit the valley, a couple of seconds before a series of booms rolled over him. He watched the fires in the field with the beginnings of a smile before he noticed something was wrong: There were only *three* fires . . . and yes, he realized now there'd only been *three* explosions, not four.

Damn it all to hell! One of the remote detonators had failed! He'd wanted four explosions and fires, one at each corner of the farm, enough to generate a vortex of inrushing air: an honest-to-God firestorm to consume every plant, every leaf within its perimeter. And now he would only burn three of the field's edges, if that. He'd even brought a spare detonator, too, if only he'd checked his equipment. Damn it, damn it, *damn* it!

He grimaced, shaking his head. Well, this really fucked things up good. Mission success was the destruction of every single mature plant, because, it had been made clear, the competition would be able to salvage usable data from even a few survivors. Well, they weren't going to have just a *few* surviving plants. They were going to have hundreds. Thousands. The damage he'd inflicted would be minimal, and they'd post a heavy guard contingent, not the single lazy bastard they had there now. In fact, Lambert could see him, awakened from the shack, standing, staring at the fires before turning and running into the woods.

He snorted at the guard's cowardice . . . and then noticed something he'd missed. Just behind the shack, an oil barrel. *Yes!* An accelerant!

He grabbed his Uzi from his pack, fired at the backlit silhouette of the barrel, but to no avail. Either he was completely missing or the bullets weren't hot enough. He emptied both clips, and then the fourteen rounds in his pistol, when he remembered the light, anti-tank weapon he'd lugged all the way up the ridge. He smiled wide, vindicated now for having bothered, and hurriedly assembled it in the dim glow of the already dying flames.

He squinted through the scope, put the bright red dot on the barrel and fired. The rocket streaked hot and yellow through the night, and he wondered whether the barrel contained kerosene or gasoline. Kerosene would just burn, but gasoline—

A loud *whoosh* sent him sprawling, as air rushed past him in a tremendous concussion. He stood, awestruck. It indeed had been gasoline, just the right amount, too, to explode in a blast of light and heat, creating a fourth pillar of fire to complete the perimeter and ignite his firestorm: a white blaze that towered high into the night. He admired the majesty of it reverently, then finally reminded himself about leaving under the cover of darkness.

Reluctantly, he turned from the leaping flames, switched off and packed the video camera, hoisted a significantly lightened pack onto his shoulders and, with a final proud gaze upon his handiwork, started down toward the highway.

FRIDAY

A heavy surf sent up a thick, cool, salty mist as it pounded damp sand, and Dolly Nichols flared her nostrils to take in as much as she could. The smell brought back decades-old memories of the South Brevard County of her youth. Melbourne Beach, Indialantic and, farther south, Sebastian Inlet. As a child her hometown had been left behind, while, just north, developers went nuts in Cocoa Beach, their excuse the glorious mission to put man on the moon. It was that accident of geography, Dolly had realized many times over the years, that had made her and her brothers and sister among the last children ever to grow up in a coastal Florida free of high rises or traffic or winter northerners.

"Aunt Doll, watch!"

Ahead, a wiry twelve-year-old in denim shorts, tank top and black backpack waited for a wave to recede, then sprinted toward the water and launched into three quick cartwheels and a flip before skipping up the sand just ahead of the next breaker.

Dolly broke into loud applause as her niece bowed modestly. "Brava, Jenn! Brava! Well done!" She resumed walking, Jennifer falling in step beside her. "I guess all those years of gymnastics was money well spent."

Jennifer shrugged. "I'm done with that now. Just wasn't into it anymore, you know?"

"Ah." Dolly nodded. "So, Miss Mitchell, what *are* you into nowadays?"

Jennifer hooked her thumbs under the straps of the backpack. "You know.

Hanging out. I'm still taking piano. And I'll probably go out for soccer next year. Hopefully, I'll get bigger over the summer. Otherwise I'll get creamed."

Dolly studied her niece's face. Small for her age, but well defined, with sharp, smart features and widely spaced green eyes. She would all too soon be a beautiful young woman and begin a troublesome patch of years during which she'd have little use for a favorite aunt. "Boys bothering you yet?"

"No." Jennifer shrugged again.

"They will," Dolly answered sagely.

"I doubt it. Not until I get boobs. Some of the girls in my class are *totally* overdeveloped. The guys all hang around and drool."

Dolly grinned and resisted the urge to pull the girl toward her for a hug. Jennifer had made clear a couple of years back she was *way* too old for that kind of stuff, and Dolly tried to respect that. She was, after all, her only niece. Her two brothers had two young sons each, but with one brother in Texas and the other in California, she saw the boys only at Thanksgiving or Christmas, if then. Plus, as unfair as it was to admit, Jenn had always been her favorite.

She had been the siblings' first baby, and Dolly had taken to her immediately, just as Jenn had taken to her aunt. Not—as Dolly reminded herself whenever she felt guilty about not getting out to Amelia Island more often— that Jennifer needed another parent. Her little sister had married well, both emotionally and financially, and consequently had one of the few households Dolly knew of personally where all was how it should be: two loving parents, a secure roof overhead, a neighborhood where it was still possible to let a child walk to the public school without fear of ending up on the evening news.

Of course, if ever two people deserved it, Anne and Michael did. Both sister and brother-in-law had done everything right, he declining promotions to spend more time at home, she interrupting a career, then slowly going back part-time when Jenn started school. Every time she heard in a Senate committee about the breakdown of the family, about children coming to kindergarten woefully unprepared, about the perilous middle-school years, it was all she could do to stop herself from holding her chin high and bragging: "Well, *my* sister . . ."

She walked with her eyes closed, her face toward the warm spring sun, and took another deep breath of the cool salt air that dampened her hair and clothes. Each time she came to the seashore, she wondered why she'd ever left. What in God's name had been so appealing about Kissimmee, one of

the few towns in Florida more than an hour from an ocean? Sure, the school
district had been hiring new teachers at a time her hometown Brevard district hadn't, but was that really enough to have given up something that, at
the end of each day, made her sane again? Then, once politics had started,
moving meant abandoning certain re-election, until one day she realized it
was mere political ambition holding her hostage to someplace she'd grown to
loathe.

"You should get out in the sun more. You don't look so good."

Dolly opened her eyes to her niece studying the pale knees and calves
protruding from her Bermuda shorts. "Thanks for noticing," she laughed. "I
don't get out much, period. Plus at work I dress pretty conservatively. Because, you know, that's what I am: a conservative."

"Even a *little* sun, I think, would make you look healthier," Jennifer declared.

"Well, you know, Jenn, a tan might look healthy, but it's not. Too much
sun can kill you."

Jennifer shrugged once more. "If that doesn't, something else will."

Dolly found herself startled, then a little disturbed, by such a statement
from someone so young. She glanced again at her niece, who seemed not to
notice the effect her words had had. Kids, Dolly decided, were growing up
faster than ever. Or maybe she was reading too much into it. Maybe it was a
popular song lyric, a bit of dialogue from television.

She changed the subject: "How's school?"

"Easy."

"Your last report card? Still getting straight A's?"

"Yup." Jennifer turned an impromptu handstand, the contents of her
backpack flopping against the sand. "I'm doing a report about you for social
studies, you know."

Dolly idly noticed the various cloth patches decorating the black nylon.
Britney Spears. Free Tibet. Tommy Hilfiger. Larry Llama. "Is that so?"

Jennifer sprung off her hands, arching her back to land on her feet. "Yup.
My aunt, Senator Dorothy Nichols, soon to become the first woman Senate
president, and then the first woman governor. Someday the very first woman
president of the United States."

Dolly laughed aloud, clapped her hands. "My, you *are* ambitious for me,
aren't you!"

A trio of seagulls glided low overhead, squawking at one another, wheel-
ing in circles out over the breakers. Jennifer shielded her eyes from the sun

to follow their flight, ahead now into a hazy mist over the deserted beach. "I brought bread, in case we see a flock." She patted the backpack lightly. "We had to write about a famous Floridian. I picked you. I'm the only one in class who could pick someone they're related to."

Dolly smiled and couldn't help reaching out to squeeze the girl around her shoulders. She had never, she was certain, mentioned anything about governor, let alone president. "Well, I'm flattered."

"Only thing," Jennifer confided, "we're supposed to include all about the person's family? You know, who they're married to, how many kids they had, stuff like that?"

From habit, the smile froze on her face, as an image of Ramon passed before her eyes. Not the Ramon as he looked now, but when they'd first met, when his eyes were still impishly bright, his hair jet-black, his shoulders loose with a careless swagger.

"So I put that you never got married because you never found the right guy. Plus you're so busy, being in the legislature and all." Jennifer glanced up cautiously, afraid, perhaps, that she'd betrayed a confidence. "Is that all right?"

Dolly flashed a comforting smile and pulled the girl close again. "That's just fine." On the sand ahead she noticed a gathering of birds standing shoulder to shoulder, beaks turned into the breeze. She cleared her throat, grateful for the distraction. "I believe I've spotted your flock."

Jennifer gasped softly. "There's like a hundred of 'em! This is going to be *too* cool!" She dropped her backpack off one shoulder to unzip the main compartment, reached in for a brown paper bag, grabbed a handful of crumbs and started to pantomime tossing them into the air. "Watch how they come!"

Dolly watched as first one, then a handful, then a dozen, finally the whole flock winged its way toward them, screeching and squawking. Then she noticed the Larry Llama patch on the backpack again, the cartoon animal's hand out, offering a packet of cigarettes. "Jenn, where did you buy that pack?"

Jennifer was busy now, picking favorites among the birds hovering above her against the wind, then tossing those lucky ones pellets of stale bread. "This? You can't *buy* one of these. I got it at a concert."

Jeena turned sideways to the mirror, scowling as she smoothed the clingy white skirt against her rear before finally giving up. It was no use. The panty lines just weren't going away. Dejectedly, she eyed the clothing in the Buy pile, all of it shorter and tighter and lower-cut than anything she'd worn since . . . well, since the publication date of a particular issue of a particular magazine.

For three hours she'd roamed Governor's Square Mall, looking for the sort of clothes her new boss wore, finally finding it in a boutique called Body Style that catered primarily to girls about a dozen years her junior. Miniskirts with off-center slits, microskirts too short for a slit, rib-hugging tops, sleeveless vests, matching jackets, all in a variety of primary and not-so primary colors.

Back when she'd worked on the legislative staff, she and the other girls in the office had had a catalog of derisive names for the fourth-floor women who dressed like this: arm candy, trophy girls, tramps, sluts. Whores. And now here she was, joining their ranks.

But no, she told herself, she wasn't. Those girls weren't real lobbyists, just little helpers for their male bosses. They brought coffee, took notes, ran copies, delivered amendments, accompanied legislators to dinner, accompanied legislators back to their townhouses. . . . She on the other hand was working for Ruth Ann Bronson, the woman who'd started as a runner for Martin Remy, then struck out on her own, a pioneer in an era when there just weren't any women lobbyists. Over time she'd learned the game better than most of her male colleagues, had earned a reputation for knowing, off the top of her head, which among the thousands of bills in play at any moment was the best vehicle for a given amendment on a given topic.

It was Ruth Ann's trailblazing that had made possible the recent cadre of female business lobbyists, a staid batch of middle-aged women in $200 coifs and $1,000 suits. They, though, were a single-issue bunch: health-care or banking. In the top tier of brand-name lobbyists, Ruth Ann was still the only woman among the Jim Bollards, the Sam Englishes, the Martin Remys.

And if Ruth Ann chose to take the fight to her male counterparts, to be easy enough on the eyes to make up for not being a good ol' boy, then more power to her. Jeena was proud to join that fight. After all, as Ruth Ann had promised, her looks were to open doors. Nothing more.

Under Ruth Ann's tutelage, she would learn The Process. Knowing how and when to massage legislation to the client's liking as it moved along. Someday soon, when a ranking lawmaker or a senior staffer saw her in a committee room, they'd know immediately that something was up, that they'd best compromise or risk seeing all their work undone.

And finally, on that day, she would erase that single, decade-old mistake.

Gone would be the days when she'd start a presentation on a billion-dollar change in tax policy, or the out-year costs of a new program, only to see in the back rows a whisper, then a knowing smile. Gone would be the days when seemingly every male set of eyes would roam her body and, no matter how schoolmarmish her attire, mentally undress her, try to imagine what she might look like sitting buck naked on a porch railing, a shy smile for the camera.

No, under Ruth Ann Bronson's wing, this town would learn to respect her. And if she had to dress a bit provocatively to get there, then so be it. It was a hell of a lot better than what those poor girls working for Martin Remy had to do. Anyway, the clothes, she reminded herself as she slipped off the white skirt and dropped it onto the Buy pile, were only window dressing. It was clear Ruth Ann valued her mind, her law school training.

Why else would she have assigned her, a rookie, the task of sifting through thirty-four boxes of Roper-Joyner's records to neuter any arguments the opposition might come up with for floor debate? Part of her had cringed at poring through all that paper. That, in fact, had been a big reason for leaving law school: too much paper having too little to do with the real world. But mainly she'd been flattered. When the matter came to the Senate Floor and the other side started lobbing charges, it would be *her* work that saved the day.

She appraised the stacks of clothing before her, the shopping bag filled with high-heeled pumps in various colors—fuck-me pumps, in her youth— as well as several pairs of strappy, impractical sandals. Wistfully, she eyed the looser, more comfortable, more conservative Put Back pile. Even those were a far cry from the Laura Ashley look she'd adopted that spring semester. Still, Ruth Ann had been plain: the barer, the shorter, the tighter, the better. And, she reminded herself, it was Ruth Ann's clothing allowance that was paying for it all.

She sighed, hung the shopping bag on a shoulder, gathered up both stacks of clothes and pushed through the fitting room door.

For eighteen minutes, Martin Remy had been sitting on the couch in T. C. Tuttle's inner office, watching and listening as the little gnome of a man called various other lobbyists in town and, with a wink for Remy, commenced to bawl out each of them over problems with his in-town apartment, his Capitol Club membership, his brand-new but glitch-ridden sport utility vehicle.

Remy uncrossed and recrossed his legs, then out a corner of his eye checked the Rolex on his wrist. Nineteen minutes. Almost noon, late for a lunch date with a new client on what should have been a day off, and here he was wasting time while Tuttle showed off. At least, he realized gratefully, he was not in the outer office, where the wait often was hours.

T.C. winked at him broadly, threw his sockless, penny-loafered feet atop his desk and let loose a blue stream of North Florida drawl into his telephone. And once again Remy found himself marveling at Tuttle's perennial ability, regardless of the Senate's titular leadership, of snaring for himself a disproportionate slice of power. T.C. for Teegan Chaunce, two names unusual enough, vaguely feminine enough to have engendered if not outright hostility then certainly suspicion in the Panhandle of the late 1960s, and therefore abandoned in favor of the initials. Governors, Senate presidents and House speakers came and went, but the Rasputin of Tallahassee, as Tuttle had dubbed himself some years back, always managed to endure.

Remy surreptitiously checked his wristwatch again, itching to turn his cell phones back on. God only knew how many calls he'd already missed, how much work was going to other, lesser lobbyists because of his unavailability. That morning he'd played two rounds of phone tag with the Christian Broadcasters of Florida and the Wine and Spirits Federation, both interested in new representation, both potentially upper-six-figure deals. But as he'd learned over the years, it paid to give T.C. every iota of your attention if you wanted any chance of eventually winning the favor of his. If he caught you looking at your watch, he would intentionally prolong whatever he was doing, be it phone call, meal or bowel movement, to make you wait that much longer. And God forbid a pager or cell phone went off in his office, particularly his inner office. Remy could remember a story a couple of years back about the lobbyist for a breast implant manufacturer who'd been working T.C. for a tax break when his cell phone rang. T.C. had thrown him out of his office, then monkeyed with that year's budget to *double* the tax on boob jobs.

From his desk, T.C. shook his head, made a yapping motion with one hand: He couldn't get the son of a bitch at the other end of the line to shut up.

Remy shrugged resignedly—what can you do?—and stole another glance at his Rolex: twenty-six minutes. Suddenly Remy's ears perked up as T.C.

made a final, parting threat about what would happen if the door ding in his metallic-blue Grand Cherokee wasn't completely, absolutely, without-a-trace removed by day's end.

"Martin Remy Cognac!" Tuttle shouted across the four feet separating them, then affected a scowl. "How come the feds haven't thrown your ass in jail yet? You ain't *co-operatin'*, are you? Ain't wearin' a *wire*, are you?"

Remy smiled, stretched his arms outward. It was their old joke: Who would be indicted first. Funny for the first five or six hundred times, now strictly habit. "Go ahead. Feel me up. I know it's something you've always wanted."

The formalities finished, Tuttle pulled his feet off his desk, ran one hand over his shiny dome, then started snapping the thick rubber bands that were perpetually around his wrists. He let out a long, fake sigh and settled back in his chair. "So who is it requires my help today? Oil company? Savings and loan embezzler? Date-rape-drug maker?"

From his briefcase, Remy pulled out a sheaf of papers stapled together and a single sheet bearing one short sentence, then passed both across the desk. "No one quite so well-heeled, I'm afraid." He leaned attentively toward T.C.'s squat frame. "My client needs a little help making sure his livelihood, and hundreds if not thousands of jobs, are not negatively impacted by a particular piece of legislation. It's the fastest-growing segment of the computer services industry, so I know the state wouldn't want to do anything to hurt it."

Tuttle skimmed through the bill, rubbed his hands together. "Computer porn! Hot damn!"

"It seems," Remy began matter-of-factly, "that a couple of your female colleagues in this chamber who happen to be, and I mean no disrespect here, charter members of the Femi-Nazi Party, are still upset about that thing at the First Coast Mall last year. You remember? That guy was busted for building a video camera into the top of his briefcase? Set it down in front of a Burdine's cash register, coincidentally enough, right beside this blonde in a miniskirt? Then it turned out there wasn't any law against it, and they had to let him go?"

T.C. shook his head thoughtfully. "A schoolteacher, right? Goddamn. Had the legs to work in a strip joint, if I'm rememberin' right."

"You are. Anyhow, instead of being flattered that her picture would be out on the Internet, where millions of guys could see it, she got all mad." Remy turned his palms skyward with a shrug. "No telling, with some women."

T.C. picked up the copy of the bill again. "So you want to keep these cameras legal. But ain't that exactly what my uptight female colleagues are tryin' to make *illegal*?"

Remy leaned forward, pointing a gold-adorned pinky at his amendment, a single word: "mobile," to be inserted into the second paragraph of the bill. "They want to make what happened in that *mall* illegal. My clients got no problem with that. They just want to be sure that cameras mounted in a *fixed* location aren't unfairly tarred by that incident."

T.C. read the amendment again. "Fixed location."

"Bathrooms, pool cabanas, underneath your secretary's desk. Wherever. My clients want to ensure that in the state's zeal to go after the perverts with their portable cameras, they don't inadvertently harm the thousands of legitimate users of secretary-cams."

Tuttle squinted, watched Remy carefully, finally shook his head. "Marty, I got to hand it to you. *Legitimate users of secretary-cams.* You even kept a straight face."

Remy grinned. "I gotta keep in practice. If somebody reads my amendment and asks about it, I have to make it sound reasonable. Of course, I'm hoping there's never any need for that. Maybe you could slip this baby in over in Bill Drafting, or maybe on the Floor when no one's paying attention. You know: one of your 'technical' amendments."

"That don't work so good no more." T.C. threw the bill on the desk, interlaced his pudgy fingers and stretched his arms to pop his knuckles. "Anytime that bitch Dolly Nichols hears me say 'technical amendment,' she sends for a copy so she can read every stinkin' word."

Remy sat a moment, waiting to hear how much T.C. was going to want for this particular favor, but T.C. was too busy digging through a drawer, finally pulling out a stick with an alligator claw affixed to the end and using it to scratch his back. Remy held his tongue. Speaking too quickly would demonstrate a high level of interest and thereby drive up the price.

"The bill already passed Judiciary," Remy said finally, defeated. "It goes to Appropriations on Monday, and I thought—"

"Don't worry about it. I'll add it in Bill Draftin', after it gets outta Appropriations and before it hits the Floor. No big deal. What *I* can't understand is why everybody's so hot to see what kind of underwear their secretary's wearin'."

Remy adopted an amused smile, leaned forward conspiratorially. "It's because, my over-the-hill fossil, a lot of chicks, especially the real hot ones, don't *wear* any anymore."

T.C. slammed his hands onto the desk. "Go on!"

Remy rose, walked to the corner of the office to a huge, nineteen-inch computer monitor, beckoned T.C. with a finger. "The taxpayers of this state have given you one of these at great expense. You know how to turn it on?"

"Great, big, Jap paperweight." Tuttle took the chair beside Remy. "What, you goin' out on the World Wide Web?"

Remy's hand moved the mouse, sliding and clicking, then his fingers flew over the keyboard. "Direct Internet access. Only the best for our public servants." He paused a moment as a picture started filling in. It was a split screen: the top half the head and shoulders of a striking blonde wearing a telephone headset, the bottom half a shot from under her desk, up between long, long legs inside her miniskirt. "As you can see, she really is blond."

T.C. whistled softly between his teeth. "Jesus H. Christ in a sidecar . . . She know the camera's there?"

Remy studied the picture which, as they watched, updated itself, the angle of the girl's head shifting, her knees moving slightly but not enough to obstruct the view. "This one, yeah, I think she does. You can tell because it's so well lit under the desk. Who works with a light on *under* their desk, right? So sure, this picture's better than most. But I'm telling you: There's hundreds of these sites, *thousands*. And is *this* really the sort of the thing the State of Florida ought to be outlawing?"

T.C. sat transfixed by the blonde, then glanced down to study the keyboard. "You s'pose we could pick up Ruth Ann Bronson on this? I confess I've had the hots for her since I seen her in that *Playboy* way back when."

Remy typed a few keys and clicked the mouse. "It doesn't quite work that way. But here . . ." A new image appeared on the screen, this one a dim but anatomically complete view of an anonymous crotch. "These are just the URLs I know by heart. But trust me: There's zillions of these sites. More pussy than there's time to look at."

"I'll give you this, son." Tuttle clapped a hand heartily on Remy's shoulder. "You sure know how to argue your client's case. The art of gentle persuasion. I like that."

Remy stood as Tuttle slid in front of the computer. "So you'll take care of it?"

T.C. leaned his head close to the screen, waiting for the picture to refresh itself. "Now, Marty, you know I always been on the side of free enterprise and the small businessman." He turned his head for a quick wink. "Maybe I'll have one of our computer *goo-roos* set me up here on this machine. Make it easy for an ol' dog like me to get on the information superhighway, into *cyber*-space, dawn of the new millennium, all that shit. By the way, if anybody asks, how many jobs you say ridin' on this?"

Remy snapped his briefcase shut. "Thousands.".

"In Florida, I mean." T.C. stood, one eye still on the computer monitor.

"Oh, Florida. Tens of thousands, then."

"Tens of thousands of high payin', high-tech jobs," T.C. agreed. "I like that. Makes it a economic development issue. Good."

Remy glanced at his watch. He was late, but there was one last matter, he knew. "Well, T.C., before I run, anything interesting on the export-import front? Emeralds from Colombia? Mayan artifacts? Whatcha got?"

T.C. finally turned away from the computer, broke into a wide grin. "Now, I like *that*." He moved to his credenza. "It's nice to have a loyal customer. You'd be appalled how many of your colleagues still got to be reminded of my weekly special."

Remy shrugged his don't-mention-it shrug, watched T.C. open a polished cherry box, lift what looked like a bamboo flute from the felt-lined interior and pass it to him for his inspection.

"From the heart of the Amazon, where they still take a white man's head and shrink it just for sport: an honest-to-God, gen-*yu*-ine blowgun," Tuttle said proudly, rocking on his heels. "My last one. Friend of a friend took his life in his hands gettin' hold of 'em. Escaped from a pack of cannibals like that Indiana Jones fella. For you, I'll let you have it for a thousand, even though I got a couple of museums offerin' ten, twenty grand, minimum."

Remy lifted it to his eye, peered down the hollow tube at T.C.'s smiling face, then tucked it under an arm to unbutton the double-breasted jacket and remove a money clip. With a quick lick of his thumb, he peeled off ten $100 bills.

"As always," T.C. said, tucking the money into his billfold, "been a pleasure doin' business."

Remy put his hand on the doorknob. "I'll send you the amendment Monday, all drafted nice and proper. I'll have one of my associates deliver it."

"Good. Send me one of your new ones. Nice tits, good legs, is all I ask," T.C. called out down the hallway, then shut the door and moved back to his inner office. He reached under a table into a cardboard box for another blowgun, peeled off the "Republic of China" sticker, set it into the green felt box on the credenza and then turned back to his computer screen.

SATURDAY

The toilet in the next room flushed, and Special Agent Johnny Espinosa winced, waited for the noise to subside, then rewound the reel-to-reel tape. The voices were soft but clear over the background hiss: Subject A telling Subject B he was confident he could get the wording inserted unnoticed, for a tip. For a slightly larger tip, he knew someone in the other chamber who'd do likewise.

A brief pause, then Subject B asked if the usual scale was sufficient. Subject A answered: Like last time. Subject B asked: Fifties and hundreds? And Subject A answered: *Muy bien.*

Espinosa adjusted his headphones, rewound the tape, hit Play again, this time turned the high-frequency filter up a notch. The voices became much clearer. Clear enough that not even a jury of Subject A's peers could claim any doubt. Satisfied, he rewound and hit Play again, this time simultaneously pushing the Record button on an attached microcassette player. It would take another couple of hours to type up a transcript, but then he might be able to take the rest of the day off—possibly his last down time for a while. Once contact was made, it would be uninterrupted work for several weeks, maybe even a month.

That was okay, though. Everything he'd worked toward for the past two years was right in front of him, ready to go. The first eighteen months had been on his own time: nights, weekends and vacations, interviewing sources, researching stacks of musty records, all the while working backup for other agents' cases during the day. Then one Monday morning he'd shown them what he had, what he thought he could get. That same Friday they'd cut him loose, told him: Six months. Go.

That was five months ago. As usual, things had taken longer than planned. Soon he'd have to show the bureau chief something, preferably something big enough to justify a half year in the field. He picked up a Clerk's Manual and flipped through, studying the smiling photos as he monitored the recording. Subject A was a start, but there had to be more, a lot more, and he only had a couple of weeks left.

Espinosa laid down the pamphlet and pushed the power button on his laptop computer. Waiting for it to boot, he stubbed out the Grande between his lips into a full ashtray and reached for the packet on the table for another.

Walter Soffit watched with secret relief as the governor finished cleaning his spear gun and returned it to its vinyl case atop the rough-hewn desk. Weapons had always made him uneasy, never mind one in the hands of a former ally whom Soffit had not long ago betrayed.

Not so long ago, the storied career of Strollin' Bollin' Waites was doomed, the polls had promised, predicting a lopsided loss to a younger, richer Republican opponent. Soffit had decided to be one of the first rats off. Sensing the Senate he'd longed to lead for so many years about to go Republican, Soffit had helped make it so, switching parties in the final days before the election.

Then the unthinkable had happened: The polls were proven wrong. Instead of losing by twenty points, the Granddaddy Gator of Florida politics somehow stormed from behind to win reelection. The Senate had indeed gone Republican, but only, it was clear in retrospect, because of Soffit's defection. Three Democrats who'd been counting on his help in close races instead got clobbered.

Ever since, Soffit had avoided the volatile governor at all costs, especially at the Mansion, whose FDLE guard, Soffit secretly worried, might not say a word if a turncoat Senate president were to enter the governor's private cabana but never come out.

"You like grouper?"

The words terrified Soffit because Waites was advancing on him now with a bolt-action rifle but asking him about grouper, which, Soffit was certain, was a type of fish. Soffit smiled nervously. "Love it!"

"Shot a couple of twenty-pounders in the Keys yesterday." Waites set the rifle on the desk, pulled a rag from a drawer and squirted some oil into it. "Plenty in the freezer, you want some."

Soffit nodded enthusiastically. "Fresh grouper! Great!" He gulped hard, wondering if he should ask Waites why he'd been summoned or simply be grateful that he hadn't, at least yet, been speared and fed to his hunting dogs. "I, uh—"

"Good. I'll send some over," Waites interrupted. "In return, I ask you one small favor."

Soffit listened in anticipation. Waites hadn't said more than five words to him since that afternoon he'd filed a party change card and the governor had stormed into Soffit's office and called him a worthless coward. Yet here was a request for a favor. Something that might finally let him redeem himself, put that whole ugly episode behind him, allow him to walk the corridors of the Capitol without the gnawing fear of running into the folksy, earthy governor who so thoroughly despised him and who seemed so comfortable with so many means of violent death . . .

"Two of my votes were invited to the White House next week for an education conference. Between me and you, it's bullshit, basically a photo-op for the guy. But at the end of the day, he *is* the president, and when the president calls, it's hard to say no, ain't it?"

Soffit nodded, more than a little envious. The president had never invited *him* to the White House and, now that he'd switched parties, probably never would, either.

"I told Drayer and Robeson to go on up. Now I know they'd both stay if I asked, but what the hell. How many times in your life you get invited to the Rose Garden? I told 'em you wouldn't mind postponing the vote till after they got back." Waites glanced up from his rifle to catch Soffit's eye. "You *don't* mind, right?"

Waites' fingers continued moving expertly over the broken-down gun, cleaning every part without him having to look at what he was doing, Soffit noticed with awe. He nodded assent, then remembered Simons' deadline. "I, uh, just need to do the vote before the second," he blurted. "That is, of course, if you have no objection . . . "

Waites pointed the gun at the door, sighted down the barrel as Soffit took a nervous step to the side. "Good. It's settled, then. On April first, we vote: Is Big Tobacca accountable for years of lyin', or do they buy us off and get away with it again?"

He raised an eyebrow and grinned, as if expecting Soffit to share in the joke. Soffit swallowed, obliged with a smile.

"April Fools' Day," Waites continued. "Fittin', ain't it?"

She turned the knob slowly and pushed gently, then tiptoed into the room. He was, as usual, sleeping, and she didn't want to rouse him. He would wake up soon enough, as soon as the medication wore off, and Dolly didn't mind sitting beside him, just watching him sleep.

Truth be told, that had become the most enjoyable, or more accurately, the least depressing part of her visits. Watching him rest, or holding his hand as he lay drowsy and mumbling after a fresh round of meds. During those times, she would study him: dainty, almost feminine hands, narrow shoulders, incongruously thick brow, squat nose, small mouth . . . And then she would recall how the face had, overnight almost, somehow transformed from clownish to the most handsome thing she'd ever seen. Thirty years ago, now. More than half her life.

Outside, the sky over the Gulf took an orange cast with the setting sun, suffusing the room with a rosy light. Another gorgeous spring day, much of it wasted driving across North Florida, from Amelia Island down to Carabelle. She scolded herself for complaining. It had been a wonderful visit, and she needed to make more of them. If Jennifer was growing up faster than she could comprehend, that was no one's fault but her own.

Through the window, a pair of sailboats moved silently toward the horizon, and she suppressed a sigh, reminding herself that it really had never been more than a make-pretend promise, like most else he'd offered her through the years. Really, neither of them even knew how to sail, so that the idea of their one day sailing into the sunset was as far-fetched as his actually leaving his wife and children to take her.

It had made for beautiful fantasies, though, lying in the bed of their Great Abaco cottage, lazily watching the yachts skim up and down the Sound. Mr. and Mrs. Jones, they had been to the proprietors, a demure elderly couple who spoke the King's English and kept the grounds spotless. She'd always identified with Mrs. Albury, for it was clear that in her household, too, it was she who had the head for business and therefore had to endure all the hostility that that entailed in a man's world. Their last visit had been five years ago, and even then Mr. Albury's health had been failing. He'd taken ever longer filling out the registration forms or bringing the plates of cracked conch that Mrs. Albury served up in the kitchen. It occurred to her that Mr. Albury was in all likelihood gone by now. She and Mrs. Albury would soon have even more in common.

"I didn't hear you come in."

Dolly saw Ramon's eyes were only half open. He looked tired. Just being awake was a strain. "I didn't want to wake you."

"Are there boats?"

She realized the half-open eyes, pointing right at the huge picture window, couldn't see that far anymore. "Two of them," she reported. "They're heading south."

Ramon nodded, a huge effort. "To the Canal and then the Pacific. Tahiti, Samoa, Auckland, Sydney."

He fell silent a few moments. So many times since the diagnosis he had apologized for not taking her the places he'd promised, not being the man he'd promised. She squeezed his hand firmly, said nothing.

"Or it is possible they are sailing to where I was born." He opened one eye fully, appraising her. "That is something else I must tell you before I go, Dolly. I must confess: All those times I spoke of growing up on the *pampas*, the son of a wealthy Castilian? It was a lie. Actually I was born by the seashore, in Quintana Roo. My father was a *campesino*, not a *caudillo*. I lied to you because I did not think a woman such as yourself could be obtained by the son of a peasant."

She maintained her smile, squeezed his hand again. He'd already told her this a half dozen times. She'd always suspected that his skin was too dark to have pure Spanish blood and confirmed the truth on their first exotic rendezvous, a weekend in Paris, when she saw his passport, read that his place of birth was Mexico, not Argentina. "Son of a prince, son of a garbage man. It made no difference," she assured him.

He let his eyes fall shut. "You have always been sweet to me. Why, I do not know." With a start, he opened both eyes. "Did you bring them?"

Dolly sighed softly. She loathed herself for doing it, but found she couldn't help herself. That, at least, hadn't changed. For Ramon, she always had and always would do anything. From her purse she removed two packets of Grandes. "The nurse will kill you if she finds out," she warned.

"So what? I'm already dying." Greedily, full of energy now, he tore the cellophane off one packet and reached under his mattress for a lighter.

Dolly fought down her lifelong distaste for cigarette smoke, an aversion that had only grown more intense since Ramon's illness. She resisted the urge to wave the smoke away, run and open the window. After thirty years, so close to the end, it wasn't worth the battle.

Three deep drags later, he calmed down, leaned contentedly against his stack of pillows, held the ash out over the carpeting. "How are things at the Capitol? You guys stick it to the old man yet?"

She steeled herself for the tirade. It was unfair, the abuse he would heap on the governor, but she supposed she could understand it. He had been, until the diagnosis, the industry's number-one man in Tallahassee, the guy who for fifteen years had coordinated the lobbying effort. It had been under his nose that Bolling had snuck through the Third-Party Medicaid law while keeping Ramon occupied with a bill banning smoking in restaurants—a red herring, as it turned out.

Ramon had taken the defeat personally, had vowed to undo it, promising his clients that he would not rest until it was undone. A couple of weeks later, after session was finished and Bolling had announced his lawsuit, he'd finally gone to his doctor about that persistent pain in his upper back, that nagging cough.

"The bill officially comes back to us Monday. We'll override. We'll send it to the House. They'll override, too," she reported matter-of-factly.

"Good. I wish I could be there to see the old bastard's face." He blew a stream of smoke at the ceiling. *"Pendejo."*

She looked away, across the room through the window, where the two boats were now mere specks of white on the horizon. She hated when he got like this. "Ramon, I don't think he did it to score points against you. He did it because he believed it was right."

"Bullshit. He did it for one reason and one reason only. We supported his opponent. *He's* the one taking it personal, not me. What we did was politics. What he did was criminal. *Puto.*" He nodded severely. "He lied to me, man-to-man. That, I cannot forgive."

Dolly shut up. Actually, Ramon had barely known Bolling. The great "lie" he liked to work himself up over was a casual "How are you?" in the hallway. Ramon laughingly asked if there was anything tucked in that last day's package of bills he needed to worry about, and Bolling laughingly answered, well, *he* wasn't worried.

She knew nothing she could say would make him stop harping on this. It was better just to let the mood play itself out. She glanced around the room, saw the side-by-side picture frame on the dresser. Miguel and Gabriella, from a beach trip, back when they were seven and five. Back before their mother had turned them against him.

"I asked how the pledges were coming," he repeated.

She snapped back into the present. "Coming. Twenty-two Republicans. We'll probably pick up a seat or two in November. I need thirteen to be safe. I have nine."

"If you think you need thirteen," he nodded sagely, "then get fifteen. If you think you have nine, you really have seven."

She smiled inwardly. He, who'd never even run for student council, still presumed to teach her how to run a campaign. She realized he was stroking her hand, and she felt her eyes start to well. "What am I going to do without you?" she asked softly.

He clicked his tongue several times, then dropped his cigarette into a cup of water so he could take her hands in both of his. "Didn't we say we weren't gonna talk like that, huh?"

She composed herself, let his hands wander her thighs, felt his fingers massaging through the fabric of her skirt.

"I plan on living right till the end. So come on." He slid over in the bed and pulled back the covers. "Let's live a little."

He reached forward to undo her belt, and she steeled herself. It was so desperate, this *machismo* thing he did. Half the time he didn't even have the energy anymore to finish. With a nervous glance at the door, she unbuttoned her blouse.

"Don't worry about the nurse. She won't come back for at least an hour."

She stepped out of her panties and slipped into bed. "And if she does?"

"Then she gets the thrill of her sorry old life."

On the plush crimson carpeting of the Gulfstream IV, oily gun parts laid out before him, Marvin Lambert scowled as he worked, vacillating between hope and dread.

What should have been euphoria so soon after a successful mission had instantly evaporated the moment he arrived at the front desk of his Cartagena hotel. For awaiting him was the telex he'd given up on seeing, but which, now that it was there, put him in a complete muddle. Its orders: Report at once to the airport to be flown back to the States.

Just like that, his exile was over!

Nearly two years it had been, slumming in the jungles and backwaters of South America, doing petty arsons and simple briberies. Avoiding any place with a strong U.S. presence, where a nosy embassy officer might run through the ex-pats, looking for any who might happen to have "holds" on their passports.

His boredom and frustration in the "minors," in fact, had been the main impetus for striking out on his own. If Roper-Joyner wasn't going to fully utilize and appreciate his talents, let him grow in his job, then by God he'd find others who would.

After all, if he'd been kept busy, he never would have had time to take up the South African's offer to visit Medellín and the security force he was training there, never would have taken the risky international flight to Brussels to attend that convention, never would have been intoxicated with the romance of the place names, the casual familiarity with such heavy-duty weaponry, the professionally edited and scored demo tapes that even the most humble "consultants" there were giving away for the asking.

He'd come away from Brussels with the realization that with the new global economy, there was more action in the world than ever before, just sitting there waiting for a man of ambition. And although any new business would have rough going at first, there Lambert had an advantage over most: After a decade with RJH, he'd socked away nearly $5 million in salary and bonuses in an overseas account, more than enough cushion for those first, lean years.

To go home *now*, with the plans for his grand adventure already in works . . . Even worse, having to face the chief . . .

Two weeks earlier, he'd talked himself into leaving. Just as soon as the bonus for the Colombia job had landed in his account, he'd buy a dozen connecting airline tickets in cash, pick a route as he went, and disappear off Durham's radar screen. Six months or a year later, he'd reappear, maybe in the Black Sea, maybe in Hong Kong; who could say? Maybe back in Medellín, finally his own boss.

On the other hand, he *was* going home. And he had to admit, working for an outfit like RJH had its advantages. Like when the South African arranged for transportation, it was usually a drafty cargo plane, not a luxury business jet with a king-size bed and decanters of single-malt Irish whiskey.

He had some decisions to make, that was for sure. He wondered again exactly what the chief needed done. He was on his way to Florida, and he knew vaguely that the company had some beef with the governor there. Perhaps, he dared hope, his job would be to put an end to the disagreement by taking out the governor. Now *that* would be something to write home about. There were only fifty governors in the whole country, and Florida was, what, the fourth or fifth biggest state? Sure, it didn't have the cachet of a D.C. assignment, but after Limpkin, they weren't likely to let Lambert get close to Washington for a good while. Anyway, the governor of a state was worth half a dozen *generalissimos*, easy. Of course, if the job *wasn't* the governor, was instead some chickenshit thing, that still left the problem of how to tell the chief he wanted out. . . .

He took a clean rag and wiped excess oil off various clusters of gun parts. He had brought all his weapons, just in case, and had most of them broken down in front of him: a TEC-9, a MAC-10, an AK-47, a Glock, a Sig-Sauer and a good ol' Colt .45 spread out in pieces on a surplus Army blanket.

Through the Gulfstream's windows, he saw orange clouds heralding dusk, peered forward into the cockpit. "Gentlemen," he shouted. "Could I suggest we run a dark approach? I think the chief has in mind a covert insertion."

The co-pilot leaned over to look at him, rolled his eyes and wordlessly turned back to his instruments. Lambert gritted his teeth. Fucking pilots. The same everywhere. Thought they were smarter than you just because they'd been to college. Even army pilots had been like that, and their planes weren't even that cool.

He fantasized for a moment about how some of his new friends might correct such an attitude. The South African, for instance. He'd smile, all polite. Then, as the plane started getting close to Tallahassee, he'd simply walk forward, put a bullet through both their heads, then parachute out.

He wondered if the jet even had a parachute. Probably not, he thought sourly. And even if it did, the chief would get totally pissed off about losing a $30 million plane over something like that.

Lambert shrugged it off, returned to his weapons. He started assembling the TEC-9 and noticed a snag in the gun's movement when he tried to slide the clip into place. He removed it, looked for an obstruction, tried again and got the same result. He looked forward into the cockpit again: "You fellas don't happen to know if there's a gun show in town, do you?"

With one hand, the co-pilot swung the cockpit door shut.

SUNDAY

After a good hour of studying the first page in a thick packet of newspaper clippings, Jeena finally admitted the intellectual dishonesty of pretending she could come out to the springs on a spectacularly sunny afternoon and actually get anything done. She lay on her tummy on a beach towel, feet kicking in the air behind her, eyes too often wandering to the chilly, crystal-clear water just a few feet ahead.

Children ran from the bank, shouting, cartwheeling into the water, as their parents sat in lawn chairs or floated lazily on inner tubes while Jeena read, re-read and re-read again the opening paragraphs to a *Wall Street Journal* article about Roper-Joyner's marketing push against the industry's Big Two.

She reminded herself that the four inches of clippings in her folder promised to be downright entertaining compared to the stuff awaiting her at home. Inter-office memoranda, marketing surveys, strategic plans, profit-loss statements: all of it in mind-numbing corporate-speak that took five times longer than necessary to say something, and even then used all manner of hedge words to avoid saying it definitively. Thirty-four boxes of the stuff, and so far she wasn't even through box five.

Instead she lay in her swimsuit at Wakulla Springs, renewing her tan, dreaming about cave-diving, pretending that if she physically held work in her hands and didn't actually jump in the water, then that counted as something productive. In fact, coming to the springs only reminded her that she'd been back in Tallahassee two months, yet hadn't done the one thing she most missed when she'd been away: a dive down into the hypnotically clear water, down into the grottos and even, after she'd worked up her nerve, into some of the tunnels.

As an undergraduate, she'd grown quite proficient and for one summer had actually worked with the Geology Department team mapping the underwater tunnels that radiated through the limestone. Of course, for two months there'd been a perfectly plausible reason not to dive: she hadn't found work, and it seemed wrong to go play. In reality, that had merely been a convenient excuse. In reality, the only person she knew in town with cave-diving experience was Dunbar, and so diving meant calling Dunbar, and calling Dunbar meant . . .

Well, anyway, now she did have a job, and the job would require every moment of her time for the next month, so there wasn't even any point thinking about diving, about the equipment sitting in her bedroom closet, about the full air tank still in her trunk. All of that would wait, and with it would wait the whole Dunbar question.

Pointedly, she ignored the two wetsuited guys backing into the spring from the opposite shore, ignored the droplet of water that fell on her arm from a boy's particularly boisterous splash, determinedly focused on the *Journal* article. It was two years old, from when anti-smoking activists started accusing Roper-Joyner of mimicking Reynolds' Joe Camel with its Larry Llama brand, of purposely trying to steal underage market share. The article pointed out that if Larry Llama was indeed aimed at kids, it followed the company's standard marketing strategy. The Grande brand was created for export to Latin America, then aimed at Hispanics at home. Jackpots were targeted at blacks, Princesses at young, single women. As far as mimicking Reynolds, the company had been accused of that a decade earlier when it changed its name from Southern Standard Tobacco to Roper-Joyner Holdings, thus giving it a ticker symbol nearly identical to that of its competitor. Reynolds officials were quoted saying, first, imitation was the highest form of flattery and, second, Joe Camel was not, repeat not, targeted at children.

Jeena flipped the page to a *New York Times* article about how Big Tobacco did all its research, like breeding high-nicotine strains, overseas to keep any incriminating results beyond the reach of the American legal system. About how competition for such products was so intense that all the major companies were rumored to engage in industrial espionage to—

"Catching up on your propaganda?" a voice boomed behind her.

Instinctively, a hand went to tug the leg openings of her one-piece to cover as much thigh as possible. She turned to a goateed man in wire rims, a T-shirt and a smile focusing hard on her face, on the headline of the article she was reading but not, she decided finally, on the edge of her swimsuit. She forced a smile and reminded herself that starting the next day, she would go to work wearing clothes revealing pretty much everything she was revealing now. She may as well get used to guys staring.

"Research," she said.

"Lies," he nodded. "Damned lies. Dirty, damned lies. Propagated by the liberal media that wants to rob each and every American of the freedom to make individual choices."

"Actually," she smiled again, involuntarily this time, "it's *opposition* research. You know, figure out what the anti-smoking side is likely to use and find something to counter it?"

"Ah. Another tobacco mercenary." He tapped his chest. "Me, too. Murphy Moran. Down from D.C. to take on ol' Bolling Waites."

Jeena watched Murphy's eyes, saw they still hadn't left hers. "Jeena Golden. I actually live here, but my new boss signed up with RJH, which makes me a mercenary, too, I suppose." She nodded at her articles. "Though the more I read, the more I want to shower off. I mean, they sound so *sleazy.*"

Murphy lifted a palm. "Not another word. Roper-Joyner Holdings is an honorable corporation upholding the Dow Jones, Bartholomew Simons is a fine American, and I don't want to hear otherwise." He grinned widely. "All right, so they're sleazy. But you know, even the sleazy have a right to the legislative process. Plus, what the hell, a paycheck's a paycheck. Anyway, I didn't come out here to get all depressed about the sort of client I have yet again. I came here to check out an honest-to-God swimmin' hole. You been in yet?"

Jeena shook her head. "I'll warn you, though. On a day like this, when it's not real hot, it's going to feel chilly. The water's seventy-two degrees, winter or summer."

"Sounds about perfect." He watched a child clinging to a rope swing out over the water in a high arc, let go, tumble in with a splash. "Jesus! Is that deep enough out there?"

"Oh, it's deep enough," Jeena said authoritatively. "This hole here is over two hundred feet to the bottom, with some tunnels going even deeper."

Murphy scratched his goatee. "Yeah, now I remember. This place was in *National Geographic* a few years back. . . . "

"They were following the team mapping the caverns. The writer needed special certification for the helium-oxygen mix they use. With plain air, you'd get nitrogen narcosis at that depth, not to mention your bottom time on a single tank at a hundred fifty feet is about two minutes."

Murphy studied her anew, impressed. "Don't tell me *you've* dived these caves."

Jeena shrugged modestly. "Not down to two hundred feet. But I was an assistant on the research project back in school. Stringing safety lines, ferrying cameras and lights through the mapped tunnels. Stuff like that."

Unbidden, her mind recalled that one awful night, how she and Dunbar were called out to help find a missing diver, a friend of theirs. How his body had surfaced a couple of days later, miles downstream. How he'd obviously been sucked into a tunnel by a strong current, then swept along through the darkness, knowing the whole way he was doomed. How just a week later, she herself had suffered a panic attack at depth when her shoulders got wedged in a tunnel they were exploring . . .

"Wow. Scuba," Murphy said. "Always wanted to learn, but never made the time. Well, except for one of those resort courses once in the Caymans. You know, learn just enough to get yourself killed?"

She swallowed uncomfortably at his choice of words, put on a brave smile—and noticed his eyes starting to stray down her back, her buttocks, her legs. And, she noticed to her surprise, she didn't mind it so terribly much.

He grinned, eyes back on hers. "Maybe you can teach me sometime."

She made a show of flipping a page, of barely having noticed his overture. "Maybe."

Murphy turned again to survey the water. "Seventy-two degrees, huh? Well, having come all the way out here when I should be working, I guess I don't have any choice." Self-consciously, he pulled off his shirt, dropped his Bermuda shorts to reveal a pair of yellow swim trunks and stepped out of his boat shoes. "Come get me when hypothermia sets in?"

Jeena pretended not to watch from behind her Ray-Bans, then casually turned another page. "Of course."

Murphy stepped to the edge of a rock outcropping, took several deep breaths, clapped his hands a couple of times, jiggled his shoulders and finally threw himself in. He surfaced a moment later with a yelp, frantically treading water.

"Feels great!" He forced a grin. "Chilly right at first, but once you get used to it . . . Come on!"

Jeena said nothing, waved her fingers at him instead. She'd studied him as he'd stripped down, had seen nothing remarkable. The start of a bulge around his midriff. Good shoulders. Shortish but muscular legs. And, slowly, it occurred to her what it was she found intriguing. It was the boyish enthusiasm, the almost shy manner of flirting. It was, she remembered, the way Dunbar had first talked to her, years ago. . . .

"I understand," he continued. "You probably want to get good and warm before jumping in. Can't say I blame you. Well, I'm gonna swim across and back, just to get some exercise for a change, and uh, well, we'll talk again."

And with a quick grin, he was stroking steadily across the spring, face down for three, up for one, methodically, not looking back. Quickly, she slipped into T-shirt and shorts, gathered up her towel and accordion folder and made her way to the parking lot.

"*You know* what my problem is? I wasn't born in Cuba." Agustin Cruz shut up a moment as T.C. started his backswing, pulled the club through a funky arc and gave the ball a solid whack. "If I'd been born in Cuba, then I could talk about Castro and stuff and people would take me seriously."

Tuttle watched the ball sail down the fairway a bit, then hook deep into the forest. He teed up yet again. "Gus, if you'da been born in Cuba, you'da been one of them fool refugees tryin' to cross over in a inner tube. You'da drowned in a storm or dried out in the sun. Either way, you'd be dead. Be glad your granddaddy came over on a airplane."

Gus watched glumly as T.C. wiggled his club, swung and hooked another ball into the palmettos and pine trees to the left of the fairway. A round of golf with T.C. was a frustrating chore in general, and getting off a tee was the worst. Gus wasn't much better, but at least he didn't care how badly he did. T.C., on the other hand, was obsessive, hacking and whacking until a ball wound up on grass. He teed again, swung again, hooked again.

"But if I was a real refugee, then the governor would respect me. He don't respect me now. You know he stranded me at the airport?"

T.C. snorted as he gave yet another ball a flailing whack. "It ain't 'cause you wasn't born in Cuba that Bollin' don't respect you. He don't respect you 'cause you're a greasy, low-rent Meskin." He watched the ball arc into the woods to the right this time, then turned to see the next foursome on the green behind them. "Aw, fuck it," he said, and waddled to the golf cart.

Gus glanced back at the previous hole, recognized two senior House members with a pair of phone company lobbyists, one of whom he'd been eyeing of late as a potential patron, then scampered after Tuttle. "How do you mean, low rent?" He eyed T.C. enviously as he turned the key and released the brake. "And when do I get to drive?"

"Low rent," Tuttle explained, as he cruised toward the elevated green a couple of hundred yards away, "low rent means you think small. If you think small, you are small."

Gus considered this. "So instead of asking for less money, I should of asked for *more?*"

Tuttle smiled, tapped his nose with an index finger. "To *be* big, you gotta think big. You ask the governor for twenty-five grand to change the world, he knows you're scammin' him. You ask for a couple mill, why, hell, who knows? Maybe you really are fixin' to change it."

Gus mulled on this. "Think big."

"Think big. And often. You can't put all your eggs in one basket. You gotta diversify, in case one p'ticular thing don't pan out." Tuttle drove right on past the general area where most of his balls had gone astray, Gus noticed. "Me, for instance. I always got somethin' cookin'. Real estate, commodities, gold, a little personal finance, antiques. You name it."

Gus watched how Tuttle handled the cart with one hand on the wheel, up a hill and around the edge of a bunker. Like a pro. Then he hit the lip of the green and kept on driving. Gus looked around nervously. "I thought we weren't supposed to drive on these."

T.C. drove to within a couple of yards of the flag, set the parking brake and shuffled toward the pin. "Normal folks ain't. We ain't normal folk. We're legislators, doin' the people's business." He popped a couple of balls onto the closely mown grass next to the hole. One stopped about a foot away, the other three feet. Studying his putter, he stood over the nearer ball. "I know, in Mi-*yam*-uh they all came to you. Money fallin' outta their pockets."

As a full-time city commissioner, Gus had made fifty grand a year above the table, about four times that under it, mainly from developers of strip malls and flimsy subdivisions. He'd thought by going to Tallahassee he'd broaden his horizons. Instead, as a part-time state senator, he now made only twenty-five grand salary and barely that much in tips from grateful lobbyists. He hadn't dared ask either wife or girlfriend to cut their expenses accordingly.

"Well, this ain't Mi-*yam*-uh. Here, nobody knows nothin' 'bout you, other than that you're a greasy Meskin. So you gotta be more enterprisin'. Hell, you think I always been on easy street? Shit, when I first got here, I was poor as you. Poorer. Fuck." Tuttle had missed his putt, knocking his ball a good two feet beyond the hole. He kicked it with the toe of one shiny golf shoe a few times until it plunked into the cup. "Your turn."

Gus stepped up to his ball and, so as not to make T.C. mad, took three strokes to sink it. He retrieved both balls. "More enterprising."

"Two for me, four for you." Tuttle scratched at the scorecard with a pencil, looked up with a grin. "It's like fuckin' the prom queen in high school. It ain't never gonna happen unless you ask."

Gus recalled the prom queen at his high school, a gorgeous Colombian named Carlita. She'd laughed aloud the one time he'd tried to ask her out. They walked back to the cart, Gus eyeing the driver's seat, the cool little steering wheel. Almost a year of golf, at least once a month, usually more, and T.C. had never yet let him drive. He shook off the memory of Carlita's rejection, took a deep breath. "All right, I'm taking your advice: *I* wanna drive."

Tuttle beamed, then held out the keys. "Now you're learnin'."

Lambert stood feet apart, hands behind his back as Simons wandered the rented mini-warehouse into which Lambert had unloaded his gear. Every so often, he stopped at a crate or duffel bag and opened it up for a look, and Lambert patiently explained what it was and how it worked.

"L-A-T-W?" Simons asked, pointing to the stenciled label on a box.

"Light anti-tank weapon, sir," Lambert recited.

Simons nodded. "In case they call out the National Guard on us?"

"It's effective against other conveyances as well, sir."

"That's good to know." Simons moved to a suitcase containing wire, connectors, a crimping tool and an assortment of various electrical components, then played with a skeletal sniper's rifle before laying it down and pulling himself up onto a bare metal desk. "All the cool *stuff* you get to use. You know sometimes, Lambert, I really envy you. Your job."

Lambert forced a smile. "Like any job, chief, it has its pluses and minuses."

Simons laughed. "Just make sure the former outweigh the latter, right? Well, I like a man who enjoys his work. Which brings us to the point of our convergence in this lovely little town. We have a situation to correct, and I need your assistance."

"Anything I can do to help, sir."

"Good. There are a couple of elements to it. One is more up your alley than the other, but both are equally important. First, there is a certain influential senator. Her vote is evidently critical to our goal, and she seems a tad reluctant to promise it to us. That despite the boundless generosity we've shown her political career over the years. We need to procure . . . material to make her less reluctant."

Lambert felt his face fall, worked hard not to show it. "And the other?"

Simons stood again, began wandering amid the crates of equipment, stopped at a pile of mountaineering gear. "The other thing. There is a single-page memorandum, something that admittedly should have been destroyed a long time ago but which nonetheless wasn't, which if it were to become public would have grave consequences for this corporation. What we need to do . . ." Simons picked up a carabiner, snapped it open and closed a few times, then turned to face Lambert. "What we need to do is find and retrieve this item, and then . . . sanitize its route."

Lambert let the words bounce around his head a moment as he decoded. "You want I should get rid of everyone who has seen it."

Simons dropped the carabiner and gave Lambert a fatherly pat on the shoulder. "I knew you'd understand. That's why you're my go-to guy."

This time, Lambert couldn't hold it in. "That's why you sent me off to Bum Fuck Egypt?" he muttered. "Bring me back to do scut work . . . "

Simons sighed. "You're disappointed. You were hoping for something else? Something more dramatic?"

Lambert shrugged. "I figured, you know, if it's the governor we got a problem with, then. . . . I mean, I already did half the research. Every Tuesday morning's a Cabinet meeting in the basement. He walks down this corridor with a clear line of sight from the balcony. If not there, then shoot, you seen the stupid little plane he flies around on? It's this little Beechcraft prop job. I wouldn't even need anti-aircraft missiles. Just a couple hundred rounds from the fifty-cal would do the trick. Sir."

Simons took off his glasses, breathed on the lenses and wiped them on his tie. "I appreciate your enthusiasm. Alas, we don't need for anything to happen to the governor. I've already explained what we do need. You're to gather intelligence on the senator woman, and I've already narrowed down the other item to two or three possibilities."

Lambert nodded, thought: *Now!* Here was the time, the perfect opportunity. He stole a glance at the television, at the VCR where the tape was already cued up. He'd decided overnight it would be best for the tape to do the talking. He could never get his mouth to work right with Simons.

"What?" Simons demanded. "More money? All right, fine. Insofar as I've assigned you two separate tasks, and given the overall importance of the mission, instead of the usual five hundred grand bonus, let's call it an even mill."

Lambert swallowed softly, unable to start. What was he waiting for? This was precisely the reason he'd begun considering leaving RJH: lousier and lousier assignments. So what was the problem?

"Okay," Simons sighed. "One-point-five mill. There. Happy? You bargained yourself an extra million. Don't spend it all in one place."

Slowly, Lambert walked toward the TV, flicked it on, hit the Play button, and stepped aside to give Simons an unobstructed view. Exciting TV-news music accompanied footage of Lambert in camouflage running up a hill, Lambert rappeling down a cliff, Lambert firing an M-16 from the hip on a rifle range, Lambert lecturing a group of admiring Colombian peasants on the proper use of a Stinger missile. An announcer boasted of Lambert's experience, as the screen showed clips of a commuter plane exploding, of a medevac helicopter rising from a forest clearing, of paramedics dragging a stretcher down the steps of the U.S. Capitol and, finally, a still unedited snippet of a dark valley bursting into flames. The words "Lambert Security Ltd." flashed on the screen.

Simons waited for the screen to turn to snow, then walked forward to turn off the television and pop out the tape. "A Thompson gun for hire, fighting to be done, eh? So that's what this is about."

Lambert shrugged. "You said it yourself, sir, your job's gotta give you more pluses than minuses."

"I was only making conversation." Simons hopped up on the desk, dangling his legs and holding the videocassette between his fingers. "Just out of curiosity: That plane in the video, that was McHenry's?"

Lambert hesitated, then nodded.

"So I guess the hunting accident was Bergstrom and the guy in D.C. would be Limpkin."

Again, Lambert nodded.

Simons looked thoughtfully at the ceiling. "So you've been lugging around a camera with you, shooting your own video, for, what, six, six and a half years? Well, I have to admire the forethought."

Lambert blinked, returned a cautious smile. The old man wasn't taking it so bad, after all. . . .

"Colonel, I think it's time we reviewed a history lesson. One, you're not really a colonel."

The smile disappeared, and Lambert saw it was going to be as bad as he'd feared. "I know that. There's no reason—"

"Two, you're not really a Gulf War hero. Yes, you received a concussion *during* the time we were bombing the shit out of Iraq, but falling off a boot camp obstacle course doesn't really count, does it?" Simons slid off the desk, started looking through the crates again. "Three, if it weren't for my intervention, you'd be on Death Row for murdering your foreman at the Jackpot packaging plant. Four, I still safeguard the arsenic-laced cigarettes he had in his pocket, as well as the reprimand he'd written you a month earlier, which, coincidentally enough, was just before the clinic logs show he started getting sick. Am I missing anything?"

Lambert stared sullenly. Occasionally, he'd let himself believe that there was no way Simons could get him sent up using evidence he himself had squirreled away for ten years. And then he'd remind himself how easily Simons had headed off a criminal investigation in the first place.

"In summary," Simons continued. "A forty-year-old with a mere GED, no real military record, who could easily have been strapped to the gurney and gotten the needle by now. Such a man is instead a multimillionaire and works a couple of months a year, tops. I'd say you've done pretty well for yourself, no?"

Simons found the crate he was looking for, pulled out an attaché case of 8mm videotapes and walked back to the desk. "I thought I saw these." One by one, he broke open the cassettes and peeled out ribbons of brown tape into a wastepaper can. "Son, these are the property of Roper-Joyner Holdings. The events depicted were authorized and *paid* for by Roper-Joyner Holdings. Any recording, rebroadcast or other use without the express written consent of Roper-Joyner Holdings is strictly . . ." Simons dropped a flaming lighter into the waste can and let the plastic tape ignite with a *poof*. " . . . prohibited."

Silently, Lambert watched years of documentation go up in a pall of acrid black smoke. He considered mentioning the proximity of the flames to a box of C-4, then decided against it. What the hell.

"Marvin, by any objective standard, I treat you pretty damn well. All I expect in return is a little loyalty. See, if you hadn't fallen on your head in boot camp, one of the things you would have learned is that when the DI tells you to jump, you're supposed to ask: how high? So as long as whenever I say jump, you say how high, we'll get along just fine. In the meantime, make

yourself an expert on one Dorothy Marie Nichols. Also, I expect I'll be lo-
cating thirty-four boxes of legal records in the next day or two. Prepare yourself for a fair amount of drudge work. I'll handle the actual retrieval. I want
to watch their faces when I ask who, exactly, was privy to the documents.
And that observation should provide me with the names for your sanitation
list." Simons stood and headed for the warehouse's garage door. "Just to show
you I'm a nice guy, we'll keep the mission bonus at a mill-and-a-half like you
negotiated for yourself earlier."

Simons reached the door, stopped and turned. "Oh, there's one other
thing. I got word that my plane's co-pilot is in the hospital with a ruptured
spleen. It seems he had a car wreck in his rental. It seems, somehow, the
brakes failed and he ran into a parked truck."

Lambert just stared.

"Cigarette factory foremen, ten bucks an hour, you can knock off a dozen
and I won't blink. But pilots for my jet." He shook his head, disappointed.
"Son, I have to compete with Delta and American for these men. It's a serious pain in the ass when something like this happens. I trust it won't happen
again."

With the sun gone, the evening chilled quickly, and Dolly Nichols wrapped
her arms around herself and wished she'd brought a sweater. She could, she
supposed, ask Bolling for one, but that meant interrupting his enthusiastic
tour of the formal garden he'd cultivated behind the Mansion, and she hated
to do that. He was on a roll, having finished with the more common vari-
eties—the dogwoods, the azaleas, the camellias—and was now into more exotic specimens—orchids, birds of paradise, clematis.

Occasionally he'd tramp off the brick path, tussle with a plant and return
with a leaf or petal or piece of bark for Dolly's examination. She had for a
while been tuning out his monologue, every so often offering up an "Oh?" or
an "Aha," enjoying instead the flowers' heavy scent in the still, cool air.

"Really?" she asked, sensing a pause in the governor's prattle.

Bolling regarded her severely. "You ain't been payin' the least bit attention."

"I have so."

"What's the last thing I just said?"

Dolly strained her memory. "The roses ought to be out in another week."

"Ha! I knew it. What I said was: Wally Soffit would make a better Senate president if he wore women's underwear." Bolling grinned triumphantly. "Gotcha."

"You're terrible," she scolded. "Okay. I admit it. I lost you back in the orchids. It's hard to be enthralled when you're freezing."

In an instant, Waites had removed his jacket and draped it over her shoulders. "Dolly, you just gotta say the word, and your every need is taken care of."

"Ever the gentleman." She pulled the coat around her, glanced skyward at the first stars. "Actually, I was just enjoying the evening. There really is something about springtime in Tallahassee."

Waites grunted. "Enjoy it while you can. Another two weeks, it'll be ninety degrees, thanks to the global warming those good, business-friendly Republicans are denyin' even exists." He grinned again. "Present company excluded, of course."

"Of course. Which reminds me. A couple of my Jacksonville colleagues want to exempt Duval County from auto emissions inspections. I told them you were certain to veto it. I hope that's all right."

"All right? A bill like that, you tell 'em not only will I veto it, I'll personally come round their house and beat the livin' daylights out of 'em, too. Then come election time, I'll make sure they can't get elected dogcatcher."

Dolly laughed aloud, then listened to the crickets fill in the silence. "I'm going to miss you, Bolling."

"And I you, madam." Waites began walking slowly back toward the Mansion. "I've said it before, Dolly, but I can't tell you how many times I've regretted not snaggin' you. By rights, you shoulda been one of ours. Schoolteacher, workin' class family. We was robbed. And now the other side's gonna get the first woman Senate president, the first woman governor. I frankly wouldn't be surprised to see you on a national ticket soon."

She smiled at him. "You're the second person this weekend to say that." She fell silent, thinking of his words, of how, when she was twenty-three and not even registered to vote, the older man she'd fallen for happened to be a Republican committeeman. How the rest, as they said, was history.

"How is Ramon?" Bolling asked softly.

She blinked, wondered if her face was so easily read, forced her trademark smile. "Fine." Then the smile faded. "Not fine, actually. They've pretty much given up. He's on pretty heavy pain meds now, but that's it."

Waites reached a fatherly hand out to her shoulder. "I know how much you've sacrificed for him, and how hard this must be for you. Bix and I had that scare a few years back. The tests, the nights in the hospital, the drugs." He shook his head. "We just want you to know our prayers are with you."

She felt her throat tighten and her eyes start to well. She tried to steel herself. After all, what kind of Senate president-designate cried on the governor's shoulder? "So," she began bravely, her voice only barely cracking. "Did you invite me over to look at your flowers, or was there something else?"

Bolling grinned and held back a rose branch that had grown out over the path so Dolly could step by. "Now that you mention it . . . Two of my solid votes are in Washington this week on a White House junket. They'd stay if I asked, but they're both young and think this is a big deal. Long and short of it, I need this vote to wait a week."

Dolly mentally ran through the coming agenda. "Shouldn't be a problem. We're tied up with the budget through Wednesday, thanks to T.C.'s shenanigans."

"I already told this to Walter, but I trust him 'bout as far as I can throw him, which at my age ain't so far anymore."

"So you need me to keep Walter in line. What else is new?" She recalled the meeting with Roper-Joyner's CEO, how Soffit had been unable to contain his boot licking. "I think his only deadline is the one Bartholomew Simons gave him: April second."

"Figures. The bastard is s'pposed to testify that day. I bet he'd do pretty much anything to stay off that witness stand."

Dolly thought about the dictatorial little man, how much fun it would be to make him testify, make him sweat a little. "So once again we have the Republican Senate Rules chairman doing the Democratic governor's bidding. Sounds about right." She laughed, reached out to take his arm. "You know, Bolling, this week or next, you still lose. You don't have the numbers."

"Give an old man some credit, Dolly. I only gotta flip two votes."

"You've already flipped the ones you're going to. And some of your own votes are pretty soft. Plus, Bolling, on this? You're on the wrong side."

Waites turned his eye skyward, gazed at a rich canopy of stars. "Oh, right. Freedom. Personal responsibility. I forgot. Hey, you ever notice how that group of stars, right there." He pointed, turned her head toward the eastern horizon. "Yeah, those; how much they look like Joe Camel?"

Dolly broke into a peal of laughter, pulled off the sport coat and handed it to him. "Good night, Governor."

Waites pointed at another clump. "And there's the Marlboro Man . . . and Larry Llama!"

Still laughing, Dolly started toward the iron gate in front of the driveway. "Give my love to Bix."

"No vote this week. I got your word, right?"

She made an X over her chest as she walked. "Cross my heart. I'll see you tomorrow."

MONDAY

In black pumps, black sheath dress and ivory jacket, Jeena realized she couldn't move. Without thinking about it, she'd taken a seat across from a young man representing the home builders, and now she was trapped.

As per her boss's fiat, she wore no underwear, and any move from her cross-legged position on the vinyl chair meant flashing the smug-faced asshole. Somehow the dress had ridden up the back when she sat down, and she could feel her bottom sticking to the chair. She tried again, discreetly tugging at the hem, but it was no use. She'd had no idea that dressing like a slut would require so much strategy. The only way to fix things would be to uncross her legs, partially stand, then pull her dress down. And the only way to do that would be if her new admirer looked somewhere else.

Once more she glanced over the top of her manilla folder, but, nope, Mr. Gentleman, pretending to read the office copy of *Florida Trend,* still kept a beady eye on the point where her thighs met. She took a deep breath, frustration now becoming anger. An invasion of her privacy, was what it was! How would he like it if his pants fell open and she stood there staring at his dick? The pervert. Probably would love it.

A schoolyard taunt kept coming to mind: *Take a picture, it lasts longer.* She savored the prospect of shouting it, of watching his face redden, of his eyes finally dropping to the floor. And then she thought of the possibly devastating retort: *Someone already has!*

She swallowed shamefully, glanced around the room, wondered which of the others had already recognized her. She knew intellectually the answer almost certainly was none. Martin Remy had known because, according to Ruth Ann, the sick bastard kept an up-to-date file of all FSU girls appearing in *Playboy* over the past twenty-five years. The people in this room had no reason to know her name, let alone anything about her. No, the attention she earned from the forty-something woman beside her was jealousy, the fifty-something receptionist was disapproval, and her thirty-something admirer was lust. Pure and simple.

And yet . . . *Ruth Ann* had remembered her, hadn't she? Who's to say the dark-suited lobbyist across from her now hadn't been a ball-capped, T-shirted frat boy back then? Hadn't been among the throng of like-minded FSU males who'd mobbed a local bookstore that had held, of all things, a magazine signing featuring six of the seven girls appearing in the pictorial? Hadn't been one of God-knows-how-many guys on campus who, failing to get a Friday night date, had made out with her picture, instead?

With all her might, she pushed the thought from her head, ignored the dull pain in her top leg that was now falling asleep and focused on Ruth Ann's file on Senator Rex Kelsey, Democrat from Palatka. One of the few remaining Yellow Dogs who hadn't yet been either lured or coerced into switching parties, his record was as right-wing Republican as they came: anti-abortion, pro-school prayer, anti-environment. With one exception. On the tobacco law, he had so far voted with the governor. A matter of personal loyalty, Ruth Ann had concluded, but one possibly overcome with some new voter data RJH's political research division had come up with. It seemed Kelsey's district had changed through the years and was now almost fifty-fifty Democrat to Republican. In other words, Kelsey was vulnerable, if an opponent could find, say, a deep-pocket source for campaign money.

That was the stick Ruth Ann had given her. The carrot was a million-dollar riverfront park in downtown Palatka, complete with old-fashioned bandstand. A perfect platform for an incumbent senator's stump speech come re-election time. Ruth Ann and the other tobacco lobbyists could probably work very hard to make such a park a reality in the budget.

Jeena's assignment was simple: Get in the door, explain the deal, then leave with a smile. Instead, she again found herself second-guessing her whole return to Tallahassee. Another two semesters in Gainesville and she could have gone anywhere she wanted, a professional woman, able to write her own ticket. Instead, she was a glorified messenger. A messenger in a minidress and high heels to make up for her lack of clout. One among dozens in the Capitol. Why, she realized with a sinking feeling in her gut, should Kelsey or any other senator even give her the time of day, what with all the lobbyists they'd known for years also vying for their attention?

No, the only people she was impressing in her ridiculous getup were hormone-crazed, developmentally arrested guys, like the moron across from her maintaining the vigil on her hemline. She would say something to him, she decided. Something nasty. Something about his pecker, and how those who couldn't, watched. And then over to Ruth Ann's office, tell her sorry, it just didn't work out, and back down I-75, try to get into a couple of classes for the summer term.

She looked up to see Rex Kelsey in the room, bidding farewell to the Hallandale Greyhound Track lobbyist he'd had in his office, getting a stack of phone messages from the fifty-something receptionist, listening to her explain that the lady from the Wine and Spirits Federation had been waiting nearly an hour, but that the gentleman from the home builders had an appointment. But Kelsey, short and dumpy with a dozen improbable black hairs combed over a bald spot, was already standing before Jeena, hand outstretched.

Jeena returned his smile, ignored Home Builder Boy's look of outrage and, in a single fluid motion, tugged her dress down over her rear as she stood and followed Kelsey into his office.

Murphy Moran waited on the couch in Simons' penthouse, eyes on the big windows overlooking the city but mind back at Wakulla Springs, back on the stunning woman who'd fallen to him like manna from heaven. Long blond hair in a ponytail, a swimsuit model's figure. Reading up on tobacco, no less. He couldn't have asked for an easier setup. Somehow he'd blown it anyway.

In his mind's eye, he saw her on the bow of his sailboat, stretching by the first rays of the morning sun in a carelessly buttoned cotton shirt, trying to decide whether she'd dive for lobster that day, or conch. He wondered, when she went diving, if she'd do so nude. What the hell; it was *his* fantasy. She would dive nude.

"High ground? What high ground are you talking about?" Simons' voice intruded.

Murphy returned from the gin-clear Caribbean to Simons' penthouse, saw a wiry man in camouflage glance at him anxiously, then point a finger at something on Simons' desk. Simons brushed the hand away, and quickly rolled up what Murphy saw was a large aerial photograph.

"Do what I tell you and never mind the war games, okay?"

The camouflaged man's eyes flashed a moment, then he gathered his map and sulked away. Murphy watched him close the door behind him before turning to Simons. "Who's G.I. Joe?"

Simons rolled his eyes. "Don't mind him. You have something for me?"

He stood behind his desk, a busy man in shirtsleeves and suspenders. Murphy for the first time noticed the nonexistent belly, the thick arms that couldn't quite hang straight down. He decided Simons hadn't been exaggerating about the weight lifting and the sit-ups.

Murphy moved to the television set in the corner, opened the FedEx package under his arm and popped a videocassette into the VCR.

The picture panned a deserted grocery store as a somber announcer described a world of $1 carrots and $10 tomatoes, priced to pay for lawsuits over pesticide residue. Of day-care centers boarded up and abandoned because of litigation over the spread of coughs and colds. Of $25 hamburgers packaged in boxes with large-print warnings about heart disease.

Think this is far-fetched? Think again! The announcer tone's deepened ominously: *Once Big Government can soak adults who've made the adult choice to enjoy tobacco, the only question is . . . who's next?*

The words STOP BIG GOVERNMENT NOW! came up on the screen over a toll-free number that Murphy explained rang a Tallahassee phone bank. Operators stood ready to switch callers to the elected official of their choice.

Simons nodded, impressed. "How do we know it'll work?"

Murphy handed him a thin binder. "Our focus group says it will. I got two other spots in the studio right now. All three use that toll-free number."

Simons skimmed through the pages rapidly. "Good. I want it on the air immediately. All markets."

"It's being hand-delivered to every affiliate as we speak. Pensacola, Panama City, Jacksonville, Orlando, Tampa, Lakeland, West Palm, Miami. Every available slot, twenty-four hours a day. By week's end, you'd have to be living under a rock not to have seen it a dozen times, minimum." Murphy waited for Simons to ask how much it would cost, instead watched him sit down, take a sip from a glass of ice water and return to his three computer screens. "I don't have to tell you that crashing these into production costs a pretty penny."

Simons waved carelessly. "Send the bill to Durham."

Murphy watched Simons scowling at his stock quotes, then pulled a folded sheet of paper from his jeans. "Listen, Bart—is it okay if I call you Bart?—there's something I need to know here."

Simons raised one eyebrow, regarded Murphy suspiciously.

"In my research, I found some things that frankly got my curiosity. Like it says here you guys have been sued more than five hundred times over the last decade. Five hundred times, and you've never lost. Okay, so Waites' law gives them an edge. With all your legal horsepower, I'd say the odds still favor you."

Simons checked his watch, typed at one of his keyboards. "I didn't lift RJH from a second-tier dog into one of the top five tobacco companies by playing odds, Mr. Moran. I play certainties."

"Fair enough." Murphy nodded. "But still I gotta wonder: Why? Why even bother with a repeal right now? You could lose the lawsuit, tie it up in appeals, then, next year, when Waites is out of office, come back and get the law repealed retroactively. No harm done."

Simons ignored him, so Murphy continued. "Okay, worst case: You lose and lose big, say a couple billion, and can't find a way to undo it. All right. So what? You raise the price of smokes a dime and pass the whole thing along to your customers. Plus you got your secret high-nicotine leaf under development in Brazil, maybe six months, a year behind the secret, high-nicotine leaf the competition has got cooking down in Colombia. So you're second in the field, win thirty percent market share. That's not even *talking* about a billion Chinese who smoke like fiends—"

"Who said," Simons frowned, finally turning away from his computers, "who said anything about being *second* with high-nicotine tobacco?"

Murphy blinked uncertainly. "I just figured, y'all are six months behind, the other guy will have the market to himself at least that long—"

"You know, Mr. Moran, Latin America is wild. It's not like here. Things happen down there. *Lots* of things." He shrugged. "Six-month lead one day, years behind the next. Let's just see who gets to market first."

Murphy glanced between his single page of notes and Simons' amused expression. The man was fooling with him, he decided. "All right, for argument's sake let's say you *do* get out first with this new cigarette. That makes my point even—"

Simons quickly whirled back to his computers and began typing, playtime over. "No, it does not," he said flatly. "Let me be blunt: You're not here to be making points. Whether we do or don't have a new leaf under development has got nothing to do with you. You're here to run a political campaign. Run it. I'm paying you enough, am I not?"

Murphy could only nod. For the amount of work, it was better money than he'd ever made in his life, or ever would. "Yes, sir, you are."

"Indeed I am. And I might remind you there are a thousand guys out there who would give their left nut to do the job at that level of remuneration without asking me a lot of stupid questions." Simons continued clacking at one of his keyboards, stopped for a moment and took another sip of ice water. "By the way: Bart is a character on *The Simpsons*. Bart is the subway system in San Francisco. I am not Bart. To you, Mr. Moran, I am Mr. Simons."

Murphy suppressed a sigh, stood to leave. "Well, Mr. Simons, FYI, I called up to your D.C. lobbying office to be on the lookout for senators Robeson and Drayer on Wednesday. I doubt we can turn 'em. They're pretty solid Waites supporters. But I figured, what the hell. Can't hurt to try."

Simons said nothing, and Murphy couldn't help take some joy in the hint of confusion in his expression. "Oh, you hadn't heard? They're up on some White House junket. Apparently, Soffit promised Waites he wouldn't hold the vote while they're away. I guess the old man's got some hold over him. Too bad, huh?"

Simons pursed his lips. "I believe our business for now is over. I expect to see those ads on the air this afternoon and a progress report on my desk tomorrow morning."

Jeena craned her neck, trying for the optimum view through a thicket of lobbyists at the bald little man in the lavender sport coat. She caught her glimpse, decided it was still pointless, then sipped from her wineglass instead. A half hour she'd been there, trying to get a minute with her final assignment of the day, the one Ruth Ann had warned would be the toughest to nail down.

Every lobbyist in town would swarm him at every available moment, Ruth Ann had said. Sure enough, they were. The men stood in a respectful circle, laughing at his jokes, buying him drinks. The women sidled closer, playing with their hair or occasionally reaching out to touch his shoulder. She thought after they'd been with him for ten or fifteen minutes, they'd leave and she could walk over and introduce herself. Instead, a fresh group had replaced the first, and he was holding court all over again.

She sighed, reminded herself that even if she didn't get him tonight, her first day had been an unqualified success. She'd met with three senators, and all three had promised their votes. True, all three were middle-aged men who'd winked and hinted, and true, the second one, a Vero Beach probate lawyer who told her she could call him Sam, had in fact propositioned her. Still and all, it hadn't been that bad. Her job was to give them the pitch, and she'd done it. Nothing more. By the end of the day, she'd even learned to sit down and stand up without flashing the planet.

Of course, she reminded herself, there was still one major task she needed to get to, especially now that she'd be spending so much time in the Capitol.

Dunbar.

She needed to call him, if nothing else for the courtesy of letting him know she was back in town, so he wouldn't find out by bumping into her going around a corner, flustering them both. Of course, calling meant explaining how she'd abandoned law school. Meant explaining how she'd joined the miniskirt-and-heels set she used to make fun of. Meant deciding whether she was going to see him again . . .

She took another sip, leaned off the barstool to see around a knot of legislators slapping each other's backs and saw the baldheaded man now wrapped up with a strikingly exotic brunette in a skirt slit clear to her waist. Jeena wondered how in the world she could compete with *that* when a throat cleared behind her.

"If I'd of known that being five-five, bald as a cue ball and dressing like a used-car salesman attracted women like that, I'd of tried it myself."

She began a laugh, turned to a goatee and mustache on a vaguely familiar face when the laugh caught in her throat. It was the guy from the springs. The one who wanted to learn scuba. The one she'd run from.

"Murphy." He extended a hand. "Murphy Moran. From the other day."

"I remember." She shook his hand lightly. "Listen, I'm sorry if I seemed rude. It was just, well, I lost track of time, and I really had to get—"

He raised a hand stoically. "Not another word. I was intruding. No apology necessary." He grinned. "Besides. I'm used to it. I seem to have that effect on women."

An obvious line, terribly overused, but Jeena struggled to keep from blurting the obligatory response, that no, that wasn't true at all. She studied his eyes, realized after too long a moment that he was equally raptly studying hers, and quickly dropped her gaze. "No, that's not true at all," she said lamely.

"Oh, you just say that because you're supposed to."

She looked up to a safe smile she found so familiar and let herself relax a bit. "I'm Jeena—"

"Jeena Golden, tobacco's warrior princess. How could I forget?" He took the stool beside her, nodded at one of the televisions above the bar. "See that? My weekend's work."

Jeena glanced up to the ad she'd seen on seemingly every television she'd happened across that afternoon, a shot of a boarded-up day-care center, an exhortation to Stop Big Government Now. "You did that?" she asked. "This weekend?"

Murphy shrugged carelessly, a bottle of Sam Adams at his lips. "Had a lot of time on my hands. Don't know anybody in town. The one nice girl I meet runs off while I got my back turned."

She blushed a touch. "I didn't run off," she started, then stopped, not wanting the conversation headed that way. She returned her eyes to the television, which was playing the same ad again, back-to-back. "Roper-Joyner must like it, from how much it's running. God, they must be spending a fortune."

"They've never lost, and they don't want to start. They've got this aura of invincibility. Lawyers probably tell their clients: Don't bother suing RJH, it can't be done. They lose one here and there, they'd see a thousand new cases, and they'd start losing even more." He took another swig of his beer. "But what do I know? I'm just the publicity guy."

She watched as the television finally went back to a basketball game. "Maybe they *ought* to lose once in a while. Between you and me, it seems like they've done some pretty sleazy things. You know: covering up medical research? Trying to hook kids?"

Murphy slammed his beer bottle on the bar in mock anger. "Heresy! Does RJH know you think like this?"

Jeena smiled. "I guess I've read too many newspaper articles."

"The liberal media," he nodded. "That'll do it every time. Turn your mind to mush. Me? Don't take a paper, don't associate with anyone who does. Only way to stay pure."

She leaned over the bar to look for Senator Tuttle again, saw him even further engrossed with the slit-skirted brunette.

"What *is* it with him?" Murphy complained. "Why is every gorgeous woman in this place fixated on *him*?"

It took a moment for Jeena to register the roundabout compliment and decide she didn't mind it. "It's because he's the sneakiest bastard in town. An encyclopedic memory, a mind like a steel trap. Wrote the book on getting a bill passed. Or killed. Or so says my boss." She sighed. "I should be over there."

"So why aren't you?"

At·the other end of the room, Tuttle had his hand on the brunette's knee, then just slightly above her knee. Jeena shuddered at the thought of walking over and introducing herself. "I can't stomach it."

Murphy smiled. "Me neither. Have you eaten?"

Dunbar Richey moved the curtain just a hair, just enough to see a pair of long, tan legs slide gracefully into the BMW convertible, then the door pushed shut by the son of a bitch who'd ever-so-gentlemanly held it open for her.

Was it her? There was no streetlight above that particular parking spot, so he couldn't say for certain. Rather, his *brain* couldn't say for certain. His gut had known the instant·he'd spotted the back of her head, the only natural blonde in a bar famous for the bottled sort.

He'd ducked down, then crept to the opposite side of Clyde's, the smoky pub that each spring became the Capitol's favorite watering hole, the place where lobbyists plied their favorite lawmakers with free booze and pretty playthings and got them to promise all manner of things they might never have done in the sober sunshine. He'd peeked around the edge of a booth and his heart had nearly stopped a second time. The man Jeena was with, if it *was* Jeena, was none other than the slimeball political consultant who'd run the media campaign against Bolling three years earlier.

Murphy Moran, top-dollar hired gun who helped elect right-wing wackos all over the country, the guy who'd nearly ended his boss's thirty-year-career with the nastiest mudslinging Florida had ever seen, *this* guy had somehow ended up with Jeena?

Then he'd convinced himself to calm down. Jeena was in law school two hundred miles away, getting the degree that would give her a new start. That would get her away from Tallahassee . . . from him. Plus Jeena wore high-collared blouses and long skirts, not slinky dresses and high heels.

Then he'd seen her get off the stool, walk through the crowded bar. The way she stepped, bare shoulders swinging confidently, it *had* to be Jeena, but a new, sexy-and-proud-of-it Jeena, bringing up torrents of lust mixed with jealousy mixed with God-only-knew-what as she walked out with that scum carpetbagger.

He watched through the curtain but still hadn't had a clear view of her face as Moran started the car, popped the headlights and backed into Adams Street. Dunbar bumped the table of lobbyists he'd squeezed past on his way to the window, muttered an apology to their dirty looks and started toward the door when his cell phone rang. He debated whether to ignore it, decided on the third ring not to.

"You near a TV?"

It was Bolling, and Dunbar tried to compose himself, turned slowly back to the bar. Over the bottles of liquor and casks of wine was a series of televisions, each showing the same ad. The same ad, but on three different stations, he realized, because none of the sets was in synch with another. He saw the toll-free number, recognized the exchange as that of a political phone bank in Tallahassee, and knew instantly why Moran was in town.

"Yeah," he sighed. "I guess it's the ad we figured was coming. Says if we sue tobacco now, no telling who—"

"I know what it says," Waites interrupted. "I want to know what we're doin' to stop it. I just called down to communications, and they tell me we're getting calls from all over the state, askin' if we plan on suin' their business, too."

Dunbar saw that obsessing over Jeena would have to wait a while. "I'm on my way," he said into his phone before sticking it back in his pocket.

He pushed open the door in time to see the light turn green and the Beemer turn onto College Avenue and disappear.

Left hand holding a hunk of prime rib at the end of a fork, right hand caressing a lobster tail, Agustin Cruz knew that after five years in Tallahassee, he'd finally hit his stride. God damn, if that T.C. hadn't been right. Sure enough, all he'd had to do was think big. And this, he decided, was thinking *huge.* On the table before him was the surf-and-turf *and* the filet, the remnants of a crab claw cocktail *and* smoked oysters, a bottle of Bordeaux *and* a Chardonnay.

He was stuffed but stoically kept eating. In the past, he'd contented himself with the most expensive thing on the menu, typically ringing up a $50 or $75 bill. Tonight he'd decided to shoot for $250, a goal he could hit without breaking a sweat in the Gables or South Beach, but, he realized halfway through his appetizers, was perhaps unattainable in Tallahassee.

"Have some lobster," he urged his dinner partner, a gold-cuff-linked, Rolex-wearing, yet somehow uptight representative of Southern Telecom, a newcomer to Tallahassee and therefore a perfect candidate for Gus's new persona. He lifted his plate and held it across the table. "Really. There's plenty."

The lobbyist managed a strained smile. "No, thank you, senator. I'm fine."

"You say so." The guy had only ordered grilled snapper, hadn't even touched any wine. He had a lot to learn about expense account living. "So you guys want to break into the local phone market. You've come to the right place."

"That's what we heard. As I mentioned, Southern Telecom wishes to expand into South Florida. We believe this area holds strong growth potential over the next twenty years. Unfortunately, the current tariff structure makes it difficult for a new entrant. We believe modifying the rate structure as we've outlined would increase the upside for our investors."

Gus nodded. "You want to double phone rates," he said from around a piece of meat.

"We like to think of it as rate *rebalancing*," the lobbyist said. "We believe ultimately the consumer will benefit from increased competition."

Gus chewed thoughtfully. "With more competition, will the rates come down to where they are today?"

The lobbyist shrugged. "In a free market, who knows?"

Gus considered this. "You know, folks back home don't like higher phone bills." He let that hang there, sipped his Bordeaux. "So you understand, the political *downside* of getting on board something like this."

"We always do what we can for those candidates who share our philosophy." The lobbyist smiled nervously. "I believe you'll find our candidates have a ninety-nine-percent success rate."

"You know, I happen to know a little bit about telecommunications myself," Gus said, trying to gauge the man's temperament. What would fly here: ten grand? Twenty? And then T.C.'s words came back to him, and Gus thought *big*. "I could help out with some consulting for, say, five hundred thousand?"

Immediately, Gus felt his mouth go dry, his heart miss a beat. Five hundred thousand! *Jesucristo!* What was he thinking! He had to say something, a lower number, anything! But then, across the table, the lobbyist pulled out a checkbook, began writing with a gold fountain pen.

"We were hoping your expertise might be available to us." He tore off the check and held it at Gus with a shaking hand. "Our binder. The rest due upon delivery of your, ah, report?"

Gus didn't notice that the hand proffering the check was shaking. Nor did he place any significance on the beads of perspiration on the man's upper lip, so fixated was he on the small blue paper rectangle: a two, a five and one, two, three, *four* zeros! It had been *so* easy! T.C. was right! A little big thinking was all he needed. He contained yelps of laughter, nodded seriously.

"This is acceptable? You'll manage our legislation in your chamber?"

He nodded more rapidly. "No problem," he said, still not quite believing it. A half-million dollars, from just one client! How many more were out there, hanging from the tree, waiting for him to reach up and pick? Shoot, he was only a plain old member of the Telecommunications Committee, but the friggin' *vice*-chairman of Health Care. And HMOs had at *least* as much money to throw around as the phone companies. . . . He smiled conspiratorially across the table, stuffed the check into his breast pocket: "In the Senate, you got nothing to worry about."

The lobbyist seemed to relax suddenly, a great weight lifted from his shoulders. He smiled. "Then we have a deal! Is there anything else we need to discuss? Anything else we can get you?"

Gus finally abandoned the lobster. It was overdone anyway. Tomorrow, once he cashed the check, he could call Maine and have an entire crate flown in fresh. He let out a satisfied burp. This lobbyist, he was a good guy, Gus decided. He wished he could remember his name. "Not unless you can get me a good Cohiba."

The lobbyist grinned, glanced out over Gus' shoulder. "You know, senator, Cuban cigars are contraband. There's a federal embargo."

Gus waved a hand magnanimously, leaned forward to clap the man's shoulder. "Doesn't apply to me. I'm Cuban!"

He leaned back in his chair and laughed heartily, barely noticing his dinner partner excuse himself to visit the restroom. The meat and shellfish felt good in his belly as he thought about all the calls he'd make the next morning. Two HMOs wanted waivers to Medicaid eligibility requirements, another wanted to restrict patients' ability to challenge coverage denials. Each legislative change would net the company tens of millions. Surely it would be worth a small fraction of that to ensure their bills got proper attention. . . .

In his mind, he was comparing prices of bayfront homes in the Grove, so he didn't notice the mulatto with a close-cropped Afro and a dark suit until he was standing beside him, pumping his hand.

"I *thought* I recognized you!" the black man enthused. "You probably don't remember, but I met you last election. I voted for you."

"Oh, yeah!" Gus feigned recognition, the politician's instinct to be liked overcoming anxiety about the man's sudden appearance. "Sure. You doin' okay?"

"Yeah, yeah. Just up here on business." The black man glanced behind him, where another table of legislators and lobbyists concentrated on their food, then back at Gus. "Well, I just wanted to say *hola*. I'm sure I'll see you again, and . . ." He fished a business card from the pocket of his suit coat and handed it to Gus. "I think maybe you should call. Okay? It was great seeing you."

With a final squeeze of his hand, he was gone, Gus still wondering where he'd come from and when exactly they'd met. He sure didn't remember meeting him. And then it occurred to him that the man had never mentioned his name.

He lifted the card and read it. And read it. And read it a third time before his brain finally accepted what he was seeing and began signaling his armpits to start pumping sweat and his heart to race into overdrive. Because there, in incontrovertible black letters, were the four words dreaded by any Miami politician: FEDERAL BUREAU OF INVESTIGATION.

Panicked, Gus stood, searched the room, but Special Agent Johnny Espinosa was gone. He flipped the card over, saw a handwritten note, and sat back down in a stupor.

The others on the sidewalk offered no resistance, quickly melting out of Bartholomew Simons' way as he strode down Adams Street. For that he was grateful. He wanted to reserve his anger for one particular sycophant, not some random dickhead on the street.

The offending piece of information was bad enough. Making it even worse was its source: the increasingly bothersome Moran. Something about his attitude, a vague smart-alecky superiority complex that he had neither time nor inclination to correct. It was getting to be a toss-up, between him and Lambert, which one was going to be the bigger pain in the ass.

Lambert, with his sullen, put-upon demeanor—attention-needy, was what the bastard had become. Like that afternoon, the dumb shit had come to the hotel for his debriefing, head to toe in his jungle cammos. Turns out he'd walked around all day in the Capitol like that, like some sort of deranged NRA wacko. When he'd scolded him for it, out had come the mopey shoulder shrug. "You never told me what to wear. . . ."

Simons shook his head, strode across College Avenue against the light. He glared at a car that honked as it passed, then brushed aside an elderly lady emerging from the double doors before storming past the captain and into the private room where the Florida League of Pawnbrokers was holding a fundraiser for Soffit. A gaggle of pawnshop owners stood around Soffit, their polyester suits shiny under a bright chandelier, while the little suck-up listened to their tales of woe at the hands of burglary victims and their police allies.

Simons let his anger build for half a minute until Soffit finally noticed him in the back of the room with an effeminate wave. Then he rushed him, bursting through pawnshop people, dragging the mumbling, apologizing Soffit into an alcove.

Simons saw the man was terrified; he glowered at him, let him steep for a while. Finally, Soffit couldn't take it anymore, began babbling incoherently. Simons cut him off with a death stare.

"I have learned," he began softly, "that you scheduled the override vote for next Monday."

Soffit's face melted with relief: "Absolutely!" he exclaimed. "Monday, two o'clock. Just like—"

"And I have learned," Simons interrupted, "that the governor is down two votes the latter half of this week."

Soffit saw now where Simons was headed, decided to dissemble. "Yes, but, you see . . . it wouldn't even be possible to schedule an override for *this* week, not this late. What, noticing requirements, plus the House—"

"The House," Simons breathed. "The House is not something I lose sleep over. If I called Speaker Powers over right now and told him to suck my dick, he'd be on his knees in a second."

Soffit looked unhappily at Simon's crotch. "You want me to suck your dick?"

"I *want*"—Simons rolled his eyes, wondering why in hell they couldn't buy a better class of politician these days—"you to schedule the override Wednesday morning. If the governor's only got eleven or twelve votes in town, then we only need twenty-five, correct?"

"Oh, no. The governor made me promise. He said Drayer and Robeson would have stayed in town if he'd asked, and I know they would have, so it really isn't fair going back. . . ."

Soffit shut up as Simons darkened to where it was clear he would either have a stroke, right there in the Henry Flagler Room, or kill Soffit with his bare hands, right there in the Henry Flagler Room. Simons took several deep breaths, eyes closed, teeth clenched. "How much are you raising from your pawnshop pals? Five thousand? Ten?"

Soffit's face twitched. "Something. Somewhere in there."

"We do the override Wednesday morning. Or your opponent for insurance commissioner finds himself with five or ten *million*." Simons mimicked Soffit's nervous grin. "How's that for fair?"

Soffit quickly doubled back, as fear of the here-and-now Simons outweighed fear of the absent governor. His mind bumped up into sycophantic high gear. "Mr. Simons, let me just say, sir, that you've been nothing *but* fair. I won't let you down. And I think the governor knows this process enough to know that plans change. As a matter of fact, if you'll give me"—he checked his wristwatch—"ten minutes to call some of my leadership . . ."

But by the time he looked up, the curtain to the alcove was open and Simons was gone.

Jeena watched Murphy shyly raise his gaze twice, drop it twice, lift his eyes a third time before working up the nerve to ask. "If you don't want that last piece of garlic bread . . ."

She held the basket across the table and let him retrieve it. Thirty minutes after their food had arrived, her dinner partner was still tucking into it with enthusiasm. She'd long ago stopped after barely denting an enormous plate of linguine, and now quietly enjoyed the glow of the red wine in her belly as between bites Murphy held up both ends of the conversation.

"Success breeds success, and the further you go, the easier it gets." He pried open a mussel and popped the bit of flesh into his mouth. "Most of my work is reelecting pretty much sure things. They're ahead twenty, thirty, sometimes forty points in the polls, and they just want to ice it. They go out and spend a fortune to hire me or somebody like me. Then they sleep easier at night."

Jeena toyed with the spoon on her plate, realized she had no idea what time it was but still had boxes of documents to plow through once she got home. Oh, well. It could wait. Her evening had taken a wonderfully pleasant detour, and she was reluctant to let it end. On the drive out of town the wind had blown gloriously through her hair; she'd whooped that her uncle had had an MG once. The restaurant had been her suggestion, an off-the-lobbyists'-track little place way out east of town, and she couldn't recall a tastier meal. Or perhaps it was just the company.

Murphy Moran had let her talk when she wanted, had taken up the slack when she didn't, in general had been a complete gentleman. Like at the springs, his eyes stayed on hers, she noticed, not her chest. She knew in her mind she was wearing the same absurd outfit she'd had on since morning, but somehow around this guy it didn't seem to matter. After a day of feeling like the display in a butcher's window, the ability to relax was priceless.

"Why," she asked, her hands returning to her lap, "if they have a huge lead, do they need you?"

He waved a piece of calamari at the end of his fork as he finished chewing. "Excellent point. Two reasons: One, these guys can't imagine not being in office. And two, it's not their money. They can't legally keep it. They can spend it on their campaign or they can give it to charity. An opponent, even a weak opponent, is still a disaster waiting to happen. So they hire me to squash him like a bug."

Jeena grinned. "So you're kind of the Orkin man of politics."

"Exactly. And they hire me, instead of somebody cheaper but probably just as good, because I'm the best. And you gotta pay for the best." He sipped his Sam Adams. "Please forgive the boasts. You won't believe this, but once upon a time I actually was modest. Then I realized that in this game, perception was ninety percent of it. Tell enough people you're the best and, after a while, they believe it. Then the newsmagazines start printing it, so, by God, it must be true."

She laughed again, vaguely remembering that she'd read about him a while back, maybe in *Time* or *Newsweek*. The article had called him ruthless, one of the new breed of campaign wizards who went for the jugular, found the most damaging tidbits about a candidate and turned them into unimaginably nasty attack ads. Jeena tried to reconcile that with the warm eyes and the slight overbite that now made short work of the last of the garlic bread.

"And you?" he asked. "How does a young, idealistic woman out to change the world end up among the black hats?"

She dropped her eyes, more than a little uncomfortable with that transformation herself. "I guess I decided law school wasn't for me. But the people who lent me the money to go there—they kind of want it back."

"Ah." He nodded. "So it's the money."

"Well, it's not *just* the money," she insisted, too forcefully. "It's not like I live an extravagant lifestyle. I'm renting this old duplex and driving this piece of junk. It's just that I have some debt right now—"

He reached across the table and grabbed her wrist, startling her into silence. "Jeena, it's okay to pick a life that pays well. Certainly, *you* don't have to justify to *me* about money."

He withdrew his hand; Jeena reacted first with relief, then half wished he'd left it there. "Well, it's just, you know, to me it's more than money," she continued. "I was here for years before I went to law school, watching how things got done, and swore one day I'd—"

"You know, money gets a bad rap," he cut in with a grin. "But money, especially a whole *pile* of it, is actually a good thing. I mean, forget for a second about the stuff it can buy, the big house, the nice car, the boat. That's all nice, don't get me wrong, but the single best thing about money is the ability to say, excuse my French: Fuck you."

She blinked in amusement. "Fuck you?"

"Fuck you." He nodded. "A pile of fuck-you money is absolutely wonderful to have around. If you have a boss, or in my case, a client, who tells you to do something wrong, or silly, or something you just plain don't want to, you look him in the eye, say fuck you, and walk away. Money, Jeena, is independence. Me, for instance. I could walk away right now and go into the desert and do rock sculptures the rest of my life, and still be comfortable."

Jeena smiled, intrigued with this philosophy, and turned her chair sideways to stretch her legs. "So why don't you? Do rock sculptures, I mean."

Murphy inverted his beer to drain the last of it, shrugged. "Guess I never much liked rock sculpture."

"Oh. Well, how about, say, sailing around the world. On the boat your money bought but isn't important to you." She nodded at the pendant around his neck. She'd noticed it back at Clyde's. "Or are the little anchor and the boat shoes just for show?"

"I guess you caught me." He grinned. "Yes, I have a boat, and, yes, if sailing means knowing where the beer is kept and what to hang on to to keep from falling overboard when you're peeing over the side, then yeah, I know all about sailing. If on the other hand you mean can I get safely from point A to point B, without ramming point C or freighter D, then, technically, no." He grinned again. "Anyway, sailing around the world's a lonely business, unless you find somebody to help you. How about you, you know how to sail?"

She shrugged modestly. "A bit. Back in the summer after graduation—" She realized she was about to mention Dunbar, quickly caught herself. "Uh, a friend and I loaded his trailer sailer with food and water and our scuba tanks. We left from Shell Point, and we were gonna gunkhole all the way to the Keys, a whole month. Well, the second night was a full moon, and we anchored all snug up in this cove. At low water, we were hard aground. Come high water, we were still aground."

Jeena laughed, recalling how angry Dunbar had been with himself, how they'd spent five days on the shoal until finally a passing fishing boat had pulled them off the bar. How those days that followed had been the best days of her life. How, when they'd finally made it as far south as Cedar Key, he'd asked her to marry him, and she'd said yes . . .

She came out of it with a start, saw Murphy quietly studying her face. "Anyway. I'm no offshore expert, but I know my port from my starboard, my jib halyard from my boom vang."

"That's already more than I know," Murphy joked after a pause, then cleared his throat after another one. "And your, uh, friend? He still have this boat?"

Dunbar had hauled it onto its trailer at the end of the summer, driven it back to his dad's place in Winter Haven. "I don't know." She crossed her arms uncomfortably. "We kind of . . . lost touch."

"Ah."

He stretched his arms over his head, checked at his watch, and Jeena sensed that some subtle thing had happened to the spell that had enchanted them all evening. A thing with a name. A name that began with a D. She scolded herself for even bringing up that sailing trip.

"So why tobacco?" she asked, eager for a new subject. "If you make all your money, excuse me, your *independence*, helping candidates coast to reelection, what are you doing in the middle of a legislative fight?"

He grinned, then picked up the hand card that stood between the salt and pepper shakers. "Remember I said there's nothing to be ashamed about doing something for the money? I think I'll fall back on that one. This tobacco thing is more money, pardon, more *independence*, than I can make in two years of helping weasels hang on to their jobs. Plus if I win here, there are forty-nine other states itching to sue tobacco. I could retire in three years."

He flipped the card over, studied a picture of a chocolate mousse. "Besides, there *is* one non-monetary element. I was in Florida last governor's race, doing media for the Republican. Remember him? Slade Moore? I came down here, he had a fifteen-point lead. Then I got to work and made it twenty. Then Bolling Waites got to work and undid it all. I couldn't figure out how to stop him."

Jeena remembered the campaign well. Dunbar had been too busy to listen to her worries about their relationship. By the time Waites had eked out his win and Dunbar had come home, exhausted, Jeena had already applied for law school.

"So the Old Granddaddy Gator and I, well, we got a score to settle. You want some mousse?"

Murphy looked up, and with great effort Jeena pushed Dunbar from her mind and forced a smile.

Agustin Cruz stepped out of his Town Car, pressed the key ring to make it yelp and started through the darkened parking lot at Lafayette Park. He'd needed a map to find it because, in all his time in Tallahassee, he'd never strayed beyond the restaurants on the main thoroughfares. The mere idea of being in a park at night unnerved him, and he tried to remind himself he was in North Florida, not Miami.

Then he remembered Ted Bundy had once roamed North Florida, and he lost his nerve again, stumbling backward over an oak root at the hoot of an owl. He cursed the bird as he brushed leaves and Spanish moss off his clothes, cursed Special Agent Johnny Espinosa for making him come out there at all. He edged forward, and as his eyes adjusted to the dark, he began to make out a somewhat brighter patch that suggested the outline of a softball diamond.

He stumbled over more roots and down a small slope into the third-base dugout. On the narrow bench was a bundle of rags smelling vaguely of booze and urine. He shook his head disgustedly, then came to the frightening realization that if this guy was so hardcore that going undercover meant actually *smelling* like a wino, God only knew what else he was capable of. Such a man was dangerous. More than dangerous. He gathered up his courage and reached out to shake the bundle.

"Special Agent Espinosa? Wake up, sir." He wiped his hand on his pant leg as the form began to stir. "May I compliment you, sir, on your disguise? You really look like a bum."

From across the diamond came a high-pitched whistle. "Hey! Great DiMaggio! That *is* a bum. I said *first*-base dugout."

Gus backed away from the now-mumbling wino, muttered his apologies and scampered across the brick dust to the relative safety of the other dugout, where the FBI man stood smoking a cigarette.

"I thought all *cubanos* loved *beisbol*."

Gus shrugged unhappily and squinted to study Espinosa's features in the gloom. He'd barely even noticed him in the restaurant, had assumed he was just black. But now he connected the man's looks and his speech and slowly and dejectedly realized his ethnicity.

"You see who I am now, don't you?" Espinosa asked softly. "Maybe one little tiny part Castile, everything else from the heart of Africa. When Castro came down from the hills and your people called him a devil, my people called him a hero."

Espinosa pulled a microcassette recorder from his pocket and pushed a button. Gus sat down heavily as he heard his own voice from two years ago negotiating with a West Dade home builder, from eighteen months ago shaking down the waste haulers, from a year ago wheedling a rent-free condo out of a dog track owner. The tape kept going, snippet after snippet, a greatest-hits of graft, and Gus felt the nausea build. He pictured all that prime rib and lobster coming back up, and the nausea built some more.

"Pretty nickel-and-dime stuff. Couple grand here, five grand there. Nothing a Miami jury's gonna get too worked up about. You know: There but for the grace of God." Espinosa took a final drag from his cigarette, ground the butt into the dugout's dirt floor. He put away one recorder and pulled out another. "Then there's tonight."

Gus heard himself chewing, asking the phone lobbyist if he wanted some lobster, asking him for half a million dollars, asking for a Cuban cigar. Without warning, a mixture of medium-rare beef, steamed lobster and 1993 Bordeaux rushed up his throat and sprayed across the dugout and into the on-deck circle. With a pained groan, he accepted the handkerchief in front of his face and stuffed it in his mouth.

"A half-million. Not bad. *And* soliciting to violate the embargo. *And* you do it all here, in Bible country." Espinosa shook his head solemnly. "Up here? I think a jury of your peers throws your sorry ass in jail. What do you think?"

Gus thought he would vomit again, leaned down between his knees. A spark of courage flashed somewhere inside, and he vowed not to take it, thought of ways to fight it. He was entrapped, that was it! The feds were always doing that to innocent people! The IRS, the FBI. Even up here in Anglo-land, they messed with people. He thought of the lawyer he'd get: a real good one, somebody who could charm the mean old Crackers on a jury up here. He thought of the Crackers hearing Espinosa's tape, hearing him ask for half a million dollars. He thought about going to prison for a long, long, time. He thought about large black men staring at him hungrily in the shower.

"Back in the old days, my family worked on your family's plantation. Maybe your sugar mill. Maybe your casino." Espinosa smiled. "But now, *mi amigo*? Now your ass is mine."

Gus vomited again, a less robust stream this time, not quite making it out of the dugout. He gasped for breath, wiped the tears at the corner of his eyes, sniffled through a suddenly stuffy nose. The spark of courage had been snuffed out. "What do you want?" he asked meekly.

Regional sales, projections versus actual, quarterly, annually, long-term trends, comparative cost analyses, market share analyses, sales versus profits, by state, by region, by nation, excise tax versus sales, by region, by nation . . .

Jeena struggled to stay focused through each mind-numbing sentence, or at least one sentence in each paragraph. She tried various tricks to avoid losing her place: forcing herself to keep eyes wide open through the end of each page, then rewarding herself with a blink. Concentrating through three pages, then allowing herself a sip of tea.

None of it worked. She'd been curled up on her couch for five hours now, having vowed to get through at least four boxes. Four boxes tonight would leave her twenty-five for the rest of the week. That pace would let her report to Ruth Ann by Sunday, and then she could go the rest of her life without ever reading another piece of paper about the cigarette industry.

The documents, Ruth Ann had explained, were duplicates of the discovery material turned over to Florida's trial team. Those lawyers likely were looking out for anything useful to the governor in the political fight, so RJH had passed a set to its own lobbying team, which had assigned the dreary task to Ruth Ann, who in turn had given it to her new, law-school trained associate, who, as the night wore on, wished she'd never even mentioned the words "law school" in her interview.

Through seven of thirty-four boxes, she'd found maybe a half-dozen memos that the other side could use, and had easily thought up counter-arguments to those. It was clear RJH had used the standard tactic of flooding your opponent with paper, of interpreting a subpoena as broadly as possible and hiding whatever was sought among reams of dross. Company lawyers had seemingly produced every single piece of paper even tangentially related to its marketing strategy, right down to the invoices it received from its advertising agencies for employee expense accounts.

Each document looked the same, from the standard header to the little yellow sticker in the corner marking it as property of Roper-Joyner Holdings. Each document was written in the same corporate-speak that induced sleep from the first sentence. It had taken her five minutes of staring at the last piece of paper to realize it was a memo from a regional marketing director to an advertising rep advising that in-room movies would no longer be reimbursable, pursuant to Legal Department's interpretation of reasonable and customary expenses.

All the while, her mind kept wandering back to Murphy Moran's shy smile, his funny little goatee. He'd dropped her at her car, hadn't even tried to kiss her, had just given her hand a squeeze as she got out of the convertible. Had waited there, ever the gentleman, until Jeena had started her car and was safely on her way home.

He was here through the override, another week at most. And then? she'd asked as casually as she could manage. And then, well, the governors' races wouldn't get going until winter, and here he'd have made enough in Florida to let him sit back, maybe take it easy for the first time in years. Maybe fly out to meet *Dark Horse* in the Azores or Gibraltar or Ibiza or wherever she happened to be.

Jeena's eyes had widened at the vision of Murphy's Hinckley sailing past the Rock, had seen herself going forward to douse the jib, and then she'd turned back to the cockpit . . . and suddenly it wasn't a polished and refined Hinckley she was on at all, but a tubby little Catalina, and at the helm was Dunbar, wearing a goofy smile and sunglasses and nothing else, as he steered across the wind, spray flying over the high side.

Dunbar the grad student, newly arrived in Tallahassee, who couldn't understand Jeena's reluctance to swim and sunbathe *au naturel* when, after all, it was just the two of them out on the shallow backwaters of Florida's Big Bend. And even if some fishing boat happened to pass by close: so what? He didn't mind if other guys saw her naked. . . .

Dunbar the new grad student, who a couple of months later learned what all the knowing smiles were about whenever he mentioned his new fiancée. Who decided that he *did* mind other guys seeing her naked, after all, and why in hell hadn't she told him? Imagine what he felt like when his "buddy" had shared his collection of "Women of the ACC" spreads that always gave prominent billing to Florida State's finest.

Though it lasted nearly five years, their engagement never really recovered from that blow, she'd always thought. Early on, she'd blamed herself. If she'd been up front, admitting it right off the bat, even *bragging* about it, like some of the other girls, then it would've been different. Then Dunbar never would've had call to question his trust. But more recently she'd decided it wasn't her fault. She'd neglected to tell him, true, but because she was ashamed: a perfectly reasonable attitude. A good husband-to-be would have understood.

And there, she ultimately decided, had been the root of their problems. Dunbar hadn't been ready to be a husband, and Jeena hadn't been ready to be a wife. He'd still been searching for perfection, instead of a good fit, and she hadn't been sure enough of herself to tell him he wasn't going to find it.

If only, she told herself for the millionth time with a sip of tea, they'd met now, instead of eight years ago. They'd be mature enough to see each other's qualities instead of failings. More important, they wouldn't have the baggage of the pain they'd caused one another.

On the other hand, she reminded herself with a final swig of the now-tepid brew, if she was still with Dunbar, she'd never have gotten to know Murphy Moran and his chipmunk smile and devil-may-care attitude and luxury yacht. . . .

She glanced drowsily at the wall clock, saw it was almost three a.m. and calculated she'd wasted ten, maybe fifteen minutes on Dunbar-Murphy, Murphy-Dunbar, while reading not a sentence of the annual sales summary in her hand. She perused it quickly, laid it face down on the completed stack, took up the next piece of paper. She noted the standard format and numbering system that identified it as an RJH-generated document, began skimming—

She stopped, went back to the top, started anew, and this time when she got to the middle, she sat bolt upright, started from the top a third time. Slowly and carefully, breath held in her lungs for fear that even a slight movement would alter a letter here, a punctuation mark there, she went back through, word by word . . . finally blew out a long, low whistle.

Squinting, she studied the initials on the sheet, realized it was real blue ink there next to the title, vice-president of marketing, atop a synopsis of a field study justifying a $500 million advertising campaign aimed at "consumers" aged nine through fourteen. In cold statistics-ese it described marketing research on 2,012 elementary and middle-schoolers, half of whom the company's own surveyors had surreptitiously introduced to cigarettes, then followed over five years, proving the following: If a child had not started smoking by age twelve, his probability of becoming an adult smoker was thirty percent. If a child had not started by fourteen, those odds decreased to eleven percent, and by sixteen they were down to three percent.

She ran a finger over the penned initials, BS, read the name again, Bartholomew Simons.

Bells went off in her head. Feverishly, she dug through the pile of documents she'd already skimmed, finally found one that confirmed it: The man who'd invented Larry Llama to hook kids on Roper-Joyner cigarettes was now chief executive officer.

What would Dunbar and the governor give to see *this*? They'd go nuts! Here was documentary proof of everything their side had been saying for years. She could run off a copy for them in the morning. . . .

The idea had barely coalesced before she scolded herself: What the hell was she thinking? She was *working* for Simons! Indirectly, perhaps, but working for him just the same. But Jesus Christ, they were going after children! They'd even addicted a thousand of them as part of their science project!

Over and over, she read the piece of paper, but it refused to transmogrify into its wordy and meaningless fellows. It was real. She hadn't imagined it. She laid it carefully on the end table, stared at it some more, began to wonder: If *that* was in there . . .

Wide awake now, she flung the crocheted blanket off her bare legs and threw herself at box number eight.

TUESDAY

Whoever they were, they were relentless; she had to give them that. Ring, ring, ring, ring, ring. She'd lost count, it had rung so many times. But really, how the hell was she supposed to answer it when she was a hundred feet down? With a novice student, no less. Just a basic lesson she was trying to finish with her new pupil, the cute, famous, wealthy yachtsman Murphy Moran, when the damn phone had started ringing. Really. How rude. Probably just a telemarketer anyway.

She turned to motion to Murphy the importance of ignoring distractions, to stay focused, when she realized with alarm that he was gone. She turned this way and that, but she was alone. And then alarm became panic when she realized she had no regulator in her mouth. She felt back with an arm and, sure enough, she had no tank either. She was holding her breath, staring upward now at the tiny disc of light filtering down from the top of the spring, a hundred feet away, and she so badly needed air, but how to get back up? Had she free-dived? If so, she could shoot upward without worry. But if she'd come down on compressed air, then an emergency ascent from this depth would put her in the hospital, or worse, if she didn't remember to blow out the whole way up. And that damned phone . . .

Finally she opened her eyes, let the air out of her lungs and sucked in breath after breath. Outside was still dark, and the alarm clock by her bed said six-thirty, meaning she'd gotten a grand total of an hour of sleep. By noon she'd be hating life . . . and then she remembered what had kept her up so late, and thoughts of weariness disappeared.

With a blink, she realized her phone *was* ringing and reached over to answer it, then sat up, speechless, at the familiar, awkward good-morning.

"I, uh, heard maybe you were back in town," Dunbar explained after a long pause. "I figured I'd give you a ring . . . I mean a *call*, except . . . my God, it's not even seven! Hey, Jens, I'm so sorry, I didn't even think."

Jeena blushed; she'd nearly forgotten the pet name. "It's okay. I was awake," she lied graciously.

"Because, you know, there I was this morning, and there was the new phone book, so I figured: well, let's just see. And sure enough, there was a J. Golden, and I guessed it must be you. Well, I figured it was a woman, anyway. You know, because of the initial?" He paused a moment. "You know, I hope serial killers don't get wind of all these single girls listing themselves that way." Another pause. "But hey, here I am presuming you're single. I mean, after all, it's been, what, a couple of years? And who knows what could have happened . . ."

Jeena laughed inwardly, suddenly remembering why she'd so loved him. "How are you, Dunbar?"

And Dunbar went into free-form monologue about his eighth year in a football-crazed city, about the weasels in the legislature up to their old tricks, about the governor still the same old governor. Jeena listened, recalling Dunbar's unshakeable loyalty for that one human being. Through grad school, into his first job in Growth Management, even talking about his own father, he'd never shown anyone the downright awe he'd always reserved for Bolling Waites.

Not without reason, she had to admit. In a day of blown-dry TV politicians, Waites was one of a kind. He'd taken on the darkest dark knight in the land, Big Tobacco, long before it was popular, and pushed to the brink of victory before they'd regrouped and set their pawns in the legislature to work. She thought of the memo she'd found, played with the notion of a Bolling Waites getting hold of something like that, and here she was on the phone with his deputy chief of staff, the man who directed Waites' legislative affairs office. . . .

What was she thinking! She sat up straight, remembered what she'd vowed before finally nodding off. She'd take the memo to Ruth Ann, show it to her, let her deal with it. After all, her loyalty wasn't to Roper-Joyner or Bartholomew Simons, but to the woman who'd given her a chance when no one else in town would. She glanced at the clock, saw it was nearly a quarter to seven, cut into Dunbar's nervous prattle, told him she had to get going.

"Well, sorry, didn't mean to keep you. I was just wondering if maybe sometime I might drop by, you know, if that's all right—"

Her eye was on her closet, mentally picking out an outfit, as she hurriedly agreed and hung up.

Balanced precariously atop high-heeled sandals, Jeena tugged her microskirt downward, clingy top upward, and threw on a cotton jacket before slamming the door to her rusting Toyota. She was late for the 7:15 that Ruth Ann held each morning to finalize the day's schedule, but was confident that once she showed her the reason, all would be understood.

She'd only briefly considered what her boss's reaction might be to the memo, had even in a moment of clarity realized it might not be all she hoped for. After all, Ruth Ann had a business to run. Wasn't she likely to take the client's side and help them hide their warts? On the other hand, she'd been so fair to her, so generous, that Jeena could almost convince herself that Ruth Ann would see the memo, fly into a righteous rage and denounce Roper-Joyner at a press conference, the damning piece of paper held high in the air.

She knocked once on Ruth Ann's door, started to exclaim what she'd found but immediately shut up. Behind her desk was Ruth Ann, her mouth pinched and eyes wide. Across from her was a stocky balding man in steel-rimmed eyeglasses, navy suit and oddly threatening smile.

Ruth Ann waved an arm at him. "This is Mr. Simons, from Roper-Joyner. He's here about those boxes."

Simons stood and bowed toward Jeena, waved her toward the seat. She slid past him to take it, pulling her skirt down as she sat, and looked up with a dry swallow. She'd considered bursting into the office waving the memo. Now she was glad she'd left it in her purse.

"I was just telling Mr. Simons how I'd turned over the boxes to you with the idea of looking for things we'd need to deflect on the Floor." Ruth Ann smiled nervously. "He just came by to check on our progress. I told him, what with how hard I'd been running you, I didn't think you'd made much headway. . . ."

Jeena watched Simons casually, the unblinking gray eyes, the thin lips curved into a grin that failed to disarm. . . . Yes, it was just the sort of face that would purposefully hook middle-schoolers on cigarettes.

She thought of how she'd kept the papers in the exact order they'd come in, replaced them in their boxes just as she'd found them. All, of course, but one, which now seemed to burn ever hotter in her handbag . . . In the reckless blink of a manufactured smile, she decided to lie: "Mr. Simons, I am so sorry, but Ruth Ann is right. Every night I've meant to start in on your material, but I haven't even opened the first box." She shrugged, in the process letting her handbag slide a little behind her. "I swear, though, tonight I'll start in if it's the last thing I do."

Simons studied her a long moment, waiting, finally broke off with a laugh. "Well, Miss Golden, you can thank me for saving you many tedious hours. Because, as I was about to explain to Miss Bronson, those documents had no business leaving Durham."

Jeena glanced at Ruth Ann, pulled her handbag tighter. "Oh. Well, like I said—"

"You see, our Legal Department is quite possessive of anything that falls into their little fiefdom. Once they found out their stuff was missing, they got all bent out of shape. Started writing nasty e-mails accusing Governmental Affairs of mishandling documents, saying how they can't possibly win the West Palm trial without them." Simons rolled his eyes. "So here I am, getting their precious papers back so they'll stop bothering my secretary."

His eyes wandered toward her purse, and Jeena hoped to God he was merely staring at her legs. She began wagging a sandal-wrapped foot to encourage him.

"Legal discovered their absence last week, immediately decided they needed them back last month. So, if you could show me to them, I'll have them flown back to North Carolina, and you can get back to the important work I'm paying your boss an arm and a leg for."

"Well . . . they're at my house. After work, I could bring them to you," Jeena offered. "They're all in the living room, by the front door, so it shouldn't take me but—"

"Actually, Legal is pretty insistent. They say now that we've tracked the boxes down, we need to take custody immediately. I don't wish to keep you from persuading the good members of the Florida Legislature of the justness of our cause, so"—he held out a palm—"if you just lend me the key to your house, give me an address, we'll be out of your hair for good."

It had to be the memo, she thought, then dismissed the notion. If it was the memo, they'd never have let the boxes out of their sight, not with the trial going on in West Palm. Plus the yellow sticker's number had been out of sequence from its neighbors. It was there by mistake, and the company lawyers probably didn't even know it. They just wanted their stuff back because that's how lawyers were about their stuff. On the other hand, the CEO personally breaking up a corporate pissing match? How much sense did that make?

"Miss Golden, please, the jet's waiting at the airport." Still his hand was out. "We both have busy days."

Jeena appealed to Ruth Ann, who responded with the barest shrug. Slowly, she moved her purse to her lap, opened it just enough to slide her hand in and, with an uneasy grin for Simons, felt around inside, past the folded sheet of paper that seemed to singe her hand, past the makeup case, past the lipstick cylinder, finally found her key ring.

Slowly, she removed the key to her front door, dropped it into the waiting palm, and gave him her address. "The boxes are right in the living room." She was most worried, she realized sheepishly, that he'd see the dirty dishes she'd left, the clothes that always seemed to scatter. "The place is a mess."

Simons pocketed the key. "No need for apologies. We're the ones intruding. I'll make certain my people don't step one inch further into your house than they need or stay one second longer than necessary. We respect your privacy." He nodded. "Just as we know you'll respect the confidentiality of those documents that we burdened you with."

She listened to the words, thought about them, realized she was admitting something with her silence. "I never even saw the first piece of paper." She shrugged again. "So I guess keeping your secrets should be pretty easy."

Simons turned the doorknob, opened the door, then shut it. "I don't mean to be a pain in the ass, but Legal insists: The documents in your custody are the privileged communications of Roper-Joyner Holdings. Any unauthorized disclosure of their contents will result in action by Roper-Joyner Holdings, both legal and extralegal, to limit such disclosure. Heavy-handed, I know, but moot, right? I'll get the key back by lunchtime, leave it with your receptionist."

He nodded again and made his way out the door, pulling it closed without a sound.

Ruth Ann recovered first with a convulsing shudder and a reach across her desk for her cigarettes. "That guy gives me the willies."

Jeena thought back through the conversation, remembered now that Ruth Ann had never introduced her. "How did he know my name?"

"Jeena, he was *here* when I came in this morning. Right in that chair. He said the door was unlocked." Ruth Ann sucked down a long drag from her Princess. "I've *never* left it unlocked. Not in fifteen years, not last night."

Jeena considered the piece of paper in her purse, wondered how Ruth Ann would react now, after Simons' visit. Before, it had been merely an item entrusted to their possession. Now it was contraband. She wondered again if Simons wasn't specifically after the memo, that the legal department stuff wasn't just a cover story. . . . "What do you suppose that meant, legal and *extra*legal?"

Ruth Ann shook her head, started loading her briefcase. "I have no idea. All I know is: I never opened his boxes, you never opened his boxes. Now we never have to see him again. We've got a lot to get done today. Let's go."

Jeena pulled her handbag close and stood to walk with her boss to the Capitol.

A slow scan of the ballroom finally revealed a flash of kelly green and a shiny dome, and Martin Remy plotted a course between legislators wolfing down free hors d'oeuvres and representatives of the Florida Chiropractors Guild trying to convince them to let children's health insurance cover spine adjustments.

With a minimum of glad-handing, he reached his target, who was chatting up one of the group's sundress-and-heels lobbyists, explaining to her the virtues of catfish farmin' and dirt-track racin'. Remy stood patiently until T.C. finally squeezed the girl's ass as she walked away.

"That legislation we talked about," he began, T.C. still waving at people over his shoulder. "You get those changes done?"

Tuttle began playing with the rubber bands on his wrist. "Well, Martin, it's like this. I had my staff take a look, and they tell me it'll be considerably harder to slip in language like that than we figured."

Remy read T.C.'s smile and his shoulders fell. "All right, what do you want?"

"Cheer up, Remy!" T.C. chucked him on the arm, then winked hideously at a passing redhead in a particularly brief skirt. "That one, boy howdy, I'd like to do a bit of *nude* catfish farmin' with her, I tell you what."

"What do you want?" Remy repeated, checking his Rolex. "I got three other weasels to track down after you."

Tuttle finished his bourbon, set the glass on a nearby table. "Well, Martin, first off, I gotta thank you for openin' my eyes to this Internet stuff. I admit I was kinda slow on the uptake, but I'm there now." He graciously accepted another bourbon from a waiter. "See, I been doin' some surfin' on that World Wide Web of late, and you were right: I couldn't *believe* how much pussy there is! So I get to wonderin'. All those sites askin' for a credit card so you can look at nekkid girls: Those things really make money?"

A consortium of them based in South Florida paid Remy a six-figure retainer every month. "None of their checks has ever bounced. I'd say yeah, they make a bit of money."

"A bit of money, is all anybody needs in this life." T.C. winked at another passing girl, this time a busty blonde. "That and a woman or two. Now whatcha suppose these outfits need to get themselves set up?"

Remy checked his watch again impatiently. "A computer. That, and either naked girls or pictures of naked girls."

T.C. nodded thoughtfully. "Yessir, I do believe that's something would fit real nice in my portfolio. Marty old boy, I believe it's time ol' T.C. diversified into computer services, you get my drift."

Remy didn't, exactly, but knew Tuttle well enough to know he wasn't going to like it. "What, exactly, do you propose?"

"Them secretary cams you workin' so hard to protect." T.C. caught sight of a stunning brunette, at least five-ten, at least half of that in her legs, in a skirt so tight it effectively hobbled her. "Jesus H. Christ, would you look at that. . . ."

"Secretary cams?" Remy prompted brusquely. "What about 'em?"

T.C. shook his head to free himself of the leggy brunette. "I'm wonderin' if you couldn't lay your hands on one."

Now Remy saw where T.C. was headed and knew he didn't like it. "Maybe. Probably." He sighed resignedly. "Why?"

Tuttle's round face broke into a wicked grin as he snagged a stuffed mushroom off a passing tray. "Up on the fifth floor, in the phone and fax center? That booth all the girl lobbyists use 'cause it's got a mirror?"

The pack of blue-haired nags had the system down, Gus realized. Each had her piece, each waited for the one before to finish before jumping in. The effect was an uninterrupted stream of New York Jewish prattle, varying in intensity, but wearing him down, until he'd promised to kill a bill requiring vision tests for drivers over sixty-five, to pass a bill providing a bigger parking lot at Wolfie's and to make the state fix the lights at their shuffleboard courts.

They'd chartered a bus from North Beach, armed themselves with AARP pamphlets with pictures of all their legislators and now were running loose. There were a dozen of them, tapping wizened fingers on his chest, dangerously close to where the tiny, watch-battery-sized microphone had been sewn into his tie. One of them, he just knew, would feel the bump of metal, grab at it: *Senator Cruz, what's that in yuh tie? Hey, Margie! Come lookit what Senator Cruz's gawt in his tie!*

He backed up slowly, until he was against a wall and could retreat no farther, and finally he saw his salvation: the home builders' chief lobbyist, the man he'd been hoping to run into all day. He excused himself from his crush of Forest Hills–via–Miami Beach constituents, sprang beyond the reach of clutching hands and strode rapidly after the retreating form of the blue-suited president of the Florida Association of Home Contractors.

All morning he'd tried to engage various lobbyists in legally questionable relationships. And all morning, to his mounting dismay, he'd struck out. Not the liquor wholesalers, not the phosphate miners, not the sugar growers, not even the dog track people. It was like they could sense he was dead meat, stuck with a hook and rotting away around it. Bait that just smelled wrong and that they simply weren't going to take.

Gus brushed aside negative thoughts as he followed his prey down a corridor. The home builders were the sleaziest lobbyists in town, always out for a tax break and willing to pay top dollar to get it. Snagging this guy would be a breeze, a quick catch to show Espinosa he was serious about cooperating. His target turned into the men's room, and Gus straightened the knot on his tie and followed.

The lobbyist was at the last urinal in the row. Gus eased into the one beside him, unzipped, waited for the guy washing his hands at the sink to finish and leave. "How you doin', Kenny?"

"Better once session's over. You?"

Gus breathed out, relieved the lobbyist had asked. His whole approach depended on it. "Oh, I shouldn't complain. You know how it is. They pay us a measly twenty-five grand, expect us to interrupt our lives, rent our own place up here during session. I suppose it would be okay if the business was doing better." He paused, got no response, continued. "Like right now, I got the bank hounding me: Pay us our money, pay us our money! I just don't got it, won't get it until after session, when I can go home and close a couple of deals."

The lobbyist grunted but said nothing. Gus began to panic. It was the same line he'd used on him the previous year to pull in three grand.

"Well," the lobbyist muttered quietly. "I suppose I can loan you a couple thousand."

Gus perked up. The words were right, but they'd been so soft. Had the mike picked them up? Gus leaned his torso toward the lobbyist so his tie dangled by the man's waist. "A couple thousand, you said?" Gus asked loudly. Loudly and clearly.

"A couple thousand." The man looked suspiciously at Gus, who now hovered within inches of him, the two men still holding their respective dicks. "Whatever you need."

There. Gus was sure the mike picked *that* up. Now for the second half. The payback. The quo in the quid pro quo. He let go of his penis and gregariously clapped his urinal mate on the shoulder, leaned even closer: "And if there's anything you need in return, anything *I* can do for *you,* a bill you need run, an amendment," he winked garishly, "just let me know."

The lobbyist stared glumly at Gus' hand on his suit coat, nodded as he shook off, zipped up his trousers and hurriedly rushed from the men's room.

Jeena blathered on autopilot, the same speech she'd given more than a dozen times in the past day and a half, while her mind returned to the piece of paper in her purse. All morning, through four meetings with senators, she'd gone back over it from Simons' point of the view, and each time concluded unhappily that Simons was right.

However the papers were sent to Ruth Ann, accidentally or otherwise, she, and by extension Jeena, were agents of Roper-Joyner Holdings, accepting payment in consideration of certain services. The papers had been given to Ruth Ann for the purpose of advancing Roper-Joyner's interests. They had *not* been given so her employees could evaluate them and, based on that, decide whether to support or oppose the client. If she were their lawyer, she could be disbarred for releasing privileged material.

Then the other side fought back: She *wasn't* RJH's lawyer, she was their lobbyist. There was no legal privilege between client and lobbyist. Roper-Joyner officials had lied under oath every time they'd told a court or Congress that they hadn't targeted minors. If she were subpoenaed, she'd have no choice but to produce the memo.

Of course, Roper-Joyner could then pursue a civil theft claim and almost certainly win. Ruining her. Bankrupting her. Not that she had much to lose: a beat-up seven-year-old car she was still paying off, a net worth in the negative five figures. *Let* them sue. She had nothing for them to win.

But, she thought with an inward sigh, Ruth Ann Bronson did. The woman who'd let Jeena cry on her shoulder, given her a chance when no one else would, hired her at a dazzling salary, big enough to pay off her debts within two years: She'd risk ruining *her*?

No. She couldn't. When she got home, she'd write a letter to RJH's Legal Department in North Carolina, enclose the memo, explain that she'd removed it from the file as potentially sensitive, but was now returning it, and that would be that.

She'd chosen to become a top-shelf lobbyist, and that choice necessarily led to developers and agribusiness and insurance companies and, yes, tobacco. She knew that going in. She could have worked for the Cancer Society or the Heart Association, but she hadn't. She'd become a black hat, and this is what black hats did. The big boys would always get top-notch representation, and if she didn't work for them, somebody else—

"Miss Golden, are you here for the proponents or the opponents?"

Jeena shut up, confused, tried to recall what she'd just said. "Excuse me?"

Dolly Nichols peered over her reading glasses, then took them off and folded them. "I couldn't tell whether you're arguing *for* the veto override or *against* it."

Was this a trick question? She'd clearly announced herself: Jeena Golden, Roper-Joyner Holdings. "For."

"Ah." Dolly set aside the sheaf of papers she'd been reading, opened a new folder. "You seemed uncertain."

Jeena murmured an apology, picked up where she'd left off, the part where she asked about the fairness of attacking an industry that produced a legal product, and if that could happen to tobacco, then weren't grocery stores and day-care centers next, and—

"Do you really believe that?" Dolly cut in. "Do you believe Bolling Waites would sue day-care centers because of germs that children pass around?"

Jeena also had considered that a rather silly example. "Well, perhaps not Governor Waites," she allowed. "But the *next* governor, maybe. The question is do we let government do something like that on a mere whim."

Dolly nodded, impressed. "Good answer."

She looked Jeena up and down, and Jeena tugged at her skirt uncomfortably. Nichols was only the second female senator she'd visited. The first wore high heels, a short skirt and a gold ankle bracelet, and Jeena had felt right at home. Nichols, though, with shoulder-padded jacket over plain blouse, silk scarf around the neck, sensible shoes—Jeena felt virtually naked, tried to hide her bare legs beneath her briefcase, tried to pull bare toes back underneath the skinny straps of her sandals.

"You used to work for Senate Finance and Tax, right?" Dolly asked finally. "Went to law school or something?"

She nodded, flattered that Dolly had remembered, wished even more that she'd worn something else. "Halfway through, I decided I wasn't sure I wanted to be a lawyer."

"So instead you joined our esteemed lobbying corps. Let me offer some advice. Take it for what it's worth, coming from a fuddy-duddy like me." Dolly opened the manilla folder, began to peruse a packet of Floor amendments. "I've been in Tallahassee almost twenty years. I've seen hundreds, maybe thousands of young women come and go. Once it was bleached blond hair, then braids, then big hair. Push-up bras and bikinis, padded bras and thongs. I guess the latest thing is no underwear at all."

Jeena reddened, tugged futilely at her skirt.

"Whatever," Dolly continued. "I guess if I still had—listen to me, *still had*—if I *ever* had had it, I probably would've flaunted it, too. Point is, there's one thing in common I've seen in these chicklets over the years: They turn thirty, they get a couple of wrinkles around the eyes, maybe a gray hair, boobs start to sag, and they're done. Finished. And they haven't learned a damned thing. Except maybe how to fake an orgasm."

Jeena opened her mouth to protest, that no, Ruth Ann Bronson had specifically promised she didn't—

"You're different, Jeena. With a law degree, with your background, you could do anything you wanted here. Staff director, policy coordinator, general counsel. I don't know why you left law school. I'm sure there's a good reason. And if lobbying's what you want, then that's what you should do. Just one thing." Dolly lifted her gaze from her work, found and held Jeena's eyes. "You have to believe in what you're selling. You come in here, talk about personal responsibility and fairness. Thing is, I already believe all that. But you know what? It's obvious you don't. If that's true, you ought to go work for the white hats."

Then Dolly's face softened. "There. Now I've made a fool of myself. Once a schoolmarm, always a schoolmarm. Tell Ruth Ann to stop worrying. I'm not likely to change my views in the next week. As for my lecture: Remember what they say about free advice. Worth exactly what you pay for it."

Dolly put her reading glasses back on and returned to her papers. Jeena realized with relief that her allotted time was up.

Murphy Moran eagerly attacked the rare rib-eye on his plate, took a long pull on his Sam Adams and only then noticed the disapproving expression across the table. "Missed breakfast," Murphy explained, as he cut another generous bite of steak and offered it on his fork. "Taste?"

Simons had already finished a plate of baked fish and steamed vegetables and was sipping idly from a glass of ice water. "If it's for health reasons you don't smoke, then I'm afraid I'm missing the point somewhere."

Murphy shrugged and ate the bite himself. "I'll go on a diet after the vote. I need to keep my strength up for the fight."

"Discipline, Mr. Moran, discipline. It's what separates Superman from the herd." Simons removed a tiny notepad from his breast pocket, clicked open a pen. "In any event. We are, Mr. Moran, in what I like to call the endgame. I expect I will not see any letup until the votes are counted."

Murphy took another bite of steak, gazed out at the Capitol complex through the window of Andrew's Second Act, the more upscale version of the sandwich shop below. Both were magnets for lobbyists taking a midday break before returning to the carpeted corridors and marble rotunda to wheedle for favors. How Jeena managed to get through a single day of it was something he simply couldn't understand. And then he found himself wondering what she was wearing, and where she was at that moment, and what her body might feel like under those clothes.

"*Hello?* Are you listening, Mr. Ten-Grand-an-Hour?"

Murphy hadn't been, tried to think of a bone to toss. "I checked with our phone bank this morning. Still two hundred calls an hour. Half to the governor's office, half to—"

"Pardon me, but does this look like the face of someone who gives a shit? Just tell me: Did you do like I asked? Buy more air time?"

Murphy bit his tongue. He hated high-maintenance clients. Why did they hire him if they weren't interested in his advice? "I called some of the major markets. They said we can have cancellations, but otherwise we've booked every available minute. If we want, they'll ask their other advertisers if they'd sell their time to us. They said if we offered twice the going rate, we could probably free up another couple dozen day-part slots, maybe a dozen primetime. Personally, I don't think it's worth it. We're already saturated—"

"Do it." Simons took a final gulp from his glass, then poured out some more from a plastic Evian bottle.

Murphy raised a finger. "Let me finish: To buy back time between now and Monday will double what we've spent for TV, for a real marginal return."

Simons stared imperiously. "Who said anything about Monday? Buy for tonight and tomorrow morning."

"How does that help us?"

A slow grin spread across Simons' face. "No point running ads after they've voted."

"They're voting *tomorrow*?" Murphy watched Simons' grin widen as he sucked down more water. "You got Soffit to double-cross the governor. How?"

Simons shrugged, jotted something in his notebook.

Murphy began to press further, stopped himself. He didn't want to know. Promise or threat, either was definitely unethical, probably illegal. His long-cultivated reputation was that of a mean son of a bitch, but a clean one: an important distinction to an incumbent politician with everything to lose and little to gain by playing dirty.

And then a tiny item he'd seen in that morning's *Wall Street Journal* came back to him: A certain stock falling on word that its tobacco project in Colombia had suffered a catastrophic fire, ending its hopes of being first to market with a high-nicotine cigarette. He recalled again Simons' cryptic remark about South American lawlessness . . . then reminded himself of the bonus million, now just a day away, and decided not to ask about the *Journal* item, either.

"Well, with Waites down two votes, it's in the bag," he said finally. "The lawsuit is annulled, and you don't have to go to court."

Simons' good cheer passed, a momentary break in the overcast on a gray day. "Let me decide when something is in the bag, if you don't mind. In the meantime, I wanted to ask you something. It seems we're not using a certain lobbyist that my industry colleagues all rave about, one Martin Remy. Why is that?"

Murphy could see it coming, like he'd seen so many times before as election day drew near. The candidate would start losing faith, started believing any and all hints of defeat, would want to change the whole strategy in the final days. Well, this was where he'd have to draw the line, and in so doing risk his million.

"It's because, like I alluded to the other day, Remy has a criminal record. He was convicted of making illegal campaign contributions. He was never formally accused of this, but the scuttlebutt is he's willing to pay cash money for a vote, if it comes to it. That's a federal offense. There's plenty of lobbyists in town with impeccable reputations. We don't need the likes of Remy."

"My colleagues say Remy gets things done. That he's a winner. That he is, in Nietzsche's parlance, a Superman."

Murphy kept his chin forward. "We're getting things done. We're on the brink of winning. Without Martin Remy."

Murphy watched Simons watch him for a long, long moment. His eyes began to water, they were getting so dry. Finally, Simons looked away and Murphy blinked with relief.

"Okay, hotshot. You win. No Martin Remy. But some of my industry colleagues also advise we hold a special thank-you dinner for the senators supporting us. The path to a legislator's heart, they point out, is through his bloated belly." Simons nodded around the room, at knots of lobbyists whispering into legislators' ears, the lawmakers nodding sagely between bites of grilled swordfish and rack of lamb. "I was thinking tonight. Lobster, king crab, shrimp, the works. You have any ethical problems with that?"

Murphy shrugged. Simons had already decided. "It's your money."

"Yes, it is. Call that club down the street. Have them arrange it. Then call our lobbying team, have them make sure our esteemed senators know there's *free* lobster. If that doesn't clinch it, I don't know what will."

Gus paced back and forth across the empty reception area of T. C. Tuttle's office, occasionally glancing at the clock above the door, occasionally hearing T.C.'s drawl rise to an abusive string of profanity from the inner office. Each time he came to the far end of the room, he had to beat back the impulse to grab the doorknob and escape while he still could.

T.C.'s capacity for retribution was legendary, and he was terrified by what he might unleash. Still, Espinosa had been clear: He was working against a deadline, and when it came, if Gus Cruz was the biggest fish Espinosa had, then Gus Cruz was going down.

He'd made his way to T.C.'s corner office in desperation after an entire morning of striking out. He had promised Espinosa he would snag at least a half-dozen dirty lobbyists, who would in turn lead to other, more senior legislators. In exchange, Gus would be off the hook, looking at maybe probation, maybe not even that. It occurred to him that that could be the way to explain it to T.C., too. Tell him Espinosa had promised T.C. the same deal: Bring in someone bigger and get off the hook.

That should help defuse things, Gus told himself. He was doing what he had to, and if T.C. did the same, neither had to go to jail. Plus it wasn't like T.C. was blameless. After all, if he'd just kept his stupid ideas to himself, Gus never would have been in this fix. Think big. Think big and you are big. Yeah. Real big. So big he'd finally given Espinosa the outrageous dollar amount he'd needed to put him beyond even the most forgiving jury. Asking for a grand or two, the feds wouldn't even have sneezed. Five hundred grand, and he was on his way to being some large man's wife in a federal pen.

The unfairness of it all overcame his innate fear of his golfing partner, so that when the Panhandle drawl called out his name, Gus adjusted his tie, gently fingered the tiny microphone and strode in, certain now that Tuttle fully deserved what was about to happen.

T.C. sat on his desk, his speakerphone finally silent, a bamboo tube against his lips, blowing homemade darts at a portrait of Senate President Soffit on the opposite wall. "Whatcha been up to, ya greasy Meskin?" T.C. puffed mightily, gave a whoop as a tin foil-finned dart appeared on Soffit's forehead.

Gus shut the door behind him. He hoped Espinosa heard that part about greasy Mexican. Let him see how contemptuous T.C. was to Cubans. He wondered if he should try to egg T.C. on, try to get him to repeat it. He sidled closer, casually leaned over the desk so that his tie hung within inches of Tuttle's lips. "That's pretty good, T.C., calling me a Mexican. I guess all us Latinos pretty much look the same, huh?"

T.C. ignored him, instead fired another dart. This one hit the wall beside the portrait and fell harmlessly to the carpet. Gus decided to get down to business. After all, being a dumb redneck wasn't indictable. He cleared his throat, dangled his tie even closer. "Hey, T.C., I was thinking about that jellyfish harvesting scam you were talking about last week. You know: sticking a couple mill in the budget, then setting up that dummy corporation—"

"Later." T.C. wagged a finger, snapped a rubber band over his wrist. "Got somethin' to show ya."

He waddled to a wall cabinet, where he pulled open a door to reveal a radio console. "A buddy of mine in the surveillance industry set me up with this."

He flipped a switch and a pair of voices came through the speakers. Gus listened, realized he was hearing Walter Soffit and Dorothy Nichols. They were arguing about something, Soffit saying he had to do it and Nichols warning him not to. Gus looked up at T.C. with renewed awe. No *wonder* he always knew what Soffit was going to do!

"He's gonna fuck the governor." T.C. chuckled. "Old Bollin', he's gonna have a stroke. With Drayer and Robeson up in D.C., ain't no way he's got the votes to sustain." T.C. twiddled with a couple of the knobs. "Never had this damn hummin' before, though."

Nichols argued that changing the date of the vote wasn't fair to Waites, and Soffit suggested she shouldn't be too vocal about that, not if she wanted to be Senate president.

Curious now, Gus approached the radio. Was is Soffit's office that was bugged, or Nichols'? The background hum grew louder, and T.C. grew more irritated. "Goddamn piece of shit Jap radio," he fumed. "Ain't had it but a month and already it's on the blink!"

Gus took another step, leaned toward the console, and the hum became a screech. T.C. inspected the radio, then Gus, then grabbed hold of his tie and pulled it right up next to the speaker only to let go and clap his hands over his ears to protect himself from the deafening howl.

Then T.C. lunged at Gus, knocked him over, tore at his tie and began stuffing it down Gus' throat.

Lambert stood against the wall, a thick research report in hand, waiting for Simons' attention to return his way, telling himself that he had done worse than this. That this, too, would pass. That $1.5 million for a week's worth of work was nothing to sneeze at, regardless of how far beneath him it was.

Even if it meant driving the old man around like a fucking chauffeur, like he'd had that morning. Or picking a lock for him like a nickel-and-dime sneak thief. He, the man who'd single-handedly brought a country to the brink of revolution, who'd put a rifle slug through the chest of a man from a thousand yards, who'd taken out a Congressional witness *in* the Capitol and managed to make it look like natural causes . . .

He sighed, continued, at Simons' nod, to read aloud page after page about Dolly Nichols' various business interests. He still couldn't understand what Simons' deal was. If the woman was a problem, then she should be gotten rid of. End of problem. That, he'd be happy to do. But no, instead he'd spent the rest of the day staking out her office again, logging who went in, how long they stayed. Sitting there with a Clerk's Manual and Lobbyist Guide to match faces with names.

But that's what the old man wanted, so that's what the old man was going to get: She met with a bunch of people in her office. Then she sat in a committee room and listened to a bunch of speeches. The end. My day in Tallahassee.

Lambert flipped a page, started on another company, Nichols and Henderson, some data processing firm founded in Melbourne but with offices statewide, and stopped when he saw Simons' scowls grow more severe.

"Wonderful. I think I get the gist here. She's a good businesswoman. Unfortunately, I don't give a shit." Simons slammed his copy of the inch-thick dossier on his desk. "Isn't there one *useful* piece of information in this? Her insurance company never cheated anybody? Her data-processing company never rigged a bid? Aren't there any fucking lawsuits? What has our crack corps of research specialists been doing all this time?"

Lambert shrugged uninterestedly. "Yeah, a couple of lawsuits. But it says her companies never lost or settled out of court. Also, it says she personally has not been sued. Or sued anybody. And her credit history has no black marks." Lambert shrugged again. "Sorry, sir. Just reading what it says."

"With such enthusiasm, too." Simons shook his head, arms folded over his chest. "Perhaps instead of digging up dirt, we should just give her some sort of award. Cleanest Legislator on the Planet. What about her personal life? Surely there's *something* there. Busted for pot when she was a kid? A DUI maybe, before she ran for office?"

Lambert read some more. "Nope. Social drinker, doesn't smoke, no drugs. No criminal record at all. Not even traffic tickets."

"*Damn* it!" Simons fumed, his face darkening.

Lambert had a thought that perked him up: Maybe if they couldn't blackmail her, then Simons would have no choice . . .

Simons removed his glasses, pinched the bridge of his nose, hard, for a few seconds, then opened his eyes. "Fine. She's clean. What about her husband, then? We're not picky: maybe *he's* a drunk or a junkie or a molester. Have you checked him?"

"Nothing about a husband," Lambert answered, paging through the report again. "Says there never has been."

"Whoa, whoa, whoa, whoa. Let's do that one again." Simons shut his eyes a moment, opened them with a gleam of victory. "She's fifty, fifty-one years old, but never been married?"

"What it says." Lambert nodded.

A broad grin spread across Simons' face. "That's what it says. And what, pray tell, did our crack team of researchers infer from that little fact?"

Lambert flipped forward, then back, then shrugged. "Beats the hell out of me. She never found the right guy?"

Simons let the grin widen. "Never found the right guy. That's good. I've another theory: She's a lesbo. A bull dyke. A muff-diver. Any of those work for you?"

Lesbian, Lambert thought with mild interest. Yeah, no husband. Made sense. And then something from earlier in the day connected with something from the day before.

"Well? Any relevant intelligence?"

Lambert offered another shrug. "Maybe."

Simons stared coldly. "I'll have an engraved invitation delivered tomorrow. In the meantime, why don't you tell me?"

Lambert thought for a moment: Could he barter what he knew in exchange for something? Maybe Simons' promise to let him leave RJH after the mission? He studied the old man's hardening scowl, decided: No. It wasn't enough.

"Yesterday, at approximately oh-nine-thirty," he began self-importantly, "I overheard Senator Nichols telling her aide about her weekend, and spending time with Jenn, but how hard that's gotten since she started running for Senate president, but how she's gonna make time tonight, no matter what. Then this morning, at approximately eleven-hundred, I see this chick go in to see her, totally hot."

He recalled the tight little dress, how it hugged her ass, recalled deciding he wouldn't mind stakeout duty so much if he could look at someone like her the whole time. "I had been timing how long visitors spent with Nichols. All the others were in and out in five minutes. The longest was five minutes, forty-six seconds. This woman was in there thirteen minutes, thirty-three seconds. Her name was Jenna. I looked it up in the lobbyist book."

Simons nodded at Lambert with surprised admiration. Lambert, in spite of himself, felt a glow of pride. "Not bad, Colonel." Simons leaned back in his chair, stared at the ceiling for a time, then stretched his arms high. "Well, my brash soldier of fortune, I have some so-so news, some bad news and some good news. The so-so news is that we need to make a point of being there tonight when Miss Nichols makes time for her little friend. I know that mere peeping-tom photography is beneath you. I also know that if things go according to plan the whole exercise may be moot, if the vote is held as scheduled tomorrow morning. Still, it may be a useful photo to have on file. It never hurts to be able to put the hooks into a state Senate president, no? A little blackmail? Now there's a felony you can sink your teeth into, yes?"

Lambert shrugged noncommittally.

"The next part I don't expect you will like, but what the hell. This is why I pay you. This morning we reacquired the thirty-four boxes of documents. They're downstairs, in the ops room. Tonight, after your surveillance of Miss Nichols, I need you to go through them until you find the one we discussed." Simons lifted a hand. "Now I know your feelings about paperwork, that it's beneath your pay grade, et cetera. But . . . we must take the bad with the good. Look at it as an affirmation of my confidence. After all, you think I would trust just anyone to locate an article that, in the wrong hands, could lead to the downfall of Roper-Joyner's management team?"

Lambert found himself nodding at the praise. God, he hated how the old man could tweak him like that. . . . "And the good news?"

Simons grinned. "After you bring the item in question to me and I've determined its authenticity, I need you to sanitize the person who may have seen it. I don't believe she did, but . . . I didn't get to where I am by taking foolish risks. I'll give you her address. I'll even give you her house key. Make it look like an accident. Be creative."

Finally, after more than seventy-two hours back in the States, Colonel Marvin Lambert cracked a smile.

Dunbar Richey rapped twice on the cabana door, then strode to the desk where the governor sat in a green madras shirt, reading glasses on the end of his nose and red pen poised over a thick bill. Dunbar waited quietly. He was not going to interrupt the old man with bad news.

Waites slashed at an entire paragraph on the page he was reading. "Phone lobbyists! Don't know if I've met a greedier bunch of bottom feeders. It ain't enough they're makin' twenty, twenty-five percent profit. Now they want to charge extra if you live more than three miles from one of their exchange centers, which, near as I can tell, covers nine out of ten people in this state." He shook his head and flipped the page. "I guess you got bad news, otherwise you'da already told me."

Dunbar cleared his throat. "It's about our response ad. It's all ready to go, but I couldn't buy a single slot before tomorrow, noon. I know you wanted it up ASAP, but every station clear down to Key West told me they're booked solid until tomorrow."

"No doubt our friends at Roper-Joyner had somethin' to do with that." Waites marked up another section of the bill, scribbled in the margin. "My old pal Bartholomew Simons, workin' hard to maximize shareholder return. I always loved that name. Wonder what his middle name is. Luke, maybe. Or Judas."

"But if it's tobacco, then how come they haven't bought up everything right through next Monday?" Dunbar puzzled on that a moment, and then his eyes grew wide. "Unless . . ."

"Unless is right. That bastard Soffit screwed me. The Senate's votin' tomorrow mornin', nine a.m. Probably threatened to support his opponent for insurance commissioner or something." Waites flipped through more pages. "You know I took him huntin' five years back? Shoulda just shot him when I had the chance."

Dunbar was still in shock about the vote, suddenly only hours away. "Governor, what are we gonna do? Can we get Robeson and Drayer back?"

"They got that Rose Garden ceremony tomorrow. Get a nice plaque from the president. Don't wanna take that away from 'em. Besides, I still got a couple cards up my sleeve."

Dunbar thought feverishly. "What about Senator Nichols? You want me to run her down? She can talk to Soffit—"

"No, don't bother Dolly. She's got enough to worry about. Plus I know she'd have tried to keep Soffit from doing this. If he's doin' it anyway, well . . ." The governor looked up over his reading glasses, narrowed his brow in concern. "Dunbar, you're gonna have to learn to take these things more in stride or you're gonna give yourself an ulcer by the time you're thirty."

"I'm thirty-seven," Dunbar said unhappily.

"Well, forty, then." Waites returned to the telecommunications bill. "Besides, we got one strategic opportunity. I heard Simons is hosting a lobster dinner somewhere for all the tobacco votes."

Dunbar groaned. He knew if there was one thing that could buy the hearts and minds of legislators, it was steamed lobster served with drawn butter, freshly shucked oysters on the side. "Governor, excuse my language, but we're fucked! You *know* what those weasels will do for a hamburger and fries, let alone lobster! You want me to leak it to the media? Tell them the Senate's violating the open meetings law?"

"Nah. You just find out for me where they're holdin' it. I'll take care of the rest."

Dunbar still wasn't satisfied. The previous year, lobbyists had held a secret lobster dinner the night before the vote on a bill protecting from lawsuits nursing homes whose caregivers happened to rape an elderly resident. The bill had passed with only two dissenting votes, that despite pressure from the normally feared AARP. It was the lobster, Dunbar had concluded.

"What if *we* held a lobster dinner for our side?" he suggested.

Waites flipped the last page of the bill, capped the red pen and folded his reading glasses. "No need to waste taxpayer money encouragin' a Florida legislator's natural predilection to gluttony." Waites lifted the thick sheaf of papers, now decorated with red ink, and pressed it into Dunbar's hands. "Stop worryin', Dunbar. They ain't gonna hold that vote tomorrow mornin'. Wally Soffit promised me, and I'm gonna hold him to it."

"But, Governor! It's *lobster!*" Dunbar protested. "We can't compete with just talk! Shoot, I wouldn't be surprised if some of *our* soft votes show up—"

The governor clapped a hand on Dunbar's shoulder. "No more of that. You just find out where they're holdin' that thing. And here, go find whoever's the top dog in this phone fight, I think maybe it's Sam English. Tell him these are the changes that need to be in whatever hits my desk, or I'm gonna veto it so fast it'll make his head spin."

Dunbar glumly looked over the phone bill, wondered who would know where tobacco's lobster fest was going to be, who within that group might tell him.

"Hey, Dunbar."

Waites stood by his desk, phone in hand. "Remember that out-of-season red tide in Louisiana a couple weeks back? You know if they banned shellfish harvesting right away, or if it took 'em a while to get to it?"

One eye on the clock, the other on the lookout for her missing earing, Jeena struggled to finish dressing. She needed to find sandals to match her sundress and touch up her makeup, all while trying to appear not frantic, not in a rush to push out the door her onetime fiancé who'd shown up unannounced on her doorstep.

Jeena had checked anxiously up and down the street but had seen only Dunbar's piece-of-crap Toyota parked at the curb. Years earlier, it had ferried them to weekends at St. George Island or lugged their scuba gear to Wakulla Springs. Now it would merely be the first flashpoint of conflict when Murphy showed up to take her to dinner. An unplanned, unnecessary meeting of old and new.

He'd explained how he happened to be driving through the neighborhood and realized he was just one street over from where J. Golden in the phone book lived and decided to come on over, like, if she recalled from their conversation that morning, she'd said would be all right if he did sometime. Wasn't she going to invite him in?

So Jeena had, futilely trying to pick up the mess that was her house as she made small talk. No, she hadn't been diving yet, but then was stumped by his suggestion that they go. Yes, she loved her new job, but then remembered that pesky memo in her purse, almost asked his advice on it, then stopped herself: He was the *last* person she should mention the memo to. Telling Dunbar meant telling the governor, which meant his calling a press conference, which meant neither her nor Ruth Ann's ever working in Tallahassee again. Then she recalled Senator Nichols' advice to lobby only for those things she believed in, and wondered how anyone could make a living at that.

"Nice house," Dunbar said, walking behind Jeena holding a glass of ice water, the offer of which he had, to Jeena's dismay, accepted.

"I was lucky to find it. There isn't much for rent this close to downtown." Discreetly, out the corner of her eyes, she searched for her missing earring, then noticed that Dunbar, too, was nonchalantly but methodically scanning every room. Finally, she realized what he was doing: looking for the second coffee cup, the extra toothbrush, the tiny hairs in the sink. The subtle signs of another male.

Her anger flashed. "I've only been here a couple months. In other words, I haven't had time yet to have a man over."

Dunbar lowered his eyes guiltily, protested too loudly. "That's not what I was doing. Anyway, you have every right to. I mean, it's been two years since you gave back the ring, right?"

"Twenty-two months. Going on two years." She brushed past him into the bathroom to check her mascara, found the missing earring on the vanity and pushed the stem through her earlobe. It had taken but a few minutes to fall back into the bickering that had marked the final months of their relationship.

"Whatever. Point is, we're not together anymore, so if you want another guy over, I don't have much say in it, do I?" He leaned against the wall in the hallway, brooding. "So if you want to have Consultant Boy, whatsisname, Mr. Convertible BMW, over, then you go right ahead. That *is* why you're getting all dolled up, right? For him?"

A wave of guilt unexpectedly washed over her, and she found herself wanting to deny Murphy's existence. She scolded herself. Murphy was a nice guy, and she had every right to be interested in him. "I've seen him once or twice," she admitted carelessly, then squeezed past Dunbar again to her bedroom to look for pale blue sandals.

Dunbar followed her, stood at the threshold. "Well, which is it? Once? Or twice? Not to be a stickler, but twice *is* a hundred percent more than once. And seeing as how he's only been in town a few days, twice is a lot more significant than once, no?"

"Okay. Twice, then. Tonight makes twice, if you really must know." She checked her appearance in the mirror, decided pearl earrings didn't work with the dress, took them off and started digging through her jewelry case, then recalled suddenly it had been Dunbar's first real gift to her, a Christmas present. She hoped maybe he wouldn't remember, but saw from his stare that he did. Quickly, she picked a dangly, blue ceramic pair and moved away from the bureau. "Murph's a nice guy."

"Oh, *Murph*, is it? And what does he call you?"

Jeena fought down a blush. "All right. Murphy. Murphy's a nice guy."

"Really." Dunbar lifted his chin into confrontational mode. "So tell me, if *Murph* is such a nice guy, then how come he's a high-priced hired gun for fucking tobacco?"

Her first instinct was to deny it. She suppressed that, let herself get mad. If Dunbar wanted a fight, then a fight he was going to get. "There's nothing wrong with being high-priced. You'll recall that you, too, once upon a time planned to leave state government after a few years and move to the private sector. Remember? And anyway, to Murphy money means freedom, nothing more."

"He gets paid to *lie*!" Dunbar shouted. "Look what he did to Bolling three years ago!"

Jeena remembered the ads, a series of vicious attacks that all but accused Waites of molesting children. She shrugged. "That's politics. No worse than you and the governor gave his guy."

"Okay, fine. That was politics. What about *this*? This isn't politics. This is corporate scum that's lied for years, gotten rich off the backs of working folks and doesn't give a damn that their product is killing them."

The words struck a chord. It was an argument she'd shared right up until a few weeks back, before she'd sworn off moral arguments in favor of a living wage. "No one made them smoke," she answered automatically. "Government has no business interfering between willing seller and willing consum—"

"*Listen* to yourself!" he fumed, then blinked, his jaw falling in astonishment. "Wait a minute. You're *one* of them, aren't you? Ruth Ann Bronson. Of course! She's registered for Roper-Joyner, isn't she? And you agreed to work that account?"

She gave up on matching sandals, sat on her bed to slip her feet into a pair of white leather thongs. "It's my job," she said defensively. "Plus they're entitled to representation in the political process, just like anybody else."

Dunbar started to applaud. "And there you have it, ladies and gentlemen. The young idealist goes off to law school, and this is what comes back."

She didn't look up until she'd heard him slam the front door on his way out.

The Capitol Club had rolled out the best silver and Irish linen for the night. One entire wall of the Andrew Jackson Room was lined with warming trays of marinated salmon, baked grouper, stuffed shrimp, Alaskan king crab. But the stars of the evening were on a table to themselves: a rapidly diminishing pile of steamed Maine lobster and an equally popular tray of oysters on the half shell.

The bar was open, the drinks flowed, and no one among the tobacco lobbyists smiling congenially or the state senators eating greedily seemed to notice a slight ammonia odor, which servers quickly masked with healthy doses of lemon juice and Tabasco.

One of the identically dressed waitresses would later report to her boyfriend in the governor's office that, of the twenty senators in attendance, all but two enjoyed at least one oyster.

Fingers weary, back stiff, Lambert mechanically paged through ream after ream. His eyes focused on the upper right hand corner, just below a small, self-adhesive label marking each piece of paper as RJH property, at the unique code identifying each particular document's department of origin.

He paged slowly and dutifully, gritting his teeth, most fearful that somehow, amid a daydream, he would miss the stupid thing, have to start all over. It was damned hard to stay focused, though, especially after the great success earlier that evening. True, he hadn't been allowed to use any firepower beyond the Nikon's motor drive, but what the hell. He'd gotten out of town for a bit, crawled around in the woods some, acted stealthy.

It had been eighty clicks southwest of Tallahassee, just beyond the small town of Carabelle, over one bridge and then west off the main road. A gated resort called Gulf View Estates. He'd expected a long, slow surveillance, possibly requiring a bribe or two for information. But on his preliminary exploration of the perimeter, there she'd been, right in the second-floor room on the southwest corner.

Lights on, curtains open. It couldn't have been easier. She was already unbuttoning her blouse, Jenna already pawing at her, pulling her into bed. He slapped on the telephoto lens and fired off an entire roll of 3200 film within a minute. Then the lights went off, and he left after an hour to get the film to the airport.

It had all gone off without a hitch, and yet . . .

Something kept nagging him. He was supposed to catch her in the act. In the heat of the moment, he thought he had. But looking back now he wasn't so sure. Like that girl, Jenna: Back staking out Nichols' office, she was a blonde. A real, natural honey blonde, he remembered, with a deep, rich tan.

But earlier, through the window, had he actually seen blond hair? He'd been so hyped up about finding Nichols so quickly, about rushing to get the camera configured or risk missing the shot . . . that now he couldn't honestly remember. The frames he could remember taking for certain: The girl was already in bed, and from Lambert's angle on the ground, he could only see Nichols. They were embarrassing, as those kinds of things went: boobs hanging out, Jenna's hand reaching up from the bed to grab them.

Still, it would have been a lot better to have the girl's face, too. . . . Well, fuck it. If the chief had wanted to be sure about the pictures, he should have brought in a professional photographer, not a security specialist. Plus Simons had been clear: He wanted all the boxes gone through by morning. That was Priority One. Okay, fine, here he was, slowly going blind as the night wore on.

He pushed self-pity from his head and concentrated anew, returning a stack of papers into the expanding folder and a stack of folders into a box. He put the box in a growing pile on the left and lifted another box from the dwindling pile on the right.

He sat back down at the desk, with deep breath removed the cardboard lid and pulled out yet another folder. Five boxes down, twenty-nine to go.

Jeena fumbled with the key, she was so nervous, before finally getting the knob to turn. She was certain her heart had been hammering loudly enough to awaken everyone in the darkened, families-with-young-children neighborhood from the moment she'd asked Murphy if he'd like to come in for a cup of coffee.

"I'd love to." The words still echoed in her ears. Would you like to come in for some coffee? *I'd love to.* Would you like to come in and make love to me? *I'd love to. . . .*

But that's not what she had asked, she reminded herself. She'd said coffee, and he'd said yes to coffee. Maybe that's all he wanted, and did she really want anything to happen tonight, anyway? So soon? It was only their second date. Third, counting Wakulla Springs. But how could anyone count that as a *date*? They both happened to be there. That wasn't a date.

"Regular or decaf?" she heard herself ask, flipping on lights and closing the door behind him.

"Whichever. Either's fine."

She eyed the wall clock. It was already eleven-thirty. "I guess this late, it ought to be decaf. Got to get up early again." Immediately, she wished she could take the words back before he took them the wrong way, as a hint to leave. "I mean, it's not *so* late—"

"Decaf it is," he said with a grin, saving her from having to find a graceful finish to the sentence. "I'm easy."

She slipped off her sandals and padded to the kitchen, leaving him to study the family photos in the living room. The evening had gone so easily, all her worries slipping away as they chatted about sailing and diving. That would be the ideal vacation, he had mused: load up *Dark Horse* with dive tanks and compressor and head for some deserted island. Belize, she had pointed out, had the best barrier reef in the western hemisphere and the fewest tourists.

It had been hours since the folded square of paper in her purse had crossed her mind, along with the alternating visions of what to do with it: Send it with a letter back to Roper-Joyner. Send it anonymously back to Roper-Joyner. Send it anonymously to the governor. Burn it.

She pushed it from her mind again, scooped coffee into the filter, filled the reservoir with water, allowed herself to mull the implications of Murphy Moran's financial situation. He could quit right now, never work another day in his life and be quite comfortable. What would it be like to be with a man like that? Could they really get along as well as they seemed? And wouldn't an extended sailing trip really be the best way to find out? She stopped, scolded herself for notions that bordered on gold digging, flipped on the coffee machine. Still . . . He *was* a nice guy. He *wasn't* married or otherwise entangled. He *was* ridiculously rich. . . .

He was standing before her bookcase, scanning the titles, and she spotted her running shoes on the rug in front of the couch, a dirty pair of sweat socks on one of the cushions. Silently, she kicked the shoes beneath the couch, pushed the socks between the cushions, just as Murphy turned around.

"It's a mess, I know." Guiltily, she pulled the socks out, threw them down the hall toward the laundry room. "I don't usually entertain. At least, I haven't since moving back to Tallahassee, and then, well, you know, with session—"

"Jeena, please. Shoot, my hotel room, it'd be condemned by the health department if professionals didn't come once a day with industrial-strength cleaning equipment."

She turned toward the kitchen, remembered the two days of dirty dishes in the sink, decided she wouldn't show him around, after all. "Coffee should be ready in five minutes. I'd give you the tour, but everything's so filthy. . . ."

And she realized he was behind her, hands on her neck, her shoulder blades, gently kneading, telling her to relax, and for God's sake please stop with the messy house already. She had indeed stopped, the instant his fingers touched her skin. She arched her back, luxuriated in a massage that felt like a caress, and she thought it had been too long, far too long. . . .

Next thing, she was on the couch with him, her hands wandering over his back, onto his chest; she felt a tingle, realized his hands were exploring her, too, timidly at first, then more bold, over her belly, under her cardigan, and she knew it had been much, much too long, and she'd missed him so, and why did she ever leave him in the first place?

She opened her eyes and saw in a terrible moment of confusion and embarrassment that it wasn't Dunbar. She stood, nearly fell over backward, pulled her sweater closed, fluffed her hair. Murphy gazed back at her calmly.

She swallowed hard, searched for something to say, almost said that the coffee was ready, then realized if she said the coffee was ready, then she'd have to serve it, and he'd stay that much longer.

"I don't know what I was thinking," she muttered, immediately realized how awful that sounded. "I mean: I have to get up so early tomorrow morning, and it's already so late, and," she pinched the bridge of he nose, "I'm sorry, I've had the hint of a migraine all day, and . . ."

Murphy smiled. "And you need to wash your hair. Jeena, don't sweat it. I should go. No big deal. Things got a little carried away, is all."

He tucked a bit of loose white fabric back into his trousers, zipped them shut. Jeena was suddenly mortified. It was her hand that must have pulled it out. She squeezed her temples, shook her head. "I'm so sorry."

"Hey, kiddo, it's okay." Murphy stood, hands on her shoulders, and lightly kissed her forehead. "I'll call you sometime."

WEDNESDAY

On the raised dais behind the walnut lectern, Senate President Walter Soffit was a broken man. In theory he presided over the most significant event of the legislative session, an event so important it was going out live over C-SPAN 2. At his right hand was the gavel, with which he would bring the Senate to order, and at his left was the script to take up and pass Senate Bill 104, the governor's veto notwithstanding, and make Florida safe for Big Tobacco again.

In reality, Wally Soffit had been neutered, and he stared blankly out over the forty desks trying to understand how and why. For each time he thought the votes were there for a quorum and gripped the gavel, one or two or three senators would clutch at their bellies and lurch out of the chamber, replacing those who'd just managed to stagger back in.

Dolly Nichols watched in bewilderment from her front-row desk on the aisle, microphone in hand, ready to make the motion to take up the report of her Committee on Rules and Calendar, a resolution regarding gubernatorial vetoes. The packed spectator gallery had a while ago started to murmur, and now was in open laughter as yet another senator would cry out in pain and waddle out the doors toward the restroom. A virus, she'd assumed at first. A late-season bug, and she wondered if she would come down with it, too.

And then, as another one left the room, it occurred to her it was only Republicans who seemed afflicted by whatever malady had overcome the Florida Senate. Yes, sure enough, there was Jacksonville's Jumbo Johnson and Miami's Roberto Garcia and Sarasota's Sammy King: each a vivid shade of green, each holding a hand over his abdomen, each emitting a low, bovine moan.

But no, there was perennial womanizer Rex Kelsey, Democrat from Palatka, doubled over in pain and headed for the swinging doors, and it dawned on her that the mystery ailment hadn't struck *Republican* senators, but *tobacco* senators. The governor's votes, in contrast, seemed perfectly fine.

She tried to recall her pro-tobacco colleagues' common experiences over the past day or so, quickly came to the previous night's "legislative appreciation dinner" at the Capitol Club. She'd made but a courtesy appearance before starting the hour-long drive to Carabelle. She hadn't eaten a thing, and she was fine. Walter Soffit, too nervous about his impending double-cross of the governor, hadn't even attended. And he was fine. In fact, the one or two other pro-tobacco votes she couldn't remember seeing at Roper-Joyner's lobster fest seemed fine as well.

So as a new round of moans arose from the chamber and another pair of senators headed for the doors, Dolly Nichols couldn't help a smile as she wondered how Bolling had done it.

Lambert finished yet another folder, closed yet another box, took yet another gulp of room service coffee and wished yet again he'd simply ignored the order bringing him home. He could have checked out of the hotel and, as far as the chief knew, just dropped off the face of the earth.

But he wasn't in South America anymore, and getting out now would be impossible. He'd become so reliant on door-to-door transport from the RJH fleet, never a worry with customs or immigration, that he didn't even have a passport. Plus Simons had at least a dozen people in Special Ops stateside who he could sic on an AWOL agent. That wasn't even considering that damned pack of poisoned cigarettes in his safe. . . .

Lambert shook his head absently, half his brain focused on the upper-right-hand corner of each paper he scanned, the other half kicking himself for not having had the presence of mind seven years earlier to keep some sort of evidence linking Simons with his first two major assignments: Brent Bergstrom and Marcie Simons. The former had been the CEO of Roper-Joyner whose retirement Simons had grown tired of waiting for. The latter an ex-wife whose appetites Simons had grown tired of paying for.

He should have carried a microcassette recorder to the meetings where

Simons ordered the jobs. Hearing a tape with his own voice would have gone a long way toward making him more reasonable, Lambert bet. Anyway, it didn't seem fair that Simons should treat Lambert as his property just because of one stupid murder. . . .

With a flick of his wrist, he finished another ream, replaced it into its expanding folder, only then realized it was the last one. There were no more boxes. He was finished. Thirty-four boxes, a dozen folders in each box, about four hundred sheets of paper in each folder . . . more than 163,000 pieces of paper in thirteen hours, and not one of them was marked MRK93-1321.

He squinted at the light streaming through the vertical blinds as he massaged his neck. Now what? Was he sure he hadn't missed it? Well . . . yes. He'd been an inspector on the Jackpot assembly line, looking for defects on the filter ends, and had an eye for detail. He hated tedium, but he was good at it. He'd been looking first for the "MRK" abbreviation, and when he'd found it, he'd always been on the alert for the numeric portion. . . . But was he sure enough to say that if Simons asked him?

Lambert was still pondering the answer when the door swung open to Simons' red-faced scowl.

"We got screwed," Simons fumed. "It was all set, but Soffit never got a quorum. The senators kept getting sick. Not all the senators. Just *our* senators. The Capitol Club thing last night. Had to have been. But I'll take care of that personally. In the meantime, it looks like our decision to strengthen our hand with the Honorable Dolly Nichols was the right one. The pictures, Lambert. You have them?"

"Should be back from Durham within the hour, chief."

"Some frames we can use?"

Lambert tried again to remember seeing blond hair through the viewfinder, again settled for the suntanned hand reaching out for Dolly Nichols' bare breasts. "Yes."

"Have them sent upstairs. I'll schedule a meeting." Simons nodded authoritatively once. "And oh, yes: You have that item yet?"

Lambert glanced again at the boxes against the wall. "It's not in there."

Simons' eyes narrowed to slits as his lips hardened to thin, pale lines. "You've been through all the boxes."

"Yes, sir."

"You didn't miss it?"

Lambert took a breath for confidence. "No, sir."

Simons stared at the open box on the desk, the thirty-three closed ones that Lambert had stacked with military precision. "She kept it." He turned to Lambert. "It's at her house. I'll have the key brought down. Go get it."

The Senate chamber below them was empty, save for a cleaning lady scrubbing at patches of blue carpet near the desks of senators who hadn't made it to the bathroom in time. Food poisoning was the verdict. Most likely something from the Members' Lounge, Walter Soffit had pronounced from the dais, that despite the numerous senators who'd taken their breakfast there that morning but *hadn't* gotten sick.

"So now what?" Jeena sat beside Ruth Ann in the deserted viewing gallery overlooking the chamber. "Work other issues until Monday? Or stick with tobacco?"

Both mentor and protégé had picked white that morning, Ruth Ann a sweater vest and microskirt combo, Jeena a low-cut tank dress. The fabric barely covered her buttocks when she stood, but she'd come to accept that as normal.

Ruth Ann finished with her cell-phone messages, punched a few buttons and replaced the phone in her purse. "Well, since Roper-Joyner accounts for ninety percent of our receivables this session, they probably deserve our undivided attention until that vote."

Jeena sighed. After Dunbar's scolding, and then the fiasco with Murphy, then another restless night, she'd awakened with the pilfered memo weighing all the more heavily. She'd muddled through the morning, knowing that by noon, it would all be over and behind her and nothing could be done. Now, with the Senate's mystery illness, it would be another five days for the sheet of paper to sit there, searing into her conscience. She peeked at her boss, made herself believe that just maybe she was taking on too much by herself when she didn't need to. After all, a woman who played it so straight in her own business, surely she'd insist her clients did the same. . . .

"Can I ask you something, Ruth Ann? After all these years, how have you managed to deal with the sleazy things some clients do?"

"Sleazy like . . . illegal?" Ruth Ann asked suspiciously.

"Not necessarily illegal." Below them, the cleaning lady vacuumed up rug shampoo. "Certainly immoral. Definitely wrong."

Ruth Ann shrugged, smiled. "I see we've developed second thoughts about our number-one customer. Well, it's like this, Jeena. We're a service industry.

We exist to serve. There are laws and rules governing our business. As long as people play by those rules, moral and immoral just can't come into it."

Jeena mulled this, tried to make sense of it. It wasn't proscribed by either law or rule not to sleep with legislators, yet Ruth Ann made it her rule. . . .

"Look at dog tracks and gambling boats. Or the car-title loan outfits. Talk about sleazeballs." She shrugged again. "You sense a double standard. Or perhaps a lowered standard. Well, perhaps it is. But girl, we gotta eat, and if you rule out clients who do sleazy stuff, that's about ninety-five percent of the folks who need a lobbyist. Like right now, the Internet porn people are trying to sneak through an amendment letting them use 'secretary cams' to look up women's dresses. That scumbag Remy's working it."

She paused to open her purse, remove a Princess from a nearly empty packet and tap the end of it with her finger. "But, hey, know what? If they'd come to me? I would've represented 'em, too. It's how things work in this town. Well, I'm gonna go downstairs and give myself cancer."

Jeena fixated on the rolled-up cylinder of paper in Ruth Ann's fingers, long and thin to make it more appealing to women, or so the theory went. "Why do you do it, then?" she blurted.

"What, smoke? I guess about thirty years ago it seemed pretty cool. The bigger kids were doing it. The TV said it soothed your throat." Ruth Ann gathered her handbag and briefcase and stood. "Trust me, if I could quit, I would. Anyway. Gotta go. Oh, hey, by the way: Did you see how they screwed up your name in the Lobbyist Guide? Sorry about that. They promise they'll fix it for the next edition in a couple weeks. In the meantime, if any of the weasels call you Jenna, you'll know why. Ciao."

Jeena pulled out her copy of the pamphlet to see for herself, glumly tossed it back into her purse. In more of a muddle than ever, she climbed past the four rows of orange seats, through a glass door and toward the elevators. Ruth Ann, it was obvious, didn't share her moral qualms about Roper-Joyner's marketing. Ruth Ann was her employer. Ruth Ann had the right to set office policy.

But Ruth Ann didn't *know* about the memo, didn't know RJH brazenly had gone after the middle-school set to replace its loyal but dying cadre of customers . . . a group that someday might include Ruth Ann herself, if she kept up her pack-and-a-half-a-day habit.

She moved slowly past the Sprint Phone and Fax Center, absently took a seat at the "Lipstick Booth" to touch up her face before starting her rounds.

She reached into her handbag, groped for her lipstick case, and as she pulled it out saw the folded rectangle of paper fall to the floor.

She pounced on it, glanced around to make sure no one was watching and placed it on the desktop. Like a bad penny, it was becoming. Constantly in the way whenever she was looking for something else. That's all she needed was for it to fall out in front of a senator or Ruth Ann . . . or one of Bart Simons' minions. She pulled the cover off her lipstick and twisted the knob, only to watch a pink stub fall out onto the desktop beside the phone. Great. So much for looking her best. Well, perhaps she'd run into Ruth Ann and borrow hers.

She started to tuck both empty lipstick tube and folded memo back in her purse when she stopped . . . unfolded the memo, stared at it in one hand, the lipstick tube in the other. . . . Then she wound the knob on the tube back to the bottom, rolled the memo into a dense cylinder, crammed it into the empty metal tube around the still-waxy red stem. So it would get a little lipstick on it. At least now it would stay out of the way.

Jeena puckered her lips in the mirror, rubbed them with a finger to evenly distribute what color was left, dropped the tube into her purse and went off to her first appointment.

Martin Remy heard the ring of cell phone number three while talking on number one and keeping number two on hold. He made an excuse to one client, told another he'd call back in five, when an arm reached into the corridor and dragged him into a room. It was, he realized after a few orienting blinks, T.C.'s inner office.

"Just the slimeball I wanted," Tuttle said, as he waddled toward the corner, Remy in tow. "I could hear you way down the hall. You know you're a loudmouth? I guess you likely do. Comin' from New York and all. Check this out."

T.C. stood before a chair at the corner table, yanked a towel off a brand-new twenty-one-inch Sony monitor displaying a split-screen view of a gorgeous redhead. In the top half she stared into the camera, touching up her eye shadow. In the bottom was a dim view of a woman's crotch bisected by a strip of hot pink.

"I'd pay cash money to know if she's a real redhead," T.C. drawled.

She was a runner for Sam English's firm, Remy recognized, formerly one of his own. "She is."

T.C. elbowed him in the ribs. "You old dog. Shoulda known there ain't a chick in town I want that you ain't already fucked. Prolly did her at one of your sex parties."

He began moving the mouse with remarkable ease, Remy thought, for someone who just days earlier wouldn't have been able to find the power button. "They're not sex parties. They're pool parties, for some of my clients, and some of my younger associates."

"Sure, right. And your associates just happen to be nekkid and passin' out blowjobs like they was some kinda *horr-derve*." T.C. clicked his way back to the site's main page, a nicely done graphic titled "Tastee Tallahassee—The Capital's Finest Movers and Shakers" on a black field. "Speakin' of which, that was some big mess this mornin', huh? People pukin' left and right. I guess ol' Bollin' ain't goin' down without a fight."

Remy let the remark pass. It was, he knew, an old T.C. trick. On the tobacco vote, like everything else, Tuttle was working both sides, trying to jack up the bidding for his vote. "You're barking up the wrong tree. I already told you, I'm not in that fight. Asked for too big a retainer, I guess. Plus the word is they won't reimburse a dime on anything even remotely hinky. Some goody-two-shoes kid, media consultant from D.C., wants everything by the book."

"You don't say." T.C. stopped for a moment at a crotch in a sheer pair of pantyhose, resumed clicking. "I hear they're throwing money around like it's goin' out of style. Sounds kinda like a great big waste, to me. Figure you take all that money, divvy it up forty ways . . ."

Remy could only shrug. He'd suggested as much to Murphy Moran, had gotten nowhere.

T.C. patted the top of the computer case. "So whatcha think of my setup? Best the Florida Legislature Tech Support has got to offer: high-resolution Jap pi'ture monitor, five hundred megabytes of RAM, B3 line to the Internet, best the taxpayers' money can buy."

Remy studied the Web site closely. It was quite professional, with simultaneous images of women sitting, he saw with a squint, at the Phone and Fax Center booth with the mirror at the back. One camera must have been installed behind the mirror, the other underneath the little desk. "I think you mean T3 line."

"Whatever. Point is, I got one." T.C. clicked to the archive section, clicked on "Ball-Buster Bronson" and waited for the dual images to fill in. "Check out this one. You remember tellin' me how some chicks don't wear no underwear? Well, damned if you wasn't right! My tech boy checked this morning, and we had eight hundred hits and seventy-two new members. Seventy-two, in just a coupla hours! Seventy-two members, nineteen-ninety-five a pop: fifteen hundred bucks. Not bad work, if you can get it."

Remy watched as T.C. pointed and clicked away, paging back through a string of underwearless lobbyists. He squinted at the address, memorized it so he could browse at his leisure, when he had time to linger over his female colleagues' girl parts.

"So now that my client came through with the cameras," Remy reminded, as T.C. pushed his nose close to the monitor to study a blonde, the chief lobbyist for the Hotel Association, "you'll take care of that little amendment, right?"

T.C. pulled back from the computer with a frown. "Cuffs don't match the collar. All these years I thought she was the real thing. Makes you wonder." He glanced up distractedly. "Sure, I got your amendment all taken care of."

Remy smiled cautiously. With T.C., it was never over until the final vote. "Good, I'll tell my clients —"

"Course, there's maybe one or two details still need to be worked out."

Remy sighed. He knew it had been too good to be true. "What?"

"I was thinkin'." T.C. stared wistfully at the Hotel Association's ersatz blonde, then looked up with a sly grin. "We could discuss it at one of your *pool* parties."

Dolly Nichols tried to keep amusement off her face as Bartholomew Simons stalked the hardwood floors of the Andrew Jackson Room, the "scene of the crime." Lined up against the wall where the previous night there'd been mountains of seafood was the Capitol Club staff who had worked the appreciation dinner, ending with captain, chef and, finally, the club director himself.

"On behalf of myself and every member of this establishment, our most heartfelt apologies for any inconvenience this incident has caused," the director apologized again, as he already had a dozen times since Simons' arrival.

"It was not an *incident*. An *incident* is something that just happens," Simons said. "Here, you poisoned us. Roper-Joyner paid you twenty thousand dollars for a seafood buffet. Instead you poison us."

"That's not known for certain," Walter Soffit piped from beside her, grinning nervously. "In fact, I'm personally leaning toward the Members' Lounge."

Dolly bit back laughter. Wally was in a bind, wanting so badly to agree with Simons but also needing to stand by the club director, who'd given both Wally's wife *and* girlfriend full food and beverage privileges.

Simons shot him a glare, and Wally doubled back. "Although your theory does seem the most likely, based on the evidence."

"Evidence. Precisely what we don't have." Simons walked down the line of uniformed servers, scowling at each waiter and waitress in turn. "Because this kitchen staff *conveniently* dumped it."

"It wasn't evidence, it was half-eaten food," the club director said testily. "And we dumped it because that's what we do at the end of each night: We throw away stuff that doesn't get eaten. Because it goes bad. That's what happens with seafood. It goes bad."

Simons walked back the other way, giving every staff member a second look. "Some seafood goes bad. Some evidently starts out that way."

That got the chef's back up. "Bullsheet! We use zee finest ingredients, only zee freshest feesh! My kitchen is famous for zee feesh!"

"It really is fresh, Mr. Simons," Soffit offered helpfully. "I remember one time I had some wahoo. Caught that morning, isn't that right, Andre? It had to be tasted to be believed! A better fish—"

"Is everyone here?" Simons demanded. "From last night?"

"One's out sick," the director said. "The guy who was shucking the oysters."

"Oysters." Simons sneered. "I should've guessed. Fucking, disgusting, bottom-feeding—"

"Sir," the director interrupted, "I can personally vouch for the oysters. In my fourteen years here, we've never had a single complaint about our shellfish."

Simons turned on the line of staff. "Anybody eat oysters last night?" A dozen heads shook no. "How about crab legs?" Three hands went up. "The fish? Lobster? Mussels? Shrimp?" Soon all the hands were raised, and Simons turned toward the director again. "And where, pray tell, did you acquire these magnificent oysters?"

And Dolly had a sudden recollection of a road trip with Bolling years ago, a long discussion of their parties' relative fortunes over oysters and beer. She cleared her throat to interrupt the club director's defensive harrumphing. "R&W Seafood, Apalachicola. Am I right?"

The director stopped, mouth open. Simons spun on her, face dark with suspicion. "How do *you* know?"

Dolly adopted her standard smile. "Anyone care to guess what the W in R&W stands for? Here's a little hint: Waites. As in Bolling's brother, Arlo Waites."

The veins on Simons' temples throbbed as he glared at her, then Soffit, then the club staff. Dolly laughed. "Face it, Bart. The old man got you."

Lambert walked purposefully up the street, turned the corner like he'd done it every day for years. Not too fast, not too slow, was the trick. Purposeful but not hurried, and no one paid any attention. Today was a day for fitting in. Mindful of the bigotry against people in camouflage, he'd even made the effort to dress in civilian clothes.

Another perfect spring morning, the air thick with pollen, and he suppressed an urge to sneeze. That would have to wait. An otherwise forgettable man in civilian clothing who sneezed gave witnesses something to remember.

With his peripheral vision, he checked for traffic and casually made his way toward the tidy brick duplex, one hand in his pocket to remove the key Simons had given him. Past two hydrangeas and a tea olive, he was up the two steps to the front door. With a quick turn of the key, he was inside. He stepped to a living room window to scan the street for passersby, saw none.

He removed a small wooden wedge from the pocket of his windbreaker, knelt to jam it into the crack under the door, kicked it lightly with his toe to secure it. Finally, he stood and turned to face his day's project. Two bedrooms, one and a half baths, upstairs and downstairs townhouse. Eleven hundred square feet of drudgery.

Another bush-league gem. A continuation of the wild goose chase he'd wasted his entire night on and from which he was still exhausted. Again he couldn't understand the point. If the woman had stolen something, eliminate her and be done with it. What was the point of this?

Lambert chafed, but pressed on. He'd wanted to toss the place, in and out in an hour. Simons had nixed that: "Not an object out of place. If she doesn't have it, find out what she did with it." He'd thought, but not dared ask, how in hell he was supposed to do that, unless the girl had thoughtfully left them a note, explaining what she'd done with the damned thing.

Lambert lifted his left wrist, set the alarm on his watch for 1830 hours, the earliest time a certain Miss Golden could be expected home. He had six and a half hours. With a deep breath, he headed for the stairs.

Simons furrowed his brow and pretended to study the contents of his computer screen, as Dolly Nichols sat in the leather chair across from him. It was a trick he'd used for years: invite someone to his office, then keep them waiting. The management expert he'd learned it from at a seminar had guaranteed its effectiveness. The person kept waiting began to question his worth, then lost his composure and ability to negotiate.

Only this time, it wasn't just a management trick. It was honest-to-God stalling. Of all the goddamned days for the Gulfstream to break down. It had taken them five hours to have the part flown in and installed. Last he'd heard, they were still a half hour out of Tallahassee. And, of course, Nichols *would* come fifteen minutes early. . . .

Out the corner of his eye, he watched Nichols flip another page in her appointment diary and scribble a note. He glanced down at his wrist, back up at his computer. Come *on* . . .

"You seem terribly busy," she said finally, standing. "I know I am. I'll leave you to your work, and we'll chat some other time."

Simons suppressed panic, calmly manufactured a predatory smile. "Were I you, I should stay. This is a rather urgent matter."

"So your message said. 'Extremely urgent,' my secretary told me. Then I get here and you ignore me. Obviously, either something even more urgent came up, or I guess it wasn't all that urgent to begin with."

Simons strained his face muscles to maintain the smile for another few seconds, then felt everything relax with Andrews' effeminate knock at the door. "Come."

Andrews scurried in with a shy nod to Nichols, handed Simons a sealed brown envelope and scurried out again.

Simons waited for the door to latch shut, then cleared his throat, focused on Dolly Nichols' shoes, a pair of black, short-heeled pumps, thought of the contrast between her plain-jane image and the contents of the envelope, wondered idly how she would react. . . . "Actually, it's about the override vote," he said.

"What a surprise. I never would have guessed. Well, my advice is to forget this morning. Bolling is far too clever to have left a trail leading back to him. I wouldn't bother trying to pin it on him."

Simons tilted his head at an angle, as if the idea hadn't even occurred to him. "Actually, it's about *you* and the override vote." He eyed the envelope on his desk. He'd asked for eight-by-tens, and to judge from the thickness, they'd done up the whole roll. Ideally he would have had a chance to open it, evaluate Lambert's handiwork, maybe arrange the photos in an order maximizing their effect. Well, next time. With luck, Lambert would have shot the best pictures last. "Actually, I need a firm commitment as well as your help with some old-fashioned, hardball lobbying of some of your colleagues. I was thinking, for instance, you could make their committee assignments next year contingent upon their vote?"

She blinked at him uncomprehendingly. "That's it? You asked me here for that? I thought we'd already had this discussion: I never give a commitment, and I don't lobby my colleagues. I vote my conscience. I expect them to vote theirs."

"Yes, but you see, I was thinking in light of the importance of this vote, and given this morning's unfortunate fiasco and how it might cost a vote here and there . . ." He shrugged, stared down at the envelope in his hands. He reminded himself how she had called him Bart earlier, at the Club, almost in derision. He would let himself enjoy this, a little. "Well, I thought you'd make an exception."

He glanced up from her milky white ankles to see her shaking her head at him, annoyed. She reached for the doorknob again. "You thought wrong. I've said no about as many times—"

"I wouldn't go just yet." Simons tried to display anguish, like he was genuinely unhappy about what he had to do. He affected a sigh, walked around the desk, held the envelope with the very tips of his fingers, so as to minimize his contact with whatever might be inside. "Senator, let me be blunt: How you take your pleasure is really none of my concern."

He passed her the envelope, saw the smile finally disappear. He watched her open the envelope, flip through the eight-by-ten prints, couldn't help himself as he rose on tiptoes to peek at what she was looking at. . . . "My associate just happened to be in Carabelle last night—"

Smack!

The slap seemed to come from nowhere, but his brain processed the following data: No one else was in the room. Andrews was parked outside the suite, away from any potentially felonious activity. Therefore it had to be Dolly Nichols' hand that had knocked his head off to the side, and then: *Smack!* came the backhand follow-through, knocking it back the other way.

He reeled backward against the desk, gingerly put a hand to his cheeks. They were on fire, and his gaze rocked back and forth, but in the middle of it she remained, red-faced, livid, shouting. Gradually, the noise coalesced into words. Words like "sick" and "monster" and "asshole."

"Have you no decency?" she screamed, as the room slowed its rotation. "For God's sake, the man is *dying!*"

With a parting glare, she stormed from the room and slammed the door behind her. Simons took a minute to regroup, ran his hand along his jawline to feel for broken bones and let her final sentence replay itself several times before sitting back down at his desk.

The man is dying. The man. Man. Not woman. Not girlfriend. But man.

An unpleasant name association came into his head, old, nearly forgotten rumors, gossip considered unimportant at the time. . . . He punched up Andrews on the intercom. "Our former chief lobbyist in Florida. The one who got sick? Remember him? Ramon Garcia? Get his current address, would you?"

Silence for a minute. "Gulf View Estates, sir. It's a hospice."

Simons pinched the bridge of his nose. "And that's in, let me guess, Carabelle?"

"Yes, sir. You want his number?"

Simons sighed and opened his eyes. "Thanks, no. But when our genius colonel checks in, send him to me immediately."

In a single fluid motion, Jeena snapped the deadbolt, pushed open her door, flicked on the living room lights and kicked off her heels. She was exhausted, the lack of sleep over the previous two nights finally catching up. A steaming cup of decaffeinated tea, and then to bed.

All afternoon she'd gone from one senator to the next, retracing her route from the previous days to remind her assigned weasels that whatever had occurred at the Capitol Club didn't change her client's interest in their support. It had been a grueling gauntlet, with one male senator after the other, emboldened by her repeat visit, suggesting they discuss the issue *in depth* over drinks. *Explore common ground* over dinner.

She padded to the kitchen, flipped through the mail as she set the tea kettle to boil when she noticed the two other pots already on the burners. Pots that had sat there, encrusted with rice and black-bean soup, at least a day and a half. Pots that sat there on the left-hand burners with handles pointing right.

Jeena was left-handed, and always put pots on the stove with the handles turned to the left. She set the mail down, carefully turned the handles to the correct side, stood studying them for a moment.

The kettle began to whistle, and she turned the gas off, stepped to the fridge to get some milk when she saw the cartons of orange juice on the top rack. The new, unopened carton in front of the old. Just the opposite of how she always arranged them.

She stared at the scene in silence for a long minute, closed the refrigerator door, slowly turned around to study her kitchen. For a while, nothing. And then she began noticing things. The bay leaves in the bottom row of her spice rack, not in the top with her other spaghetti spices. The salt shaker to the right of the pepper mill.

A sudden chill passed through her, and she ran her hands over bare arms. She needed to call someone. The police? They could come over with all their police stuff, dust for prints, do whatever else police did. Like ask her why, ask if there was anything she had that someone might want . . . Ruth Ann? No. Same problem. She studied the spice rack again, the pots on the stove, the salt and pepper, and then picked up the phone book.

Dunbar bent his closely cropped head to the doorjamb, then over to the door lock, then back to the doorjamb. "How'd they get in, then?" he asked finally.

Jeena shifted her weight from one foot to the other. She'd changed out of her skimpy day clothes and into a T-shirt and sweat pants immediately after hanging up the phone. "I told you. I don't know."

Dunbar closed the door, snapped the knob for the deadbolt, snapped it open again. "Well, I don't get it. This burglar magically comes in, rearranges a bunch of your stuff, then leaves. Why?"

He'd arrived not ten minutes after her call, in jeans and a golf shirt, carefully avoiding any physical contact and quickly exposing the inconsistencies in her story. Calling him, she soon realized, might have been worse than calling the police. At least the police didn't have a vested interest in destroying her boss's client.

Jeena pursed her lips, studied the plain but wholesome features of her former fiancé. Nothing particularly good-looking. Nothing off-putting, either. A face she'd at one time found irresistible. He could have asked: Why not call *Murph*? but hadn't. It'd been obvious that when she really needed someone, that someone had been Dunbar. She let her gaze fall on the little black purse sitting on her couch, moved it off when she saw his eyes follow hers.

"Okay, what? What's in there that someone's gonna want that bad?"

Only after the question was out and she released the breath she'd been holding did she realize she'd been waiting for him to ask it. She moved to the couch, sat, played with the leather strap, the chrome buckle. "You've got to promise something. What I show you, you can't breathe a word of. In fact, you can't know this as the governor's deputy chief of staff. Only as . . ."

"As? As what? The guy whose ring you gave back?" His face flashed through anger, then frustration before settling on resignation. "I should have seen this coming. All right, sure. Not a word."

Silently she removed her lipstick container, pulled out the rolled-up memo, wiped smears of Pomegranate Passion on her sweats, passed it to Dunbar. She sat with hands clasped around her knees, noticed that his legs were nearly grazing hers, thought about pulling away, decided not to. Decided that having him that close was almost comforting. Wondered if he, too, noticed that his fingers had touched hers when he'd taken the cylinder of paper from her. Their first physical contact in two years.

"Jesus Christ . . ." He blew a soft whistle between his teeth. "I can't believe this. . . . This for real?"

She shrugged. "I can't imagine why they'd want to fake it."

"Holy, shhhhh . . . It looks like the original, too! Our lawyers had heard they might come up with this if they looked hard enough, but they were just flooded with paper. Semi-trucks full of paper . . ." He glanced up again. "How in hell did *you* find it?"

"A mistake, I'm sure. My hunch is certain people don't want it around. Where I found it, it didn't belong." She saw his brow crinkle. "What I mean is, I had all these boxes of documents, okay? Supposedly stuff turned over in the last round of discovery, and I'm supposed to look for anything you guys might use in the override fight. So I'm going through this one box, and there this is." She pointed to the yellow sticker. "This number? It was totally out of sequence with the stuff on either side. Plus this originated in marketing, and all the other stuff in that box came from finance. Somewhere along the line, somebody up at Roper-Joyner lost it."

"And now you found it." Dunbar eyed the memo enviously. "And you rolled it up in a tube of lipstick because . . ."

Jeena recalled Simons' polite manner, the dark vibrations she'd picked up nonetheless. She shrugged helplessly.

"Because you guessed *somebody* up at Roper-Joyner might want it back," he answered himself, looking around the room. "So where are these boxes?"

"*Somebody* came to take them back. Yesterday."

"Ahhhh . . ." He nodded. "Things get more clear. They came, said there'd been this mistake, and took back their boxes of documents. But you'd already pulled this one out. Then you come home, think somebody's broken in and start getting the guilts."

She hadn't thought of it that way, but now that he mentioned it . . . She thought back to the pots, the orange juice. She'd been so exhausted; *could* she have left them that way?

"So naturally, you call me, who works for the one man who can probably best put this to use, but then you say, oh no, it's a secret. You can't tell anybody. Great. Now what?"

Jeena studied her feet, well groomed, what with the sandals she was wearing most of the time now, but still decorated with the same toenail polish she'd applied over the weekend. Ruth Ann's toes always accented her outfit. Jeena wondered how she found the energy: morning workout, at the office by seven, eleven-hour day, stacks of reading when she got home, painted toenails.

Dunbar bent his head down to catch her eyes. "Helloooo? Anyone there?"

Painfully, Jeena finally looked up. "I don't know, is what."

"I don't *know*?"

"Dunbar, somebody broke into my house. I think they know I have it. . . ."

Dunbar scoffed. "Right. We're back to that. They broke into your house, moved your orange juice carton and your pepper mill. Of course, they got in without leaving a trace, and then left. Don't you think that if they thought you had it, they'd just *ask* for it back? And didn't you just get done telling me it was in with a bunch of unrelated stuff? Like it was lost?" He flung the memo at her, watched it bounce off her knee and settle to the floor. "Christ, Jeena, here you've got something that could change the world, and you don't *know* what to do? The hell's happened to you? Where's the Jeena I once knew? What happened to the girl who interned for the Cancer Society her freshman year?"

The words jabbed at her, and she folded her arms over her chest. "She grew up, is what happened. She's got car payments and rent and college loans she needs to pay off. *Some* of our parents couldn't afford to put us through school and grad school and law school," she fired back. "And it's not going to change the world. It's just going to help Bolling win his lawsuit. The two don't always necessarily coincide."

"So you need to work for the fucking evil empire? That's the only way you can stay solvent?"

"Ruth Ann is not evil. No more so than criminal lawyers are evil. She's a first-rate lobbyist and she works her ass off."

Dunbar snorted. "Ruth Ann Bronson is a whore. She'd lobby against her own mother if somebody paid her to. You want to come back to Tallahassee, okay. You want to be a lobbyist, fine. But you can't find a single white hat in town to work for?"

Jeena dropped her eyes again. She hadn't even approached any of the dozen or so white hats. She knew what kind of money they themselves made, let alone what they could pay a junior associate. "I told you, the car, school loans, plus law school wasn't cheap, either. And they expect full payment, the bank does, even if you don't finish."

"Fine, you got obligations. Join the club. But total, those debts come to, what, eight hundred a month? Nine hundred? And Ruth Ann's paying you . . . a thousand a week? Eleven hundred?"

Jeena said nothing, kept her eyes on her right foot, now partially tucked beneath left thigh on the couch. The skin on her ankle was dry, she noted. She'd need to apply lotion before she went to sleep or it would crack and peel. Not terribly attractive.

"Twelve hundred? Thirteen?" Dunbar continued. "More?"

"Almost fifteen," she answered softly, but with more than a hint of pride.

"*Fifteen!*" Dunbar screamed. "Fifteen hundred a week? So like . . . seventy-eight thousand a year? More than *I* make? And I've been doing this now for five, six years?"

He stomped around in silence while she sat. Yes, calling Dunbar had been a mistake. She should have known better. Or maybe, she thought with a sigh, it had been just what she deserved. In a sense, he was right. The Florida Children's Campaign, the Heart Association, the Florida Food Bank: all had been looking for legislative relations people. All were offering in the low twenties. It had been a choice between paying off her debts while living hand to mouth and paying off her debts while living in style.

"This was always the problem, wasn't it?" Dunbar faced her now, hands in his pockets. "I'm the guy who never wanted to grow up, get a real job, enough to support a family. Enough to afford a decent car instead of a rusting piece of crap. I guess old Murphy, old Murph, he's more what you need, huh? Made enough to retire by the time he's forty. You could stay home with the kids. Hell, you could *both* stay home with the kids. Or take his fancy yacht and go off sailing."

She wanted to contradict him, tell him all the right things, that no, that wasn't it at all, that those things weren't important to her. Instead she imagined herself on Murphy's boat, hearing his mellow voice explain about money and freedom, and not worrying anymore about what people in Tallahassee thought of her, or about that stupid little piece of paper in her hands. Instead she said nothing as Dunbar flashed her a brave smile, pulled open the front door.

She glanced up in a panic. "Dunbar, you can't say anything. . . . You promised. . . ."

"And if I do anyway? Then what? You'll never talk to me again?" He laughed bitterly and shut the door behind him.

Outside the penthouse windows, a red light atop the Capitol blinked on, and off, and on, and off. Warning the planes that must loop overhead to line up on the airport runway, Lambert realized, then tuned back in to his boss, who slouched in his executive chair, patent leather dress shoes up on his desk, glasses off, eyes closed.

"I woke up this morning," Simons mumbled, "I figured I'd be on my way home by now. Waites' law off the books. The memo gone away. All the loose ends nicely tied up. Instead . . ." He waved an arm, the enormity of the world's woes. Then he opened his eyes to study Lambert. "When you got to Gulf View Estates, didn't it say anywhere that it was a hospice? A place where sick people go to die, as opposed to a place to have trysts with your lesbian girlfriend? Oh, and the 'Jenn' that Ms. Nichols spent time with over the weekend? That would be her niece, Jennifer. A key fact missing from your report that may well have led us to a different conclusion. I am, by the way, still trying to comprehend how you mistook a terminally ill, black-haired cancer patient in his late fifties for a 'totally hot' blonde in her twenties. I can't decide whether it was an honest mistake or merely your oafish attempt at avoiding future photography assignments."

Lambert said nothing. It had brightened his day immeasurably when Simons described how Nichols had reacted to the pictures. He wished he could have been there to see it. He half wanted to point out that it wasn't his suggestion the woman was gay in the first place. That had been the chief's own brilliant deduction. He rolled back and forth on his heels, stared back out the window.

"I suppose I mustn't blame you completely. It was I, after all, who leapt to the conclusion regarding her sexual orientation. Anyway, I don't pay you for your cognitive skills. I pay you to blow things up, make people go away." Simons put his glasses back on and sat up straight. "Which means, I imagine, you're taking great pleasure in this turn of events. How so, you ask? Well, it seems the way things are going, I may have need for more of your mayhem than I originally anticipated.

"First, the memo. Okay, if Golden doesn't have it, then she must have given it to somebody. Find out who, then deal with it. Start with whoever has the memo and work backward to Miss Golden." Simons reached for a bottle of mineral water and poured himself a glass. "In the meantime, there is another task, one I think you'll find quite challenging. Now that your little debacle with the photos has alienated the Senate president-designate, we may have to deal with her a bit more severely. I don't know if she'll vote with the governor, but if she does, she could easily take a dozen others with her. We cannot allow that. We need a contingency plan."

Lambert nodded, his interest piqued. "Such as?"

Simons leaned back in his chair again. "I was trying to remember. The unfortunate Dr. Limpkin. He didn't have any history of heart problems before the myocardial infarction in that stairwell, did he?"

Lambert grinned, shook his head with pride.

Simons returned the smile, took a sip of water before turning to gaze out at the setting moon. "It's the damnedest thing. You look at Senator Nichols' medical records, and she's never had any heart trouble either."

THURSDAY

T. C. Tuttle yawned expansively, shook his head in an attempt to wake up and glanced over at the governor. "Don't suppose you brung coffee in that pack."

Bolling Waites sat patiently, black eyes locked on a patch of fog in the mid-distance, the spot where he absolutely guaranteed a ten-point buck would appear. "Nope. Coffee back at the cook shack when we make breakfast."

Tuttle wished again he'd never answered his damn phone. But he had answered it, and it was his old pal, Bolling, who'd heard Wally Soffit had canceled Senate for the day to let everyone fully recover from their food poisoning. So Bolling had suggested an early morning of hunting, for old times' sake. T.C., after hemming and hawing at the six a.m. rendezvous, had finally agreed, for old times' sake.

Now he found himself sleepy and irritable and hungry and cold, sitting on a damp log on the governor's seven hundred acres northeast of town, his hands numb from holding the damn rifle. Beside him, Bolling acting like the cold and the damp didn't bother him one bit, just sitting there chewing his wad, occasionally spitting behind him into the thick mat of decaying leaves.

"T.C., I hate to say it, but you just don't look happy," Bolling said finally. "Like you've gotten so caught up bein' a big-shot legislator that you forgot the simple pleasures. Like for instance, when's the last time you caught a fish, or shot an animal, and gutted it with your own two hands and ate it right out of the pan?"

T.C. thought about it, realized he couldn't remember the last time he'd done such a thing, but that it didn't bother him nearly as much as the fact he couldn't remember the last time he'd had use of one of Martin Remy's young associates. One of those limber little things in one of those easy-on, easy-off outfits . . . "Too long," Tuttle muttered, blowing into his hands.

"I can tell. You gone lost your common sense, is what happened. Look at you: foggy mornin' like this, but you don't wear an orange safety vest? Ain't you afraid of gettin' shot?"

T.C. replayed the question as he studied Bolling. The governor's face was unreadable. No upturned lip, no twinkle in the eye. The old man wanted something, that was for sure. He should have known an out-of-the-blue hunting invitation had to be more than just social. He replayed Waites' question a second time, swallowed uneasily at the flat tone, then let out a too-hearty laugh. "Bollin', I figured I'd stick close by you and I'd be okay."

Waites stared out at the patch of fog again. "Well, you worry me, is all." He stared some more, then checked and cocked his own rifle. "I'll tell you what else is worryin' me. It's that damn vote. See, I had a deal with Wally that he'd hold off till next week. Then the son-of-a-bitch cuts me off at the knees anyway. Now that don't necessarily surprise me, comin' from him. What surprised me was I had to hear it from people who heard it from someone else, who heard it from . . . You get the picture."

T.C. did and swallowed again, knowing what was coming. Desperately, he tried to think of excuses. "Well, Bollin', it's like this—"

"And the whole time, I ain't gettin' any heads-up from My Man in the Senate, my good friend and confidante Teegan Chaunce Tuttle, my go-to guy, my old roommate from the Pork Chop days?"

T.C. said nothing, felt something vaguely resembling guilt as he recalled the phone call that morning as he was dressing for the drive out to Bolling's hunting reserve, how Martin Remy had told him The Call had finally come, that he was about to become not just a player but *the* player, that he was talking six figures, easy. "A lot's changed, Bolling."

"Sure has. Your party affiliation, for one. I—"

"Chrissakes, Bollin', how many times I gotta tell you?" T.C. complained, glad to be on the offensive. "Active and retired military make up thirty percent of my district. How many of them you think vote Democrat?"

"I was about to say, T.C., that I couldn't give a rat's ass what letter's after your name: D, R, whatever you like. But loyalty, that's somethin' else. How many of the crazy boondoggles for your district have I let through over the years? I bet you can't even count 'em. I always said: If T.C. can snake 'em past the Legislature, far be it from me to take 'em away. More to the point, how many times have I run across your business schemes and turned a blind eye? You think that was easy? Me, bound to uphold and defend the Constitution blah blah blah, seein' the goofy shit you pull and still stickin' up for you? Think that was easy? You been indicted twice since I got elected. Each time, here I am, tellin' the press: innocent till proven guilty, let the facts come in, et cet'ra, et cet'ra, like some fuckin' moron."

"I was found not guilty. Both times," T.C. protested.

"Yes, you were." Bolling nodded. "And I'm glad you got the intellect'al honesty to say *not guilty*, rather than *innocent*."

T.C. sat quietly, deciding now just to take it. The governor had some bug up his ass, no doubt about it. Probably figured out that T.C. planned to sell his tobacco vote to the higher bidder. Well, nothing to be done about it now other than take his lumps . . . along with Roper-Joyner's cash.

"It's come to this, T.C." Waites set his rifle down on the log. "You and I, we been friends a long time. Longer than maybe we shoulda been. And it was you who got my tobacco law through in the first place, and I'm in your debt for that. But that law don't mean squat unless I keep it on the books. So let me make myself clear, for the record: I intend to win Monday, and I'll play hardball, softball, whatever the hell kinda ball I need to play to do it."

Slowly, Waites lowered the zipper on his anorak, pulled out a twelve-inch bamboo tube, held it up to examine it. "You are aware of Florida's fraud statutes? Of the penalties for false advertising? Of the enhanced penalties for elected officials convicted of participating in a fraudulent enterprise?"

T.C. wondered where Bolling had gotten it. One of the lobbyists, no doubt. They were the only ones he was selling them to. He'd have to track down whoever it was and make them pay. "No fraud there, Bollin'. A little souvenir, is all."

"Really?" Bolling held it to one eye, peered through at his companion. "Souvenir as lethal as this probably comes under the dangerous instrumentality statutes. Don't by any chance got a license to sell lethal weapons, do you?"

"Lethal?" T.C. grinned nervously, wondering where this was headed. "Chrissakes, Bollin', they made in *China!*" And then he realized he'd just admitted to fraud, added quickly: "Course, people who buy 'em *know* that. They're just wantin' a *replica* of a real Amazon blowgun. . . ."

The governor pulled an eyeglass case from a pocket, opened it to lift out a metal needle balanced by a nub of red plastic. T.C. wondered where the old man had been able to find them. He himself had looked for weeks without luck and was just about to ask when Waites reached into the eyeglass case for a small medicine vial, poked the tip of the dart through the lid.

"You know; well, I'm sure you do, seein' how you're the expert on Amazon Indians. But did you know some tribes of the Amazon basin still use curare to kill their prey?" Bolling carefully loaded the dart into the base of the blowgun. "You got any idea how hard it is to get curare here in the States?"

T.C. watched in morbid fascination as Waites stood, lifted the tube toward his mouth. "See? That proves I didn't sell a lethal instrument, 'cause you just said how h-h-hard it is to find the p-p-p-poison," he stammered. "All I did was sell a h-h-harmless souvenir. Ask 'em, ask any—"

"Back to the tobacco vote," Bolling said softly. "Come Monday, you with me? Or agin' me?"

T.C. hemmed and hawed, babbling as he recalled reading about the deadly poison, how it paralyzed animals instantly, killed them within minutes, letting the hunter approach at his leisure. He thought of the rifle in his hands, remembered he hadn't even loaded it, threw it aside and fell to his knees, begged Bolling to let him explain, wondered if the old man had finally gone off his rocker, had decided the only way to win the vote was to kill off those senators planning to vote with the industry—

And he felt the stick in his neck, looked up in horror to see Bolling lowering the tube, his cheeks still puffed from that one, single, fatal little exhalation . . .

T.C. clawed at his neck, realized he couldn't feel the touch of his own hand on his skin. He fumbled with the dart, yanked it out, stared at it, his breaths coming fast and shallow, no doubt an effect of the lethal curare . . . the old man just watching him calmly, watching him die, the cold-blooded bastard!

"You crazy s'um bitch! I'm goin' numb! You done killed me!" he spluttered, his hands on his neck, his eyes almost pure white. "You crazy s'um bitch! You crazy, arrggghhhh . . ."

Bolling watched impassively as T.C. dramatically fell backward over the log, landed on the soggy ground, hands still clutching his throat, eyes wide open but almost completely rolled back under his lids. Bolling tucked the blowgun back into his coat, reached to picked up his rifle before he stepped toward T.C.'s sprawled body.

None too gently, he kicked T.C. in the butt. "Gotcha, you old fool. You ain't dyin'. That's benzocaine you're feelin', like the dentist uses."

T.C. let his hands wander away from his neck, down his chest, pinched through his jacket. Sure enough, Bolling was right. He still had feeling there. The old man had gotten him good, he realized. He forced himself to control his breathing, finally focused on the lanky figure who was now pointing a rifle at his crotch.

"I just want to reiterate." Bolling spat a stream of tobacco juice off to the side. "It's true we been friends a long time. But if you double-cross me, so help me God I'll hunt you down and shoot you like a dog."

Murphy Moran pushed the door open after knocking twice and saw it wasn't Simons behind the desk at all but the sullen camouflaged man. G.I. Joe.

"Sorry. I was looking for Simons," he muttered.

Lambert glanced up for a moment, returned his attention to the desktop. "Ain't here."

"Know where I can find him?"

"Not my day to watch him."

Murphy edged closer, squinting to see what the little man was hunched over. "It's, uh, about the governor's TV ad. You know, about the tobacco vote? You happen to notice the phone number that flashes on the screen?"

He'd seen the ad for the first time that morning, a fifteen-second spot with Bolling Waites talking directly to the voters, telling them how "Big Tobacca" was buyin' their legislature, usin' ill-gotten millions to overturn the one law that could make them pay for the death and destruction they'd wreaked through the years. Bolling urged viewers to call their elected representatives, then recited a toll-free number—the same one Murphy had set up days earlier.

"No," Lambert said.

Murphy took another step toward the desk. Where the hell was Simons? G.I. Joe kept his head down, taking notes. Beside him was a cardboard tube, the sort used to mail posters. "Any idea what Mr. Simons wants me to do about it?" he asked finally.

Lambert offered the slightest of shrugs. "Not a clue."

Murphy edged closer, his view of the desktop still blocked by stacks of paper. "Well, *has* he been here? We had an appointment."

"He left. You can wait if you want. Or you can leave a message."

Murphy nodded. "Okay, tell him this. I started doing like he called about last night. Hiring *all* the lobbyists in town for the weekend push. So far, of the 1,387 private-sector lobbyists out there, 976 are now on the RJH payroll."

Lambert traced his finger along the desk, muttered absently: "I'll tell him: 976 out of 1,387. That it?"

"Of the 411 we don't have," Murphy continued, "some work for do-gooder outfits. Some are so busy already that the fifty grand we're offering doesn't mean anything. And then there's Martin Remy and his ilk, the ones a step away from getting indicted. I'm not even talking with that bunch."

G.I. Joe said nothing, and Murphy went on. "I'm going to ignore the Cancer Society crowd. There's only a couple dozen of them anyway. As for the rest, a lot of them have hundred thousand dollars retainers. If Mr. Simons really wants it so a senator can't even ask for a free cup of coffee without getting reminded which way to vote, then we're looking at a couple more million." Murphy watched Lambert ignore him for a few moments. "How about if I just write all this down?"

Murphy scribbled a note on his pad, propped it up against Simons' pen and pencil holder and started for the door, perplexed at why Simons would leave his office to such an oddball, even more perplexed by the large-scale blueprint on the desk that so captivated the oddball's attention.

The steel-gray door stuck in its frame, and Simons lowered a shoulder and gave it a satisfying shove out onto gravel floor and blue sky.

He picked up his briefcase, adjusted his jacket and strode toward a bearded man in a tailored Italian suit leaning carelessly against the east railing. Little glints of gold flashed from fingers, neck, wrists. "Mr. Remy, I presume?"

Remy raised his hands, stopping in mid-gesture to turn off a cell phone that began ringing. "You got me."

Simons glanced around the rooftop, the highest point in Tallahassee. To the south, a slight haze obscured the Gulf of Mexico's marshy shore, while rolling hills spread to the east, north and west.

"You wanted a private place in the Capitol." Remy shrugged. "It was either a broom closet or this."

Simons set the briefcase between his legs, said without preamble, "I need to know if you're still interested in working for Roper-Joyner."

Remy snorted. "I was interested a month ago. I offered you a complete package, guaranteed success. But no, you wanted a big gun. So here you are. He the one told you to hold a lobster dinner at the Capitol Club? Didn't anyone tell you Bolling's brother has the seafood contract there?"

Simons forced a thin smile. "You were in hindsight correct. Shall I grovel?"

Two more of Remy's cell phones began ringing. He held up an index finger for Simons, answered one, told the caller it was already in bill-drafting, checked the display on the second, decided that person could leave a message and turned off the ringer.

"No groveling necessary. United States currency will be sufficient." He shoved the phones back in his pocket. "But I'm not working with that pussy Moran."

"No one's asking you to. You do whatever needs doing. However you think is best. Five hundred grand for six, or two-fifty to twelve. Or two hundred for ten, and fifty for twenty—"

"It's gotta be the same for everybody," Remy interrupted. "Otherwise the ones getting less find out and want whatever the ones getting more are getting. Keep it simple: one fee."

"Whatever. I leave it completely in your hands. So we have a deal? Two mill now, two on delivery?"

Remy shook his head. "Three."

"Three?" Simons scoffed. "You want five million dollars, for a weekend's worth of work?"

"No, I want six million. Three now, three later, plus expenses. Look, time's money. I gotta rearrange my schedule, disappoint other clients. This late, my own costs go up. It's gonna take me more to get it done." Remy shrugged carelessly. "Of course, you're free to try the market, look for somebody else. Of course, you come begging Sunday, it might cost eight, maybe nine . . ."

Simons squinted silently for a minute, then nodded slowly. "I cannot resent a man for knowing his worth. Fine. Three now, three later." He bent for his briefcase. "I only brought five. Two for you. Three for your, uh, expenses. I'll have the rest flown down."

Remy eyed the briefcase quizzically. "What are you talking about?"

Simons flipped the snaps and lifted the lid.

"Whoa, whoa, whoa, don't show me that shit!" Remy averted his eyes.

"Where the fuck you think we are, Baton Rouge? Think twenty-first century, my friend." He scribbled on the back of a card. "Here's a phone number in Nassau. Read that second number to the man who answers."

Simons studied the lengthy bank account number. "Our, uh, clients are equipped to accept payment like this?"

Remy laughed, stepped over the briefcase on his way to the door. "These days, any Florida politician worth his salt knows all about Bahamian banking laws. Cheers."

Dolly Nichols sat in perfect comfort atop the old, much-nicked wooden desk, let the warmth of the sunshine pouring through venetian blinds and the smell of old textbooks soak into her skin. God, it felt good to be back in front of a classroom, enjoying the rapt attention of three dozen sixth-graders.

"The young lady in the pink blouse, toward the back," she called, and watched as a mousy girl with braces and thick eyeglasses stood. The girl had caught her eye as a virtual clone of herself at that age, and Dolly had made it a point to make frequent eye contact with her, to call on her the first time she worked up the courage to raise a hand.

"My name is Melissa Arnold, and I have a couple of questions. Why did the Republicans oppose the governor's plan to build new schools, and is the governor still mad at you because of it?"

The question jabbed unexpectedly, and Dolly flashed a look of pained surprise at Jennifer's teacher at the back of the room, then recovered her professional smile. The girl obviously wasn't as shy as she looked. Just like Dolly.

"Good question, Melissa, and one that goes to the fundamental difference between the two parties. Public schools have traditionally been a duty of local government, and we Republicans thought it inappropriate for the state to get involved."

In truth, her vote with party leadership and against Bolling had been a tough one. She knew Florida's high concentration of retirees, the "greedy geezers," made local property tax increases next to impossible, leaving schools, even in rich communities like Jennifer's, deteriorating and woefully short on even the basics. She'd noticed as she'd come in that students were doubling up on old, taped-together math and science texts, and it hurt her to the core. Had she voted the other way, and persuaded just two colleagues to do the same, Bolling's school bill would have passed the Senate.

"That doesn't mean the governor was wrong or we were right. In politics, sometimes you have to agree to disagree. It's happened before; it'll happen again." She thought to the coming week, to finally getting that damned tobacco thing behind them. "It'll happen again next week, in fact. But that doesn't mean the governor's mad at me. In fact, I consider him a good friend. And you had another question?"

The girl smiled now. "Yes. Is it true you're going to be the first woman president of the United States, like Jenn says?"

Nichols made a mock scowl at Jennifer, who reddened and shrugged. "Well, Melissa, I know I should never back away from anything my niece the campaign manager says, but I'm afraid that all I can say right now is that I have a decent chance of becoming the next president of the Florida Senate. After that? Well, you'll just have to ask Jenn."

She smiled at the round of laughter, checked her watch, realized she needed to get moving. Jennifer's teacher had asked for a visit preceding the class trip to Tallahassee the coming Monday, and Dolly had begged off for weeks, finally accepting the previous night after Wally had canceled the next day's session. But she'd enjoyed her visit more than she thought possible and vowed to make a return appearance soon.

"Time for one last question." Her eyes searched the room, settled on a gangly redheaded boy in a Marlboro T-shirt. "You, sir."

The boy grinned sheepishly as he stood, his weight on one leg. "Uh, when you're in the Senate, do you have to wear a white robe?"

Dolly interrogated the teacher with a look as laughter erupted again. The teacher explained the class had just seen a PBS production of *Julius Caesar*, and Dolly raised an understanding eyebrow, then shook her head firmly.

"Nope. Robes went out with the Middle Ages. And with that, as much as I'd like to stay, I'm afraid I have to hit the road. You've been a wonderful audience. I might have to come back and try out my political speeches on you."

The class broke into sustained applause. In the front row sat Jennifer, beaming proudly. Dolly winked at her, then gathered her handbag to leave.

T. C. Tuttle stormed the length of one empty corridor, down another, and stood before a locked door, fumbling with the set of master keys he'd had made for himself two decades earlier. Most lawmakers didn't even know where the Florida Archives were, let alone the fact that one entire floor was designated to keep every scrap of paper produced by the legislature for the statutory hundred years before shredding and incineration. T.C. not only knew where the skeletons were buried, he even had keys to the cemetery.

He cursed as he tried one after another, his hands still shaking from the anger that had overcome him a few moments after Bolling had spit his last stream of tobacco juice, hoisted his rifle and walked away. Still wheezing from the trauma, T.C. was afraid he'd wet himself, staring up alternately into Bolling's bottomless black eyes, then up the equally black, equally bottomless barrel of his rifle. Sheepishly, he'd thrust a hand down his pants to check as soon as the governor had disappeared in the morning mist. And then shame had quickly and violently metamorphosed into anger. The hell did the man think he was, treating him like that? And all because T.C. had had the presence of mind to maximize the value of his vote?

Fuck that. And fuck Bolling Waites. All right, they'd been friends, once. And yeah, the governor had helped him out of a couple of jams. But dammit all, he'd already repaid that. A year ago, sneaking his tobacco law through the Senate in the first place. Bolling should have known that leadership would have a total meltdown when they realized what had happened. He should have hurried it up and won his lawsuit before session started, if he knew he didn't have the votes. Or settled. Whatever.

Either way, he didn't have any goddamn business threatening T. C. Tuttle. Nobody threatened T. C. Tuttle, a little fact Bolling was about to remember.

Finally he found the right key, kicked the door open and stomped into the musty room. He counted bookshelves as he walked, stopping at the fifth stack of bound Journals. He dropped to his knees, pushed aside boxes of budget amendments from the mid-1970s, back when he was but a mere freshman, and dug at the loose floorboard beneath.

Carefully, avoiding the tips of rusted nails on either side, he reached down to remove a manilla envelope closed with a length of string looped around two cardboard tabs. He blew off a layer of dust, opened it, removed a sheaf of papers. He flipped through to the final page and smiled at Bolling's familiar signature.

Step one complete. Now to find the greasy Meskin.

Marvin Lambert worked quietly and contentedly, finally on a project worthy of his talent and experience. A tiny head-mounted surgeon's lamp provided a circle of illumination enough for the wire strippers, crimping tool and solderless connectors that flew through latex-gloved fingertips.

On a tripod beside him was a Florida Public Television camera that pointed through a small, smoked-glass window overlooking the Senate dais. At the desk was a computer for the camera operator's use. And in a spark-proof metal box beside the window, as promised by the blueprint, were the electrical buses for the vote tabulation buttons and individually keyed microphones on each of the senators' desks.

From a jacket pocket he removed a plain metal box the size of a cigarette packet: a battery, built to the peculiar design requirement of delivering the bulk of its charge in a fraction of a second. From a trousers pocket, he removed a ceramic cylinder the size of his thumb: a capacitor, to build up voltage to a predetermined level before letting it complete a circuit. And from his billfold, he removed a black disk just larger than a dime: an infrared sensor, which he stuck to a lower corner of the glass window with self-adhesive tape.

With easy familiarity, he stripped the ends of some blue wire, began linking the components together. It was, after all, an almost identical setup that had dispatched the conscience-ridden Dr. Limpkin some two years earlier. That battery had been larger, more the size of a small telephone, and therefore harder to hide. Since then the state of the art had advanced, although that was sort of moot, given how many nooks and crannies the utility room offered. Not that too terribly much electricity was needed in the first place. Half an ampere or so at several hundred volts, no more than enough for a powerful light bulb, was enough to make a human heart fibrillate.

Carefully, playing his headlamp from battery to capacitor to junction box, he checked the wire run, made sure it crossed nothing sharp, had no nicks in the insulation, before finally attaching the leads to the terminal in the column marked "MIC," in the row marked "6."

He took out a multi-meter, checked for continuity, taped the components to the underside of the desk. There. Finished with Dolly Nichols. Now he could move on to the task of tracking down Miss Golden and the purloined memo.

But first he had to make certain he hadn't left any more evidence for crime-scene techs than absolutely necessary. Slowly, methodically, he played his headlamp beam back and forth, looking for scraps of wire insulation or sticky-back paper or any other leavings. He stood back, tried to imagine a newcomer's perspective, immediately noticed the little black disk on the window. He thought for a moment, then slid the computer monitor several inches to the left, obscuring the disk from casual view.

As he was backing away, he saw his move had bumped the monitor off its screen saver and onto a Web page featuring a number of thumbnail photos of women's crotches. He bit his lip a moment, checked his watch, finally sat at the desk and clicked on a thumbnail.

With the lightning speed of a direct connection, a split-level photo filled in, the lower half a dim view up some brunette's skirt, the upper one a shot of her sitting at a desk talking on the telephone. Lambert clicked back to the menu, clicked on another thumbnail, then back to the menu, read the names besides the photos, scrolled down . . . saw one labeled "Naturally Golden" and given a promising five stars, and clicked on the tiny picture.

The photo filled in—and he blinked rapidly: He knew that girl!

He stared some more, both at the top half of the screen, her head and torso, and the bottom, a low-light shot between her legs. And it came to him: the chick from Nichols' office, the one in the skin-tight skirt. The one he'd told Simons was Nichols' lesbian girlfriend. Jenna something. He bent closer to the monitor, studied the dark area where her underwear would be, began suspecting that maybe she wasn't wearing any, squinted, tried to make out some detail. . . .

Or maybe it was dark because there just wasn't enough light for the camera. His eyes finally moved back to the top half of the screen, which was when he noticed the girl wasn't talking on the phone like the others. Instead she was concentrating on a piece of paper. He squinted some more. . . .

And his jaw dropped. Because after a whole night searching through those boxes, a whole day in that girl's house, here it was, right on the goddamn Internet! A single white piece of paper with a tiny yellow rectangle in the upper right corner!

He looked at the girl's face some more, and some previously unconnected details linked up in his mind: Jenna something, Miss Jeena Golden. He patted his pockets, pulled out his Lobbyists Guide, paged through until he found her photo. Then he pulled out the city utility records for the house he'd searched. Then he nodded with a sigh. Okay, so she wasn't Nichols' girlfriend. But she *had* spent almost fifteen minutes in her office that morning. What could they have talked about for fifteen whole minutes? Maybe . . . a stolen RJH memo she happened to have?

Lambert allowed himself a satisfied smile. He'd run by her house, just to make sure his theory was correct, and then he'd tell the chief. Finally a piece of information juicy enough to bargain with! He pulled a pen from his pocket, jotted down the Web address on the cover of the lobbyist booklet, then tucked it and the utility bill back in his pocket.

Still smiling, he removed headlamp and surgical gloves before grabbing the knob through the sleeve of his jacket and slipping out into the empty hallway.

Fingers jabbing calculator keys, Jeena went through yet another permutation of her budget, this time cutting groceries to $35 a week, plus $2 a day for a packed lunch. Utilities, rent, auto insurance, car payment, student loans, dry cleaning . . . She hit the equal key and sighed. Nope. No mistake. At the salary the Cancer Society could afford, she'd barely make it each month. Barring unexpected expenses, she'd be able to put away a grand total of $240 a year.

She crossed her arms, threw her feet on an adjacent kitchen stool, stared glumly at the figures. She'd signed a year's lease on the townhouse, and it would cost nearly as much to break it and find a cheaper place than to stick it out another ten months. A roommate could possibly take the spare bedroom, but the place only had one real bathroom. Plus she was tired of putting up with someone else's leg hairs in her bathtub, someone else's dirty dishes in her sink. She was an adult, dammit, not a college student. She shouldn't have to live like one.

She'd spent the unexpected day off studying legislation pertaining to Ruth Ann's other, non-tobacco clients. Time and again, though, she'd found herself re-living Dunbar's lecture, each time growing more ashamed of what she'd sacrificed for a comfortable bank balance. She'd thought, perhaps, that Ruth Ann might grant her a mini-leave until after the tobacco thing was finished. But even if she went for it, which she doubted, what was she supposed to do? Just sit the thing out? Pretend like she didn't know about the memo?

Finally she'd called the legislative affairs director over at the Cancer Society, found out, yes, the position was still open, and boy could they use someone right away. She'd mulled the idea over, had even thought of how the Cancer Society probably shared information with the Heart Association and the Lung Association. How if—somehow—a blockbuster secret document were to be released by one of those other groups, no way could anyone make a connection to Ruth Ann Bronson . . .

And so, eventually, she'd decided. The next day she'd go tell Ruth Ann she was quitting. Simple, to the point. Ruth Ann would be annoyed, maybe even upset, but she'd understand. She might not even ask for her clothing allowance back, Jeena dearly hoped, as she'd already worn most of the clothes and would have a tough time returning them. Then she could spend the rest of the day, the weekend, Monday morning, undoing her work of the past four days. Finding a way to get the gist of the memo out without it coming back to Ruth Ann. Finally, maybe Sunday or Monday, turning the thing over to someone at one of the nonprofits on the other side, making them promise to fudge where they'd gotten it.

And then, after the vote, she would go take the Cancer Society job, start bringing home $500 a week instead of $1,500 . . . She considered the display on the calculator again with a sigh. Thirty-five dollars a week for groceries. A lot of beans and rice. A lot of pasta.

Jeena looked to the pile of dishes in her sink, willed herself to get her lazy self up to wash them, for once, rather than putting them off till morning. She glanced at the salt shaker and the pepper mill, still reversed in the spice rack, and managed a slight smile. It was her paranoia over stealing that memo that had convinced her tobacco goons had broken into her house, which in turn had made her call Dunbar, which in turn had exacerbated her guilt about working for tobacco, which in turn . . .

In retrospect her fear seemed ridiculous. Okay, so the salt and pepper were in wrong, and the orange juice. Which proved what? That she'd been in a frenzied hurry all week, new job, new look, new boy interest, new everything. It was a wonder anything was in its proper place at all.

On the other hand, the pots had been on the stove the wrong way, too. She never, *ever* left them like that. . . . And the pen by the phone was moved. And the phone table itself had been dust free, even though she couldn't remember the last time she'd cleaned it. And that memo probably *was* worth hundreds of millions, so why *wouldn't* tobacco goons be looking for it?

Well, Sunday, she resolved, she'd get rid of the thing. One way or another, turn it over to someone else.

She'd just pulled herself to her feet when the doorbell rang. For a moment, panic: tobacco goons, returned for their property! She scanned the room for her purse, saw it hanging from a dining room chair, walked to the peephole and released a sigh of relief.

She opened the door to a grinning Bohemian college student with an earring and goatee standing behind a bundle of roses in each arm. "Either two different guys are sorry for whatever they did, or one guy is *really* sorry," he said.

Jeena laughed, accepted the bouquets, held them simultaneously to her face to inhale as the deliveryman walked back to a pickup truck and drove off. She shut the door with her back and set down her flowers to read the cards. The one in the yellow roses read: "Still friends, right?" It was from Murphy.

Then she opened the card amid the salmon and crimson blooms. It was from Dunbar, and said simply: "I'm sorry."

She took another deep breath, intoxicating herself in a sense of warm fuzziness, all her concerns slipping away for a minute. . . .

And she recalled the scene as she'd opened the door for the florist guy, tried to figure out what was wrong . . . finally put her finger on it. The outstretched limb of the live oak in her front yard. Even in the gloom, the bump where the large branch split off seemed bigger than normal, as if . . .

She ran back to the front door and threw it open, squinted at the tree.

Nothing. She stared, but nothing changed. She'd imagined it, was all. Or whoever was there had left, perhaps to a better location, closer to the house, under the azaleas. Suddenly, dropping her roses, she slammed the door shut and set the chain, ran to the kitchen to do the back door.

FRIDAY

Dolly Nichols finally lay her pen on the desk and dropped her chin into the ledge formed by her clasped fingers. "I'll give you this: You're persistent. They say that's the most important thing."

Jeena shifted one crossed leg for another, moved her purse into her lap, played with the buckle that held it closed. She should just bring it out and show it to her, she thought again. Just let her read it for herself. Her hand moved to the flap . . . then stopped, settled on her lap. No. She wasn't going to do that. She wasn't going to do anything that could hurt Ruth Ann's career. She owed her at least that.

"Thanks for agreeing to see me," she said.

Dolly shrugged. "I see anyone who can knock. Even some who can't. That's my policy. But I have to warn you, Jeena, persistent or not, I just don't promise votes. Never have, never will. And if Roper-Joyner can't accept that, and if Bart Simons wants to keep me from getting the Senate presidency, then so be it."

Jeena took a deep breath. "Actually, I'm not working for Roper-Joyner anymore." It was something she'd yet to tell Ruth Ann Bronson, who hadn't been in her office when she went in early that morning to tell her. Jeena watched Nichols raise an eyebrow. "Actually, I'm not working for anyone, right now. I represent only myself."

"Fair enough." Dolly nodded. "I take it that you, representing yourself, now advocate a position contrary to the one you advocated representing Roper-Joyner Holdings?"

"What if I were to tell you Roper-Joyner is flat out lying when it says they never targeted minors?" Jeena bit her lip, tried to gauge Senator Nichols' response, but got only the inscrutably serene smile. "What if I were to tell you that they carefully researched the nine-to-fourteen-year-old market when they developed Larry Llama? What if I were to tell you that the CEO himself personally signed off on the project?"

Dolly Nichols laughed. "That's a whole lot of what-ifs. I don't suppose you're actually going to tell me these things, are you. 'What if' is the best I get?"

Jeena avoided the question, instead studied her fingernails. Dunbar's visit and its aftermath had taken them to a new nadir, and she'd worked in Ruth Ann Bronson's waiting room that morning trying to salvage what she could with an emery board. A half-hour later, Ruth Ann still hadn't shown up, and Jeena, nails trimmed to the quick but neat again, decided she was wasting precious lobbying time.

"Of course, your new allies, the Cancer Society, the Lung Association, they've been saying these things for years, but have yet to provide one shred of evidence. Against that, you have sworn testimony by RJH executives that Larry Llama is aimed at young adults, not children." Dolly shrugged. "Let's set that aside for a moment. For argument's sake, let's say Roper-Joyner *did* target children. Okay. That's sleazy and underhanded. But it's legal, isn't it?"

Now Jeena looked up from her nails. "So it's illegal for them to *sell* cigarettes to minors, but it's not illegal for them to market them to minors."

"An interesting contradiction. And perhaps for consistency's sake, such advertising ought to be outlawed. Okay, let's pass a law saying that. You've got my support. But that's not what you're asking me. You're asking me to let Bolling sue the pants off the company because we don't like how they used a legal loophole."

Jeena let out a breath dejectedly. She'd hoped, given Nichols' refusal to promise her vote to Roper-Joyner, that she might have been amenable to voting against them, thereby dragging a bunch of Republicans pledged to her presidency with her. . . . Well, she should have guessed it wouldn't be that easy. She'd need to spend the rest of the day, the rest of the weekend, hitting all the senators she'd helped persuade to vote one way to now vote the other.

"Well, thanks for your time." She gave a pre-standing tug to her skirt. "I won't keep you."

"I'm sorry I can't help. But like I said, I believe what I believe and no lobbyist on either side of an issue is going to change that." She smiled again. "Even if that happens to be the same lobbyist."

Jeena stood to leave, shook Dolly Nichols' hand briefly and turned to the door.

"Just one more piece of advice, if I may? Your 'what if' from earlier? If on the one hand you can't prove what you're implying, then I'd be careful of what I said. You lose someone's trust just once, and it's gone forever. Down that road are the Martin Remys of the world." Her smile disappeared now. "On the other hand, if you *can* prove what you were implying, then I'd be *real* careful. Period. Pretty much any time you can prove a CEO of a multinational has perjured himself, particularly one who got his job after his predecessor died in an unsolved hunting accident, you need to be careful. Okay?"

On first hearing, the words didn't register. Jeena was in such a rush to move on, find some senators whose minds she *could* change, that it was only on her way to the Senate Office Building, cutting across the bright blue carpeting of the Senate Floor that Dolly Nichols' warning began worming its way into her mind.

A chill passed through her as she remembered the rearranged stuff in her house. . . . "Be real careful." Against something like *that?* Or much less dramatic, like getting blackballed on the job front?

At a polished walnut desk two rows down stood Senator Afumi Booteme, holding court with the troupe of capital press that turned to him daily for wisdom and an "urban black" sound bite. Senator Afumi Booteme, who in a former life was Leroy "Choo-Choo" James before finding Allah just after getting indicted for stealing money meant to redevelop a train station in his district. And in the front row was Senator T. C. Tuttle, gathering the papers on his desk, trying to leave, while another bunch of reporters squeezed him for a typically outrageous quote for their stories.

She needed both men and leaned against the desk next to Tuttle's to lift one sore foot out of a torturous sandal and rub it against the other. One day, her new footwear would be broken-in and comfortable. That same day, she knew, it would be out of style in favor of some new but equally painful look. She leaned over to massage her instep . . . and for just an instant she saw it: a skinny face peeking through the double doors opening onto the rotunda.

She stared now, but whoever it was was gone. The uneasiness from Dolly

Nichols' warning intensified . . . and she remembered the day she first went to speak to Nichols, when a short, weird-looking guy in full cammos and combat boots had lurked in the hallway, turning away each time she looked at him. At the time she'd assumed it was one of the NRA's band of "citizen-lobbyists," the handful of survivalist wackos they always deployed during legislative sessions. But then, a couple of days later, she thought she'd seen his face again. Where? The Capitol? No. It had been on her street, as she drove to work, strolling casually, as if toward the park. . . .

The same day, she realized with a cold feeling in her belly, that she thought her house had been searched. She hugged her purse close, stole glances around the Senate chamber. Both senators were still engrossed in conversations with reporters. No one else in the room. No one up in the viewing galleries. *Be real careful*, Dolly Nichols had said. Why? Had Roper-Joyner's goons been to her house, too? Had she come home one day to find some camouflaged thug escaping out her back door?

She peered out the doors, saw nothing. But that damned memo, still burning a hole through her purse . . . She sat, casually, in the overstuffed leather chair at the desk, realized it was Senator Nichols' desk, the traditional desk of the Rules Chairman, front row, on the aisle. And she noticed the microphone in its receptacle . . .

Casually, under cover of one arm, she tugged the mike out on its retractable cord, unscrewed the round foam ball on top. Sure enough, it was a hollow metal tube, the microphone's sensor way at the bottom. Under Nichols' desk she pulled the lipstick cylinder out of her purse, dropped it into the tube, jammed it down until it was snug, carefully rescrewed the foam ball, and, with a long sigh of relief, let the mike slide back into its receptacle on the desk.

"You waitin' for me? You got thirty seconds. Go."

She glanced up to Senator T. C. Tuttle's cueball head, stood, almost weightless, her purse once again merely a harmless accessory in which to carry girl things. She took a final look out the chamber's doors, then turned to Tuttle and began her pitch.

His arm ached, Gus had held it up for so long. But there was nothing he could do. No way to prop it up, nothing to rest it against. He lay wedged, forehead and nose mashed against the base of the couch, the back of his head against the Members' Lounge's elaborate floor molding, his left arm extended straight, holding up his tie like an aerial.

He'd been waiting hours it seemed, even though a sidelong view at his wristwatch told him it really only was about forty-five minutes, and not a single senator had mentioned something untoward, let alone indictable. Five, maybe six pairs and threesomes of senators had sat on the couch, discussed golf games, vacations, their kids' educations. But not one word about which lobbyist was picking up the greens fees, which political action committee was paying for the airfare and hotel, which professional association was taking care of the tuition. The bastards! The craven, venal, lying bastards! Letting him go down for something they all did, not lifting a finger to help. . . .

Gus squirmed against the bottom of the couch, blew away a dust bunny that threatened to make him sneeze, glanced again at his watch. Getting on ten. Seven hours to Espinosa's deadline, when, unless he had another couple of names, the young and ambitious special agent would turn him over to his bureau chief.

Beads of sweat squeezed onto his brow, began to trickle down the bridge of his nose as he once more pictured himself as the girlfriend of large, violent black men. Large, violent black men with nothing better to do than pump iron and sodomize Cubans. He grimaced as he imagined how much it would hurt, one large convict throwing him over a bunk, or worse, *two* large convicts, taking turns—

And suddenly he was being dragged, feet first, and for a moment he panicked: It was *them*! The large black convicts! They couldn't even wait for him to get sent up! He drew in a lungful of air to scream, scream as loud as he could for one of the guards, maybe he'd be lucky, find a Cuban one to take pity on him. . . .

"Stop your whimperin', greasy Meskin."

It was T.C., Gus saw with a mixture of embarrassment and dread. He'd been avoiding him since the day T.C. stuffed his tie down his throat. But now here he was, dragging him out from his hidey-hole, grabbing him by the tie, sitting on his chest . . . *Jesucristo!* He was going to do it again, suffocate him with his neckwear!

"Hey, T.C., come on, man! It's not what you think. I'm not wired. I mean, I wasn't *last* time, either, and—"

"Be quiet, you stupid beaner, and listen up." T.C. straightened, adjusted his sport coat. Fuchsia, today. "Your fed friends still wanna nail someone big?"

Gus shook his head in fear. "No, T.C., you have it all wrong! I don't even *know* any feds!"

T.C. lifted Gus's tie to his mouth. "Hello? Can you hear me? You guys still want a big enchilada? Well, I got one! Three o'clock, janitor's closet off the Cabinet room. Be there or get screwed."

Simons squinted at the monitor, then at Lambert, then back at the monitor, where there was indeed a sheet of paper in the girl's hand bearing a small yellow label, just like the kind Legal used.

"That's why I didn't find anything at her house. Because she's carrying it around in her purse. See how it looks like she's rolling it up? I bet she put it in that lipstick case there next to the phone. By the way, our Jeena is the same girl I saw that time. Her name is spelled wrong in the Lobbyists Guide." Lambert sat across from Simons' desk, legs stretched out, confident. "I did a little research on that Web site, too. It's only been up this week. Which means that picture's at most a couple days old."

Simons turned to him and Lambert felt a twinge of pride as he saw the old man clearly was impressed.

"Nicely done, Colonel. Above and beyond the call. Above and beyond." Simons turned back to the computer screen, thumb on his chin, index finger on his upper lip. "She has the memo. Yet she hasn't come to me. Our lobbying team hasn't mentioned talk of any 'smoking gun' in the opposition camp. So what the fuck is she doing with it?"

Lambert blinked. What did it matter what she was doing with it? Wasn't it enough that he'd found it? That *he'd* found it while an army of RJH's private investigators hadn't?

"You know what it is?" Simons asked. "Misguided loyalty. She knows those documents were given in trust to Ruth Ann Bronson. That if something damaging were to be leaked from them, that Miss Bronson's reputation in this town would be shot. She's hanging on to it because she's not sure what else she can do with it. Foolish girl."

He clicked the mouse back to his stock updates and turned to Lambert. "Well, you'll teach her an important life lesson?"

Lambert grinned.

"Sooner, rather than later. One never knows how long her conscience will hold. Try to minimize reasons for police to investigate, will you?"

Lambert grinned again. "Standard operating procedure." He watched

Simons pick up something from his desk to read it, felt his throat go dry. He had to strike now, while Simons' praise was still fresh. "Chief, I thought in light of what I've done so far on this that you could maybe reconsider about my future."

Simons raised his head slightly, enough for him to squint at Lambert over his glasses. Lambert plunged ahead.

"I was thinking . . . you don't really use me more than a couple months a year anyway. So what if I sort of freelance for you when you need me, and work for myself the rest of the time? Something like that could benefit the both of us—"

"Marvin," Simons interrupted. "Did you ever read the story of Dr. Faust?"

Lambert could already guess the answer. "No, sir."

"Well. Dr. Faust sells his soul to the devil in return for knowledge and power. Later, he tries to break the deal." Simons continued with his reading. "Back when you agreed to work for me, rather than explain to the police about arsenic in cigarettes, you sold your soul. Do you understand that? I'm your devil, and a deal's a deal. Now go do your job."

Lambert felt himself redden with rage and humiliation and, ultimately, impotence. He stared hatefully at the shiny top of Simons' head, then turned for the door.

"One last thing. That device you prepared to guard against Dolly Nichols' defection. Do you have it?"

Lambert felt the lump the television remote made in his jacket pocket. If he had any balls, he'd destroy it. Destroy the whole rig. Quietly, he pulled out the plastic rectangle and tossed it on Simons' desk.

Simons studied it. "This works as one might imagine?"

Lambert nodded meekly. "If she starts saying something you don't like, just make sure she has the microphone in her hand and hit the power button. And she'll turn off."

Ruth Ann Bronson poked her head into Duplicating, yelled, banged the bell on the counter, was rewarded with silence. She scanned the desktops for a stapler, saw none. Increasingly cranky, she adjusted the stack of papers she held against her chest, got a new grip on her briefcase and with one hip knocked open the swinging gate through the counter.

It had been that kind of day. One thing after another. Speaker Jon Powers had without warning skipped a meeting, leaving her sitting at the breakfast table for a half hour before a waiter finally gave her the message. Then a nursing home bill that should have been drafted by nine of course hadn't been, and she'd spent an extra forty minutes there, waiting for it.

And still unresolved was that note from Jeena a day earlier, asking for the day off, giving her time to think. She hadn't liked the sound of that at all, so close to the tobacco vote. The poor girl had probably been poked or pinched one too many times by slime-bag senators. Or perhaps one of them had gotten wind of that *Playboy* picture, had left it on his desk when she came in for an appointment. Poor girl. She herself had faced similar bullshit, but had quickly developed a thick hide and a fuck-off attitude to protect herself. Not everyone, she supposed, was mentally suited to handle that.

Well, she'd page Jeena, just as soon as she found a stinking stapler to assemble the packets of paper now rumpling against her chest. She approached a door and was nearly bowled over by a pair of red-faced, blue-suited guys bolting from the room the House Clerk had put at the lobbying corps' disposal. Puzzled, she watched them retreat through the swinging gate, then stepped into the room where, beside a computer mouse pad, she finally saw a stapler.

She arranged the sheets in alternating stacks and began stapling that day's set of bills, bill analyses, amendments, and amendments-to-the-amendment. One by one, collate, staple, collate, staple . . . And she noticed that although her hand had bumped the mouse pad, the monitor hadn't come to life. She studied the screen for a moment, saw that the little LED indicator wasn't glowing.

She crinkled her nose, recalling the two lobbyists who'd run from the room as she entered. One represented trailer park owners, the other the Florida Consortium of Bailbondsmen. Both total sleazeballs. With a forefinger she pressed the button, heard a crackle and saw the indicator light shine a steady, bright green. On the screen appeared two views of Melanie Kristal, one of Martin Remy's fresh, young girls: one of her face, and the other, Ruth Ann saw with rising anger, a sneak shot up her skirt. She studied the image of Melanie applying lipstick, knew instantly where the picture had been taken.

Hands trembling, she grabbed the mouse and clicked the "page back" button, saw the marquee "Tastee Tallahassee" unfold as she scrolled down the alphabetized listing, came to "Ball-Buster Bronson" and clicked on it long enough to see herself in her black tank dress. She clicked back to the list, scrolled down, found the line: "Naturally Golden."

Ruth Ann clicked the mouse again as the pictures filled in, then clicked back to the main page. Her breaths came shallow and fast, and she noticed a curious red twinge to everything. . . . No *wonder* poor Jeena needed a day off! The bastards, the absolute, bottom-feeding, cocksucking bastards! Small incidents from the previous week needled her now, and suddenly she knew. . . .

She yanked out the power cord from the wall, gave the computer case on the floor a sharp kick for good measure, then hefted the stapler, slapping it against her palm, and marched out the door on her way to the fifth-floor Phone and Fax Center.

Special Agent Johnny Espinosa maintained his practiced look of supreme indifference, or as close as he could manage, given the circumstances. The closet was barely six-by-six and largely filled with mops and cleaning supplies. A single bare bulb lit the room from above, letting Senator T. C. Tuttle's pinkish-purple sport coat dominate the scene.

"Well, Mr. Special Agent, know why I picked this room to talk?"

Espinosa shrugged. "I'd guess we're in a dead zone for radio transmissions."

T.C. nodded at Gus sitting wedged in the corner on an overturned bucket. "Pretty sharp. I guess the Federal B-I don't recruit dummies." He removed an envelope from his jacket, passed it to Gus. "What we got here are *pho*tocopies of the contract between His High and Mightiness and the ambulance chasers he hired to sue tobaccy."

Gus leafed through the pages, puzzled. "What do you want *me* to do with 'em?"

T.C. jerked his head at Espinosa until Gus sheepishly handed up the documents. "Stupid Meskin. On page eleven, in the paragraph marked by that there yellow sticky, there's a clause requirin' that the lawyers assist in the passage of the third-party liability law. For such effort, they shall be awarded a bonus of five percent, if and only if the law's passed without any changes."

Espinosa read page eleven, shrugged. "So?"

"*So!*" T.C. snorted. "*So,* that just happens to be illegal, is what. A felony. Thou shalt not use a contingency fee award in any legislative or executive lobbyin' contract. Florida Statutes two-forty-point-oh-six. Bollin' pushed that law through himself thirty years ago, back when he was House speaker. So there you go: the governor of Florida, conspirin' to commit a felony with out-of-state shysters. And look here: a fax distribution list. Makes it wire fraud, a federal offense, if I ain't mistaken. So, Mr. FBI man, is that a big enough fish for you?"

Espinosa checked the documents again, tried to contain his building excitement. Tuttle had helpfully included the relevant pages from Florida Statutes showing that it was, indeed, a felony. Five years on the state charge, plus, say, another three or four on conspiracy and wire fraud . . . he was looking at maybe eight or nine years behind bars! For the *governor* of Florida! He felt a flush in his cheeks. *Finally,* on the brink of disaster, of facing his boss with yet another corrupt Miami pol, he instead was on the verge of a major coup. . . .

"And what," he began, still trying to sound bored, "do you get for giving me this?"

T.C. smiled wide. "*I,* and may the good Lord strike me dead if I'm lyin', *I* didn't give you nothin'. Gus over there did, as he had every reason to, your havin' his ass in a sling and all. But I'm thinkin', if he were to get you the originals, I'm thinkin' your jack-booted thugs could get their damn noses out of my export-import businesses."

Espinosa recalled that the Northern District U.S. Attorney had all but closed the many investigations into Senator T. C. Tuttle for want of credible witnesses. He made a show of weighing T.C.'s demand, finally nodded. "When can you get me the originals?"

T.C. grabbed his hand and pumped enthusiastically. "Looks like you and Gus got a deal!"

The crack of light beneath the door said Ruth Ann finally was in her office, and Jeena sucked in a breath to rally her courage. In her head, she'd gone through what she needed to say dozens of times. Now all she had to do was open her mouth, let the words come out.

It occurred to her that the closed door meant Ruth Ann was on the phone or had someone in with her. Perhaps she should wait. She let that comforting logic settle in her brain, then noticed there was something in her mailbox. She stood on tiptoe to reach it, read the brief memo . . . then read it again.

It was from Ruth Ann and stated that, effective immediately, Bronson and Associates had a new dress code: All women employees would wear skirts no higher than one inch above the knee, and all blouses would be opaque, and underwear, including hose, would be worn at all times.

She heard a rustling in Ruth Ann's office and knocked on the door before entering to find Ruth Ann primping herself in a hand mirror. Her boss turned, and Jeena's mouth fell open. The shortest black skirt she'd ever seen left little to the imagination. A see-through blouse left nothing at all.

"You need me?" Ruth Ann asked, turning to her desk.

The reason for her visit had completely escaped her as she stared at her virtually nude boss rummage through a drawer. The skirt was really more a wide belt; the top a piece of gauze with a few buttons sewn on. She looked down at the memo, back up at Ruth Ann.

"If this dress code thing is on my account," she said at length. "I mean, I really don't mind it anymore. Besides, I—"

"Do as I say," Ruth Ann said, pushing the drawer shut with a thigh. "Not as I do."

She worked the handles on a pair of locking pliers, shoved the tool into her purse and strode past Jeena out the door.

All his colleagues and almost all the staff had already left for the weekend by the time T. C. Tuttle took his sport coat off his hanger and heard the knock on his door. He made an exasperated noise, then remembered he'd let his secretary head home almost an hour ago.

"I was just leavin', and I'm already late, so—"

And then he saw Ruth Ann Bronson in the most amazing outfit he'd ever seen in the Capitol, lounging in the door frame with one foot up against the doorjamb behind her, chest thrust out against a top so transparent it was like it wasn't there at all.

"I just need a couple of minutes."

The voice was soft but deep, and he found himself in a trance, watching one sexy foot climb ever higher up the doorjamb, the microskirt inch correspondingly higher up her thigh. He saw his jacket had fallen to the floor; as he reached down to retrieve it, he realized he was as stiff as a board.

Carefully he pushed his arms through the sleeves and flashed a generous smile as he adjusted the lapels. "A coupla minutes never hurt nobody!"

He moved to his desk, motioned her to the chair opposite, wondering what good thing he'd done to deserve such a day: revenge on Bolling, an end to the chronic worry that the Feds were about to indict him, and, now, this! Ruth Ann Bronson, for all intents and purposes, naked! In his office!

"How can I help you?"

She pushed the door shut behind her, sat in the proffered chair and leaned forward. He realized the top buttons of her blouse were undone, and he could clearly see one brown nipple. The left one, he determined after mentally switching places with her. If he leaned his head to one side, like so, he probably could see—

"I wanted to tell you I'm honored to be on Tastee Tallahassee, and I wondered if you might be interested in an idea I had for additional revenues from . . . shall we say, *action* pictures?"

Part of his brain screamed warnings at him, but T.C. was well beyond warnings. Control had fully transferred from his head to points south. "Action pi'tures?" he repeated.

A wicked smile spread across Ruth Ann's face as she stood, leaned way over the desk. T.C. realized he could see both nipples. "Let me demonstrate," she whispered.

A soft moan escaped his lips as she moved around the desk, wordlessly squeezed in beneath it, gently pulled down the zipper on his trousers. . . .

And then his world exploded in a flash of white, hot, agonizing light, blinding him . . . He was shrieking, blubbering for it to stop, or maybe he was just imagining he was screaming, and really he was sitting there in silence, his mouth open but unable to utter a sound—

"Shut up, Senator," came the suddenly business-like voice from under the desk.

So he *had* been screaming. . . . He shut up, glad for the moment of relief, then realized there *was* no relief, that the pain continued unabated, and he opened his mouth to resume yelling—

"Okay, mister encyclopedic memory," the voice continued. "Who's my New Hampshire–based client?"

T.C.'s brain whirred, stalled, and the pain intensified. "Tip Top Tools!" he screamed.

"Very good. So you'll remember, the next time they have a legislative request, just how well made their vise grips are? How sturdy, how strong, yet so delicately balanced that even a dainty girl can operate them without breaking a nail?"

T.C. tried to make sense of what he was hearing and, in a sudden flash of dread, connected "vise grips" with the pain spreading out in waves from his groin. . . .

"Now that we know your brain still works, I want the name, address and phone number of whichever computer geek set up Tastee Tallahassee."

T.C. groped for his Rolodex, imagined he felt Ruth Ann's fingers twisting the screw on the pliers, the jaws clamping down ever harder. . . . With shaking fingers, he handed the card down between his legs.

"Thank you kindly. Now I want you to sit very still and keep your eyes straight ahead."

Tuttle nodded, stared at the closed door ten feet away. He needed to mollify this woman, he realized, before she did something drastic. "Look here, Ruth Ann. I know you're upset, but—"

"Shut up," ordered the voice from beneath the desk.

He shut up, thought he felt something pricking his testicles, and then Ruth Ann squeezed past his legs, out from under the desk. She pushed his chair forward until his chest was against the desktop.

"Hands flat on your desk," she commanded. "Comfortable? Good. Don't move."

She reached a hand down between his legs again, and he heard some metallic scratching and felt another vibration in his balls. And then she was walking toward the door, slipping the Rolodex card into her purse. She reached for the knob and turned to him with a soft smile.

"It's important for you to sit very, very still. You think you can do that for a few hours? Good. Because, I'm sure you know, another of my clients is Freedom Fireworks, which, I'm sure you also know, manufactures the M-80, which is illegal in Florida and most other states because, I guess, it's the equivalent of a quarter stick of dynamite." She opened the door a few inches. "Oh yeah, there's an M-80 attached to a battery-powered ignitor, with the contact wires about a millimeter apart. I think if you don't move, and try to breathe without using your diaphragm, you should be able to keep from blowing your nuts off. I'll come by in a few hours and see how you're doing."

T.C. watched in horror, the breath trapped in his throat, as Ruth Ann Bronson playfully flicked a strand of hair from her eyes and, with a slam that nearly gave him heart failure, yanked the door closed behind her.

With both head and feet aching, Jeena leaned heavily against her door and for a moment lay her head back against the wood with her eyes closed. It had been a long, largely fruitless, decidedly humbling day. Male senators who so eagerly stared at her body and hung on her every word when she represented a big-money contributor couldn't be bothered with her now that she represented only herself. After all: with so many women to lust after in the Capitol, why not lust after those whose clients would give you a lot of money?

She leaned over to peel off one painful sandal, then the other, and started toward the kitchen when she heard it again . . . a soft footfall or the scuffing of a boot on her hardwood floor. She thought she'd heard it when she first came in, but had ignored it then . . . wanted to ignore it this time, too.

She continued toward the kitchen, flicked on the light, not wanting to turn, knowing that if she didn't turn, she wouldn't see him, and he wouldn't be there. Finally, she turned, and even though she fully expected it, the actual sight of him still made her heart skip, then leap into overdrive. It was him, the weirdo in the cammos, except now he was in her living room, a big gun in one hand, waving it carelessly at the front door, at the kitchen, at her. . . .

"I was starting to think maybe you lived in the dark."

She crossed her arms over her flimsy dress against eyes that seemed to bore through the fabric. "Take anything you want," she said softly. "Money, there's a little bit of jewelry, the TV. It's yours."

"If it was your stuff I wanted, I would've taken it when I was here a couple days ago." He held the gun like a lethal extension of his finger. "I think you know what I came for. Eight-and-a-half by eleven? Yellow sticker in the corner? Not yours to begin with?"

The words chilled but didn't surprise, and she thought of Senator Nichols' ominous warning. "I don't have it," she said truthfully.

"Have you looked? Maybe you just misplaced it. How about in a . . . empty tube of lipstick?"

Her breath caught, and she felt dizzy. She grabbed for a wall to steady herself. How in God's name had he known . . . ? "It's not here," she said truthfully.

"Let's go get it."

She couldn't take her eyes off the gun. It was so damn big. People had no idea from TV. "Then what?"

He blinked, stared at her neutrally. "You let me worry about that. One thing you *can* tell me right now: How many copies you make?"

"None," she answered, realized immediately it was the wrong thing to say, that lots of copies would help guarantee her safety. "I mean, none that I have here, but—"

"No," he cut her off. "I think you told the truth the first time. Let's quit screwing around. Where is it?"

She swallowed hard, realizing that once he had the memo back, there was no good reason for her to remain alive. She thought of her chances of finding a security guard at the Capitol on a Friday night . . . concluded, yes, he probably would be able to get her in and out of there unnoticed. She needed to think of someplace, right now, where she could somehow reduce the lethality of that enormous gun, give her at least a fighting chance. . . . And suddenly she knew.

"I'll take you," she said softly.

Gus paced the outer office for a while, mulling T.C.'s prohibition against knocking on his inner door if it was closed, weighing that against their date to celebrate their dispensing of the FBI man with a night of chicken wings and ogling at Hooters.

With the nearest topless joint more than two hours from Tallahassee, Gus had spent all afternoon daydreaming of perky little co-eds with their perky, not-so-little breasts tied up in those white T-shirts. T.C. was to have met him in the parking garage an hour ago so they could drive over together. Instead, Gus had spent forty-five minutes in his Town Car before hunting down T.C.'s spot, finding his latest-model Grand Cherokee still there.

He bent his ear to the inner door, listened, heard nothing. The light was on inside, he could see from under the door. Maybe the son of a bitch had keeled over, dead from too much dirty living. He wondered about his obligations in that case. Did he have to call the police? He preferred not to have anything to do with police for a while, especially if there was going to be a scandal. Well, maybe he could check to see if T.C. was okay . . . but if he was dead from kinky sex or something, he could get out quickly and pretend he'd never been there.

He nodded to himself, pulled his sleeve up over his hand so he wouldn't leave any prints, slowly turned the knob. . . . And there was T.C. at his desk. Gus grinned and strode in. "Man, I been looking all over for you!"

"Stop!" T.C. whispered hoarsely. Sweat poured off his head and drenched the lapels of his purple jacket. "Don't touch the desk! Crazy bitch wired me to go off at the least bump. . . ."

Gus froze, quickly gauged the distance to the desk. As a Miami Cuban politician, bombs and how to deal with them had never been far from his consciousness. He turned silently to calculate the distance back to the threshold. He could make it in two big steps or a single dive. The dive might be better, as he would already be low to the ground—

"Don't even *think* about leavin' me here, you greasy Meskin bastard, or I'll have your dick cut off in your sleep!" T.C. screeched softly.

Gus wrung his hands, stepped from foot to foot. "*Jesucristo*, T.C.! What can *I* do? They got *bomb* squads for shit like this!"

"Bomb squad, my hairy butt. You think I wanna see this in all the papers tomorrow? Here, just come move the desk away."

"I thought you said you'd go off at the least bump?"

"I didn't say *least* bump."

"You did. I heard you: 'least bump.'" Gus whined. "You just want to take me with you."

"Git *over* here!"

Gus started to, then stopped, considered the situation for a moment and remembered T.C.'s advice about having to ask for something if you wanted it. "Hey, T.C., I was just thinking. Here you really need my help, right? So I was thinking, maybe you could do something for me. . . ."

T.C. rolled his eyes. "What?"

"Well, it's that thing you always call me. Greasy Mexican. You know, there's a big difference between Cubans and Mexicans. I mean, you listen to the language, it ain't nothing alike, not to mention the customs and traditions. I mean, I'm three-quarters Spanish, like the old country, and the average Mexican . . . well, anyway, I was thinking that maybe if I help you out here, maybe you could stop—"

"Now you listen to me, you greasy, ingrate slime-bag Meskin: I got your ass outta the sling, and if you don't help me, I'm gonna throw it right back in. Now *git* your ass over here!" T.C. growled. "I'll lift my hands up, then you, real slow-like, pull the desk away. Got it?"

Gus sourly mulled his failed gambit, wondered for a moment how T.C. could get anybody's ass in a sling if he was dead, then decided he oughtn't risk it. What if T.C. were only *maimed*? That would just make him madder. With shaking hands and sweat beading his own brow, Gus approached, grabbed the lip, gently pulled the heavy desk over the carpeting until T.C. was sitting in his chair, clear, his privates hanging out of his trousers, a large, metal device hanging from his privates.

Gus leaned in for a closer look. "Hey, how come you got a pair of pliers on your *cojones*?"

T.C. kept his head level, his eyes focused on the opposite wall. "Look again," he whispered. "There's an M-80, and a ignitor, and all kinds of other shit to blow 'em off."

"Nope." Gus leaned down even closer. "Ain't none of that stuff. Just pliers on your nuts, is all."

Slowly, T.C. turned his gaze downward, saw that Gus was indeed correct. For an instant, his face melted into relief, then immediately moved to rage. "Goddamn bitch *lied!*" he bellowed. "I can't *stand* it when a lobbyist lies to me!"

Dry pine needles crackled beneath her feet along the familiar sand trail, and Jeena again considered the steel tank in her right hand. How far back was the psycho? Close enough to swing the tank and crack him in the skull? But what if he were too far, out of reach . . . then he'd simply raise his pistol and shoot.

"How much farther?" he demanded.

"Not far." She leaned to the left as she walked, balancing the weight of the tank. Her other arm carried mask, snorkel, buoyancy compensator, fins and a shorty wetsuit. "It wouldn't hurt for you to offer to carry some of this."

Her captor merely grunted, and they soon came upon a clearing. At its center was the spring, shimmering beneath a gibbous moon. She dropped her equipment and straightened to stretch a crick away. The psycho squinted out over the water. He wore the same camouflage outfit she'd seen in the Capitol, a colonel's eagle on the collar.

"Where?"

She pointed to the center of the spring. "Out there," she lied, realizing how lucky she'd been that he hadn't seen her ditch the memo. On the other hand, if he *had* seen her, maybe he wouldn't have shown up in her house. Or maybe he would have anyway, to keep her quiet. She swallowed hard. It was too late for maybes. "I told you. On a ledge, in a Tupperware box. Eighty-three feet down. It'll take me a couple of minutes to get down, but about twenty to come back up. You know. For decompression."

"Okay." He played with his gun again, checked the magazine. "Go get it."

She bent for her wetsuit, realized he wasn't going to look away, turned around to change, slipping out of her dress before tugging on the stretchy hot-pink neoprene. She turned back to a flat stare.

"Still no underwear, huh? Just like on the Internet."

The words rang for a while in her head, and she felt her ears flush with embarrassment. Snippets of conversations she'd heard over the past days, conversations that abruptly ended when the male participants saw her approach, now began to coalesce. "Excuse me?"

"You don't know?" The psycho waved his gun casually. "W-W-W dot Tastee Tallahassee? The Capitol's Tastiest Ladies? You're *uuugggghhhh . . .*"

It happened instantly. Shame became anger, and one bare foot lashed out, just like the self-defense instructor had taught back in college, and caught the psycho's groin with a powerful instep. For a second, she thought of finishing it with another kick to the crumpled figure's midsection, but then she was staring down the blacker-than-black muzzle. His hand began to squeeze, and she felt her heart stop as the gun finally pointed away.

"Bitch! *I* didn't post the damn picture up there," the psycho managed, finally rising to a squat. "You don't know how close you just came. . . ."

But Jeena did know, and it terrified her. She still wasn't certain what the psycho had been talking about and had a feeling she didn't want to know. Either way, here, now, none of that mattered. Here was an armed nutcase, and she'd very nearly pushed him over the cliff. Her one chance was to dive into the spring and yet, at water's edge, she'd almost blown it. "Sorry," she stammered. "Really, I didn't—"

"Just fucking go get it," he ordered, his free hand caressing his privates. "Now!"

Silently she donned her gear, spit in her mask and rinsed, turned on the flashlight and tank valve and, eyes still on the gun, backed into the water until she was waist deep. And suddenly she sank into a crouch, turned and kicked as hard as she could to where the bottom became sheer drop-off. Down, down, down she sank, the flashlight's beam playing against the rising wall.

She struggled with her pounding heart, tried to keep it from racing, tried to pace her breathing. Finally, she checked her depth gauge, saw she was at one hundred feet. Surely a handgun's bullet couldn't reach this deep, could it? She forced herself to put it from her mind. For what she was about to attempt, every extra minute at depth increased the amount of dissolved nitrogen that could come bubbling out of her blood, swelling her joints, her brain. Crippling her. Killing her . . .

She lifted the flashlight's beam, began swimming along the wall, until, there, above a narrow ledge was the black hole she would never be able to forget. The one she'd started up all those years back, only to lose her mask and then her nerve. Twelve hundred and fifteen feet, that much was etched in her mind. A quarter mile long, three feet wide at the start, narrowing to half that just a few yards in . . . so narrow, in fact, that wearing a tank was impossible.

Jeena set the light on the ledge, pulled off her tank and dive vest, took one final breath, then carefully laid the regulator on the ledge so the valve remained open and a stream of bubbles rose to the surface. With a final glance upward, she swallowed her fear, pulled herself into the black tunnel, felt her way to the narrowing where the current increased, drew her in. . . .

Instantly she was scooting along the underground stream, fending off rock sides with her hands, but even more important: blowing. Constantly, never stopping, overcoming the primal instinct to hold it in . . . knowing that if somehow she forgot, the air would continue expanding as she surfaced and, unable to escape through her trachea, would explode her lungs instead.

Jeena blew and blew and blew, kicking gently to keep some control, the rocks cutting and bruising her hands, back, shoulder, until finally one arm got bent behind her and her head grazed the side of the tunnel. Her mask was gone, she realized with terror, then realized with even more terror that she was holding her breath. She forced herself to open her mouth and continue blowing a stream of bubbles, arms in front again, gazing ahead and upward into the black.

Why was it still black? Surely there should be moonlight shining down through the pool . . . something cold as ice gripped her gut as she wondered if she hadn't picked the wrong tunnel, one that ran not a quarter mile, but a half mile, or two, or ten. . . .

Marvin Lambert rocked back and forth over his heels in a crouch, one hand still comforting his privates. She had no business kicking him like that. Hell, it wasn't like *he'd* taken the damn picture or, for that matter, made her go around without any panties in the first place.

The pain had spread through his lower abdomen, and he wondered if she hadn't really hurt him. Ruptured his spleen, maybe. Well, he'd have to grin and bear it. Wasn't like he could go to the emergency room, complain to the nurse: Excuse me, but the woman I was kidnapping kicked me in the nuts, gave me internal injuries. . . .

It was, he knew, his own damn fault. What he'd said lacked professionalism, something he prided himself on. Do the job quickly, efficiently, move to the next one. It had kept him out of trouble for years. Hell, the one thing he'd ever done based on emotion, his factory boss, was going to haunt him till the day he died.

He brooded on that again, on how he was never going to get out from under Simons. The man was relentless. Someday, he knew, he was going to have to work up the nerve to take him out. A quick, clean job, something that gave him a day or two to run . . . He shivered, terrified of getting to the moment where he had to squeeze the trigger, hesitating . . . and then Simons would look up at him, annoyed, tell him to put the gun down, and he would.

Lambert sighed, peered out at the water. He checked his watch, saw it had been a full twenty minutes and played the flashlight beam out over the spring. He scowled at the bubbles that still broke the surface, the tiny point of light still visible in the depths. The hell was she doing down there? How long did it take to dive down and bring something back up? She was yanking his chain, was what it was. Well, it didn't matter. Her air couldn't last forever. She had to come up eventually.

Or . . . did she? He recalled reading somewhere about freshwater springs, and underwater rivers, and how they were all interconnected and water could disappear into a crack one place and come out miles away. . . . He stood as straight as he was able, pointed the light across the spring to the opposite shore, which was when he heard a car door slam behind him.

For one foolish second, he wondered who it could be: He didn't remember any other car in the dirt lot when they'd come in. Then he was running, stumbling bowlegged down the sandy path as an engine cranked to life, the flashlight beam bobbing ahead until he saw the vague outlines of a car backing and filling through a K-turn, then speeding off toward the highway.

Lambert dropped to one knee, brought up the silenced Sig-Sauer in a two-handed grip, then put it back down. She was already way out of range. Any lucky shot that got near the car would simply lodge in the metalwork, ballistic evidence for the police to collect. . . . The red taillights finally came on as the car turned onto the paved road toward town.

He shoved a hand down into his pants pocket to remove the set of keys he'd demanded from her as they got out of her Toyota. In the beam of the flashlight, he counted a house key, a deadbolt key, an office key, a small, locker-type key . . . but no car key. Of course not.

A dull roar of embarrassment filled his ears as he realized how she'd played him. In all likelihood, the damned memo wasn't even down there.

She'd just told him it was to get someplace a nine-millimeter bullet couldn't follow. Beautiful. She'd tricked him into letting her escape and ditched him fifteen miles out of town, all at the same time.

He shook his head to himself, started trudging toward the road. First things first. He needed to get back to town to his own car, then he needed a fallback plan.

He thought as he walked, and he thought as he held a thumb out at passing headlights. She'd probably passed the memo off to somebody. When? Probably that morning, when she'd glanced up just as he was looking in the Senate chamber, tailing her . . . Who'd been in there?

He squinted, called back the memory into his mind. Two senators. He pulled the Clerk's Manual from his inner pocket, put names to remembered faces. Afumi Booteme and T. C. Tuttle. Both had voted with the governor a year ago, according to the creased newspaper clipping he kept folded up in the pamphlet. But Tuttle was actually the governor's point man, he read. The guy who flat-out lied on the Floor to sneak the law through the Senate.

He nodded to himself. He had to move, and he had to move fast.

He glanced up at the road, just as a muddy pickup truck sporting a rebel flag on its antenna honked and stopped to give him a lift.

T. C. Tuttle leaned on Gus as they made their way past the smiling Hooters girls holding the doors open for them, nearly stumbled as they crossed the lot toward his Jeep. A night at Hooters, he allowed grudgingly, maybe hadn't been such a hot idea, given the condition of his male organs. Every time a tight T-shirted, orange-bunned waitress had stopped by the table, he'd started to get a hard-on. And each time he'd started to get a hard-on, his whole groin had pulsed with waves of pain.

"You doing okay, T.C.?" Gus asked as they neared the truck.

T.C. grunted, reached into his pocket for keys and pointed them weakly at the driver's door until it squeaked. "My nuts ache."

"Well, you gotta expect that," Gus said soothingly. "They been through a lot."

Tuttle grunted again, fumbled with the door handle, then groaned aloud as he climbed into the driver's seat. The ache had spread from just above his knees to halfway up his torso. Gangrene, he guessed, with his luck.

"And hey, thanks for getting Espinosa off my ass. That was pretty decent.

Anyway, I'll see you at Remy's pool party Sunday, huh? It's supposed to be a hot one." Gus eyed T.C.'s crotch skeptically. "You sure you don't want a ride? You don't look so good."

T.C. waved him away, then pulled the door shut. He bent toward the ignition slot with his key, then sat up straight to feel cold metal at the base of his neck. He let his shoulders slump, more weary than scared. Of all the nights to get carjacked . . .

"Son," he told the ski mask in the rearview, "I'm sorry to bring you the bad news, but I only got eight dollars in my pocket. Plus, after the day I had, I honestly don't give a shit whether you shoot me or you don't."

"Sir, that makes two of us," a cold voice replied from the backseat, and T.C. felt himself tense at the unexpected answer.

"You Senator Teegan Chaunce Tuttle?"

"*T.C.,*" T.C. said, and grew even more anxious. Clearly, this was no random carjacking.

"Well, Senator, if you do as I say, everything will probably be all right. If you could go out to Capital Circle and turn east on U.S. 90, please."

T.C. put the car in gear and drove quietly, occasionally trying to catch a glimpse of his abductor in the mirror. He thought about that word, "probably." *Probably* be all right. Like it wasn't up to him. Spicy chicken wings churned in his belly, and his testicles throbbed. "Could I ask how much you're gettin' paid for this, perhaps have an opportunity to bid—"

"Shut up," the voice cut him off. "Sir. Left up here, sir."

At least he was being polite about it, T.C. thought. He switched on the high beams as they went deeper into the woods, and he remembered an article a while back about a carjacking victim who'd intentionally rammed a big oak tree, and how he hadn't suffered a scratch because of the airbag but how the gunman had gone through the windshield, landing with a broken neck. He glanced in the rearview, saw his kidnapper was leaning against the back of the passenger seat, not anywhere near a seatbelt. . . . He began scouting the narrow road for an appropriate tree, tried to work up the nerve—

"Sir, if this vehicle moves an inch toward that shoulder, I'll put a bullet through your brain."

T.C. heard the determination in the voice, and it turned up the anxiety level another couple of notches, until, finally, he was good and scared again. As scared, maybe even a bit more scared, than when he thought his nuts were wired to blow up. He tried to swallow, considered another attempt to barter for his release, when Ski-Mask Man told him to measure exactly four-tenths of a mile beyond the speed limit sign and then turn right.

T.C. eyed the odometer, slowed the truck to take the turn, and only then realized with horror that he knew exactly which dirt road he was on and exactly where it led.

Dunbar Richey finished the final collar on the final shirt, turned off the iron and draped the shirt over a plastic hanger. He flicked off the light in the laundry room and grabbed his beer on the way out. Plopping himself into an easy chair, he silently drained the last of his Heineken.

She wasn't going to call.

At first he'd tried to invent excuses. She didn't want to call too late at night or too early in the morning. She was busy all day, no time to call. In the last hour or so, he'd finally let reality settle in. The flowers had been delivered a full twenty-four hours ago. If she was going to call, she already would have. Dunbar snorted disgustedly. Of course, why should she? Him with his sanctimonious, holier-than-thou bullshit. If he were her, would he?

All his years in Tallahassee, he could have at least learned polite empathy for those whose work made them do the bidding of politically incorrect clients. After all, not everyone could work for the high and mighty Bolling Waites. And even Bolling sullied himself with politically expedient alliances with the unsavory from time to time. Hadn't T. C. Tuttle, of all people, carried the original tobacco bill through the Senate?

Dunbar lifted the green bottle again, forgetting he'd already finished it. There was no more in the fridge either. Of course not. A night he needed to get good and plastered, he'd have to wallow through on one beer.

He put himself in her shoes again, and again he felt a twinge of shame. *Sure*, she should just leak the memo. Give it to the governor. Give it to the media. What the hell. What did *he* have to lose? It wasn't *his* word, *his* career, going down the toilet. At the end of the day, he wouldn't have even known about the goddamn thing if she hadn't told him. And yet he had a right to preach?

He sighed, recalling the hurt on her face when he'd left. He'd been so close, too. When she'd really needed someone, she hadn't called Murphy boy. She'd called him. So what had he done? Made fun of her. Ridiculed her fears. Attributed them to a guilt he then tried to convince her she ought to feel.

Good. Nice going.

Dunbar rose to do the dishes and get to bed by a reasonable hour for Bolling's Saturday morning staff meeting. He'd just turned on the tap when he shut it off again, curious and a little annoyed at the late-night ringing of his doorbell. He swept aside the curtain over the glass front door, then hurriedly worked the latch.

Jeena stood on his stoop, shivering and damp, clad only in her wetsuit. Bravely, she attempted a smile, then collapsed into his arms in tears.

SATURDAY

By the fifth knock, Special Agent Johnny Espinosa realized it wasn't part of his dream. He snapped his eyes open, saw the glowing numbers 4:45 on the nightstand, pulled on a pair of pants and went to the door with service weapon drawn.

Two guys with earpieces flashed badges at him and asked if he wouldn't mind accompanying them. Espinosa thought about protesting, then decided against it. He'd known from the start it was only a matter of time before the Florida Department of Law Enforcement got wind of his activities. He made himself presentable and followed the state cops out of the hotel and into a Crown Vic waiting in front of the hotel lobby.

Espinosa grew a little nervous when they didn't turn down Tennessee Street toward FDLE headquarters, and a lot nervous when the car instead zipped down a deserted Adams Street and through the main gate of the Governor's Mansion. One of the agents went to the guard shack while the other led him through a manicured formal garden to a large pool cabana.

There, sitting in a warmup suit at an old pine desk, reading a worn Bible, was the new target of his corruption investigation, the governor of Florida. Behind the man was an exercise bike, a weight machine and a treadmill, but Espinosa's eyes fixated on the Bible.

"I try to cleanse myself each morning before I go trade with the Pharisees up the hill," Waites drawled. "I ain't sure the Good Lord buys it . . . but what the hell."

Espinosa stretched himself as tall as he could manage, thrust his chest out and tried to appear relaxed. He crossed his arms, uncrossed them. "Can I ask, sir, why I'm here?"

Waites smiled wryly. "Word is there's this young, upwardly mobile FBI man looking to take down a top Florida politician to fast-track his career. Word is this fella's got his sights on yours truly. Don't happen to know where I might find him, do you?"

Espinosa tried to hide his astonishment, opened his mouth to deny it, shut it again.

"You see, Agent Espinosa, when the folks in this town ain't stealing the people's money, what the hell else is there to do but gossip? You can meet in basement closets, you can meet on ball fields in the middle of the night, you could meet in bathroom stalls, for all anyone cares, and people still gonna hear about it. This is Tallahassee."

Agent Espinosa folded his arms again, fumed inwardly at Gus. The slimy little Cuban must have talked. How else would the old man know? Well, it didn't matter. Whether he knew or he didn't wouldn't change the illegal contingency clause in those original contracts.

"I'm sorry, Governor, sir. I can't comment on an ongo—"

The old man stopped him with a raised hand. "Save it. I, uh"—he grinned— "*asked* you here this mornin' to give you my side of the story."

Espinosa opened his mouth to object, then shut it and listened as Waites launched into a history of tobacco legislation in Florida, about the essential sameness of Republican and Democratic legislators when it came to their number-one sugar daddy.

"Legalized bribery," Bolling thundered, his face dark. "Four years in a row, we tried to pass a bill bannin' smokin' in hospitals, schools, that sort of thing. All out in the open, press conferences, lots of bully-pulpit lobbyin'. Four years in a row, we get our heads handed to us. And every goddamn year, tobacco used a contingency arrangement with their lobbyists: a big, fat bonus, I'm talkin' mid–six figures, sometimes seven. Illegal as hell. But who's in charge of policin' the lobbyists? The presidin' officers of the legislature."

Bolling folded his hands atop the closed Bible. Espinosa tried to avoid his gaze, found he couldn't.

"And so, Agent Espinosa, I did what decent men have done through the ages when they went to war. They used deplorable, ruthless tactics, the same tactics used by their enemies. And then, when it's over, they go home and reflect, and they're none too proud, but they're at peace with the fact they did it."

Espinosa stubbornly kept his chin up. "What you did broke the law, sir."

Bolling nodded. "Yes. You're right. I did. But I want you to think of somethin'. For years and years, the industry I'm fightin' has been hooking kids on cigarettes. Replacement smokers, is what they call 'em. Sorta like replacement parts. Essential to the economic well-being of the company. Now the only reason that's been legal is that decent people stood by and did nothin'.

"I like to think of myself as a decent man, Juan, but I know I did indecent things. I lied to get that law passed. I offered a contingency-fee contract when that was illegal. It's the kind of stuff the industry's been doin' for years, but I ain't gonna be a cry-baby about it." Bolling opened his Bible to the red velvet bookmark. "You need to take me down, fine. I broke the law, and I'll suffer the consequences. All I ask is you hold off till after the vote."

Dolly Nichols stared vacantly out at the Gulf as Ramon greedily sucked down the first Grande in the packet she'd smuggled him. She tried to ignore the sound of his breath as it rasped up and down his throat, carrying his favorite poison to his lungs. She felt awful, a pusher still unloading product at the deathbed. . . . But she hadn't been able to resist his urges for thirty years. Why should now be any different?

Ramon started coughing violently, and she turned her head away. The cancer was in its final stages now, and the pain would be unbearable, even through the medication.

"All those books I always told myself I'd read when I had time? Now I got the time, but my eyes can't focus on a page for more than a minute." He laughed ironically. "I got *One Hundred Years of Solitude*, but I won't even get through the first week."

She glanced at the book on the nightstand, the only object there save for a reading lamp. No flowers, no cards, not even a recent photo of his children. Dolly had hoped his wife might, at the end, find a way to forgive him, let him say good-bye to his babies. She'd even offered to track her down for him and call, but his pride wouldn't allow it.

She felt him dropping off, gently removed the unfiltered cigarette from his lips and crushed it against the rim of a water glass he'd been using as an ashtray.

"Dolly, *Dolita*, could you look out the window and describe it for me? Maybe if there's any sailboats? I'm gonna rest my eyes a bit. . . ."

Outside, a gray overcast blanketed an equally gray, deserted ocean. Instead, Dolly reached back to Abaco Sound and drew in detail a limitless blue sky over turquoise sea, a graceful white sloop running downwind behind a brilliant yellow-and-red spinnaker.

On the bed beside her, Ramon had fallen fast asleep. Dolly watched him awhile, then climbed in beside him.

The FDLE agents had offered a ride back to the hotel, but Espinosa insisted on walking. He needed a smoke, bad, and was ashamed to let the governor's people see him. He checked over his shoulder, made sure the guard hut at the Governor's Mansion was out of sight, then pulled a Grande from its packet with his lips and struck the lighter.

He let the smoke linger in his lungs, felt the nicotine's soothing touch, blew out, thought about the governor's request, then tried not to think about it. That was a decision above his pay grade. If he started asking himself those kinds of questions, how the hell would he ever put anybody in jail?

He took another drag, idly glanced up Monroe Street, slowly took notice of the giant billboard with the dark-haired Latina in a wet swimsuit, back arched, bosom out, a long thin cigarette between her fingers. He began to wonder if it was new or if he'd just now noticed it when a city bus passed, Joe Camel on the side with hand outstretched, offering a smoke from an open box.

Espinosa recalled his youth, when his aunt, his uncle, all the bigger kids in the neighborhood, *everybody* smoked. In his part of town, it was Grandes, and he and his buddies would steal and beg them. He blew another lungful of smoke into the air, a bit queasy now, the governor's words rattling around in his brain, and flicked the stub to the sidewalk and ground it beneath a heel. He continued walking, then stopped, looked back with disgust at the sorry wad of squished paper. With a glance to make sure no one was looking, he bent to pick it up and throw it in a trash can.

Espinosa started toward the hotel again, his alliance with Cruz and Tuttle weighing ever more heavily, when he saw the trio of boys by the brown dumpster behind the convenience store. Each held a lit cigarette.

Blood raced through his ears, and Espinosa broke into a sprint. The boys saw him, saw his expression, then turned to run.

"FBI! Freeze!" he shouted, then tackled the closest kid as the other two escaped on skateboards. Espinosa threw him against the brick wall of the mini-mart, frisked him, yanked a pack of Larry Llamas from the kid's pocket. He pulled his badge, held it in front of the kid's face, saw his eyes bulge and knew he'd made an impression. "Where'd you get these? This place sell 'em to you?"

The kid thought about it, thought about lying, shook his head no, explained that they got some guy walking into the store to buy them.

Espinosa nodded as severely as he knew how. "You know it's illegal for you to have these?" The kid nodded, scared, and Espinosa shook out the cigarettes and slowly tore up each one. "All right. If I *ever* catch you with these again, I'm gonna take you down. We're talkin' five to ten in the big house. Got it?"

The kid nodded rapidly, and Espinosa stared off in the direction his buddies had taken off. "Go tell your friends."

Murphy Moran scanned the two columns on the top page of his clipboard, mentally double-checked his tally, then delivered the bad news: "One vote."

Bartholomew Simons, to Murphy's continued bewilderment, not even for a moment dropped the easy grin he'd worn since waving him into the inner office. "One? Really? That close, eh?"

Murphy scratched his head, glanced down at his clipboard, back up at Simons. Something was wrong. The man had been on edge all week. Yet now, the weekend before the vote that would either cost or save his company billions, he was almost sedate. He wore a soft chambray shirt, tan twill trousers. The most relaxed he'd ever seen him. Murphy couldn't understand it.

"Well, yes." He cleared his throat. "Naturally, I hoped to have been a bit further ahead, but, well, to be perfectly candid: I think we lost a couple of votes with the food poisoning—"

"Oh." Simons waved a careless hand. "I don't think we necessarily *lost* them."

"—and then there's Senator Nichols. I tried to talk to her, and she threw me out of her office. I have no idea what's going on there, but it makes me nervous."

Simons reached into his drawer, pulled out a strap of wooden beads, draped it around his neck and began pulling it back and forth. A massage tool. Murphy cleared his throat again. "Because, as you yourself have pointed out, Dolly Nichols is key. She's in line to be Senate president. She turns against us, she takes a bunch of votes with her—"

"Oh, I shouldn't worry about Dolly Nichols." Simons smiled anew. "I don't believe she'll vote against us. In fact, I'm certain of it."

Murphy stared at the man as he lifted canvas deck shoes up onto his desk, and decided something was definitely weird. He flipped a page on his clipboard. "The good news is of fourteen hundred lobbyists, all but a hundred and two are working for us now. Twenty-nine, the real anti-smoking ideologues, are still working the other side, but the other seventy-three have agreed, for a nominal fee, to stay out of it. Now what I'd like to do is set up a schedule to have them start calling the senators from now until Monday mo—"

"You know, Murph? You work too hard," Simons announced. "Why don't you take the rest of the weekend off? Go out, get yourself laid or something. You've done a great job. Trust me, everything's going to work out."

Murphy nodded politely and pointed to the top page of the clipboard again, the bottom line. "With due respect, I have to disagree. One vote's way too thin. Frankly, I don't understand why you're as confident as you are, given the circumstances."

Simons laughed, tossed the beads onto his desk and stretched his arms. "Son, I didn't get to the top of a Fortune 100 company by delegating everything."

The statement floated in Murphy's head, and then he recalled the strange man in cammos, a *Newsweek* item from years ago, felt a connection click almost audibly. "That guy who was here before, G.I. Joe, he wasn't by any chance the one who torched the tobacco plantations down in Paraguay five or six years back, was he? Nearly started a revolution? What's his name, Lamar, Lambo . . ."

"Lambert," Simons corrected. "Colonel Lambert, to you."

Murphy was about to follow up when three sharp knocks sounded on the door. It pushed open, followed by a small bearded man in pricey leisure wear. On either arm was a stunning young woman in a flimsy sundress, one a strawberry blonde, the other a dark brunette.

"Excuse me," Martin Remy said to Murphy, then grinned lasciviously at Simons. "We had a lunch date?"

Simons nodded. "On my way. Meet you in the lobby in five."

"Okay, but hey, I got something for you. Lemme go, girls." Remy pulled his arms free, handed Simons a sheet of paper he dug from his pocket.

"Those four, uh, individuals we were talking about?" Remy flashed a thumbs-up sign, retreated to his women.

"Good." Simons dropped the paper to his desk. "I'll see you downstairs."

Murphy heard the door shut behind him, watched Simons with one eye, the sheet of paper with the other. It was a list of names, he saw, a bit longer than the "override" column on his own tally. And beside about half the names was a figure in red ink: 250.

"So, Mr. Moran, are we finished?" Simons asked, rising. "As you can see, I have a rare, much anticipated social engagement."

"I, uh, thought we agreed we weren't hiring Martin Remy." Murphy watched Simons fold the list, shove it in a pants pocket. "That I wasn't working with anybody with a criminal record."

Simons moved toward the door, ushered Murphy out. "*Criminal* makes it sound so awful. Like he was holding up liquor stores. A slightly larger-than-recommended campaign contribution was all it was. Not even a felony."

Murphy stopped at the threshold, nodded at Simons' pocket. "He's paying out bribes, isn't he?"

"Bribes." Simons shook his head. "Those are illegal in this country. I have no idea what you are talking about. Now, if Mr. Remy is facilitating the transfer of perfectly legitimate consulting fees from one bank not in the United States to another bank not in the United States, I really don't see what that has to do with anything."

"Mr. Simons, I have to protest—"

"Look, you're not working *with* Martin. You two are working independently toward the same objective. If that's not satisfactory, you're free to waive your bonus. Or even return your fee, for that matter." He pulled the door shut behind him and locked it. "If you'll excuse me, I'm hungry."

Ruth Ann Bronson rang the bell a third, fourth, fifth time, until finally the door opened inward a few inches and still-sleepy eyes squinted out.

She put on her friendliest face. "Good morning, Mr. Stephen Brechner, senior executive service making $81,476 a year, yet with no civil service protection against hasty firing. Or actually, good afternoon." She peered over his shoulder. "Where's Mrs. Brechner today?"

Stephen Brechner studied her suspiciously, lingered on long, tan legs extending from the ground to insubstantial white minidress. "Visiting her mom. In Orlando." His eyes couldn't move off the dress. "For the weekend."

The door opened a bit more, an invitation, what with the wife safely away. Ruth Ann's smile turned sarcastic. "How convenient. You inviting me in? Or you just interested in girls on your computer?"

His eyes narrowed for a moment, clearly conflicted. There was her outfit and her offer to come in. Yet there was also her predatory attitude, her knowledge of his name and salary. "Who are you?" he demanded.

"You don't recognize me?" She tilted her head coyly. "Maybe you need a look up my snatch to remember?"

She watched his interest pique at the word "snatch," then melt into suspicion again as he considered the context. "What do you want?"

Ruth Ann studied him up and down. At least a couple of inches taller, easily fifty pounds heavier. What the hell. She reached back and slugged him in the jaw, knocking him backward. "I'm Ball-Buster Bronson, Tallahassee's *tastiest* 'chick' lobbyist. It's so nice to finally meet you in person."

Diary at one hand, expense log at the other, Murphy Moran tapped at his laptop, preparing his invoice. He flipped pages in the diary and realized just how little actual work he'd done for the amount of money he was getting, compared to the typical political campaign.

A whole pile of money, compared to campaigns, which themselves paid extremely well, compared to any normal job he might have hoped for. A lot more rewarding, too, with new challenges, new goals every few months.

But what goals . . .

Getting this weasel elected to Congress or that weasel to a governorship. He hardly knew the candidate beforehand and left town immediately afterward, so he never had to suffer the consequences of his work. How many good, decent leaders had he helped elect? How many had merely been ambitious or lucky or rich?

Murphy recalled Simons' attitude and knew the only way he could be this relaxed this close to the vote was if he had it in the bag. Paid for and delivered. Some thirty names on a list, half with a dollar figure beside them. How many were votes the governor was counting as his own?

He rolled his fingers on the keyboard: *asdfjkl;asdfjkl;asdfjkl;*. And then he moved the little trackball with his thumb, clicked to a new document, increased the point size to forty-eight and clicked on boldface. He typed: IT's 11 O'CLOCK. DO YOU KNOW WHERE YOUR VOTES ARE???

From his briefcase, he removed the latest *Guide to Florida Government,* entered the fax number for the Governor's Mansion in the appropriate field, plugged the computer into the room telephone and hit the send button.

Dunbar walked slowly toward the Mansion, mind in a stew. With Jeena's story in the hands of a master like Bolling, they'd have a fighting chance. The headlines in every paper would scream about tobacco's secret memo and armed goons: enough to swing at least one or two borderline senators back their way.

And yet—he'd promised again not to breathe a word about it, not until they'd tracked down Ruth Ann Bronson, made sure she was okay, warned her about the psychopath who, having failed to find what he was looking for with Jeena, might very well try her boss next . . .

Face streaked with tears, unable to speak coherently, she'd fallen asleep on his shoulder, right there on the couch in the T-shirt and sweats he'd lent her. He'd moved her to his bedroom, then climbed in beside her, fully clothed.

She'd awakened in a panic, grabbing for the phone, calling Ruth Ann's house, Ruth Ann's cell phone, Ruth Ann's pager, over and over, leaving message after message. Finally, he'd made her stop, and she'd told him the whole story. The drive out to the springs, her escape up the side tunnel and her wrenching fear that the guy would go after Ruth Ann. They went to her house, saw nothing unusual except for the fact she wasn't there, and then to the office, before he was able to persuade Jeena that she needed to go to the Governor's Mansion, immediately, and stay there until they caught the bastard. She'd agreed, but on the condition he renewed his promise: The reason for the psycho's visit, that memo, had to remain secret until they'd tracked down Ruth Ann. He'd argued until he was blue in the face, told her that having the governor publicize the memo, make a big deal out of it, *that* was the best way to take the heat off of Ruth Ann. Once the word was out, then there'd be no advantage to silencing Ruth Ann or anyone else. But Jeena stood firm, pointing out that perhaps logic and clear thinking weren't the psycho's forte, and Dunbar gave in for the sake of getting her behind a patrolled iron fence.

Dunbar knocked at the cabana's screen door, then waited for the characteristic grunt before turning the knob. Bolling was behind the desk in a light gray sweatshirt and reading glasses. Casually, he flipped a page in the stack of papers before him.

"My girlfriend, sir," Dunbar began, taking a deep breath for the lie to follow. "She was kidnapped last night by one of RJH's goons. She's one of their lobbyists, and they thought they'd accidentally sent her a sensitive document. Anyway, she didn't have it, but she couldn't convince 'em. He broke into her house, took her at gunpoint." Dunbar licked his lips, wondered if Bolling was buying the *didn't have it* stuff. "Point is, she didn't have it, and eventually she got away. She got a good look at the guy. Of course, she can't *prove* he's with Roper-Joyner, but—"

"She here now? She all right?"

Dunbar nodded. "In my car by the gate. She's fine. Still kind of shaky, but okay. She's also worried about her boss, Ruth Ann Bronson. She thinks they might figure, well, if she doesn't have what they're looking for, maybe Ruth Ann does. In the meantime, I'm wondering if she can stay here. You know, until—"

"Of course. I'll have FDLE send the crime scene unit out to her place. I don't want her leavin' the Mansion grounds till we pick the son of a bitch up. We'll track down Bronson, too, invite her to stay here, if she wants. At the very least, post a guard with her till this is over." Bolling shook his head, his eyes hard and angry. "You hear rumors, you know? How Bart Simons got to be CEO. How their whistle-blowers' airplanes keep blowin' up. Now this."

He handed Dunbar a single sheet of paper from his in-box. "I'd say your girlfriend's ordeal forces us to consider a couple of interpretations we ordinarily might not have, wouldn't you?"

Dunbar flipped the paper over, saw it was a fax with no originating phone number. Then he read the single sentence in the middle of the page.

"How do you suppose the next Senate president, a closet feminist, I daresay, and a believer that pornography abuses women," Ruth Ann Bronson asked, "how do you suppose she'll react to a senior Senate staffer using state computers to propagate porn?"

Ruth Ann sat on the edge of Stephen Brechner's desk, her pedicured, spring-sandaled feet a mere inches from Stephen Brechner's groin. She'd forcefully reminded him of that proximity once already, but still his eyes lingered on the hemline of her minidress, where it lay on her lap.

"Hey! Computer Boy! I'm wearing underwear today, okay? Get over it!"

Brechner's eyes fell to the carpeting, to his own pale, unhealthy-looking, almost yellow toes. "I didn't use a Senate computer," he protested weakly. "Everything's on a server at Remy's office."

"Yes, I'm sure Dolly Nichols will agree that makes it all better. That it makes up for your installing a spy camera in the Capitol, distributing pornography from within a state building, *doing* all this on state time, when presumably you've got other, more important things to do. Or maybe," Ruth Ann studied her cuticles, "she'll decide you *don't* have other, more important things to do. Maybe you're one of those state employees who does nothing but collect a fat paycheck, like the Republicans are always talking about. Maybe firing you won't be so hard after all."

He turned quickly to the computer. "I'll get those pictures down right now. Yours and—"

"All of them."

"Right, all of them," he agreed. "And those cameras will be gone—"

"Don't worry about the cameras. In fact," she reached for her purse, removed a paper bag, emptied bits of mangled metal and broken glass all over his desk, "here you go."

He studied the mess unhappily, opened his mouth to protest, shut it again. She bent toward the computer, watched him type. "You can take files off Remy's computer from here?"

"Sure." He continued typing, then waited for the dial tone to become a shrill buzz. "Just call into his modem. Nothing to it."

Ruth Ann watched a string of gibberish scroll down the screen. "You mean, just files for Tastee Tallahassee or . . ."

"Oh, no. Everything."

"Everything?" She blinked. "Everything . . . like financial records?"

Brechner's eyes grew wide, and he shook his head fearfully. "No way. He'd kill me. I'll never work again!"

Ruth Ann leaned back, arms around her knees. "You're right. I'm sure there are *plenty* of eighty-grand no-show jobs in this town for computer geeks. Plus, I'm sure Senator Nichols will give you a *glowing* recommendation."

He turned back to the monitor with a sigh. "What do you want?"

She pointed at the computer, then the printer: "Everything. Download here, print there."

With a small whimpering noise he began typing. The printer started whirring. He typed some more, moved the mouse, clicked, then sat staring at the monitor, shoulders slumped. Defeated. "There. Done. It's printing out. And the pictures are gone."

Ruth Ann reached into the printer's tray. The first page was a ledger marked new accounts, led by "Christian Broadcasters of Florida" with an entry beside it: $500,000. She considered it a moment, glanced over the page at Stephen Brechner. "On second thought, perhaps we ought to leave at least *one* picture." She smiled mischievously at his perplexed look. "You know those sleazy pictures, with the heads of movie stars pasted on naked models? I was thinking a nice picture of Martin Remy engaged in some good, old-fashioned sodomy would be just the thing!"

"Miss Bronson!" Brechner whined. "You know how long it takes to make a good one of those? *Hours!* It's painstaking!"

She blinked at him quizzically. "And you had big plans to do . . . *what*, today?"

He sighed again. "Anal or oral?"

Ruth Ann grabbed the next dozen pages of printout. "Surprise me."

Five bras, five pairs of panties and three pairs of hose topped out the duffel bag, and Jeena pulled the zipper shut. She wore jeans, a long T-shirt and flats. In the bag were another set of the same, plus several calf-length skirts and high-collared blouses. The return of Laura Ashley.

She slung the bag over a shoulder just as Dunbar appeared at the door. "Cops getting antsy?" Two FDLE cars had accompanied them to her town house, and agents guarded both doors while she packed. "I just need my bathroom stuff. Won't be another minute."

Dunbar said, "Take your time," but his eyes were on a half-shut cardboard box on the floor. In it were the low-cut blouses, the high-heeled sandals and the rest of her wardrobe from the previous week. Jeena saw hanging out of the box a corner of the minidress she'd worn that night at Clyde's. Hastily, she tucked it back in, folded the flaps shut.

The tips of her ears burned with shame, but she realized Dunbar would have no idea why. "Just some clothes I'm getting rid of," she mumbled.

Dunbar nodded, seemed on the verge of asking something, then thought better of it. "I could run them down to Goodwill."

"No, that's all right. I thought I'd just throw them out." She brushed by him to get to the bathroom, tossed toothbrush, floss, hair brush and hair spray into a travel kit. "You think they have hair dryers at the Mansion?"

"Not if Bolling has anything to do with it."

She unplugged hers, crammed it into the case. "I wish I knew how long it was going to be. One day, ten . . . I have no idea what to bring." She slid by him into her bedroom again. "Think they have an iron I can use?"

"Jeena."

Slowly, she lifted her eyes. Her heart was pounding, she realized.

"Did that bastard do anything last night . . . to you? I mean, the clothes you packed, the clothes you're getting rid of . . ."

And she understood now and shook her head. "No. Nothing. He didn't lay a finger on me. In fact, *I* kicked *him*."

"You kicked him."

"Yeah. In the nuts. He told me . . ."

In her mind's eye, she saw again what the little shithead must have been referring to. It was a picture she'd noticed on a computer screen somewhere a few days earlier: a dark-haired woman on the phone in the top half, a shot up her skirt in the bottom. At the time, she'd assumed it was just another sophomoric hidden-cam Web site. It was only earlier, waiting in Dunbar's car while he went to talk to the governor, that she'd realized *where* the camera had been hidden, why the Sprint logo in the photo's background looked so familiar, and how the psycho had known she'd hidden the memo in her lipstick case.

"Dunbar," she sighed, taking his hand, leading him to her spare bedroom where her computer was set up. "There's something I need to show you. Better you saw it now, from me, rather than one of your friends. . . ."

She didn't mean it that way; it was a friend, or ex-friend, who'd gleefully shown him the *Playboy* picture years ago. His face fell. It was an episode they'd both rather have forgotten. "What I mean is," she said quickly, "I remember how much it hurt you that I didn't tell you up front—"

"No, Jeena, *I'm* the one who should be sorry. That picture was a long time ago. I was a jerk to have reacted—" He blinked at the computer. "That son of a bitch! He put it out on the *Internet*?"

Jeena clicked on the icon to dial her online service. "No. Well, I should say, I don't think so. I haven't looked. But I think what it was . . . Well, you'll see. It's one of those secretary-cam sites. . . ."

Dunbar watched her type in the address. "Tastee Tallahassee. So *that's* what that is. I've overheard a bunch of guys talking about it. I figured it was one of those lingerie-modeling services."

The computer screen went blank, and they watched in fascination as it filled in a giant photograph of a naked, unbelievably acrobatic Martin Remy servicing three massively endowed and equally naked young men.

"Wow," Dunbar said, impressed. "I didn't know that was physically possible."

Jeena shook her head in awe. "I didn't even know he was gay."

SUNDAY

The instant Lambert untied the knot, his captive spit out the gag and began cursing a blue streak.

"You got *any* idea who I am? I'll have your nuts cut off and fed to wild birds! I'll have you strung up by your dick," T.C. sputtered. "*Nobody* does this to T. C. Tuttle and gets away with it, not even the governor. You don't let go me *this instant*, I'm gonna have the feds crawlin' up his asshole so far he'll be lookin' cross-eyed!"

Lambert adjusted his ski mask to realign the holes with his eyes and mouth before he moved on his knees to a boat cleat he'd installed on a wall of the rough-hewn cabin. He picked up a rope dangling from the pulley he'd bolted to the ceiling and watched Tuttle for a moment.

"Boy, I'm gonna count ten. By the time I get to three, you'd best untie me. One, two, *uuuaaaagh!*"

Without warning, Lambert yanked down on the rope, pulling Tuttle skyward by his ankles until he dangled upside down, his shiny round head a few feet from the dirty wooden floor. He waited for Tuttle to stop swaying before he tied the rope off to the cleat and sat cross-legged before Tuttle's reddening face.

"I warned you! I warned you, you snot-nose bastard, you hang me up again and you'll regret it the rest of your livin' days. Okay, you did it anyhow. Now you leave me no choice. You go ahead and have fun with your torture while you can, 'cause when—"

Lambert laughed once, a single menacing snicker. "Torture? This? Senator, this isn't torture. Torture is when by noon you still haven't told me what I want, I go get the battery and the ignition coil from your car and hook it up to your dick with jumper cables. Now *that's* torture."

Tuttle blanched, stared at Lambert silently.

"That's better." Lambert grabbed an apple from his duffel and bit into it. "Now, for the millionth time, sir: Where's the memo?"

"Christ Almighty, I already told you a million times: I ain't got no memo! I remember the girl you're talkin' about, but she didn't give me nothin'. Look, if Bollin's so hot to get this, why don't he just get his fancy-schmancy lawyers to so-*pena* the damn thing and leave me the fuck out of it?"

Lambert studied Tuttle carefully. Somehow they were working on completely different frequencies. He'd hoped to make it quick: find out where the memo was, retrieve it, bury the senator out in the woods, then go figure out what to do with the girl. Instead, through a whole day and a half, this stubborn old fool kept going on about Bolling. Bolling this, Bolling that . . .

Lambert got a bad feeling. "Sir, why do you keep mentioning Bolling?"

T.C. squinted at his captor through the layer of mud he'd fallen in on his way into the cabin. "You don't work for Waites, do you?"

The bad feeling grew worse, and Lambert couldn't keep a look of momentary confusion from his face.

"Waites? Bollin' Waites? The governor of this here state?"

Lambert checked his watch authoritatively. No matter what, he had to maintain the appearance of control. "Senator, it is now 1148 hours. You have exactly twelve minutes to tell me where the memo is before we electrify your penis."

"You *ain't* with Bollin', are you?" T.C. glanced around the cabin. "Then why the fuck did you bring me to his huntin' lodge?"

This caught Lambert's attention, and he looked nervously around the single room. Nothing but plain pine furniture and a cast-iron stove. "This is the *governor's*?" How could that be? Unease threatened to become panic but he quickly suppressed it. Even if it were true, the governor would be busy this weekend. No time for hunting. He affected a careless shrug. "Twelve potential sites were identified from an aerial. Reconnaissance showed nine to have regular activity. This was chosen from the remaining three at random. Not that it's any of your business, sir."

T.C. scowled, thinking. "Well if you ain't workin' for Bollin', then . . . You fuckin' *moron*! You're with Roper-Joyner, ain't you? Don't you know I'm *with* you people?"

Lambert bristled at the insult. It was among the favorites his drill sergeant had had for him. That and dickbrain. He dug the Clerk's Manual with the newspaper clipping from a pocket of his cammos. "Says here you were quote the governor's point man in the Senate passing the tobacco law unquote. Now I may not be as educated as I might, I'll admit that. But I think this eagle on my collar can vouch for the fact I know what *point man* means. So just maybe *I* ain't the moron—"

"You dumbfuck, backwoods dickbrain!" T.C. exploded. "I wasn't on Roper-Joyner's payroll back then, was I? This time I'm takin' a quarter mill of your company's money to vote *against* the governor!"

Lambert tugged at the ski mask uncomfortably, the turmoil in his belly now a clear case of panic. If Tuttle was telling the truth, then not only was it highly doubtful that the girl had given him the memo, it also meant Simons was counting on his vote Monday . . . which meant he wasn't going to be able to shoot him in the head and bury him as planned. . . . And which still left the fundamental question: Where the fuck was the memo?

"Call Martin Remy!" T.C. demanded finally, and Lambert unhappily went to his field pack to dig out the cell phone.

Beside him, Martin Remy was explaining something to Choo-Choo James about Bahamian banking laws, but Gus Cruz couldn't follow a word of it, not with a pair of Martin Remy's associates approaching again. Each wore only a thong bikini bottom, one neon pink, the other a bright lime, and carried trays of fresh mimosas and croissants.

Gus tried not to stare but couldn't help himself. Such gloriously cheerful breasts; it made him proud to be an American, by God. Even before the pool party, he'd been having trouble digesting his amazing turnabout of fortune in just two days. First, he'd gotten out of the FBI's squeeze, then Remy had called with a six-figure "premium" for a vote he was going to cast anyway, and now this: naked girls bringing him brunch.

One of the girls, the brunette in the lime bottom, asked if he wanted anything. Gus nodded stupidly, his eyes locked on her bobbing nipples. She gave him another croissant, for which he thanked her profusely as she padded off with the blonde to the other side of the pool where Speaker Powers and a few of his House cronies sat in a cluster of chaise lounges.

"Hey, Martin, how come you never invited me here before?" Gus asked, then whimpered softly as the blonde began applying sunscreen to Powers' shoulders. *Damn!* Why hadn't *he* thought of asking her that? . . .

"Because you're a greasy Mexican."

Gus looked up to laughter, Remy and Choo-Choo James high-fiving each other. He laughed, too. What the hell? He munched on his croissant, wondered idly where T.C. was. He hadn't seen him since Friday night. They were supposed to have played golf Saturday, but he'd stood him up.

"So after my account is set up, how do I check my balance?" Choo-Choo asked.

Remy feigned disappointment. "What, you don't trust me?"

Gus perked up. He, too, needed to learn the intricacies of offshore accounts, now that he had one.

. "Piece of cake. Call Nassau, ask for Mr. Pinder. Read him that long number I gave you, then the password you picked out. That's it. Half is already there. The other half gets transmitted at three-oh-one p.m. tomorrow. Assuming everything goes off."

"Oh, it will." Choo-Choo nodded at the sunburnt figure lounging on an alligator float. "Rex Kelsey there is vote number twenty-six, I'm twenty-seven. Plus you got T.C., too, right? That's twenty-eight."

Remy shrugged. "We'll see. I been in Tallahassee long enough to know you never count your votes till the board's been cleared and the gavel's come down." He nodded at the girls, who now were letting a grinning Powers slather sunscreen on their backsides. "Best hires I've made in a long time."

Gus whimpered again, finally noticed an annoying beeping and watched Remy reach into the pocket of his robe for the cell phone.

"Colonel Lambert?" Remy asked. "Who are you again?"

Dunbar handed Bolling the list and stood by as the governor set down the fishing reel he'd been assembling and scanned the page. Already he felt the heavy weight in his belly, the certainty that if only he'd been paying more attention to the votes and less to how he could win back Jeena . . .

"So outta eighteen Democrats, only twelve are committin' to us."

Dunbar swallowed hard. All his damn fault . . . if he'd been there, riding herd on the fence-sitters, they'd still have their fourteen "As of this morning."

"And these three circled in red, you can't find? Rex and Choo-Choo—"

"And T.C., too. Sir, I tried everywhere. Their district offices, their homes, their cell phones. No luck." He bit his lip, steeled himself to broach the really bad news. "Governor, rumor is that Roper-Joyner's handing out cash money, like 250,000 each, to like a dozen senators. . . . If that's true, maybe FDLE can investigate—"

Bolling Waites shook his head. "No way in hell they can nail anything down in the next twenty-four hours. Dammit all. I shoulda known they'd play this dirty. Hell, couple billion dollars on the line, they could give all forty senators a million each and still have themselves a cheap investment." He poked at the list again. "Can't find 'em anywhere?"

Dunbar sighed. "Sorry, sir. This is all my fault—"

"Not another word. It ain't you, it's them. They promised they'd vote with us. Now they're goin' back on it, is all. How in hell we gonna compete with a quarter mill in a Swiss bank somewhere?" He shook his head again. "We get those three back, we're in business. We lose 'em, we may as well forget it."

Dunbar took the list back and turned for the door. "I'll track down their aides. See if they know where they're at."

Testicles still swollen from his encounter with Vise Grips Woman, face and neck coated with sticky dirt, the Dean of the Florida Senate pushed through his front door, hobbled to the bathroom and tossed his clothes into a soggy heap.

For the longest time, he held his face to the steaming water, let it soothe aching muscles, wash away accumulated grime and humiliation. Someone, he decided, was going to pay. Nobody treated T. C. Tuttle like that for free. Martin Remy had fallen over himself apologizing for Lambert's mistake, promising to make it right, promising to send over a couple of girls. The one thing he hadn't promised, T.C. realized later, was more money.

But more money there surely would be. A lot more. A quarter million? T.C. snorted under the stream of water. More like a half million. Yessir, Roper-Joyner was about to learn that mistakes were expensive, especially when they affected T. C. Tuttle's quality of life.

He lowered his head, let the water hit the back of his neck, unhappily regarded his privates. They hurt, but not like before. He scowled, wondering how he'd get back at the Bronson woman. He was, he had to admit, more than a little afraid of her. Part of him wanted to pretend it had never happened. She represented the country's second-biggest toolmaker. God only knew what implement she might use next. He imagined himself tied to a band saw or a table sander, the business end approaching his frightened, shrinking unit. . . .

With a shudder, he flipped off the water, only then heard the phone emit half a ring, then stop. He waddled to his answering machine, hit the play button, listened through one, two, three, four, five, six, *seven* messages from Waites' office, each demanding to know where he was, each more frantic than the last.

He sat down, recalled the look in Waites' eyes when he'd shot him with the blowgun, began to panic. What did Bolling want? Surely it had to do with the tobacco vote. Probably suspected T.C. was about to betray him. Probably planned some devious revenge . . .

Eyes bulging, he scanned the bedroom. Quick, why hadn't he called Waites back? What reason could he give?

He was back in the district. That was it. No. One of the messages said they'd tried there already. . . . There was only one explanation: He'd been consorting with Big Tobacco. He was being entertained by Remy's nymphs, in anticipated gratitude for his vote. . . .

T.C.'s breathing became shallow and his privates began spasming as his panic increased. Bolling would kill him, is what he'd do. Why the hell not? He wasn't running for re-election. He didn't need T.C.'s support out in the Panhandle anymore.

And then it hit him: He'd tell the truth! He nodded to himself. It was a desperate tactic, but he saw it might be the only way out. He threw off his towel, climbed back into his filthy, sweaty clothes, opened the sliding glass door to a tiny fenced backyard.

He fell to his knees and maniacally pulled up sod. Then he threw himself into the dirt and began rolling.

"*Ambition, is our problem*. Blind ambition is all you need. You don't gotta be caring or smart or any of that. You just gotta want it bad enough." Bolling Waites squirted machine oil onto a rag, cleaned the breech of his side-by-side for a moment, then continued his tirade. "They don't even read their own damn bills, let alone anybody else's. Their idea of researchin' an issue is havin' lunch with the lobbyist on one side, and dinner with the lobbyist on the other, then goin' with whoever promises more money for their re-election. "And you know whose fault it is? Ours."

Dunbar and Jeena sat quietly on a couch, watching the old man clean his weapons while they waited for a phone to ring with news, any news. The aides for Rex Kelsey and Choo-Choo James had claimed not to know where their bosses were but promised to let them know the governor was looking for them. T.C., meanwhile, had apparently fallen off the face of the earth, as had Ruth Ann Bronson, who still hadn't shown up at her house. The possibility had begun to occur to all three of them that Jeena's psycho had embarked on some kind of wild rampage.

"End of the day, folks get the government they deserve. How things work up here ain't exactly a secret. If they wanted, they could throw the bums out. Instead they keep sendin' 'em on back." Bolling lifted the shotgun, snapped it shut, broke it open again. "You can lead a horse to water . . ."

He pointed the weapon at the cabana door and peered down the barrel, just as the door opened inward.

T. C. Tuttle saw the gun and dove to the gravel. After the FDLE escort helped him back up, he saw Waites' expectant look, then took a deep breath: "I was kidnapped by tobacca thugs!"

Dunbar and Jeena held hands in the front seat of the FDLE van and listened to two more senators discuss in excited murmurs T.C.'s ordeal. The details had spread like wildfire, growing more dramatic each time T.C. retold it. What had started as three armed men—two of them, T.C. never got a good look at, but the third seemed to match Jeena's abductor—had by day's end doubled to six, with possibly a seventh in a black helicopter, acting as a spotter.

Dunbar glanced back at the two men, both from Broward County, both liberal Democrats with Long Island accents who wondered whether the Feds should be brought in and whether the governor's kitchen staff could be persuaded to send out for bagels in the morning.

He squeezed Jeena's hand as the van pulled through the gates of the Mansion. The two senators, each toting a garment bag, climbed out and were directed toward the cabana, where a dormitory had been set up. Bolling Waites welcomed them personally, showed them to the cots he'd had Emergency Management bring over from the hurricane operations center and pointed out the tripled guard surrounding the wrought iron fence. He patted them on the back and strolled toward the van, greeted Jeena, then pulled Dunbar aside.

"Still no word from Kelsey or Choo-Choo? Or Ruth Ann?" Dunbar asked.

"*Nada.* I think we gotta assume worst case. They've been kidnapped, won't be released till after the vote. Or worse. In Ruth Ann's case, definitely or worse."

Dunbar recalled version two or three of Tuttle's story. "Didn't T.C. say they went out to bring in some others? Which is when he managed to get away?"

"That whole thing . . ." Waites shook his head. "Bein' dragged out to *my* cabin, of all places, then *escapin'*? Tell me, you see T.C. as a big escape artist? Sort of a McGyver type?"

On the pool deck, T.C. had stationed himself by the shrimp table, where he held forth over a circle of spellbound senators. By now the abductors had probably grown in number to a small army, Dunbar guessed. "I see your point."

"Now, I don't doubt tobacca's desperate enough to start kidnappin' folks. I *do* doubt T.C.'s got the wherewithal to get away from an arthritic grandmother, let alone somebody with a gun. Plus he smelled weird."

"Weird?"

"Not right," the governor said. "The soil out at the cook shack is a red clay. That's the stuff on his clothes, all right. But his arms and face had like a garden topsoil on 'em. Didn't make much sense. Anyhow, I've never trusted the little bastard, and I get the sense now ain't the best time to start."

Waites studied his corps of supporters on the patio. "You know, the rules for override favor us. Therefore the rules for kidnapping favor us, too."

Dunbar stiffened. "Sir?"

"Well . . ." The governor offered the famous Granddaddy Gator grin. "For every two of ours they kidnap, we only gotta take one of theirs. Listen, Dunbar, we got here, even passin' the law in the first place, by playin' by their sneaky rules. I'll be damned if I'm gonna let 'em win just by taking it one more step. Tomorrow, just before the vote, let's even things up a bit."

Dunbar studied the governor nervously, then the senators by the cabana, where more and more were losing interest in T.C. and helping themselves to the spread laid out by Bolling's chef. By some definitions, he realized, what the governor was proposing was illegal. A federal crime, even, punishable by many years in a penitentiary. "How many should I take?"

Waites thought a moment. "Take one. Fair is fair." He watched his supporters in the dying light and for a moment caught T.C.'s eyes before the senator turned away hastily. "Second thought, take T.C., too. I've got this bad feelin' about him, like he's been theirs from the get-go, and today's thing was some sorta red herring. Last thing I need is that snake out on the Floor, trickin' the others to go along with him."

Through the high-powered Nikons, T. C. Tuttle wore a fresh green sport coat and snapped up skewered strips of meat in between telling senators a wild tale, gesturing dramatically with his hands.

High up an oak tree behind the Mansion, Lambert reddened with anger. What a fool he'd been, believing that lying bastard! Call Remy, he'd said. So he'd called Remy, who'd assured him T.C. was on their side. Lying bastards, the both of them. Because if T. C. Tuttle was on their side, then what the hell was he doing at the Governor's Mansion?

Lambert set the binoculars down and surveyed the armed guard patrolling the ivy-covered fence. Three, four, five, six, he counted. Probably more on the inside. A hit here was definitely out of the question.

He sighed, then from his perch looked around at nighttime Tallahassee. A few blocks up the street was Simons' hotel. A few blocks farther was the twenty-two-story Capitol, floodlit at the base, red lights flashing at the top.

Lambert turned over on the tree limb to lie flat on his back and consider the enormity of his fuckup. Fuckups, really. First the girl, now Tuttle. Both should have been dead. Instead both were under protection of the governor himself. One of them surely had the memo, which meant now the governor had it.

He thought it out carefully: He was supposed to call in immediately in the event of a problem. Strictly interpreted, that could possibly include the weekend so far. On the other hand . . . all was not lost yet. He'd seen a school bus being led into the Mansion courtyard. Obviously the means of caravanning everyone to the Capitol tomorrow.

Mission success was retrieving the memo and eliminating anyone who had seen it. The first half might no longer be possible, but he was sure Simons would understand, particularly if the second half was carried out with a certain . . . flair. He nodded to himself soberly. They'd made a fool out of him. Now it was time for payback, time to make an example out of them, remind the world that *no one* fucked with Colonel Marvin Lambert.

Plus, he thought with a smile as he stared at Tallahassee's tallest building, maybe now Lambert Security Limited could shoot some fresh, even more dramatic footage for its new demo tape. . . .

Unable to sleep, Special Agent Johnny Espinosa tossed and turned, then finally just lay on his back and stared at the hotel room ceiling. Just two days ago, it had all been perfect. He had the chief executive of the fourth largest state, dead to rights. Conspiracy. Fraud. With a friendly magistrate, maybe even bribery.

And then the old bastard had started in with stuff like truth and justice, and everything had gone to hell. He couldn't stop thinking about it. Where was the justice if corporations who made their fortunes addicting children to a poison got away with it while he sent up the one politician trying to stop them? Whose bidding was he doing then?

With a final twist of his sheets, he sat, turned on the bedside lamp and grabbed the file labeled "Waites, B." containing original contracts, notes from his interview with Tuttle and canceled State of Florida checks made out to members of the trial team. He walked to the bathroom and methodically tore up each piece of paper into the metal trash can. Then he went for his cigarettes and lighter.

One long, last look, a fleeting reminder that he could still stop, tape the torn pages back together, and then he bent down, held the lighter to the loosely packed paper, sat back on the lid of the commode, lit a cigarette. . . .

For a long minute, he watched the paper burn, took a drag from his Grande, held it before his eyes, then threw it, too, into the metal can. One by one, he tossed the remaining cigarettes into the fire, crumpled the cardboard box, threw it on as well. Silently, he watched the flames turn small bits of paper into smaller wisps of ash, knew that with the smoke went the quick promotion, the special commendation, the invitation to meet the attorney general . . . maybe even the president. Bringing in a governor was one thing. Bringing in just another smarmy state legislator, a Miami Cuban at that, was a much lesser thing. A great, big, fat hairy deal. A Quantico trainee could sting a Miami Cuban.

There was a knock at the door, and Espinosa thought: great. The fire has set off a smoke detector. End of a perfect fucking day.

He went to the door, opened it and saw the unlabeled cardboard box on the carpeting. He checked the hall, both ways, but saw nothing before dragging the box inside and pulling open the lid.

He read the top sheet of the computer printout. Then he smiled.

MONDAY

One by one, the senators under the protection of Governor Bolling Waites boarded the yellow Leon District Schools bus requisitioned for the half-mile convoy up Monroe and around the block to Duval, to the main entrance of the Capitol. There, a contingent of state troopers, Tallahassee police, humorless men in FLDE windbreakers and blue-blazered members of the Senate sergeant-at-arms were already in position, waiting to escort the precious ladies and gentlemen up to the fourth floor so they could cast their precious votes.

Dunbar and Jeena stood by the front, clipboard in hand, ticking off names as they boarded, when the governor sauntered over in a workday madras shirt and tried to pull Dunbar aside.

"Just a minute, Governor," Dunbar cut in. "Jeena has something to tell you."

Bolling glanced at one, then the other, finally settled on Jeena. She swallowed and drew herself to her full height in an old, familiar pair of flats. "I want in."

The governor lifted an eyebrow. "In?"

"Yes, sir." She nodded firmly. "If y'all are talking about getting even with the bastards who hired that little psycho, then, yes, definitely. I want in."

Bolling turned to Dunbar, who shrugged helplessly. "She knows what she's getting into. I swear to God I didn't tell her. She overheard—"

"Please, sir. I *want* to do this," she insisted. "I owe it to Ruth Ann, if something's happened to her. She was as good to me, sir, as you've been to Dunbar."

The governor eyed her critically a long moment, finally nodded. "All right. You're in." He turned his back to the schoolbus, scratched behind his ear. "Well, boys and girls, I think I know where we can take our, uh, guests where nobody's gonna trip over 'em. The roof, through the twenty-second-floor access. I'll talk to ol' T.C. myself. Tell him I want a private meetin' before the vote. It's up to you guys to persuade Gus Cruz. Tell him I wanna see him about that Cuban-American scam. Tell him I'm gonna agree."

Dunbar traded glances with Jeena. "Just one thing we're kinda not sure about: How do we, uh, *persuade* them to stay put?"

Bolling smiled, reached into a hip pocket and produced an eyeglass case, then opened it for them to examine. "The darts are loaded with an animal tranquilizer, but you tell 'em the points are dipped in a special poison flown in fresh from the Amazon basin. T.C. will know what you're talkin' about."

The penthouse had been empty. So had the hospitality suite at the Capitol Club. Finally, Murphy Moran began stalking the halls of the Capitol itself. Surely the son of a bitch would want to see this in person. . . . There! Through the glass doors opening onto the brick courtyard between old and new capitols was the man of the hour, his flunky beside him, silently observing a dozen or so of the high-rise's nicotine junkies enjoying an after-lunch smoke.

Simons saw him approach and nodded at the smokers. "Look at them all. Sheep. I could take cow dung, use it as filler, and stretch the profit margin. Call it Bovine Bliss. Menthols and Regulars. Our old friend Nietzsche would be proud."

Murphy grabbed Simons by the lapels to get his attention. "What the hell's going on?" he demanded.

Simons blinked once and looked Murphy up and down. Gently, he smoothed out the wrinkles in his navy suit coat. "Is this how we address someone who's about to sign your million-dollar bonus?"

Murphy repeated the news that had been making the rounds that morning. "There's a hundred cops waiting to escort the governor's votes up to the Senate chamber. Any idea why that might be?"

Simons shrugged gamely. "Maybe the old man heard he was down to ten votes and didn't want us stealing them in the final minutes?" He reached over, adjusted the sport coat and bright canary tie Murphy had worn for the big day, then turned back to the smokers. "Relax, would you? Just look at these saps. Mooooo! Pathetic. But, you know, I shouldn't be so harsh. They do, after all, keep me in clover. Four dollars a pack, five dollars a pack, *ten* dollars a pack. Won't matter a bit. They'll be there for me." Simons nodded. "And you know, *I* should do something for them. Once we finish with this override, we ought to push through the country's first smokers' rights act. What do you say? They shouldn't have to huddle outside, like lepers, just to enjoy a cigarette." He turned toward the crowd: "Hey, everybody! How'd you like to smoke at your desks again, like the good old days?"

Murphy ignored the cheering, pushed closer to Simons. "Then maybe you can explain something else I heard this morning. Apparently, the good senator from Chipley, T. C. Tuttle, has been telling anybody who'll listen that he was kidnapped Friday and held for two days by heavily armed camouflage-wearing commandos before he managed to escape." Murphy watched the confidence dissolve from Simons' face. "Sound like anyone we know?"

Simons seemed to ponder something and checked his watch anxiously. Murphy grew exasperated and wished now he'd insinuated himself into whatever secret plan Simons had cooked up. The bribes made sense, turning soft votes into solid votes. But then why kidnap T. C. Tuttle? What sense did that make?

Murphy waited through Simons' silent frown . . . and it dawned on him that the man was wondering the same thing. That whatever plan it was Simons had cooked up, he no longer had control of it. That his boy Lambert had gone off the reservation . . .

He scowled, wracking his brain. The lunatic had kidnapped Tuttle. So maybe he'd assigned himself the task of taking out of circulation any votes they still couldn't be sure of . . . But that had failed, and if he couldn't kidnap them quietly, his next step would be . . .

Feverishly, Murphy tried to think: Where would a maniac with a gun fetish set himself up . . . and suddenly he recalled the muttered urging for Simons to secure the high ground. He looked up—and saw a glint of metal against the sky.

Dolly Nichols pulled out her tally for the override vote, went over it a final time as her niece sat across the desk, skinny legs dangling over the edge of the overstuffed visitor's chair, explaining how her class had already seen the Supreme Court, where they'd had an oral argument, and visited the Florida Archives, and then the House chamber, where they were having a boring debate about workers competition.

Dolly smiled to herself. "I think perhaps it was workers compensation."

"Oh yeah," Jennifer continued. "Anyway, they talked and talked and talked and finally they said they'd talk about it some more tomorrow."

"That's the House for you," Dolly replied, then glanced up at her ceiling with scrunched nose. She could smell the faint odor of cigarettes, something she absolutely did not tolerate in her sanctum. Indeed, her one extravagance when she'd moved into the Rules Committee suite had been authorizing $5,000 for an in-line air purifier to make sure she didn't get any stale air from the offices of the few senators who continued, illegally, to smoke there.

Yet the air handler wasn't blowing at that moment. . . . She looked around the room, finally settling on the guilty expression on Jennifer's face. She stood, eyes locked on her niece's, moved around the desk, sniffing the whole way. Sure enough, the smell grew stronger as she neared. . . .

Jennifer held her breath for thirty seconds, a minute, ninety seconds, finally let it out, and Dolly Nichols staggered backward. She knew and could see in Jennifer's eyes that the girl knew that she knew.

For a long minute, she couldn't even speak, until Jennifer broke the spell: "Go on! Yell at me!"

Dolly counted to ten in her head, trying to let the anger subside. She kept going to twenty, then backward to zero. "I don't get it," she said finally. "Your mom and dad don't smoke. Never have. You have a good home life. You get straight A's. Never get in trouble at school. So why?"

Jennifer shrugged. "It's no big deal, Aunt Doll. Lots of kids smoke." She read her aunt's reaction, lowered her eyes and her voice. "It's no big deal."

Dolly Nichols unfolded one arm from her chest, extended it and snapped her fingers. Reluctant hands reached into the Larry Llama backpack, pulled out a hard packet of Llama Lights and surrendered them to her aunt, who peered distastefully inside to count six remaining cigarettes.

"They're *lights*," Jennifer exclaimed. "Thirty percent less tar and nicotine than regular Llamas."

"Thank the Lord for small favors."

"I only smoke like two or three a day. Four, if I'm totally stressed out."

Dolly nodded. "Stressed out. Sure. That happens." She bit back her anger, slowly shook the packet at her niece. "Jenn, these are poison. They gum up your lungs with carcinogens, they inject a drug directly into your bloodstream. This is *your* body. *You've* got to start making the right decisions to take care of it. Nobody else—"

"It's no big deal," Jennifer interrupted again, hands on sassy hips, weight on one leg. "Besides, I'm *gonna* quit. Promise, on my sixteenth birthday, I quit. Cross my heart."

Dolly shook her head, as anger became something else. "You're only twelve years old. . . ." She recalled the day Jennifer was born, a tiny, swaddled little bundle; how her sister handed her to Dolly to hold; how she'd cradled the little head against her shoulder; how tiny hands had gripped her fingers and hair . . . she felt herself reeling, grabbed her desk even tighter.

"Your mother doesn't know, does she."

Jennifer scoffed. "You kidding? She'd have a total cow. I'd be grounded for like a year."

Slowly, the hurt started swinging back toward anger, and this time Dolly stoked it. She crushed the cardboard packet in a fist, snapped her fingers for the backpack. With scissors from her desk drawer she cut away the Larry Llama logo, threw it in the trash, threw the bag back at her niece. Jennifer opened her mouth to protest, then shut it again when she saw the fury in her aunt's eyes.

"I don't *ever* want to see, or smell, or in any other way sense a cigarette in your possession again," Dolly began slowly. "I don't *ever* want to see Larry Llama or Joe Camel or the Marlboro Man or any of those other bastards on or anywhere near you again. Are we clear?" She walked back around the desk and deliberately took her chair. "Now, what happened in this room stays in this room. Forever. Unless . . . I catch you or find out or even *suspect* you've so much as touched another cigarette again. Then I call my sister, and I open my big fat mouth and don't shut it again until you've been grounded for *five* years. Understood?"

Her niece nodded, a scared expression on her face. Dolly returned her attention to the vote sheets on her clipboard.

"Now go. You need to meet up with your teacher. I'll introduce your class from the Floor."

Jennifer scurried out, and Dolly raised her eyes to watch her departing form. She rested her chin on her hands, recalling again the tiny pink fingers reaching out to her face, the little eyes and mouth screwed up in annoyance at having been awakened from a nap. . . . She slammed her clipboard shut, checked her watch and stood to head over to the Senate chamber.

The first push on the door did nothing. Nor did the second. It took a full, shoulder-down assault for it to fly open ahead of some splintering wood, and Murphy Moran picked himself off the gravel. He was still breathing hard from running twenty-two floors, after impatiently waiting a full five seconds for upper-floor elevators that would not come.

He examined the broken board Lambert must have used to wedge the door shut, then looked up to see Lambert himself in full cammos, black and green grease paint on his face. He glowered at him from behind an extremely lethal-looking automatic pistol.

Lambert grunted in recognition but kept the barrel on his chest. "What are you doing here?"

Heart hammering, Murphy threw his hands up. "You're cool! Simons sent me up. In case you needed help."

A line of doubt appeared through the paint on Lambert's brow. "The chief knows I'm here?"

Murphy thought for a moment, saw Lambert's index finger inside the trigger guard. He decided to play it bold. "He didn't get to be CEO by being *dumb,* did he." He watched Lambert for a reaction, saw the man still wasn't persuaded. "He figured with things getting so fucked up over the weekend, you were gonna need all the help you could get."

Lambert lowered the gun a hair. "I don't need any damn help. You tell him his precious memo will be taken care of momentarily."

Murphy wondered: What memo? But said: "Well, there's nothing more to do downstairs. So Simons wants me up here, make sure you don't screw this up, too."

Lambert's eyes flashed anger for a moment, then looked Murphy up and down, from boat shoes to once-in-blue-moon socks to even rarer coat and tie. "So you're here to help, huh? Why, you handy with a fifty-caliber gun?"

Murphy shrugged. "Always a first time for everything. I was pretty good at target practice in Boy Scouts."

Lambert shook his head sadly, then seemed to remember something. "You know, now that you mention it." He walked to a duffel bag and lifted out an eight-millimeter video camera. "Maybe I could use you after all. I was gonna put it on a tripod, but you miss out on a lot that way. Here. Just follow the action. Think you can handle that?"

Murphy looked through the viewfinder, hit the record button with his thumb. "This for your highlight reel?"

"All right, Mr. Boy Scout, just shut up and keep the camera steady, okay?" Lambert set the gun down and began walking toward the northeast corner of the building, where a long, high-tech rifle sat on a tripod. "Station Alpha. Here I can pick 'em off individually in the vehicle. It's a tough shot. I'm firing downward at moving targets behind glass, possibly smoked glass. Oswald had it easy in comparison." Lambert pointed across the roof. "Which is why we have fallbacks."

He walked as he talked, moving to a heavy machine gun that waited with a long belt of ammo stretched out to one side. "Station Bravo is the fifty-cal, in case I can't get a shot with the rifle. Few hundred rounds with this baby takes out a half dozen targets in under ten seconds. And if that don't do the trick, we have Station Charlie: the rocket."

Lambert stepped over to where his shoulder-launched anti-tank weapon was assembled and loaded. He stroked the rocket lovingly. "Yeah, this baby takes care of the whole bus, need be."

Murphy studied the weaponry through the video camera, then focused on Lambert. "And then? After you've blown up a third of the Florida Senate, you get away . . . how?"

Lambert nodded at an enormous coil of black rope at the northwest corner of the building. "Rappel down, got a Suzuki stashed behind a bush. Company jet flies me out of the country." Lambert stared straight into the camera. "With Lambert Security, the client gets years of operational experience. Complete planning, from reconnaissance to post-op withdrawal. A clean job, start to finish."

He walked back toward the eastern side of the roof and, with a glance up Monroe Street, noticed the approaching school bus. "Showtime!"

On the backseat, several empty rows between them and the nearest senator, Dunbar kept his voice to a murmur: "We'll get T.C. first, then we can come back down and get Senator Cruz."

Jeena shook her head. "No time. If we don't get Gus before they go into session, we lose him for good. Face it, my way's best."

Dunbar rubbed his jaw with the back of his hand, eyeing the small knapsack at his feet containing their thoroughly underwhelming kidnap kit: duct tape, hunting knife, faux-Amazon blowgun and Bolling's eyeglass case with the tranquilizer darts. "I don't like it," he said at length.

"Don't worry. I can handle it. I just wish I still had one of my slut outfits." She grinned, took Dunbar's hand. "Look at it this way: I'll finally find out if I'm really sexy or if it was just the clothes."

Lambert loaded a cartridge with the bolt and peered down the long gun through the telescopic sight. "After immobilizing the vehicle by neutralizing the driver, we can proceed to take out individual targets," he narrated. "This is the preferred method to simply igniting the fuel tanks with heavy-caliber shells. Once a fire is lit, it becomes impossible to verify whether a target has been eliminated or merely wounded. . . . Hello! I believe we have here a primary target! Maybe we'll start with her, instead. . . ."

Murphy kept the camera on Lambert with one hand and with the other picked up a pair of binoculars at his feet, focused on the bus. There, in the backseat, was Jeena, head turned away, talking to someone beside her.

He snapped his eyes back in alarm, saw Lambert's thumb flick the safety and his index finger move toward the trigger guard . . . and realized he had less than a second to act. He cleared his throat loudly: "You know, I was wondering about the clothes you wear all the time. I know cammos help you blend in with the jungle or desert or wherever. But here, in an office setting, I think *I* blend in better wearing a jacket and tie than you do in those." He reached out and awkwardly pushed Lambert's shoulder, sending the rifle barrel askew.

Lambert turned on him, eyes ablaze, lifted a warning finger: "Don't *ever* touch a man taking a shot! Just aim the damn camera and keep your theories and your hands to yourself."

Murphy muttered an apology, watched as Lambert closed one eye to sight through the scope again and saw his finger settle on the trigger. He glanced down at the bus, still in range, and gulped again, then focused on the man's temple, where a sideburn descended just past his ear, wound back his fist and let loose a wild roundhouse.

Hot pain buzzed up his arm as Lambert's shriek filled his ears. He ignored both, watched the school bus slide past and turn the corner toward Duval Street, then dove on top of the prone colonel.

Dunbar pulled T.C. aside within seconds of stepping off the bus, leaving Jeena to track down Gus Cruz. It took her all of five minutes. As usual, he was holding down a favorite spot on the fourth-floor rotunda, hitting up dog track and beer distributor lobbyists for money or a job or both.

She took him by the elbow and, with her best Ruth Ann Bronson throaty whisper, asked if he could spare a moment for the governor. She hadn't used a single suggestive word, yet she was rewarded with immediate ogling of her fully covered body as she led him to one of the upper-floor elevators.

"You sure you never worked for Martin Remy?" the polyester-suited Cuban asked conversationally.

She smiled vaguely and shook her head, eyes locked on the numbers above the elevator door that flashed upward ever-so-agonizingly slowly. She knew that letting her gaze wander even a little meant acknowledging Cruz's idiotic leer. Out the corner of an eye, she saw him trying to peek down her dress. It had a high collar and she was wearing an industrial-strength bra, but that wasn't dissuading the little pervert any.

"Maybe you got a sister works for him? I thought for sure I saw a girl looked just like you at—"

Jeena shook her head sharply, watched the indicator light climb through seventeen, blink off for a long moment, light up at eighteen.

"I knew the governor would come around," Gus boasted. "You know I'm the president of the Cuban-American Freedom Association."

She decided the elevator was *never* going to get to the top. "You mentioned that."

"I was thinking, to bring democracy to Cuba, it would be useful to have a Caribbean office, maybe in the Virgin Islands. I would need an assistant to travel with me to set it up . . . if you're not busy after session, perhaps May—"

Finally, the bell sounded and the doors popped open to Dunbar and T. C. Tuttle waiting at the landing. She smiled with relief, and Dunbar quickly led them to the roof access.

"What's the governor want with you, T.C.?" Gus asked. "I thought you were voting *against* him?"

T.C. hissed at him, grinned widely for Dunbar, forehead sweating. "Dumb Meskins. Never know what fool nonsense is gonna pop outta their mouths."

Dunbar motioned them ahead, fumbled at the backpack's zipper to remove the blowgun as T.C. pushed the door open and then froze: Framed against blue sky was Murphy Moran, one swollen hand tucked against his belly, the other unsteadily holding a machine pistol.

On the gravel roof behind him was a pile of green-and-black camouflage clothing, right beside a giant bundle of shouting rope.

One senator after another took the Floor and delivered long, rambling, artless speeches about why they were voting to lift the unfair burden the state had placed on the weary shoulders of law-abiding, taxpaying tobacco companies. Most read from a printed card of helpful "talking points" that seemingly every lobbyist in Tallahassee had been distributing that morning.

Adult decision, Dolly had heard dozens of times already. *Why should government punish an industry because individuals made an adult decision blah, blah, blah. . . .*

The vote was a lock. The governor had lost—just as she'd hoped for so many months. And yet when her turn came to speak, she planned to waive her time and sit, she was still so angry. Jennifer's cigarette rebellion had summoned memories of Ramon's latest deterioration. How he couldn't even lift his head anymore. How each breath, ever slighter than the last, wheezed in and out . . .

And those images reminded her of the slimy Bart Simons, of his insufferable smirk, of the pained look he affected when he handed her the pictures . . . Hell, she had half a mind to vote with the governor, just to pay back the man's turpitude.

Yet such a vote, she knew, would be a pointless symbol accomplishing little beyond torpedoing her own career. An industry as big as tobacco could make or break a would-be Senate president. Her colleagues would be wary of supporting anyone who crossed such an important contributor, not to mention the likelihood that tobacco would recruit and finance an opponent to run against her in her own district.

She glanced down her row, saw that T. C. Tuttle's and Gus Cruz's seats both remained empty. She smiled at the fantasy that they'd miss the vote, thus eliminating RJH's margin of victory and allowing a single senator to upset the outcome. Now *that* would be fun: hold off until the end, make Simons sweat a little before finally casting her vote to override the governor. That ought to wipe the smirk off the bastard's face.

But no, T.C. and Gus would appear as the time drew near. No way would they miss a vote like this. She listened with half an ear to a Cuban senator from Hialeah explain how his family had left Havana because of Castro and how this tobacco lawsuit was just the sort of thing Castro would do.

Then, above in the visitor's gallery, she saw Simons enter with his little lackey in tow and take his seat in the empty front row of the walled-off VIP section reserved for him. The son-of-a-bitch hypocrite was wearing another one of his "designed-by-kids" ties. She daydreamed again about holding the deciding vote, about watching him dangle as he wondered how big a mistake he'd made trying to blackmail her. . . .

"*Shut the door,*" Murphy ordered quietly. "Dunbar, right? Why are you here?"

Dunbar reached back to comply as Jeena took a closer look at the mass of yelling rope. Somewhere inside was a human, his cursing muffled by layers of cord. She noticed the camouflage outfit beside the rope and realized she knew *which* human.

"I rec'nize you. You work for Bart Simons," T.C. declared, then blinked, suddenly aware he was in the company of agents for both men to whom he'd promised his single vote. He made a show of checking his watch, turned for the door. "My goodness, *look* at the time. Well, y'all tell Bollin' I'll have to meet with him some other—"

"Stop," Murphy said, then queried Dunbar. "The governor's coming *here*?"

On the gravel rooftop, a head emerged from the rope bundle, twisted until its chin was clear, then resumed cursing Murphy. T.C. took one look and recoiled in horror: "It's *him*! The crazy s'um bitch kidnapped me! Made me miss Martin Remy's pool party!"

Murphy with one foot rolled the bundle over so Lambert's cursing was at least pointed in a different direction. "Why are you here?" he repeated.

This time, Gus stepped forward proudly. "We're here to see the governor. He has agreed to my proposition."

Murphy scowled skeptically, kept the gun pointed vaguely at the two senators as he turned back to Dunbar and Jeena.

Dunbar cleared his throat. "Actually, they're here to pass a little time. Just enough, in fact, so they happen to miss a particular Floor vote."

Gus and T.C. looked at one another in stunned silence, then at Dunbar and Jeena, finally appealed to Murphy. Murphy ignored them. "And whose idea is this?"

Jeena opened her mouth to take the blame, but Dunbar beat her to it. "Mine," he said. "All mine. The governor knows nothing about this."

"Bull-*sheeyit!*" T.C. howled. "The dep'ty chief of staff runnin' amok? That what we s'posed to believe? Forget it! Bollin' Waites has double-crossed me for the last time!"

He started for the door again but stopped when Murphy aimed the gun at the top button of his tangerine sport coat. "That's about enough." He waved the pistol toward a vent pipe sticking six feet out of the roof. "You two: over there. Dunbar, there's some rope in that bag. Also some sort of commando knife."

Jeena traded a look of amazement with Dunbar before he scrambled to Lambert's equipment bag, dug a bit and came up with one small coil of rope, about fifty feet worth. He cut off two, ten-foot segments, walked to the senators, and with seamanlike efficiency bound their hands in front of them, then the two pairs of hands to each other around the vent pipe.

Murphy watched Dunbar curiously for a moment. "Can I ask how you were planning to do this by yourselves? Without a weapon?"

Dunbar finished the knots, then wrapped them with duct tape until no rope was visible. "We brought a blowgun with some tranquilizer darts."

"Tranquilizer?" Murphy asked, eyeing the still-screaming rope bundle.

Dunbar nodded at the knapsack at his feet. Murphy with one good arm loaded the blowgun, then pulled apart some coils of rope.

"Wait!" Jeena yelled. "Ask him what he did with Ruth Ann Bronson!"

"Don't know what you're talkin' about!" the rope bundle screamed. "Don't know what any of you are fuckin' talkin' about!"

Murphy sighed apologetically. "He's been this way ever since I hit him. I haven't been able to get a single useful answer out of him." With a deep breath, he blew out the dart. The cursing stopped.

Murphy started loading the duffel with Lambert's various guns, ammo clips, rockets for his anti-tank launcher. He considered the set of camouflage clothing and boots, stuffed them into the bag as well.

Jeena studied the bit of exposed buttock between the coils of line where Murphy's dart had stuck. "Is he *naked* under all that?"

"In case he gets out, I wanted to make it harder for him to leave unnoticed." Murphy regarded Gus and T.C., who stood openmouthed at the turn of events. "I was thinking we ought to do the same with those clowns, but I guess they're not going anywhere. Your boyfriend really does know his knots.

Me, I just kept going until I was out of rope." He smiled and shrugged at Jeena. "Guess I'm really not much of a sailor."

Dunbar tucked knife and duct tape back into the knapsack and studied the bird's nest of rope wrapping Lambert. "Looks like enough line to get down this building." He blinked at Murphy. "If you're working for Simons, then how come you're helping us?"

"Formerly working for Simons." Murphy nodded at Lambert. "I came up here because I had a hunch about him. Turned out I was right. He was planning to blow up the bus y'all rode over here in." He lifted his now-purple right hand with a grimace. "I think I broke it hitting him."

Jeena moved to it automatically and had her fingers on his forearm before recalling the few short minutes on her couch just days earlier. She reddened and consciously fought the urge to let go of his flesh as if it were something infected. "You should get that checked," she said as neutrally as she could manage. "Maybe have it X-rayed."

Out a corner of his eye, Murphy watched Dunbar's reaction, then, when the coast was clear, gave her a quick wink. "I think I'll do that."

She blushed once more, then realized there was a new blue streak splitting the air, this time from T.C.:

"—a fuckin' federal offense, is what y'all are lookin' at, if you don't get your asses back here and cut me free this goddamn minute! False fuckin' imprisonment! Look it up! I made a promise I'd vote on this override, and so help me God, I'll—"

"You did more than just promise," Murphy said quietly. "You took a cash bribe, and that *is* a federal offense, so let's not start bandying around jail time, okay? Senator?"

Dunbar pointed to his watch. "We're getting close, if we want to get down there in time."

Murphy started toward the door when T.C. yelled: "I ain't takin' this shit from two flunkies and a whore, goddamn it all!"

Jeena stopped in mid-stride, stiffened. "What did you say?"

"You heard me," T.C. continued. "I seen your pi'ture up on the Internet. I bet you went up to the camera knowin' exactly what you were doin', too!"

Her face reddened again, this time with rage. Dunbar reached to grab her back, but it was too late. She pulled the assault knife from the knapsack, unsheathed it as she stalked toward the suddenly quiet senators and, ears roaring with the sound of her blood, she tore and slashed, cut and ripped amid terrified yowling, until finally she backed away, gathered her breath to survey her handiwork: two middle-aged state legislators, tied to each other at the wrists around a metal pipe, sweating with fear, and, save for their shoes, buck naked.

T. C. Tuttle and Gus Cruz exhaled with relief, then watched silently as she walked their mutilated clothing to the edge of the building and tossed it over, before she and her male companions filed through the roof access and pulled the door shut behind them.

The chamber's rhetoric had been pitch-perfect. Every bought-and-paid-for senator mouthing the lines legislative affairs had dreamed up, Murphy Moran had polished, and some 1,300 lobbyists had disseminated. The gospel according to RJH.

Through it all, Bartholomew Simons barely heard a word. The sense of serenity he'd allowed himself over the weekend was gone, thanks to know-it-all Moran. With Lambert finally getting a line on the memo and Martin Remy providing an expensive but certain guarantee of the borderline votes, he'd figured the loose ends had finally been tied up. All of that, now, had gone to hell. Because Moran's damned rumor had checked out: The governor's votes *had* been caravanned to the Capitol under police escort. And yes, the reason *was* because Tuttle claimed to have been kidnapped.

The whole project seemed on the brink of disaster. The memo, MRK93-1321, still was unaccounted for, as was Lambert. That by itself wouldn't necessarily have worried him. The man over the years had always gotten the job done, even if he'd never been particularly punctual about reporting in. But now he had to consider Lambert's tardy report alongside the troubling rumors Moran had brought to his attention, as well as the even more troubling fact that, despite the rapidly approaching appointed hour, two seats on the Senate Floor remained empty: T. C. Tuttle and Agustin Cruz. Both RJH votes. Or were they? Because why should the governor need to protect *his* votes because of something that had happened to Tuttle? Unless Tuttle was playing both sides . . .

Simons fumed inwardly at his decision to remain low-key. He should have been direct. Buy those votes he could, let Lambert take care of the problem children: Tuttle, James, Kelsey, Nichols. If he'd done that, he wouldn't be here now, sweating the final minutes. He made a mental note: The next state legislature that messed with him, no more Mr. Nice Guy.

He craned his neck over the rail to see the double doors at the rear of the chamber, but they remained closed, a blue-blazered sergeant at either side. He ticked Tuttle and Cruz off his list, quickly counted the remaining names in the two columns on his clipboard. Without them, they still won twenty-six to twelve.

Of course, one of those twenty-six was Madame Rules Chairman, their one vote who had refused to take either quasi-legal campaign contribution or extra-legal consulting fee. He remembered how she'd slapped him, the pure hatred that had burned in her eyes. . . . If she switched, that would make it twenty-five to thirteen, and RJH would lose.

Of course, she wouldn't switch. He wouldn't let her. He patted the TV remote in his pocket. Of course, if Tuttle and Cruz came back at the last minute, and they, too, switched, then he was in trouble. Then he'd need to improvise. . . . And for that he needed Lambert.

"Andrews," he snapped. "Go find the colonel."

The woman was clearly a schoolteacher, T.C. decided, the way she herded the children single-file away from the picture windows, quickly stepping between stragglers who stared back at the two naked men who'd appeared on ropes from the sky, pounding the glass, opening and shutting their mouths inaudibly. Within seconds, she and her young charges disappeared, leaving the two senators standing on the thin ledge outside.

"Not surprisin', I guess," T.C. said after a time. "Ain't exactly like seein' Redford and Newman in the raw."

"We're *not* in the raw!" Gus complained.

"Yeah, I s'pose our shoes and the socks on our peckers make us presentable."

Gus looked up angrily. T.C., as usual, had been wearing loafers without any socks, and now Gus' new wingtips were chafing his ankles. "At least we *have* socks, thanks to me."

T.C. studied himself unhappily. One of Gus's sheer black dress socks was held in place by one of the rubber bands that always lived around T.C.'s wrist. "So my dick's gonna smell like a stinkin' Meskin foot. Great."

All the windows on lower floors were covered by a strong metal grille, not that they had enough rope to get any farther anyway. They'd shimmied up the vent pipe through mutual exertion, with more genital-to-belly, genital-to-thigh, and genital-to-genital contact than he cared to remember, then used their teeth to unwrap the duct tape and start loosening their knots. They'd considered getting more rope by unwrapping Lambert, but ultimately decided to let sleeping lunatics lie.

Beside him, Gus pushed his face against the glass to look for other bystanders. "Oh, man, if I don't get down there to vote, I'm gonna be in *big* trouble. I already spent like half my money."

T.C. shaded his eyes as he peered in and realized Gus was right. They had less than fifteen minutes to get inside, find some clothes, run down eighteen flights of stairs to the Senate chamber and cast their votes. "All right," he said decisively. "Ain't no one comin'. You gotta do it."

Gus's eyes widened, and he peered over the ledge more than two hundred feet to the concrete and brick courtyard. "Come on, T.C., why me?"

"We been through this already. You got twenty pounds on me, minimum. Plus you got pointier shoes. Now go!"

With a final jerk of his hips, Lambert rolled himself right up against the wall, giving himself enough slack to wiggle his fingers free and extricate himself from the remaining coils of rope. He stood, groggy, and surveyed first the rooftop, then his own nakedness.

Over the railing he saw the two likewise naked senators on the ledge below and stepped back so they wouldn't see him. He squinted out into a bright blue sky, down at the empty courtyard twenty-two stories below, at his disabled weapons across the rooftop. . . .

With a start, it came to him: He needed to bolt.

It had always been in the back of his mind that someday an op wouldn't go right and he'd have to abort. Well, that someday was today. He was damned lucky the dart had worn off as quickly as it had, before cops showed up. Now he needed to take advantage of that break and move. . . . He still had his money safely tucked away, more than he ever could have dreamed he'd have. All he needed was to get out now, while he could use it.

He checked the roof access door. Locked, as he'd figured. He walked to one edge, peered down and saw some clothes scattered in the bushes. Quickly, he gathered up the rope, made one end fast to a metal vent pipe sticking out of the roof and tossed the rest down. Onto the bike, out of town somewhere he could regroup, figure out a plan. In a way, he realized, it was lucky he hadn't killed anybody yet. If he had, the cops would be that much more excited about nailing him . . . especially if it had been the governor or a senator or something. Then they'd have turned it into some kind of national emergency, plastered his face all over the CNN—

Senator Nichols!

The chief still had that remote! If he used it, they'd throw up a dragnet so tight there was no way he could get out. . . . He swallowed hard, considered his options, decided. He'd just have to stop him.

He shook his head to clear away the effects of the drug, got a good grip on the rope, and climbed up and over the wall.

Gus took a final look down, gathered up some slack line in his hands and moved his feet up onto the plate glass. He closed his eyes and started hopping lightly on the window, swinging out a few inches each time.

"Come on, you tubby, greasy Meskin!" T.C. taunted. "Gonna have to get a little more into it than that!"

Gus slowly increased the strength of his kicks, until he swung several feet out beyond the ledge each time before hitting the glass.

"Jump, greasy Meskin! Jump!"

Gus jumped as hard as he could . . . and his patent leather soles lost their grip on the glass . . . and Gus twisted in mid-air, grimaced in anticipation, eyes and teeth clenched tight . . . and slammed face and belly into the plate glass window. He crumpled to the ledge, emitting a long, soft moan.

T.C. studied the glass closely. As Gus hit it full on, the entire panel had shuddered. Like it wasn't secure at the far end . . . He walked along the ledge, dug his fingers into the crack and tugged. "I'll be damned," he said, sliding the window open. "I guess we shoulda checked first."

Jeena listened to the debate with mounting self-loathing. What was going on down there, she'd helped bring about. With attention-grabbing clothes and industry-written pitch, she'd lured more than a couple Democrats away from the governor, and kept more than one Republican securely in the fold.

"Bad news," Dunbar said, sliding into the seat beside her. "I can't even get Rex Kelsey or Choo-Choo James to talk to me. We got twelve votes and that's it."

"*Damn* it!" Jeena breathed. "One more. That's all we need. Just one."

When they'd gotten down to the public gallery and seen the two "missing"

Democrats in their seats, they'd at first been elated, deciding that the whole kidnapping rumor had been a false alarm, and that the camouflaged gun-nut had planned all along to kill the governor's supporters, pure and simple.

Then they'd learned the real reason why Kelsey and James hadn't been reachable Sunday, why both still looked hung over, and they'd fallen into a deep funk.

Jeena took Dunbar's hand. "Still no word from Ruth Ann?"

Dunbar shook his head. "Sorry." He nodded across the horseshoe-shaped gallery, at Bartholomew Simons in the VIP section. "It's that bastard. I just know he's behind Remy's bribes. Just like I know he was behind the psycho on the roof. Of course, it'll take months to prove it. And by then the lawsuit's ancient history."

She looked across the gallery and her grip on Dunbar's wrist tightened: "It's him! The psycho!"

"What?"

She squinted, shook her head. "I swear he was just there. . . . Dunbar, he must have gotten loose! We need to call the cops! If he hasn't done anything with Ruth Ann already, he'll *definitely* try now—"

"Try what?" asked Ruth Ann Bronson from the aisle. "And will one of you tell me what the fuck is going on? Why are there cops all over the rotunda? And why was there an FDLE agent at my house?"

Jeena jumped up into a bear hug, finally dragging Ruth Ann down into the chair beside hers. "Where *were* you? We've been looking for you for two days!"

"The beach house." Ruth Ann managed to extricate herself from Jeena's grip. "I found myself with a ton of unexpected paperwork Saturday and took it there. It's the only place I can get anything done. Why? What's up?"

"Christ, Ruth Ann, I've been worried sick! Friday night this psycho breaks into my house with a gun, and I was certain he'd come after you, too, when—"

"Jeena!" Dunbar shook her shoulder. "One vote! The memo!"

"Oh! You're right! I hid it in the microphone. . . . It's in Senator Nichols' microphone!" Jeena glanced down onto the Floor, back up at Ruth Ann, clapped a hand over her mouth, looked plaintively at her former boss. Ruth Ann studied her, then Dunbar, both watching her expectantly. "Okay. What? What are you two talking about? What memo?"

Jeena traded glances with Dunbar, took a deep breath: "The guy who broke into my house? He was working for Simons, looking for a memo . . . which I found in one of the boxes that Simons came for that day."

Ruth Ann blinked. "You took something out of those boxes?"

"I was planning to tell you. . . . That morning Simons came, in fact. I was gonna show it to you, ask what you wanted to do about it. Then after they took back the boxes, I thought my house was broken into and searched, and turns out it was, and then that nutcase came back the other night, looking—"

"What is it?"

"It's the smoking gun, is what it is," Dunbar said, pointing across the gallery at Simons. "It takes *that* man down."

"I swear, the only person I told was Dunbar," Jeena explained. "I was afraid if word got out, it would hurt your reputation in town. You know, leaking a client's confidential documents? And then, after Friday, I thought they'd come looking for you next, thinking you might have it, or copies of it. . . . Anyway, I made Dunbar promise not to say a word to anyone until we knew you were safe. And, now that you are . . ."

Ruth Ann stared with narrowed eyes at Simons. "Somehow I get the feeling there's a longer story behind this, but, cutting to the chase, if this gets out, Simons and Remy and those guys are fucked?"

"Big-time," Dunbar answered.

She turned toward Jeena with a grin. "So what are we waiting for? Get it out!"

Jeena nodded slowly, then faster, stood to climb past them to the aisle. Dunbar grabbed her wrist: "They won't let you pass a note in. I already tried with Choo-Choo. Soffit's sealed the chamber. No notes."

She sat back down, stared at Senator Nichols in her big brown chair not ten yards away, watching a colleague deliver a speech about adult choices and personal responsibility.

"All right, then, if we can't send a note, we'll just get her attention some other way."

The crowd in the noisy rotunda parted as the two trouserless men approached, then grew quiet as the lobbyists recognized them. Each wore a blue blazer with a Florida Senate crest—extras from the pages' cloakroom—and a black sock on his penis. The phalanx closed around them curiously as the two confronted the burly, unsmiling sergeant-at-arms guarding the double doors to the Senate chamber.

"Son," T.C. explained, "I been servin' behind them doors since you were in diapers. So I'll ask nicely: Get the fuck outta my way!"

The sergeant wouldn't budge. "Sorry, sir. You're not appropriately dressed. Senate rules—"

"Senate rules say gentlemen must wear a jacket." He thrust a sleeve in the man's face. "The fuck you call this?"

The guard cast a cautious eye up and down T.C.'s body. "Sir, you have no pants. No underwear."

"Fuck underwear! Rules don't say nothin' 'bout underwear! Or pants, neither! Now open the motherfuckin' door before—"

A blur of Italian silk and thousand-dollar shoes burst through the throng and knocked T.C.'s bare ass onto the cold marble floor. "Son of a bitch!" Martin Remy screamed, his hands around T.C.'s throat. "You seen that goddamn Web site? You seen what's on there? You know what the Christian Broadcasters did when they saw this this morning? Dropped me like a hot potato, you bastard! Half a million contract, out the window. You owe me, pal! Five hundred large!"

T.C. struggled for breath, thought he felt himself passing out when he heard the words he'd heard in nightmares his entire Senate career: "FBI! Freeze!"

The weight lifted from his chest as he saw Special Agent Johnny Espinosa barge through the lobbyists, badge in one hand, a fistful of clinking handcuffs in the other. With astonishing speed, Espinosa snapped cuffs over wrists, reciting from memory as he went: "Martin-Alexander-Remy, Agustin-Cruz-Valdez, Teegan-Chaunce-Tuttle, you-are-under-arrest-for-bribery-of-a-public-official. You-have-the-right-to-remain-silent, the-right-to-an-attorney, if-you-cannot-afford-an-attorney-one-will-be-provided. . . ."

T.C. watched Gus shake his shoulders, eyes wide: "This is political persecution! My family fled Cuba to escape this!"

T.C. watched Espinosa ignore his fellow countryman and instead turn to the burly sergeant: "I also have warrants for the arrests of the following senators. Under no circumstance will you allow them to leave that chamber: Rex Kelsey, James 'Jumbo' Johnson, Leroy 'Choo-Choo' James . . ."

And as Espinosa struggled with Gus and Remy, T.C. saw the befuddled sergeant wonder whether to help or stay neutral, noticed the doors behind him unguarded . . . and with a clanking noise he saw was a handcuff chained to his right wrist, he slipped as stealthily as he could manage into the sanctuary of the Florida Senate.

———

Simons was searching for Andrews when he happened to notice the blonde across the gallery, where the governor's side had staked out the first three rows. She was familiar, he thought idly, then did a double take as he remembered why.

Yes, sure enough, it was the girl on the computer, the one who Lambert was supposed to have taken care of Friday night—the one who was supposedly a lobbyist for *their* side. Son of a bitch . . . If she was still alive, it meant Lambert had fucked it up . . . probably hadn't even recovered the memo yet. At the same time, Tuttle was claiming to have been kidnapped by a gun nut. . . .

Simons stared hard across the gallery, wondering how in hell he was going to deal with her *now*, and how he was going to wring Lambert's neck, when she began waving her arms. He squinted down at the Floor, back up at the girl, down at the Floor again . . . saw Senator Nichols idly turn toward the west gallery, catch sight of the girl, smile in recognition . . . then frown as the girl started pantomiming holding something before her mouth, pretending to talk into it, pointing urgently at Nichols' desk.

Simons watched with interest as Dolly Nichols touched her microphone, lifted it, watched the girl make an unscrewing motion with her hands. As a portly senator from Jacksonville wrapped up a pompous speech explaining how voting with tobacco was voting with God and country, he saw Dolly Nichols study her own microphone. He watched her grasp the end of her microphone, start unscrewing the cap . . . and he started to get a sinking feeling in his gut.

Dolly Nichols opened her microphone, peered inside, held it upside down, shook a shiny metal cylinder into her palm. A lipstick case. She unscrewed it, removed a piece of paper and slowly began unrolling and unfolding.

Simons sucked air through his teeth, quickly patted his pockets for the television remote, found it, pulled it from his pocket, studied the buttons. . . .

And from beneath him, a bright orange arm reached up to snatch the remote away.

It was Lambert, smudges of grease paint on his face, slashed sport coat and trousers on his body. Simons wondered where he'd come from, then noticed the half-open grate over the air vent, way down on the wall at the far end of the front row.

"The fuck do you think you're doing?" Simons hissed, reaching down to grab the remote back. "And why are your clothes all cut up?"

Lambert squirmed, cramped for space between Simons' legs and the low wall along the gallery's front row. "It's complicated, sir."

"I'm sure it is," Simons said. "I see you failed in two of your primary objectives the other night. I assume there was a compelling reason which you will enthusiastically share with me. In the meantime, let go of the goddamned remote!"

Dolly Nichols read the pink-smeared sheet of paper, then looked up over it. Looked right at Bartholomew Simons with uncontrolled rage. The same look she'd had after she'd slapped him, he recalled. She read the memo again, stared at him again.

"I can't let you use it, sir," Lambert said.

Simons looked down in disbelief. "Are you kidding? She's seen the memo, now she needs to die. *Quod erat demonstrandum.* End of discussion. Now give me the motherfucking remote before I break your neck!"

He leaned one knee down on Lambert's chest and moved one hand from the remote to Lambert's throat. The shift was all Lambert needed to slide his fingers under Simons' other hand, pry the cover off and pop out the batteries.

"What in fuck do you think you're—"

It only took an instant for Simons to realize the answer to his own question, but the instant was all it took for Lambert to get one of the two penlight batteries into his mouth. Simons immediately grabbed the second battery with one hand, tightening his grip on Lambert's throat with the other. "Okay. Quickly now, what is the problem?"

In her chair, Dolly Nichols laid down the memo, calmly screwed the foam cap back onto the microphone tube and pressed the white button on her desk to indicate to Soffit that she wanted to speak.

"God *damn* it, Lambert, she's getting ready to talk! Now give me the goddamned battery!"

With his free hand, Lambert fended off Simons' free hand. With his tongue, he tucked the battery into his cheek. "Thur, wuh need to 'bort!"

Simons scowled: *"What?"*

Lambert tucked the battery deeper. "Uh-bort! The thops, thief. They're onto us."

"No, they're onto *you*. Give me the battery."

Lambert shook his head. "I'll thallow it!"

Simons peered over the wall at Soffit nodding in acknowledgment to Nichols, flashing her a single finger. One more minute. Simons took a deep breath. "Okay. What is it you desire?"

"Out. Plane thakes me to Thouth 'Merica. You doan follow."

Simons pursed his lips. "Done."

Lambert thought for a moment. "An' my millun an' a half."

"And your million and a half."

"Fromith?"

"I promise," Simons said. "Give me the battery, and I'll get on my cell phone and tell the pilot you're coming."

Lambert pulled out the battery with a finger, wiped it on his torn jacket, handed it over. Simons plugged both batteries into the remote and pushed the lid into place. Lambert watched quietly a moment, then cleared his throat. "Sir, you were gonna call the pilot. . . ."

Simons climbed back up into his seat. "I'm a tobacco executive, you moron. I lied. Get over it." He pointed the remote at the smoked-glass window behind Soffit and with a manicured thumb decisively clicked the power button. His expression flattened, then reddened as, below, on the Senate Floor, absolutely nothing happened.

"Lambert . . ." He clicked the button a second time, then rapidly, over and over. "I imagine there is a good explanation why Madame Chairman is not dying?"

"She put it down." Lambert sulked, pointing at Dolly Nichols, at the microphone which now lay on her glass-topped desk. "Glass is a good insulator. I told you to wait until she was holding it."

Simons stared at Nichols, at the instrument of her death lying harmlessly beside her. "So that's it? She's escaped?"

Lambert shrugged. "No. It's still hot. If she touches it . . . You promised . . ."

As Simons tried to mentally regroup, tried somehow to will Dolly Nichols to reach out and touch the shiny metal cylinder, a commotion began on the Floor. Three dozen heads turned toward the chamber doors.

With a shameless swagger, a bare-assed Dean of the Senate marched down the aisle and squeezed behind Nichols' chair to his desk.

T. C. Tuttle boldly planted himself in his seat, felt himself sticking to the leather, decided to stand again. He glanced up at the dais, nodded importantly at Soffit, noticed Bart Simons in the front row of the east gallery, nodded at him as well. He buttoned his blazer, reached to stick his hand in his pants pocket, remembered he wasn't wearing any pants, casually lay his hands on the back of his chair instead.

It was going to be all right. It would take more than one double-crossing, black-looking, Cuban-sounding federal cop to trap old T. C. Tuttle, that was for damn sure. As long as he was on the Senate Floor, he was untouchable. Then, once the vote was taken and the celebration erupted, he'd drift into the Members' Lounge and from there into the unmarked closet that was really a spiral staircase down to the third-floor Majority Office, itself only a few yards from the members' elevator to the parking garage. A quick flight to Fort Lauderdale, then to Nassau until the heat was off . . . Enjoy his quarter million in his Bahamian bank account, sip umbrella drinks on the beach and watch the pretty girls stroll by. Yup, you had to get up pretty early in the morning to catch T. C. Tuttle, as FBI boy Johnny Espinosa was finding out right about now.

From the dais, Soffit called on him, gave him the Floor. T.C. lifted his microphone grandly, heard handcuffs jingling, quickly switched hands and launched into his speech: "Senators, there comes a time when we gotta remember our duties as Americans. . . ."

He noticed smirks and giggles from the public gallery and realized he felt unusually chilly. He glanced down, saw that his sock had fallen off and he was dangling on the cold, glass desktop. Hastily, he bent for the sock, pulled it over his member, secured it with a fresh rubber band, then continued: "As I was sayin', like many of you in this very chamber, I'm sorry to admit we were led astray by our governor last year. Tricked into votin' for somethin' we didn't know nothin' about. Now the scales have fallen from our eyes, and we see it was all about punishin' a honest, taxpayin' business for manufacturin' a product that adults—"

Out of a corner of his eye, he noticed a disturbance in the west gallery, saw the crowd part for a lanky, silver-haired man as he strolled down the steps to sit in the front row and, with an easy smile, stare straight at T.C.

"Choice, I mean, choosin' . . . freedom . . . legal product, le-le-legal," T.C. stammered, his throat clamping shut at the sight of the governor's grin. He began to wheeze, his eyes fixated on the governor's. In his mind, the image became a vision of Bolling Waites pointing the gun at his crotch, of Bolling Waites smiling as he knelt beside him with a hunting knife, ready to skin and dress him. "Puh-puh-puh-prod—"

His breath caught again, and he realized he wasn't wheezing. In fact, he wasn't breathing at all. The governor's face started growing larger, began spinning, and T.C. reached around him, grabbing, grasping for support . . . and his handcuffs clinked against the glass of his desk, then clinked once against the glass of Dolly Nichols' desk. . . .

And with one bulging eye, he saw a white spark arc from his chained wrist, heard a loud *bang* from the vote boards on the wall, felt a terrific jolt in his chest, and, as he began falling, saw the sock pop off his penis and sail across the Senate chamber.

Dolly Nichols watched in fascination as two barrel-chested sergeants lifted the unconscious but breathing T.C. and hauled him to the rear of the chamber, laid him out on one of the blue vinyl benches reserved for the pages.

"Shouldn't we call an ambulance?" one of the freshman senators suggested.

On the dais, Soffit shrugged. "Nah. He'll be okay. Just a bit overexcited. Now, please, senators, take your seats. It is now one fifty-six. We made a commitment to vote on this at two p.m."—he flashed a nervous grin toward Simons in the viewing gallery—"and send it over to Speaker Powers' House. I intend to keep that commitment."

Dolly watched the interplay between Soffit and Simons and felt sick to her stomach. Here was the president of the Florida Senate, publicly panting and yipping to please a corporate executive who didn't even live in the flipping state. She studied Simons again in the VIP gallery, felt the loathing rise for the beady eyes, the smug mouth.

She glanced back down at her vote sheet, ran through the columns again. With a pen, she scratched off Agustin Cruz. Word was he wouldn't be coming back. That made the vote twenty-seven to twelve. And now, with T.C. out of commission, it was down to twenty-six to twelve, and that made her pulse race.

One vote. Any of those twenty-six votes switching would make it twenty-five to thirteen and throw it to Bolling. Any single vote. Her vote . . .

"What about the vote board?" one of the governor's loyalists asked. All its lights had flashed and popped as T. C. Tuttle had fallen, a concurrence the governor's senators questioned but which Soffit had already ruled was mere coincidence. "How can we vote without the board?"

Soffit grinned again. "The old fashioned way. Roll call. There's only forty of us. Actually, thirty-eight now. Shouldn't slow us down too much. We have only one speaker to go, Senator Nichols, but given where we are, I'm sure she'll agree to waive her time so we can move forward."

Dolly looked back up at Simons, felt her rage build anew. It wasn't fair, to change the rules specifically to attack a single industry as Bolling had done. . . . And yet, if any company deserved unfair persecution, Roper-Joyner sure as hell was it, the way they'd shamelessly and, judging from the memo, *methodically* gone after children, even secretly supplying a thousand of them with cigarettes for their marketing study . . .

She thought of Ramon, on the edge of death in his hospice bed. She thought of Jennifer, ready to pick up where he'd left off. A one-for-one replacement. Holding on to market share.

She studied her clipboard. One vote. It would be a doozy, she knew. United Industries would put out an alert to its members, direct them not to donate a red cent to Nichols' presidency fund, would in fact run an opponent against her in the Republican primary, would funnel millions from Big Tobacco to that opponent. . . .

She looked up at the viewing gallery, found Jennifer's sixth-grade class, found Jennifer. And she realized it was deathly still in the chamber, that every pair of eyes was on her. She blinked, turned toward the dais.

"Senator Nichols?"

"Yes?"

Soffit smiled unhealthily. "Glad to have you back. Do you waive your time?"

She glanced at the vote sheet, then at Simons, then at Jennifer, then at the vote sheet again. Dolly Nichols, Senate president. Dolly Nichols, governor. Dolly Nichols, vice-presidential material . . .

With a deep breath, she stood and held her head erect. "No, Mr. President. I do not."

Bartholomew Simons slowly stood, Lambert still prone at his feet, and with thin lips and squinty eyes watched Dolly Nichols mesmerize her colleagues.

"After eighteen years, I will not play the tobacco game any longer."

Dolly Nichols' unamplified voice rang crystal-clear. The chamber watched in rapt silence as she held aloft a single, pink-streaked sheet of paper with a shiny yellow sticker in one corner. "You all know what I mean, senators. They lie and cheat and hook our kids on their poison, then wink at us with a fat check come reelection time, and we turn the other way. . . ."

Simons eyed the remote control in his hand, gamely pointed it at the smoked-glass window behind the dais and clicked, then pointed it at Dolly Nichols and clicked. Nothing happened.

"It ain't gonna work anymore," Lambert said spitefully. "The battery's charge is all gone."

On the Floor, Nichols continued: "Well, it ends here. Today, senators, let's muster just a tiny fraction of the indignation we manage whenever we're discussing heroin dealers. . . ."

Simons watched for a long moment, a car wreck unfolding in front of him. They were about to lose the vote. . . . And then Nichols would run off a million copies of MRK93-1321 so every newspaper in the state, the country, even, could run it on its front page. And then, tomorrow, he would have to fly down to West Palm Beach and testify about it . . .

He shook the vision from his head and reached down to grab Lambert by the collar. "Get your ass down there and shut her up." He turned toward Soffit. "It's absurd, what she's saying. I don't know what she's talking about!"

Lambert hugged the metal base of the auditorium seat. "No way, sir. It's suicide. I could never get out."

"Then you'll just have to take one for the team, soldier," Simons said. "Come *on*! You call this loyalty? Now get down there!"

"Forget it, sir," Lambert squealed. "You shouldn't have lied to me about the plane. I'm not doing it."

Nichols frowned at the commotion, then at Soffit. "Mr. President, I suggest the gentleman in the east gallery is out of order and that the sergeants be directed to remove him—"

"Mind your own fucking business!" Simons growled. "And you, Soffit, *you* know how Tuttle would vote if he was awake! So vote him by proxy! That makes it twenty-six to thirteen. Veto overridden. Now *do* it!"

Soffit laughed nervously. "Mr. Simons, you know we can't vote by proxy here—"

"Mr. President," Dolly Nichols cut in, "I have to protest your giving the Floor to a visitor in the public gallery. Senate Rule fifty-three-point-oh-six clearly states—"

"Then wake the bastard up," Simons yelled. "If he's just unconscious, then get a doctor in here to wake him up and cast his vote!"

Soffit's face brightened, as if finally seeing something that had eluded him. "Right! Is there a doctor in the house? A nurse?"

From the opposite side of the gallery, a voice rang out: "Here!"

Soffit grinned, motioned her down onto the Floor. "Sergeant, open the doors for her. . . . And get a first-aid kit in here, too."

Nichols glared at him in disgust, glanced at the clock, then cleared her throat. "Members, as chair of the Committee on Rules and Calendar, I call attention to the time, which is now three minutes past the time-certain vote approved by the committee last week. I call the previous question and direct, under Senate Rule forty-one, Madame Secretary to commence a roll call vote."

The reading secretary put on her glasses and looked down at the lectern. "Senator Allman?"

"Yes."

"Senator Drayer?"

"No."

Simons stared in stunned disbelief at Nichols' parliamentary maneuver, then at the burned-out vote board. Tuttle was third from last, but at this rate it wouldn't take but a couple of minutes. "Soffit, you pussy, stop this! Who's running this show, you or her?"

Soffit's mouth opened and closed silently, just as the doors flung open and one of the sergeants escorted a sexy woman in minidress and heels into the chamber. Soffit nodded at her gratefully. "Ah, Miss Bronson. That's right, you were an emergency room nurse once, weren't you?"

Ruth Ann Bronson smiled back as she knelt beside the half-naked senator, brushed away the sock somebody had found but which nobody had cared to slip back onto Tuttle's sleeping member. Simons watched her unzip the first-aid kit, break open a packet of smelling salts, slowly pass it below Tuttle's nose.

The senator's head jerked once, twice and his eyes opened, then widened at the sight of Ruth Ann Bronson. She bent close to his ear and whispered something. With a blood-curdling scream, T.C. clutched at his privates and passed out again.

Ruth Ann Bronson turned to Soffit with a shrug, looked up at Simons with a wink.

"*Senator Foxman?*"

"*Yes.*"

"*Senator Horning?*"

"*Yes.*"

Simons sighed, released Lambert's neck to pull out a checkbook. He scribbled on one and tossed it at him. "Twenty million dollars. All right?

More fucking money than your whole backwoods family can even count. Now get down there. Go stick your pinky into her frontal lobe or whatever it is you learned from your Navy SEAL book. Just do it!"

"Senator Nichols?"

"No."

Lambert shook his head. "No way. Besides, it's too late, sir. She just voted."

Simons spun back toward the railing, studied the clipboard on his chair. Lambert was right. Seven more senators. Two more no votes. He would come up one short . . . unless he could prevent one of the no's from voting.

"Senator Soffit?"

"Yes."

One of the governor's remaining votes, Mike Uhfeld, was way on the far side of the Floor, too far for Lambert to get to in time . . . but the other, Matt Zimmer, was right below them, just a few feet beyond the rail. . . .

"Senator Tuttle? Senator Tuttle?"

Simons wrote out another check, dropped it on Lambert. "Forty million, Lambert. But I'm warning you. That's my last offer. You need to do Senator Zimmer, then get the memo from Nichols. Swallow it. Your stomach acids will do the rest."

Lambert kept his arms around the base of the chair but eyed the two checks on the carpeting. "Sir, I'd never get a chance to spend it. This is Florida. They'll fry me in the chair."

"Then you'll leave a nice inheritance for your wife and kids."

"I don't have a wife, sir. Or kids."

Simons winced. "Poor planning on your part does not constitute a crisis on mine. Now get *up!*"

Lambert glumly scooped up the checks, stuck them in a pocket of the slashed sportcoat and stood to lean out over the rail. "Which one's Zimmer?" he sulked.

Simons pointed. "There. Now jump."

Lambert considered the drop for a few moments, finally shook his head. "I don't know, chief—"

With one hand, Simons reached down, grabbed Lambert's ankle, and quickly and discreetly flipped him over the rail. "When I say jump," Simons said softly, "I expect an employee of mine to ask how high."

Lambert tumbled end over end through the air, limbs flailing . . . down, down and over the unaware senator to land on his desk, bones audibly snapping as they hit.

"*Senator Zimmer?*"

Matt Zimmer stared for a moment at the groaning body on his desk, finally glanced up at the dais. "No."

The secretary turned to Soffit. "Twenty-five yes, thirteen no. The override fails. The governor's veto is sustained."

A roar erupted in the west gallery as aides and supporters of the governor reached at him to clap him on the back or shake his hand. Simons watched bitterly as applause spread through the entire gallery, spilled over onto the Floor, where one senator after another scurried forward to ask Soffit's permission to change his vote from yes to no.

Simons crossed his arms over his chest and waited until Walter Soffit finally looked his way. "Soffit, you bastard, if you know what's good for you, you'll move for a recount right *now*. Do I make myself clear?"

Soffit studied the scene on the Floor, where governor's supporters and vote-changers both mobbed Dolly Nichols, all smiles and thumbs-up, and he banged his gavel. "Without objection, show the previous vote unanimously sustaining the governor's veto!" He glanced nervously at Simons. "Sergeants, please remove the rude gentleman from the visitors' gallery. The Senate is adjourned."

Simons felt powerful arms close on him roughly, shook them off and glared at Nichols one final time, then walked up and out of the gallery.

TUESDAY

On the barroom television, that morning's madhouse scene played itself out all over again: a pack of reporters, wide-eyed, shoving microphones and tape recorders at the smiling, silver-haired governor. Bolling Waites clearly relishing the moment, raising his arms, crowing to the crowd: "Eleven billion. That's *billion* with a *b*, make sure y'all get that down right. An eleven with one, two, three, four, five, six, seven, eight, *nine* zeroes!"

Some of the reporters shouted questions, and Bolling raised his arms again: "Maybe the jury woulda given more, maybe they wouldn't have. All I know is, we win. We had Big Tobacco on the ropes and they knew it." Bolling stared directly into the camera now. "No more concerts, car races or sporting events sponsored by tobacco. No more billboards. No more Larry Llama. Five hundred million dollars to the state of Florida for the next twenty-two years, adjusted for inflation. Not bad money if you can get it, huh?"

Another reporter shouted, "Why did they cave so fast?" With a twinkle visible through the TV, Waites flashed his wily grin, shrugged, noticed something out the corner of his eye. "Why don't you ask *him*?"

The camera shook and followed the pack as it mobbed a night-in-jail disheveled Bartholomew Simons and peppered him with questions about RJH's board of directors revoking his golden parachute, then firing him, all via a faxed letter to the holding cell where he awaited a bail hearing. Simons scowled, pushed his way down the steps to a waiting taxi.

The TV picture returned to the anchorman, who now had an FBI logo perched over one shoulder as he read: "A massive political corruption scandal in Tallahassee, federal authorities announced today. Nine state senators, including President Walter Soffit, plus prominent lobbyist Martin Remy are in custody, with more arrests expected. . . ."

Jeena and Dunbar turned from the television, hands still entwined, hers once more adorned with a half-carat, small-but-perfect stone on her ring finger, and sipped at their beers. Dolly Nichols toasted the end of the tobacco era in Florida politics, and Jeena, Dunbar, Murphy and Ruth Ann Bronson lifted their glasses with hearty cheers.

Dunbar turned toward Murphy and clapped him on the shoulder. "Thanks, man, for looking out for us. That nut really was gonna do what he said, wasn't he?"

Murphy shrugged. "Looked that way. I get the feeling we won't be seeing much of ol' *Colonel* Lambert for a good forty or fifty years." He took a swallow from his Sam Adams. "Seems the FBI guys were a bit puzzled about why he'd videotape his own crime. And they *still* can't figure out why T.C. and Gus were walking around with their peckers hanging out."

"So what's next?" Jeena asked. "Maybe a relaxing cruise on *Dark Horse*?"

Murphy laughed. "Trust me. A cruise is never relaxing for me, what with all the bruises and cuts I always end up with. But no, I heard some California legislators want a tobacco law letting *them* sue RJH, too. I figured I'd go give 'em a hand."

Dunbar whistled. "The anti-smoking groups out there have enough money to afford *you*?"

"I'm not going for the money." Murphy smiled. "I'm going for the fun."

A lobbyist behind them lit a cigarette, and Dolly Nichols turned on him. "Excuse me, but we were here first. Would you mind taking that somewhere else?"

The man instantly became indignant: "This is a *bar*, for Chrissake!"

From behind the polished counter, the bartender quickly moved in. "Yes, but it's a non-smoking bar."

"Since when?"

The barkeep winked at Dolly Nichols. "Since Madame President said so."

The lobbyist grumbled something about thought police but crushed out the cigarette and retreated to a back booth. Dolly mouthed the words *thank you* to the bartender and returned to her glass of Zinfandel.

Ruth Ann smiled at her. "Madame *President* . . . Sounds nice, huh?"

Dolly shrugged. "I suppose. But it's only temporary. The party's mad as hell at me. Roper-Joyner's their number-two contributor, nationally. They're trying to draft somebody, anybody, to replace me for the rest of this session. Then they'll run somebody against me in September, and they'll beat me."

"No, they won't!" Jeena pointed to the television, where the news replayed Nichols' dramatic Floor speech that led to tobacco's defeat. "You're a hero! People will support you, I know they will. *I'll* work on your campaign, for free!"

Dolly wagged a finger at her. "You most certainly will not. You're finishing your last two semesters and sitting for the bar, remember? Besides, I think I'm ready to leave politics." She surveyed the astonished looks, nodded. "Yup. I learned something these last two weeks: I'm not happy doing this anymore. I'm tired of compromising for the sake of winning. Plus the happiest I've been in years was at my niece's classroom the other day. I called Brevard County schools, and they've got a number of elementary school openings for the fall."

"You're leaving?" Ruth Ann asked, stunned. "You can't!"

"Oh, it's not as bad as all that. Besides. If I really miss it, I can always come back." She checked her watch, took a last sip of wine. "I need to run if I'm going to get down to Carabelle before dark. Murphy, can I drop you at the airport?"

With a hug for Jeena and a handshake for Dunbar, Murphy hoisted his bag. "Madame President, I'd be honored."

Ruth Ann approached Jeena and squeezed her hand. "Gotta run, kiddo. Remember, you need a job after law school, there's always room at my shop. You can even run the new, pro bono, white hat division. Cancer Society, tree-huggers, Save the Manatees. The whole bit. You and Dunbar both."

And she was off, too, and Dunbar and Jeena watched her leave, then turned back to the television until the stories about the tobacco settlement were finished.

"Another beer?" Dunbar asked.

"I've got a better idea." She wrapped one foot around the back of his calf and leaned to his ear. "Wanna go to the springs, and neck?"

He pulled a ten from his wallet and dropped it on the bar. "Your piece-of-crap Toyota or mine?"